"What's wrong?" I asked. "Do you have a hangover?"

"I might still be a little drunk," Dan said. "But I have to ask you something."

"Okay," I said, a bit confused by the drama in his tone.

"If we get married, how will we know that we're in the relationship because we want to be there?"

"What is this, the riddle of the Sphinx?" I joked. "I thought we already had our requisite thirty talks on this subject."

"I'm serious," he said. His tone was accusing. "How will we know that we're together because we really love each other, and not just because we promised to be?"

"You know what, Dan?" I said, voice rising. "I'm not gonna answer that question. You know why? Because that's a question about the institution of marriage, not about us getting married! Because that's a question you ask before you've found someone you really love, because when you really love a person, you want to get up in front of God and everybody and say, 'I'm gonna spend the rest of my life with this person.' Because you're dying for everyone in the world to know how much you mean it!"

It's a lot calmer on the page, believe me.

Clearing the Aisle

Karen Schwartz

New York London Toronto Sydney

An *Original* Publication of POCKET BOOKS

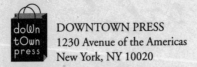

DOWNTOWN PRESS
1230 Avenue of the Americas
New York, NY 10020

ISBN: 0-7434-7110-5

First Downtown Press trade paperback edition May 2004

10   9   8   7   6   5   4   3   2

DOWNTOWN PRESS and colophon are
trademarks of Simon & Schuster, Inc.

Manufactured in the United States of America

Designed by Jaime Putorti

For information regarding special discounts for bulk purchases,
please contact Simon & Schuster Special Sales at 1-800-456-6798
or business@simonandschuster.com

Acknowledgments

Thank you to David McCormick, agent extraordinaire; Leslie Falk, his able deputy; and Cressida Leyshon for leading me to them. Thank you to Amy Pierpont, Amanda Ayers, Megan McKeever, and everyone at Simon and Schuster for guiding this book through publication and to Sujean Bruno for providing the beautiful cover art. Thank you to Laura Zigman, Mary Pat Walsh, and Melissa Bank for sage advice and words of encouragement

Huge thank yous go to fearless readers and wonderful friends Ellen Umansky, Sarah Schmidt, Martin Pousson, Mindy Schultz, Liz Craft, Tara Smith, Joanna Smith Rakoff, and, especially, Jessica Shattuck, who makes everything more delightful. Thanks to Dave Gutman for the med school consultations and to Preble Jacques, the best sport I know, for allowing his home to be converted into a writers' colony.

Thank you to my family: my parents, Jay, Judy, and Rita; my in-laws, Arnie and Sue; to Rose and Arthur and Aunt Marcia, for always being there; and, especially, to my two fantastic brothers, Michael and Stephen.

And the biggest thanks of all to Mike, for everything and then some.

For the love of my life, Michael Feldman

An engaged woman is always more agreeable
than a disengaged. She is satisfied with herself.
Her cares are over.

—Jane Austen, *Mansfield Park*

Ibergekumene tsores iz gut tsu dertseylin.
Troubles overcome are good to tell.

—Yiddish Proverb

$\mathcal{A}$t first, it's all congratulations. Congratulations punctuated with an army of exclamation marks, congratulations that sound like "Yippee!!!!" "Yippee!!!!" because you are getting married. You are *getting married!*

But that's just the pop of the cork before the champagne spills on the rug.

There was a time when we thought the big questions were "What creative thing can we do with the place cards?" and "Instead of making a toast, should we do a fun performance?," a time when my biggest fear was turning into Bridezilla.

But that soon changed. Before long, instead of skipping through a field of romantic whimsy, we were tiptoeing through an active mine zone.

Why? Because in order to get married, you must first plan a wedding.

Wedding Timeline:

Six Months or More Ahead

- Set budget and establish priorities
- Compile guest list
- Select date and reserve ceremony and reception sites
- Choose a caterer
- Choose and book officiant; discuss service
- Order dress and accessories
- Choose wedding party

One

$\mathcal{L}$ooking back, I can pinpoint the exact moment when I knew that planning the wedding would be hell. We were in Washington, standing in the foyer of the Kosmos Club and talking to Kimmy, the overly blonde, overly perky events booker whose nude stockings and curled bangs had put me off from the moment she'd stuck out her hand and said, "You must be the Bride!" in a way that you could tell meant she dotted her *i*'s with little hearts or smiley faces.

But I'm being a little hard on Kimmy. After all, she thought she was asking an innocent question when she said, "Now, how many guests were you thinking of?" How could she have known that Phyllis and I would answer in unison?

"Between one fifty and two hundred," I said.

"Seventy-five," said Phyllis.

As Kimmy's eyes darted back and forth between me and my stepmother, I turned to Dan, my fiancé, whose left eyebrow, a slightly arched "heh?," told me that he was just as bewildered as I was. (On most people an eyebrow might not exactly express bewilderment, but on Dan, who had been aptly nicknamed

Bodhisattva by his college roommates, it did.) My father, Jerry, stood behind Phyllis, who was smiling and nodding her frosted head confidently. I knew that combo. It was vintage Phyllis. It meant, "Something I don't like has just been said, and if I smile and nod hard enough, I can, by sheer force of will and faux-positive facial muscles, make it go away." Having just met Phyllis, Kimmy had no way of knowing this, and therefore assumed that the smile and nod meant that the two dramatically different numbers she had been quoted could somehow be reconciled.

"So, about one seventy-five, then?" Kimmy questioned, looking straight at Phyllis and returning her Stepford grin.

"No," Phyllis replied, the smile never cracking, "just seventy-five. We want to keep it small."

"We?" I asked, turning to face Phyllis directly as the corners of Kimmy's mouth tensed.

"Dad and I," Phyllis answered with a quick double nod and then turned back to beam at Kimmy.

Had she forgotten my father's cousins, the ones who actually flew in from places like Phoenix and Denver for all of the bar mitzvahs and weddings? I couldn't recall a family event without my father's cousin Irwin, a San Diego dermatologist, checking moles in a corner near a buffet table.

"The kids had mentioned wanting to have the ceremony outside," Phyllis continued. "Is that a possibility?"

"Well—" Kimmy began.

I couldn't let it slide. "Whether or not we can do it outside, I doubt that keeping this wedding to seventy-five people is a possibility. Dad's family alone is seventy-five people." I tried to say this in an even, nonconfrontational tone, not because I wanted to avoid a confrontation, but because of Phyllis's use of the word "kids." Phyllis was fond of saying things like, "We don't consider this a second marriage," and, "There are no stepchildren in our house, only love." But any time I wanted or needed something from my father, she cast me in the role of Willful, Spoiled Child. If I expressed emotion, I'd be playing the part.

"We'll have another, smaller party for the cousins some other time," Phyllis said. "We'll discuss it later." She turned back to Kimmy. "So, outside space?"

"What?" I asked, genuinely baffled, looking directly at my father. "Why would we do that?"

"We have to stick to a budget here, Rachel." My dad's face was reddening as he spat out his words in the I'm-breaking-my-usual-silence-to-lay-down-the-law tone that my brother Matthew and I unaffectionately called "Jerry-anal." "Now, we've thought about it, and seventy-five is the right amount of people for our price range."

"What?" I asked again, and felt Dan's hand on my shoulder. "Your wedding was seventy-five people, and that's just your guests. That doesn't include any of our friends, not to mention the people that Dan's parents want to invite—"

"You said they wouldn't have that many guests." Finally, Phyllis spoke without nodding.

"Right," I answered. "I said *not that many*. I didn't say none."

"Well, they can have twenty-five, you can have twenty-five, and we'll have twenty-five," Phyllis shot back, as if it were a solution.

Dan let out a little laugh. "Aren't you forgetting someone?" he asked.

My father looked down at the carpet. Dan and I looked at Phyllis.

"We haven't figured out how to handle Joyce yet," she said. We hadn't figured out how to handle her either, but as soon as the specter of my mother had been raised, Phyllis's plastered-on smile had vanished.

"You know, we can hold off on firming up the numbers just now," Kimmy said, pressing her clipboard to her chest as if to bolster her peppiness. "Why don't I just show you our party rooms?"

"That would be wonderful," Phyllis said.

"Right this way," Kimmy said, her relief palpable.

Dan and I had been skeptical about a Washington wedding all along. All things being equal, we would have definitely had our wedding back in New York. Actually, all things *really* being equal (or in our fantasy world, whichever), we would have had our wedding at the Central Park Boathouse, site of our engagement dinner, steps away from the Central Park Zoo, site of the proposal itself. Central Park, the place where we walked together on weekends—people-watching, holding hands, shaking our butts to the beat at the skating circle, sharing the air of contented cosmopolitanism with contented cosmopolitans.

I suppose that Dan, who grew up in Main Line Philadelphia, was a guy who'd gone to Columbia for college, and, once he'd had a taste of New York, stayed. I grew up in suburban D.C., went to Barnard, and stayed, so I guess the same could be said about me. But the difference was that New York was the only place I'd ever really considered home. I was a New Yorker held against her will in suburban Washington for the first seventeen years of her life.

My father likes to tell the story of driving down Broadway with me just after I'd moved into my first-year dorm at Barnard in 1989. My father looked out the window and saw garbage, filth, and "questionable characters," and thought to himself, "Am I leaving my daughter here?" And I turned to him, big smile on my face, and said, "Isn't New York the greatest?"

A few days later (the second day of classes, to be exact), I met Dan. It was at that "are these people going to be my *Big Chill?*" phase of college where "You like Elvis Costello? I *love* Elvis Costello!" was a commonly overheard snippet of dialogue. I was making my way through the crowded John Jay cafeteria with my new friend from Art History, when her friend motioned for us to join him at his table. There were other people with him, but the only one I can remember had messy Jew-fro hair and wore a red-checked flannel shirt over a faded Bob Dylan T-shirt and black glasses, which, while not quite fashionable, were funky by suburban standards. He stood up from the table, flashed the most beautiful smile I'd ever seen, and stuck his hand in my direction and said, "Hi. I'm Dan Gershon."

From that moment on, I referred to him as "the love of my life Dan Gershon," as in: "There's a party Friday night? Will the love of my life Dan Gershon be there?"

Eight years later, armed with a wedding date, we went to Washington to see the Kosmos Club. We'd gotten engaged three months before, and had taken the summer to "just enjoy it." But now it was fall and we had a wedding to plan. One morning of phone calls in New York had revealed that having a wedding in the city that never sleeps would cost at least twice as much as one in Washington, and there was no way I could justify the extra expense to my father, let alone myself.

It went without saying that a D.C. wedding meant Phyllis, whose life in the seven years since she'd moved from Long Island to first live with, then marry, my father consisted of near-constant redecoration of their Arlington condominium and a never-ending cycle of buying and returning things to the "fabulous" Pentagon City Nordstrom's. With the amount of time she had on her hands and the amount of money my father would have to shell out, Dan and I had known way before Kosmos Club D-Day that there was no way Phyllis was going to take a laissez-faire approach to this wedding.

But I had come to D.C. with hope. The mere fact that someone's your stepmother doesn't mean she's a *stepmother*.

"This is different," I had told a skeptical Dan on the train ride down. "This is *our* wedding. Phyllis knows that. And even if she doesn't, my dad does. He knows it's our day."

Of course, in reality, I had my doubts too.

"Anyway," I'd said, "we'll be lucky if our biggest problem with this wedding is Phyllis."

Dan and I wanted a wedding that felt like a cleaned-up version of us, a wedding more about warmth and joy than catered food and centerpieces. We were all about sacrificing formality for the sake of festivity, which is why, as I'd mentioned to Phyllis on the phone, we were hoping to have the wedding outside. I had also mentioned that we had a great potential place—the Audubon Society, better known to us as the site of the Levy-Wu wedding.

The Levy-Wu wedding was the wedding of Debra Levy, daughter of Dan's parents' oldest friends (better known as "the Levys"), and Zhang-Yuen Wu, her sweetheart from Brown. Dan and I called it "the Levy-Wu wedding" instead of Debra and Zhang's wedding, because, since they hyphenated their names, Debra and Zhang were now officially the Levy-Wus—definitely the best hyphenated name in the politically correct practice's short history. Like their name, the Levy-Wus' wedding was a sort of ode to multiculturalism. Their *huppah* was held by attendants—one African-American, one Indian, one Dutch, one Korean—all wearing their native garb; their Reform Jewish ceremony was supplemented with readings from Lao Tze; their hora was danced around red paper lanterns. The event itself, which could have come off somewhere between an intellectual "It's a Small World" ride and a computer commercial trying to evoke "the future," was actually the nicest wedding we'd ever been to.

The bridal magazines I had recently acquired emphasized the wedding as a coming-out party where you show the world your tastes as a couple. This seemed dopey until I realized that the sites of weddings Dan and I had attended had indeed said a lot about the couples who held them. There'd been my high school friend Jonathan and his wife, Leora, whose black-tie wedding at the Teaneck Hilton presaged their move from the West Eighties to a four-bedroom colonial in Englewood six months later. Then there was my cousin Lynn and her husband Mark, whose elaborate wedding at the Plaza foreshadowed their every-time-you-see-them recommendations for restaurants on Park Avenue South. And there was my stepbrother Gregory and his partner Thomas's self-described "wedding of sorts," poolside at an Art Deco hotel in South Beach, with synchronized swimmer "bridesmaids" walking down the diving board to begin their routine to a song from the *Funny Girl* soundtrack.

A wedding at the Audubon Society would have said that Dan and I were relaxed enough to brave the elements for an outdoor wedding, and maybe that we supported enriching hobbies like bird-watching in some vague sense, the type who'd have you over for a brunch of bagels and smoked salmon and serve you coffee in public television pledge gift mugs—a pretty accurate picture, actually.

We knew the Audubon Society fit our bill, but we weren't set on it. Which is why we'd agreed to look at other places.

In the wedding of our fantasies, we could see ourselves and our family and friends milling about a nice but not stuffily manicured lawn, drinking champagne as the sounds of the jazz quartet playing and the birds chirping filled the June afternoon air. In the words of Martha Stewart, we were after "relaxed elegance."

Those were not the words that sprang to mind when Kimmy unlocked the French double doors that led into the Kosmos Club ballroom. The words that sprang to Kimmy's mind, or at least to her mouth, were "Louis the Fourteenth." The words that sprang to mine were "no way, Jose."

This wasn't smoked salmon and PBS mugs; it was cucumber sandwiches and Wedgwood.

"Most of our brides make their entrance through those doors," Kimmy motioned to the back of the room toward one of the many sets of gold-paned windows, "and proceed down the length of the room and then up the stairs and onto the stage."

The stage.

"Of course, we have a lovely red velvet carpet that we lay out for the aisle, and we set up chairs like these," Kimmy pointed to a white-cushioned, gold-backed chair that sat forlornly in a corner, "on either side of the aisle for the audience."

The audience.

"Just try and visualize it," Kimmy said. "The audience—" her hand swept along in front of her for effect. "The flowers—we usually set up two large displays on either side of the staircase. The music—the accompanists usually sit right there, to the left of the staircase. Just take it in and get a picture in your head. Close your eyes if you want to."

"You know," I said, "I can really picture it. What about you, Dan?"

"Mmmm-hmmm," he said, nodding. I had to bite my lip to suppress a laugh.

Kimmy turned away and I cast a glance toward Dan, whose

pained look back told me that he was every bit as uninterested in getting married in this room as I was. Phyllis and Kimmy chatted as they made their way down the hall to the room where the reception would theoretically take place. My father hung back with us.

"Pretty nice place, huh?" he asked, looking up at the chandelier.

"Sure," said Dan the diplomat. This was the general tone of all of their conversations—my dad asking a banal but leading question, Dan being politely agreeable. "Pretty good movie, huh?" "Not bad."

"So you think you might want to do it here?" my father continued, his eyebrows raised in hopeful expectation.

"Maybe," Dan said, though it sounded more like two separate words: may—be.

"I think it's pretty nice."

"Yeah," I said. "It is."

My father really could have been thinking, not just hoping, that Dan and I would want to have our wedding in the stuffy opulence of the Kosmos Club ballroom. As an electrical engineer and designer of communication satellites, it wasn't so much that my father was out of touch with our taste, it was more that he was just out of touch. It never surprised me to hear his closest friends, the friends he'd grown up with in Scranton, Pennsylvania ("a great place to be *from*," elbow to the ribs, yuk-yuk-yuk), one of whom was Henry Kissinger's doctor, another of whom was a Connecticut State Supreme Court judge, say, "Jerry Silverstein is the smartest guy I know." My dad sat around all day thinking thoughts and solving equations that 99 percent of the world couldn't even fathom existed.

Communication satellites my father could master, but human

communication was another thing entirely. When I was a child and he and my mother were still married, he would come home from work, head to the family room, turn on *MacNeil Lehrer*, sit cross-legged on the seventies shag rug, and start dealing out his solitaire hand. And there he would sit, all night, flipping the cards and thinking. I'd sit down right in front of him, cross-legged, watching. By the time I was four, I was going to the closet and getting my own deck of free airline cards so we could play side by side. Every so often, my father would glance over his shoulder at my hand and offer strategic advice. As those glances yielded fewer and fewer pointers, he taught me to play speed solitaire and I'd sit facing him again, going head-to-head. We soon moved on to gin.

"We'd really like to do the wedding here," my dad went on as Kimmy and his wife walked down the hall ahead of us and out of earshot.

"Well, we'll have to see about it," I replied in a slow tone that I hoped conveyed a sense of letting down easily.

My father pursed his lips and let out a short breath. "We'd like for the two of you to have something that you want," he began in fully Jerry-anal mode, "but it's very important that this wedding stay within our budget. The Kosmos Club is very reasonable for members. The fee for the room rental is very low, and they only charge you what you'd pay in the restaurant for dinner, which is a lot less than a caterer."

I'd seen *Father of the Bride*—both the original and the remake. The father of the bride freaks out about money. I could handle that.

"You know, Dad," I said, our pace now slowing to near-molasses, "even if we don't have it here, we don't want some over-the-top wedding. I'm sure we can find a place we like and keep the costs down, too."

"You know, one of the main reasons we joined here is that it's a very reasonable place to hold a wedding." The Jerry-anal face was its telltale red.

No wonder Phyllis had been vague about the other places we'd be touring; there wouldn't be any.

"Well, you should have taken us on the tour then, Dad," I said. "We would have told you that if you were joining this place to have our wedding in it, you might as well have canceled your application."

"Rachel," my father's tone was stern, "the Kosmos Club is a very good deal. The amount they charge for the food is very reasonable."

There is only so much Jerry-anal I can take, and I had reached my limit. "First of all, Dad, I am twenty-six years old, so stop speaking to me as if I were twelve. Second, we did not like that room and we do not want to get married there. Besides, that room was huge and you only want there to be seventy-five people in 'the audience.'"

"If you have the wedding someplace less expensive, like this, we may be able to have more people."

I rolled my eyes. "Do you seriously expect to have a wedding and not invite the cousins?"

"I expect to have a wedding that I can afford."

"And you're willing to blow off your family?"

"If need be."

I could imagine him dragging his feet, Jerry-anally sticking to whatever budget he had pulled out from who knows where, until my aunt Natalie, his sister, called him up and told him in no uncertain terms that there was no way that he could hold a wedding for his only daughter and not invite the cousins. And I knew that at that moment, it would be back to the drawing board.

"Why don't you just save us all a lot of trouble and admit that this wedding is going to be one hundred and fifty people, and let us work from there," I said.

"Because I'm not sure this wedding is going to be one hundred and fifty people. What I am sure of is that this wedding is going to be in line with the budget."

"Okay, that's fine," Dan said, turning the heated tone a notch down. "But can I ask what the budget is based on?"

"It's based on what Phyllis and I have decided we can spend," Jerry-anal, Jerry-anal, Jerry-anal.

"And how much is that?" Dan asked.

"Ten thousand dollars," my father replied firmly.

"Ten thousand dollars?" I repeated in astonishment.

I know that ten thousand dollars is a lot of money. But ten thousand dollars was about what Phyllis had spent on the customized wall unit in their den. Ten thousand dollars was one-eighth what my father had spent on the new Lexus we'd driven to the Kosmos Club. Ten thousand dollars was probably the flower budget at most of the weddings that my father had been to in the past few years, weddings thrown by his Scranton friends and business associates. In the world of weddings, ten thousand dollars does not go very far, even for the kind of low-key event that Dan and I were hoping to have.

Which is what I was about to say, when Kimmy and Phyllis returned with their ever-present smiles.

"We wondered what was keeping you slowpokes," Kimmy said. "Come and take a look at the reception room."

"The Kosmos Club does all of the catering, right?" I asked. When Kimmy nodded yes, I continued, "So, is there any way to have a kosher reception?"

The confusion registered on Kimmy's face. "I don't see how," she said. "We don't allow any outside caterers."

I turned to my father, knowing he could tell, even before I put the card facedown, that I had gin. Grandpa Sol, my mother's father, was seriously Orthodox, which meant that in addition to putting on *t'fillin* and *davening* every morning, he only ate kosher food. How could his granddaughter's wedding not be kosher?

"That rules it out," I said, shrugging my shoulders and putting an end to whatever speck of a Kimmy-friendly façade I had left.

"We can't be bound to your grandfather, Rachel," Phyllis said.

"Excuse me?" I felt Dan's hand on my back.

"We can't be held hostage by one person's beliefs," Phyllis reiterated.

Kosmos Club aside, this was not a negotiable point. "It's not a matter of holding you hostage, it's a matter of showing my one living grandparent respect. I know he's not related to you, but you can't just ignore Grandpa Sol. Not at my wedding."

"We'll talk about this later," Phyllis said, returning again to Kimmy. "Now tell me, what about outside space?"

"Well, we don't really do affairs outside here," Kimmy explained, as if this were the stickiest point we'd touched on. "If you'd like, we could see about using the parking lot, but I think that may be a little awkward."

"That's okay," I told her. "I think we've seen enough."

Two

Back in New York Monday morning, I was still tense. I got up early and went for a prework swim at the West Side Y. That morning, two of my favorite regulars were in the sauna, sitting and *shvitzing* in their trademark foil suits.

"Look who's here!" Esther, pure Grand Concourse, beamed as I opened the door.

"Rachel, *mammilah*," said Frieda, Eastern Europe. "*Vhat a sur-price!* This isn't your normal time."

"Hi, guys," I said. "I figured I'd get in a few prework laps, start the week off with a clear head."

Frieda nodded. "*Ve* have the *vater air-o-biks* at eleven."

Esther shrugged. "You get here early, you don't have to rush."

"True," I said, seating myself on the top bench. "So how are you?"

"*Vonderful, vonderful, dah-link,*" said Frieda, a West Side Zsa Zsa Gabor.

This was one of my favorite New York things: the people-in-your-neighborhood moment.

I had been a *Sesame Street* fanatic, famously interrupting a meeting at the Pentagon to inform my father that a show had been sponsored by the letter R (for Rachel!) and the number three (my age at the time!). "Who Are the People in Your Neighborhood" was my favorite song. Fifteen years later, walking down Broadway, it dawned on me: This was what I'd been singing about—literally! Without anyone telling me how, I had managed to get to Sesame Street!

"How's that fiancé of yours?" asked Esther. They'd met Dan many times in the lobby.

"He's good," I smiled, the mention of Dan adding to the warm "I Heart NY" wave that rose in my belly.

"Such a nice boy," said Frieda. Every few times she saw him, Frieda would ask Dan if he'd seen her letter from Steven Spielberg, "*tanking* me, can you imagine?" then reach for her purse to show him the dog-eared note yet again.

I smiled wider and, relaxing my head against the wall, dropped my towel.

"You see, Frieda." I jolted a bit as Esther motioned toward me. "*This* is what I'm telling you. Exactly my point."

I wondered what exactly my naked body was proof of.

"Rachel, *mammilah*," Frieda explained, "we were just talking about you the other day."

"Oh?"

"All *dese younk gurlce*," she said, "running around with the fake breasts."

"Mmmm," I nodded, relaxing again. "It's a little weird, isn't it?"

"It's disgusting," Esther said. "God gave you what you got for a purpose. Opening yourself up, having a surgery—you do that out of emergency, not for the sake of sheer vanity. Young girls with tits made of plastic. What are they doing to themselves?"

"*Zey* think it *vill* help them find a man," Frieda said, looking at me and nodding.

I shrugged.

"What kind of man finds that attractive?" Esther railed. "I'll tell you what kind: a woman-hater, that's who. He wants plastic, I say, let him buy a blow-up doll. *That's* attractive? They should go across the park to the Met, take a look around, and learn a thing or two. There's your beauty, in all shapes and sizes. No plastic necessary."

I nodded.

"Except for that Picasso," she added. "He was a whoremaster. I have no use for him."

I nodded again, already imagining myself repeating this gem.

"When it was just the movie stars, it was one thing," Esther continued. "Fine, I said, let them make a living. Then it was the trophy wives. Fine, I said. Let them be, they're on the East Side with Donald Trump. But now it's right here," her ire was raised, "at the Y!"

"Really?" I said. This was not that kind of gym. "I would think at Reebok, or Equinox—"

"Well, sure—"

"Or maybe even New York Sports. But the Y?"

"What does it matter?" said Esther. "It's everywhere you look already!"

"But not you," said Frieda, brightening. "Not our Rachilah."

"That's right," said Esther. "We said, 'Hers are real, and they are beautiful.'" She stamped her hand on the bench beside her. "Look at them," she motioned, palm outstretched. "Real. And *beautiful.*"

"*Vondervul,*" said Frieda, shaking her head back and forth.

"Like a ripe fruit," said Esther, squeezing imaginary somethings in each hand.

"Those," Frieda said, "are breasts."

The Kosmos Club seemed far, far away.

I returned home to find the phone ringing. Dan had left for class. I picked up the cordless, fairly certain who was on the other end.

"Good morning, Charlie," I said.

"Good morning, Charlie," Laura replied.

Laura was my work friend. I wrote Young Adult novels—*Turnerville High School* novels, to be exact—and she was my editor. We both worked at home. In the two years I'd been writing these books, we'd met in person only once. But our morning phone call had evolved into a daily ritual, one that made the homeplace seem more work-like. In homage to the greatest unseen coworker of all time, we called each other "Charlie." (All right, so he was technically a boss and not a coworker—we still found it amusing.)

"How was your scouting mission?" Laura asked.

"You don't want to know," I grumbled, hanging my coat on the Mission-style rack Dan and I had inherited from Thomas and Gregory.

"Let me guess," she said. "Your mother found out that you were down there with your father and stepmother and threw a fit."

In the time-honored tradition of work friends, we knew more about the day-to-day details of each other's lives than our real friends did.

"Actually, no," I said, sitting down at my desk and starting up my computer. I ran a hand through my still-a-bit-damp hair. "But thanks for reminding me that I have that to look forward to."

"That and writing yet another 'will-they-or-won't-they' Jake and Chloe sex scene," she said, referring to *Turnerville*'s virginity-encumbered hero and heroine, who, sixty-seven books into the series, still had yet to make it past second base.

Job-related gallows humor: another work friend staple. Laura and I were roughly the same age, made roughly the same amount of money, and spent an ever-increasing amount of time wondering the exact same thing—namely, is this it?

The *Turnerville* job was comfortable enough—the money wasn't a lot, but it was decent, and, as Dan liked to point out, I could legitimately say I was a writer. But I couldn't help but feel I wanted to do more with myself than this.

Maybe I was dissatisfied because, like a precocious child star of an eighties sitcom, I'd achieved too much too early and easily.

My last two years at Barnard, I wrote a column on *Beverly Hills 90210* for the *Columbia Daily Spectator*. The column analyzed each week's episode and put it into social, cultural, political, and—of course—literary perspective. By college standards, it was a huge success. I took one week off and there were letters of protest to the editor. I was a big fish in the little pool that spanned 114th Street to 119th Street, from Morningside Drive west to Riverside, and constituted my entire world.

By senior year, word of *90210 UnZIPped* had spread so far through the grapevine that eight other colleges were running it in their newspapers. Unlike everyone else around me (aside from Dan, now my boyfriend—who'd decided that, despite an undergraduate tenure with no science classes whatsoever, he wanted to be a doctor), I didn't dread the Big "what-are-you-doing-after-graduation" Question. I was going to be a writer, and I was sure that the real world would be ready to greet me with wide-open arms.

Ha.

I spent the first year out of college seasick on uncharted waters, living in the spare bedroom of Gregory and Thomas's Lincoln Terrace co-op and hostessing at a restaurant downtown. Most people from school stayed in Manhattan, our college town, and they were shopping for new work wardrobes and upgrading their Filofaxes from rubber to leather. I wore overalls most of the time. My father began speaking to me in perma-Jerry-anal. Phyllis began giving her version of advice: "You just need to find an organization, assess its needs, and be the one to fill them!" Gregory began scolding me (and Thomas) for getting "too involved" with *Melrose Place*. The world around me was saying, "You can't just *write*. You need to get a *job*, in an *office*, on a *track*. That's what grown-ups *do*."

And I started listening. Instead of writing pieces and trying to get them published, I was set on finding myself a job. A job that would lead to writing, sure, but a *job*.

Ha again.

The packets (charming but not-too-familiar cover letters, résumé writing clips) I had so painstakingly prepared (white linen seemed so boring, ecru too formal, a dilemma until I found a stationery store on Eighty-fourth and Amsterdam that had the perfect subtle eggshell shade) were either ignored or rejected with to-the-point letters ("Dear Ms. Silverstein, While your writing shows promise, we have no entry-level positions at this time") by the mass of editors to whom I'd sent them.

"Maybe I need to switch my focus," I said to Dan. On that day's trip to the mailbox, I'd found myself in the role of "her" in "Let Her Down Easy" yet again.

"Switch it how?" he asked between bites of eggplant in garlic sauce. We were eating leftovers and sitting on his unfolded futon, one of four pieces of furniture (flea market coffee table, Ikea

chair, and fiberboard "entertainment center" being the others)
that fit in his studio apartment. Even though I was "living with
Gregory and Thomas," I spent almost every night at Dan's. But
we "weren't ready to live together." Dan liked the idea of having
his own place (though he far from minded me being there most
of the time—picking up after him and clearing out his drawers to
make room for my stuff), and I didn't want to share an apartment with him until I could split the rent.

"Well, I've been focusing on magazines and newspapers, but
people our age don't even write for them."

"So where do people our age write?" Dan had been through
enough of these "Aha! I know where I went wrong!" conversations to know that the best way to respond was with a leading
question.

"TV!"

"TV."

"Right!" I said. "It's so obvious. I love TV. My whole column
was about TV. Why write *about* it when I could just write *it*? I
don't know why I hadn't thought of this before."

So, freshly-written *Seinfeld* spec script in hand, I went on one
demoralizing quasi-writing, quasi-TV interview after the next.
The worst one was for a job as the assistant to the head of
infomercials at a big ad agency. Infomercials were on TV, somebody had to write them, and hey, I could write ones that were
like sitcoms, and then I could parlay that into writing actual sitcoms or . . . something—you get my drift. Besides, it was
infomercials—at the very least campy and fun. But my would-be
boss nixed that angle. The guy had visible nosehairs and the
worst comb-over I'd ever seen. His big selling point: "Sometimes
you have to be real creative. Like on the Bare Lady shoot. We'd
hired a Puerto Rican girl for the before and gave her three weeks

to grow out her leg hair. Three weeks, I thought, that's hairy. She was Puerto Rican, so I figured she'd be real nice and dark. And she was. Just not on camera! So everyone's running around the set, 'What can we do? What can we do?' And then it came to me." He actually *snapped* when he said this. "Mascara!"

Finally, I got a job as the assistant to the head of development at The Comedy Network. At first, it seemed ideal. I would be working with Mandy—"*With*, not *for*," as she told me in the interview. "I hire assistants who are smart, whose contributions I value, and who I promote inside of a year." Mandy was responsible for creating new shows, and under her I'd be meeting writers and producers, learning the ropes, even pitching my own show ideas. It had been a year and a half since graduation—a year and a half of living with my stepbrother (in spirit if not in practice) while everyone around me found their place in adult life, a year and a half of telling my father that it took time to break into creative professions, a year and a half of hearing my stepmother spout bizarre motivational-speaker truisms. At The Comedy Network, I finally had my shot.

For a few months, everything was great. With my newfound steady income, I finally moved out of Gregory and Thomas's apartment and into a decent one-bedroom with Dan. (When he looked at me and said, "Are we sure we're ready to take this step?" I said, "Give me a break.") Mandy included me in meetings, asked for my opinions, let me take cabs on her expense account. "You'll be running things while I'm gone," she'd say, rubbing her pregnant belly. "I knew I picked the right assistant."

And, best of all, she *loved* my show ideas.

"I *love* this one!" Mandy would exclaim. "One of these days, I'm going to be working for you!"

When she passed my treatment for a show called *Charmed*

Life (about the spoiled daughters of a famous film director coping with their ennui) on to Sheila, her boss, I was sure I was on my way. Then my would-be mentor had her baby.

During her maternity leave, Mandy would call from home and say that Sheila was insisting that she go to some meeting or other—"You know how pissed she is about the baby"—and could I please, please, please just watch little Max for the day? Lines were being crossed here, and I knew it. But these were favors for Mandy, the person doing so many more important favors for me. Sure, I'd say, again and again.

Not that I had much to do at the office. With Mandy gone, it started to dawn on me that none of the shows on her development slate were anywhere near production, and that Mandy's job was in fact a delicate shell game consisting of having meetings, going to lunch, telling me what a promising future I had, and—most important—kissing up to Sheila.

When Mandy returned to work, I'd try to follow up on *Charmed Life*, or suggest myself as a writer for the shows we were staffing. Mandy would say something encouraging enough to keep me agreeing to her childcare-related requests, which now included sending her freshly pumped breast milk by messenger from the office to her nanny at home. ("Fresher has to be healthier. I just want the best for little Max.")

Desperate, I wrote up another sitcom idea and gave it to Mandy. It was for *Downtown Cinema*, a *Cheers*-esque show about a group of misfits—lovable ones, of course—who work at an art house. After a week of "I want to talk to you about your show," Mandy sat me down in her office to give me her feedback.

"I really loved the part about the father being a director," she said, in her best I'm-so-glad-I-hired-you voice. "And about the boyfriend who's like Keanu Reeves."

She was talking about *Charmed Life*, the show I'd written up six months before, the show she'd been so crazy about she'd passed it on to Sheila, the show whose status she had been updating me on—in her own vague way—every other week for the past few months! I scanned my mind for some way to make it possible that Mandy had ever been telling me the truth as she went on and on about Peyton and Annabelle, the "brilliant" characters she'd "loved" months ago.

"I *love* this idea!" Mandy said. "I think you're really on to something this time. One of these days, I'm going to be working for you!"

"No, Mandy," I corrected. "*With,* not *for.*"

From then on, my self-assigned main duty was to watch every minute of the O. J. Simpson trial so that anyone who worked at The Comedy Network could at any time stop by my desk or phone me for an update. A month before the verdict came in, a friend from my college newspaper days told me that the publisher she worked for was desperately looking for a ghostwriter for the *Turnerville High* books. I sent my clips, and was hired that week. Feeling I had conquered the world, I quit my job at The Comedy Network—which really meant that instead of watching the trial at work, I watched it at home, and people from work just called me for updates there.

Offices, I decided, were not for me. In that way, the *Turnerville* gig was great. As I was fond of saying, I had *work* but not a *job*. There were, however, two glaring negatives. Number one: no health insurance. But this would be remedied once Dan and I got married; he was now in his second year of med school at Columbia, and as a spouse, I'd be covered on his student health plan. Number two was not so easy. I had been writing teen novels under Janet Pierce's name for just over two years now. I could continue writing them indefinitely—which would, in some ways, be fine. But it would mean Rachel Silverstein's name would continue to signify next to nothing. And, much as I enjoyed the continuing soap opera antics of the *Turnerville* gang (and I did, truly—perhaps sadly—enjoy them), I lived with a near-constant gnawing feeling that I should at least *try* to do something beyond this.

But who had the time? Since the engagement, any free time I had was spent poring over *Martha Stewart Weddings* with the trained, patient eye of a Talmudic scholar.

"So if your mom wasn't the problem this weekend, what was?" Laura wanted to know.

I told her about the Kosmos Club, the gilded room, Kimmy, my father's declaration that they'd joined only for the purpose of throwing my wedding there. She listened patiently, clucking her tongue and saying "no way" appropriately. Then I told her about the ten thousand dollars.

"Ten thousand dollars!" Laura's voice registered the shock. Her sister had gotten married back in St. Louis the year before, so she could instantly grasp the ramifications. "But that can't include your dress, can it?"

"I'm not sure," I said, remembering that Laura's sister had worn a Vera Wang. "We didn't get that specific."

"It can't mean your dress," Laura said.

"At this point, very little would surprise me."

"It can't mean your dress," Laura repeated, as if to shoo the thought from my mind. But, rather than dislodging, the thought had now wedged itself into a permanent spot in my mind. I needed a second opinion.

"I'm asking Thomas," I said. "I'll call you right back." Laura said okay, and I hung up with her and dialed the SoHo fabric store where Thomas worked. He often weighed in on the thorny matters Laura and I tackled.

"Tennison Fabrics," Thomas chirped, in full-out perky fabric butler mode.

"Do you think the ten thousand includes my dress?"

"Hmmmmm . . ." Thomas had heard what went down at the Kosmos Club approximately five minutes after Dan and I got home. He sighed. "Honey, I wish I could say no, but . . ."

The only thing worse than having Phyllis for a stepmother was having her for a mother-in-law. The two-bedroom Lincoln Terrace co-op where Thomas and Gregory lived was actually Phyllis's (inherited from her mother—hence the no-man's-land location) and, with me out of the spare room, she and my father would stay there when they came into town. No matter how clean the apartment was (and this was the apartment of two gay men, one of whom was Phyllis's son), there would always be something not up to her standards, something she'd declare "impossible" and set about righting. One time, it was Thomas's closet. He came home from work to find a third of his clothes in a bag for Goodwill and, head exploding, rushed out of the building and down to the pay phone to call me and announce that "closets are important! I lived in one for twenty-nine years! The Energizer Bunny has crossed the line!" Phyllis-commiseration was a mainstay of our friendship, much to Gregory's irritation.

When Thomas and Gregory got married, they made a point of doing it without the aid of Phyllis and Jerry. They told Phyllis and Jerry they were paying for the wedding themselves, so they could "maintain creative control." Meanwhile, the entire affair was financed "through a grant from the Alice and Clyde Hanson Foundation," aka Thomas's parents.

"I didn't think it would include the dress," I groaned.

"Don't think about it and get yourself all stressed out," he said, repeating his advice from before. "It's all gonna work out. The important thing is that you're marrying Dan."

"I know, I know, I know."

"I'm with a client." Thomas sold high-end British fabrics. Customers were clients. "I gotta go."

"Okay."

"Hi to Miss Laura."

I hung up and called her back.

"Thomas says hi," I said when she answered. "He doesn't know about the dress either."

"It *can't* mean your dress," Laura said again.

I shook my head back and forth, trying to shake the thought loose. Then I asked Laura, "How was *your* weekend?" I asked. "Did you have the dream?"

Lately, Laura had been having a recurring David Letterman nightmare. In it, Dave would be playing one of those games with help from the studio audience. Dave would approach the first contestant and, in typical fashion, ask, "What is it that you do?" The person would be a doctor or a lawyer. Dave would say, "Well, that's impressive." He'd move on to the next contestant (as Laura told it, no game was actually ever played), again asking about the person's job. The person would be a schoolteacher, or an outreach coordinator at Planned Parenthood. Dave would say, "Well, that's certainly a noble profession." Then he'd move on to the next contestant: Laura herself.

"What's your name?" Dave would ask her.

"Laura," she said.

"Well, Laura," Dave would continue, "what do you do?"

"I edit *Turnerville High* books."

"*Turnerville High* books?" Dave would say. "*Turnerville High* books?" Then he'd start laughing. As the audience began laughing along, Laura would wake up.

Being the butt of a Letterman joke was apparently the worst thing that could happen to a person who grew up in the Midwest with ironic sensibilities.

"Thankfully, no dream," she said.

"Good," I said, though I knew we both had reason to be haunted.

Three

Friday afternoon, as I put the finishing touches on the "Jake and Chloe stay at second base" scene, Phyllis called.

"Dynamite news," she said. "The new member of the condo board is a fabulous caterer. One of *the* best in Washington!"

"Oh," I said, not getting it. For Anita, the condo board was an obsession ranking right up there with Nordstrom's.

"Her name is Deena. She does affairs at the Audubon Society all the time. So I put down the deposit and booked it for your date."

Come again? "What about the Kosmos Club?"

"It's too stuffy for June. Besides," she said in secret-spy mode, "this could be a *big thing*."

I assumed that meant a discount of some sort, but when I tried to pin my stepmother down on specifics she said, "Let me finesse it a little. I gotta run. Hugs to Dan." And Hurricane Phyllis blew out as quickly as she'd blown in.

When Dan came home, I briefed him immediately.

"They've done a complete 180," I said. "I'm totally confused. I have whiplash."

He said, "Who cares? The important thing is: We're having the wedding at the Audubon Society."

"That's true," I said, only now appreciating the clear sky. "We are. Yay."

"So," he said, continuing the now-bright mood. "Look what I got." He unzipped his backpack and produced two thick paperback books. Squinting, I made out the titles: *Lonely Planet India* and *Southeast Asia on a Shoestring*. "For the honeymoon," he explained.

I took the India book in my hand. It was heavy. "Do I have to read the whole thing?"

He shrugged. "Not if you don't want to."

"Really?"

"Yeah, really. I don't mind planning the trip."

"Good," I said, surprised by my own relief.

"You just have to trust me to do it."

"Why wouldn't I trust you?"

"Okay. But no second-guessing."

"Fine," I said, baffled, as I unloaded the book on him. "No second-guessing."

He returned the tome to his bag.

"So," Dan began with forced casualness, "how do you feel about going out to dinner? Will called before . . ."

"I'm tired."

"Ray-chul."

"What?"

"Come on."

"Easy for you to say. When you're tired you just fall asleep." This was true, be it at a party, in a movie, or during a game of charades, Tired Dan plus Comfortable Chair always equaled Sleep, especially when beer was added as a variable. Anyone who knew Dan had seen this in effect; most people considered it a Zen master–like gift.

"Ray-chul," he said again.

"What?" I said. "I'm not in the mood."

"Don't be a grouch," he said.

"I'm not a grouch. I'm tired."

I *was* tired. But, as Dan knew, my wanting to blow off dinner that night had little to do with end-of-the-week lethargy. It had to do with our engagement.

When you are first engaged, everyone wants to hear "the story," and you oblige with a neatly scripted anecdote containing the where, when, and how the groom-to-be popped the question. No matter what happened, everyone sticks to roughly the same formula:

The guy is the all-planning, all-doing master of ceremonies. He goes out and plunks down a huge amount of cash on a ring that, if we're being strict here, he has no idea whether his intended will actually like. He sets the scene. He gets down on bended knee. He pops the question.

Then it's the bride's turn. She reacts with joy. She puts her hands on her cheeks like the *Home Alone* kid. To the question she says, "Yes!" To the ring she says, "It's beautiful!" She may even cry.

In our culture, this is supposed to be romantic. But when you think about what the engagement stories we tell say about relationships, you start to wonder why we hold so stubbornly to the form.

Forget the active/passive roles for a second (and the way the woman seems thrilled just to have been asked, never mind who did the asking)—let's think about the surprise. It's tempting to think that life could flow that seamlessly, that when two people come together they don't need words to know the time is right. But come on. Shouldn't people deciding to spend the rest of their lives together be close enough to suspect the direction in which things are heading? Shouldn't they have at least talked about the idea beforehand?

I'd worry about the marriage where the official story was actually the whole truth.

Dan and I had an engagement story, which I sort-of mentioned a while back. Dan told me he'd made reservations for a "nice" dinner, but wanted to go for a walk in the park before we went. We went to the zoo and watched the monkeys pick bugs off each other and Dan said, "You're the only monkey I want to pick bugs off of." And then he asked and I said yes, and we went to a dinner at the Boathouse, complete with special flowers—Gerber daisies, my favorite—on the prearranged table and a postdessert gondola ride.

That's the story, and it's true, but it's not what really happened.

What really happened began about a year before. Dan and I were having our usual diner brunch and I said, "I think five years is long enough to know whether or not you want to be with someone forever, don't you?"

We'd been together four. I'd just quit my Comedy Network job and Dan had just completed two years of postbac science courses and was applying to med schools. It was a time of talks—what kind of doctor did Dan want to be? Did writing *Turnerville High* make me a real writer? A time of dilemmas—should we get a really nice desk chair for the computer or upgrade to a real couch? A time of plans—let's go on a really big trip one summer while Dan's in school! It was a time when it was clear that we were two separate people walking down the same little back road together—a time when, it seemed to me, we should either just admit it or stop walking now while we could still see our way back to the highway. With every one of those joint decisions, we had already begun paving our little back road, so it seemed stupid to persist in pretending it was still just gravel.

"What are you saying?" Dan asked. He was a fan of the Socratic debate, and his side of discussions was, more often than not, in question form.

"I'm saying that I think there comes a time when you've been together long enough to know if this is it."

"What do you mean 'it'?"

His deliberate density was starting to get annoying. "What I mean is that by the time we've been together five years I think we should either get engaged or break up."

"Well," Dan said, "five years just seems arbitrary. Why not six years?"

"Because five isn't arbitrary at all," I told him. "When we're together for five years, we'll both be twenty-six."

"Which seems on the young side to get engaged."

"Agreed—but only objectively. If I were saying, 'I need to be engaged by the time I'm twenty-six,' that would be extreme."

"But that's effectively what you're saying."

"No it isn't. I don't need to be engaged by any specific age. But I'd never get engaged to anyone without having been with them for at least three years and I don't want to be a middle-aged bride in a suit. So if we're not getting married, I'd better get a move on."

Of course I didn't mean that. I mean, being a middle-aged bride in a suit is not dire—it's just a bit unfortunate, like a man with womanly legs.

And that's not the reason the explanation was a crock, as you no doubt already know. This was the love of my life Dan Gershon! I had no interest in finding someone else! But it's human nature to take a sure thing for granted, and when you've gone around for years calling someone "the love of your life," you need to be vigilant against becoming a sure thing.

"So you're saying that if we're not engaged in a year you're breaking up with me," Dan said.

"Basically."

"So you're giving me an ultimatum."

"You don't have to make it sound so negative," I said, picking at my poached eggs. I thought of that "I'm called a feminist whenever I express opinions that differentiate me from a door-mat" line, and tried to remember who said it.

"But that's what it is," Dan reasoned.

"Only if you look at it that way. What I'm saying is that after five years it's time to shit or get off the pot. Time for *me* to shit or get off the pot."

Dan got really quiet, so I said, "Oh come on, you have a whole year!" and we finished our eggs and went to the movies.

For the next six months, we discussed the subject of engage-ment in dribs and drabs. One time, Dan said, "You know, I'm not thinking of what you said as an ultimatum anymore. It's just the practical way for a woman to be," so I knew he'd discussed the issue with his parents. Finally, we had a breakthrough conver-sation. Dan explained that, for him, getting engaged was like going to med school. With both decisions he was saying, "This is what my life is going to be"—ending the uncertainty on one hand, but with the vague regret of "cutting something off" on the other. Not cutting off something sexual per se—"I've been in a monogamous relationship for almost five years and it's never been an issue, so I can't see that bothering me significantly in the future"—but cutting off other directions his life could take. I said that I'd never felt that way. I just thought, "I can do every-thing I want, I'll just be doing it with Dan, which would make it all the better." Then Dan nodded, said I had a point, and, after a minute added, "Well, I guess we should plan a kick-ass trip before I start rotations."

So why weren't we just engaged then? We weren't waiting until he bought a ring, because I'd already told Dan I didn't want one. I wasn't a big jewelry person, and diamond solitaires looked like big pacifiers to me. And to force Dan, who was already ratcheting up tens of thousands of dollars in med school debt, to plunk down a huge sum for a rock seemed not just unnecessary, but also a little sadistic. Besides, once we were married, I wanted us both to have the same rings on our fingers. And with the money we were saving, we could make our honeymoon that much more decadent. We weren't engaged, we were waiting for an engagement story.

A few weeks later, Dan went out with his college roommate Will. I don't know what exactly happened that night because I wasn't there, but according to Dan, he said something like, "I think Rachel and I will be engaged pretty soon," and Will tried to talk him out of it until the bar closed at 5:00 A.M. Dan has consistently refused to share more than snippets of the conversation, but between those scraps and my knowledge of Will, the gist of his arguments can be imagined.

Will Foster was a verbal Rumpelstiltskin—he had the unique ability to take the most ridiculous bullshit and spin it into something that sounded, at least to him, like the golden rule. Will loved to hold court, and his friends, Dan included, loved to let him. A favorite topic was the year he spent between boarding school and college following the Grateful Dead and developing a dubious drug addiction, one apparently cured not by twelve-steps or rehab, but by switching his "scene" from committed pot-smoking Deadheads to dabbling, alcohol-drinking Ivy League freshmen.

Since graduation, Will, an aspiring screenwriter quasifunded by his Darien, Connecticut, parents, had been temping sporadically and living with his girlfriend Lisa, a model (All-American catalogue, not emaciated high fashion), who was trying to break into acting. Her biggest role to date had been the part of "sunshine blonde" on a box of "sunshine blonde" hair color. Lisa only went out with Columbia people if I was there, which made sense since I was the only one who was actively nice to her. Sometimes Dan and I would go out with the two of them and Will and Lisa would always strike me as not being, for lack of a better word, *normal*. Spending time with them felt like being in a diorama. We'd usually meet up at their place on West Eleventh, then go out to dinner somewhere in their neighborhood. At their apartment, Will and Lisa would ask each other concerned questions—first about props, "Honey, do you think this wine's turned?," then about which restaurant was the right setting, "Sweetie, do you think Moustache or Tartine?"—always in soft voices, and always with their chins inexplicably raised. A normal couple says, "Does this wine taste funny to anyone but me?" and, "Are we in the mood for Middle Eastern or French?" in a normal tone of voice, with normal facial angles.

I imagine that to talk Dan out of getting engaged, Will would have planted himself on philosophical ground, saying something like, "Commitment isn't real unless you have to renew it every day. If you're not bound to be with someone, you're there because you truly want to be. But if you get married, you're just there because you've made the commitment. You're only in the seat because you've strapped yourself in it."

Will was the kind of guy who made you want to look him in the eye, smack him across the face, and say, "Life is meaningless! You are going to die! Deal with it!"

Will would have continued with something like: "What's the rush? Your older brother isn't even married. If Rachel is just forcing you into this you should wonder what her motives are."

You had to wonder what would have happened that night at the Dublin House if Dan's other college roommate had been there. Connor McCormick, the youngest child in a family-business–centered suburban Chicago family, was the only one of Dan's friends not swimming in a soup of self-created angst. Instead, he was applying to Ivy League Ph.D. programs in Comparative Literature. Each of Connor's four older siblings had gone to work for his father, a man who, having supplied sheets of rubber to the makers of treadmills, was known as "the rubber king." In Connor's family, graduate studies in the humanities constituted a serious, if baffling, rebellion. Since college, he had been dating Julie Montgomery, a daughter of family friends who was working as a researcher for a documentary on teenage drug addicts and considering a master's in public health. Anyone with half a brain could spend five minutes with the two of them and surmise that Connor would have had a more positive view of engagement than Will did.

Even without knowing exactly what he'd said, one thing was clear: To Will, I was still nothing more than a job description. I wasn't "Rachel"; I was "Dan's Girlfriend." Five years had done nothing to break down the "girlfriend" fence he'd put around me from the beginning.

And no matter what he said that night, Will wouldn't have given his real objection to our engagement. At the end of *Grease*, Danny and Sandy sing "You're the One That I Want." Then Frenchie says: "Kinickie and Riz made up! The whole gang's back together!" They sing "We Go Together" and start dancing, but at the end, when Danny and Sandy take off in Greased Lightnin', the whole "gang" parts their line dance like the Red Sea to clear an aisle for Danny and Sandy to drive down, and then waves good-bye to them, as if to say, "We know we're all one big gang, but you, Danny and Sandy, are the *stars*." Contrary to popular opinion, the most unbelievable part of that final sequence is not the fact that, apropos of nothing, Greased Lightnin' up and *flies* away, it's that the group of friends would actually acknowledge Danny and Sandy as the most important people at the carnival. In life, everyone thinks that *they* are the stars. There is only one time when people will clear the way to make you an aisle—on your wedding day. Once engaged, Dan and I would become Danny and Sandy, at least temporarily.

But it wasn't just that Will wouldn't be the center of immediate attention. He and Dan had been friends before we had been a couple, so while Dan and I were just going out, he could still think that their relationship was the supreme relationship in the room. But now our couple-dom would trump that. By getting engaged, we would announce our supremacy in the place that in your midtwenties counts most: the future. From now on, instead of "Dan's Girlfriend," I would be "Dan's Wife," a main character in his story for all posterity, and Will would be "Dan's College Friend," a supporting player at best.

I understood that, and I tried not to take it personally. But . . .

The next morning, I found a bleary-eyed Dan sitting in the living room smoking a cigarette.

"What's wrong?" I asked. "Do you have a hangover?"

"I might still be a little drunk," Dan said. "But I have to ask you something."

"Okay," I said, a bit confused by the drama in his tone.

"If we get married, how will we know that we're in the relationship because we want to be there?"

"What is this, the riddle of the Sphinx?" I joked. "I thought we already had our requisite thirty talks on this subject."

"I'm serious," he said. His tone was accusing. "How will we know that we're together because we really love each other, and not just because we promised to be?"

This blending of the plausible and the ridiculous was hardly unfamiliar.

"I'm not going to sit in my living room and debate Will Foster," I said.

"Just answer the question. I'm the one who's asking it."

"You know what, Dan?" I said, voice rising. "I'm not gonna answer the question. You know why? Because that's a question about the institution of marriage, not about us getting married! Because that's a question you ask before you've found someone you really love, because when you really love a person, you want to get up in front of God and everybody and say, 'I'm gonna spend the rest of my life with this person,' because you're dying for everyone in the world to know how much you mean it!" (It's a lot calmer on the page, believe me.)

"I still don't understand why it has to be *now*," Dan said. "None of our friends are engaged! My older brother isn't even married!"

"Are we living in biblical times here? Does my father need to buy you a goat? Since when are you a little sheep who needs to go along with the herd?"

"I just don't get why this is so important to you."

"You know what? I'm a little sick and tired of having to convince you to want to be with me. It's starting to feel like begging. If this is still so fucking hard for you, I'll make it easy. This can be the very last day of our relationship, and all of your problems will be over."

I went back into the bedroom and hastily packed enough

clothes to last the weekend, shouting more pissed-off things I can't remember. When I came back out, Dan said something about it being "fucked up" that I "didn't care about his feelings," to which I snorted and said something about having obviously forgotten that he was the only person in this relationship allowed to have feelings, and that my role in life was to take any shit he felt like throwing on me in the name of them. I told him that asking me how he'd know that he actually loved me once we were married kinda made it seem like he wasn't so sure about it right now. Then I told him that I wanted to marry a *mensch*—not just a good person, but literally a man and not a little boy—and wished him all of the happiness in the world living with his friend in a permanent state of late adolescence. I slammed the door on my way out and got as far as the elevator before completely dissolving into tears.

Once out of the building, I made a beeline for Thomas and Gregory's. Gregory would already be off at work, but I knew Thomas, who had Fridays off, would be home.

"Dan's just being a straight boy," Thomas told me, bringing over the honey for my "Sereni-tea." "They have to get all commitment-phobic. It's in their manual."

One of the things I liked about Dan was his apathy toward sports, but I felt myself wondering whether a lifetime of *Monday Night Football* was next. "I don't want to be married to someone so *typical!*"

I blew off *Turnerville* and lolled around with Thomas all day, eating microwave popcorn and singing along to the *Funny Girl, Sound of Music,* and *The Little Mermaid* videos. To cheer me up, Thomas said that he would marry me—if he was ever a famous Hollywood actor in need of a beard.

At around four, Dan called and said he was sorry. He told me that after I left, he reread Erich Fromm's *The Art of Loving* and took a head-clearing walk through the park. Looking at ducks in the lake, Dan realized that he'd been thinking about me only as his best friend, whom he could talk to about anything, and not as the person who'd be hurt by questions like the ones he'd asked that morning. He asked me to come back to our apartment. But there was something I had to know first.

"What did you say last night?" I asked.

"Honestly, not much," he said. "It was more monologue than dialogue, if you know what I mean. Will did most of the talking."

"I figured," I said. "What I mean is, did you leave him with the impression you thought he was right?"

Dan exhaled a quick "hah." "Definitely not," he said. "Why do you think he kept going on and on for so long? When we left, he said, 'I haven't changed your mind at all, have I?'"

"And what did you say?"

"I laughed, and Will said, 'Bodhisattva, true to form.'"

I felt better. But Dan's taking me for granted was the juice I'd been stewing in all day; I couldn't just go running right back the second he apologized! When I told him I was staying at Thomas and Gregory's for the night, Dan got me to agree to come back early on Saturday for a "special" dinner . . . a dinner that turned out to be at the Boathouse with Gerber daisies on the table, after we took our own walk through the park.

A week later, my friend Naomi threw us a party to officially announce our engagement. Will seemed to have accepted the inevitability of our decision; he offered unenthusiastic congratulations that were at least sincere. Dan had faith that he'd eventually come around.

"Once he sees that we're still the same Rachel and Dan, we're just getting married, he'll calm down," Dan had said. "By the time the wedding rolls around, he'll be psyched."

"How big of him," I'd replied, only half under my breath.

Dan continued to work this Power of Positive Thinking that afternoon. "C'mon, Rachel. You know it'll be fun."

"I do?" I was not in the mood for a diorama dinner.

"Come *on*," he mock-pleaded. "Give the poor guy a break. Lisa's out of town."

"So it's just us and him? No thanks."

"No," Dan said. "Connor and Julie will be there."

"Oh," I said. This changed everything. "Why didn't you say so?"

Dan tilted his chin. "So you're up for it."

"Sure," I said, overdoing it. "Why not?"

He shook his head—what am I gonna do with you?—then came over and gave me a two-second neck rub.

"Gimme half an hour to finish this up," I said, and he kissed my cheek. As he went off to the bedroom to watch TV, I turned back to my monitor. My smile faded. Every time I thought of Will, a sludge of bad feelings was dredged in my gut.

Why had I spent so much time with that asshole?

The question was not rhetorical. I sighed, reminding myself, for the millionth time, of its answer. One of the things I'd always liked about Dan was the way he treated his friends like family. And, like it or not, Will was his friend.

Four

For certain people our age, the place to live in New York in the mid-nineties was the East Village or one of its spillovers— Williamsburg or the Lower East Side. Most of these people were not people-in-your-neighborhood New Yorkers, they were people who came to New York to be "cool." People who, in a desperate bid to flee their upper-middle-class suburban roots, survived a dangerous Hudson River crossing and washed up on the shores of the isle of Manhattan. People whose main goal in life was to not turn into their parents, but confused "not being" with "not looking like." People who hadn't quite figured out that there's nothing more bourgeois than pretending you're not bourgeois.

Dan and I chose to live on the Upper West Side, ground zero of the left-leaning bourgeoisie, with a street named for Isaac Bashevis Singer and three full pages in the neighborhood yellow pages devoted to the psychologist/psychoanalyst category, a veritable haven for card-carrying members of the ACLU. We loved our neighborhood, and when forced by East Village types to defend it, would always mention the irrefutable benefit of living a short walk from Central Park and say, "Getting on the subway to go to the park defeats the whole purpose." Even the most fervent seventies-TV-show-logo-T-shirt-sporting Alphabet City–dweller would have to acknowledge that we had a point.

We'd never tell such people that our other favorite thing about our adopted neighborhood was a plaque hanging in Zabar's, a monument to people-in-your-neighborhoodness that read:

It is with profound sorrow that we acknowledge the passing, at 86 years old, of Sam Cohen. His illness was brief. At Zabar's for 46 years, he truly enjoyed what he did. He was the last of the old-time Jewish lox cutters. A teacher, an artist, a tummler, his banter and optimism charmed everyone he came in contact with. Sam kibitzed with celebrities, neighborhood regulars and tourists alike, educating them on the nuances of Nova while slicing the thinnest smoked salmon in the Western world. His following was very loyal—always willing to wait for his service and smile. We depended on him for his humor as well as his loyalty. We shared his simchas—the marriages of his son and daughter—and we shared his pain—the passing of his wife. We thought we would have him with us for many more years. So it is with great sorrow that we say goodbye. We will miss our tavarish greatly. From now on, this site will be known as Sam's Corner—the place where the king of appetizing reigned.

They wouldn't understand.

When most of our contemporaries thought of the Upper West Side, they thought of the bars on Amsterdam Avenue, the unfortunate results of the eighties boom which made the neighborhood safe for bankers, lawyers, and business school types, bars we wouldn't be caught dead in, ones we referred to as "part of the problem."

To my endless irritation (Dan had considerably more tolerance), many of our generational peers seemed to have come to New York on a sort-of five-year test: you get three points for an apartment in Manhattan, three points for each dinner at a trendy restaurant, two points for every treatment at a day spa frequented by Uma Thurman.

People come to New York with different ideas of what it is, then make most of their lifestyle decisions to conform to those notions, and are therefore living in their New York. In the late nineties, you could determine what New York a person was living in by figuring out which decade's stereotypes they bought into. Unless you were gay (in which case you probably played eenie, meenie, minie, moe between a handful of acceptable cities), if you were a person in your twenties living in New York at the turn of the Millennium, you were either a Seventies, Eighties, or Nineties New Yorker.

Seventies New Yorkers wanted to live in either the West Village or Upper West Side, but in reality lived wherever they could get the best deal. If they lived in Brooklyn, they were in Park Slope. To find out the goings-on about town, they read the listings in *The New Yorker*. Their pop cultural apex was *Annie Hall*, with the hope of evolving into *Hannah and Her Sisters* and, while opinions on *Stardust Memories* varied, Seventies New Yorkers could at least appreciate it as part of the oeuvre. Dan and I were Seventies New Yorkers.

Eighties New Yorkers lived on the Upper East Side, or in SoHo, and had regrettably established beachheads on the Upper West Side and in the West Village (which raised the rents and made it hard for Seventies New Yorkers to live there—and forced me to have to say, time and time again, "there are Seventies New Yorkers in the West Seventies, they're just closer to their seventies"). If Eighties New Yorkers lived in Brooklyn—which was doubtful—they'd only be in Brooklyn Heights. They took their cues on what to do from *New York* magazine, and, depending on their line of work, their pop cultural apex was either *Bright Lights, Big City* or *Wall Street*.

Nineties New Yorkers lived "downtown"—in the East or West Village, the Lower East Side, Alphabet City, Chelsea, or Tribeca—or, if they were lawyers or consultants, on the Upper West Side. (The Upper East Side wasn't "cool" enough.) If Nineties New Yorkers lived in Brooklyn, they really could have been anywhere, though Williamsburg tended to raise the most suspicion. They read the listings in *Time Out New York*, and, whether they knew it or not, their pop cultural apex was the very troubling *Friends*.

Friends was vexing because it combined things that, like milk and meat, just should not go together. Normally when you have good-looking, magazine-cover–ready people running around fretting about their love lives in the latest impossibly expensive trendy clothes, you have a show produced by Aaron Spelling. And when you have a smart sitcom, a sitcom like *Mary Tyler Moore* or *Seinfeld* that's funny because the people creating it were inspired by something real in their lives rather than a prepackaged *Brady Bunch*–esque "how 'bout a show about a step family—he has three sons, she has three daughters!" concept, you have people on it who look and act like real people. But *Friends* wanted it both ways—"*Melrose Place* with a laugh track!"—and that's just *wrong*. (By the way: As huge a hit as it was, nobody my age moved to New York for *Seinfeld*. And, if someone actually had, they would be a Seventies New Yorker, because *Seinfeld* was a show about Seventies New Yorkers who lived in New York in the eighties, which aired in the nineties.) A few seasons in, I cracked and watched *Friends* and was horrified to discover that, despite the fact that there's no way the other four would be friends with the two-dimensional "wacky" Phoebe (an airhead like that would last two days in this city) or "dumb" Joey (at least they tried for an outer-borough, *Welcome Back, Kotter* kind of thing), the show was actually funny. But I still had to be against *Friends* on principle, if only because it brought the wrong element to New York—the element that thinks New York is just a place for the young and the trendy and that people that chipper and tan can be found anywhere but in Los Angeles.

With their naked materialism so in conflict with the left-leaning semi-intellectualism I felt was the spine of the city, you'd probably think that a Seventies New Yorker like myself would be most vehemently opposed to Eighties New York types. Not so! Eighties New Yorkers were so easy to spot, and therefore avoid, that they were almost benign. Like *Friends*, the insidious Nineties New Yorkers were the real enemy. They were Eighties New Yorkers in Seventies New Yorker clothes. Nineties New Yorkers ate at down-and-out diners and scrappy Cuban restaurants—but only the ones with Zagat's ratings or *Time Out* reviews posted in their windows. Nineties New Yorkers went to movies at Lincoln Plaza and the Angelika—but the independent films, not the foreign ones. Nineties New Yorkers loved *Annie Hall*—if asked, some would even cite it as their cultural apex—but they often found *Hannah and Her Sisters* "not that funny" or "just okay," and had never even heard of, much less seen, *Stardust Memories*, and therefore smacked of *Friends*. Nineties New Yorkers loved people-in-your-neighborhoodness the way a tourist in Italy converts to gelato for the duration of his trip—"when in Rome do as the Romans do." And that was exactly the problem.

Their concept of New York was a place of impermanence, a place to be before you "settled down."

Dan and I were already pretty settled down. We basically lived like the senior citizens in our neighborhood. We'd check out books from the library, have lunch specials on Columbus, or grab smoked-salmon sandwiches from the concession stand before taking in matinees at Lincoln Plaza, then go for our afternoon swim at the West Side Y, where I'd sit in the sauna with Esther and Frieda.

There was no doubt that a big reason we could live this kind of a New York life was because, having gone to college here, we'd been living here longer than most people our age. Our roots had already been laid down.

"Hey, you guys," Julie called brightly as we entered the restaurant, a small candlelit exposed-brick Argentinean steakhouse in the Hundreds on Amsterdam. The three of them had already gotten a pitcher of sangria, so after the hugs hello, I poured myself a glass.

"Where's Lisa?" I asked. Clearly a question for Will, but one I addressed to the table at large.

"L.A.," Will said. "Auditioning for a movie with Sean O'Malley."

"Who's Sean O'Malley?" Dan asked. He had the worst pop-cultural vocabulary of anyone our age—this wasn't a matter of literacy, it was a matter of retention. "Sean O'Malley . . . it sounds familiar . . ."

"He did that schmaltzy *Love Song* movie that was a huge deal when we were like three," I explained. "My mother had a crush on him."

Dan's face was still scrunched in confusion.

"And he's married to Mara Austin," Connor added. "But not technically. They've got that Goldie and Kurt thing going on."

"Ah." Dan nodded, lips pursing, face returning to neutral. "Gotcha."

"That's exciting," I said. See how nice I am about your girlfriend, jerk?

The waiter came and took our drink orders, and Julie said, "I'm gonna go wash my hands."

"That's a great idea," I said, getting up to join her.

"How hard did Dan have to twist your arm to get you here?" she asked with a good-natured smile. As always, I was simultaneously relieved to have Julie around as a friend and ally and conscious of the way we were playing the hand we'd been dealt—the girlfriends squawking in the bathroom together.

"Whyever would he have to do that?" I said in my best eye-batting Scarlett O'Hara.

"Well, I give you credit," she said. "Connor's still annoyed Will said all that stuff to Dan when he wasn't around." Julie had mentioned this before, but I couldn't figure out if Connor was annoyed because he thought his exclusion was somehow deliberate or simply because he'd missed something big.

"Honestly," I said, "I would not have come if you weren't going to be here."

We soon rejoined the others.

"So how's the wedding planning going?" Will asked once the food arrived.

I said, "It's going." I thought: *Like you give a shit.*

"My parents are coming up next week for a powwow," Dan said.

"How does that work?" Will asked. "Do they throw something the night before? Like a rehearsal dinner for the wedding party?"

"We're not so sure about that," I said. We weren't. With the wedding in Washington and most guests coming in from out of town, it seemed that whatever we did the night before would have to include everyone.

"Hence the need for a powwow," said Dan.

"What do you mean?" Will asked. "The bride's parents pay for the wedding and the groom's do a rehearsal dinner. Isn't that always the way it works?"

"Not necessarily." I shrugged.

"But traditionally," he said, his tone heating up.

"I don't know," I said.

"What do you mean, you don't know? It's *traditional*. You don't have to do it that way, but it is."

I shrugged.

"Speaking of tradition," Connor thankfully changed the subject, "this will be my first Jewish wedding. I'm psyched to wear a beanie."

"Jewish weddings are fun," said Julie, a veteran of the Montclair, New Jersey, bar mitzvah circuit. "You break a glass. And you have that little hut, right? What's that called?"

"The *huppah*," I said, smiling. I loved Julie.

"The hut," Dan giggled. "I think I like that better."

"And the procession is different, too, right?" Julie continued, inquiring WASPs want to know. "Because at my friend Kira's wedding she and her husband each walked down the aisle with both their father and mother."

"Yeah," I said. "I mean, some people do have the father give the daughter away"—I decided to not even get into how lame that sounds—"but the way your friend did it is really more traditionally Jewish."

"So is that how you're gonna do it?" she asked.

"In some permutation." With the complication of my parents, I hadn't yet figured out who would walk me down the aisle.

"That's cool," said Connor. "I like that idea." He was the kind of guy who wanted to come to your Seder.

"I like it too," I said. "It feels—I don't know—*truer* to what's really going on somehow."

"Enough wedding talk," Will grumbled.

"I agree," said Dan.

"So," Will began, chewing his carne asado, "when do you think you guys will move out of the city?"

It was clear that by "you guys," Will meant Dan and me. It was also clear he hadn't given up on challenging us about our plans. Only now Will would put down our engagement through the back door, in discussions that were ostensibly about other topics.

"We're not moving," I said, cutting into my pollo and bracing myself.

"Right," said Will. "Not now. But soon, you'll be outta here."

"What makes you say that?" I asked, taking a bite.

"Come on," said Will with a shrug. "It's really expensive to live in the city long-term."

"That's true," said Julie. "Look at my brother and sister-in-law. They were the total East Village, five-floor walk-up couple. Then she got pregnant and it was bye-bye walk-up, hello, West Orange." Julie's brother and sister-in-law always made their way into these conversations, signposts of life five years down the road.

"Did they try to find another apartment first?" I asked.

"I don't know." Julie shrugged.

"It would have been pretty expensive to find a two-bedroom," Connor said.

"Not necessarily," I said. "Not in Brooklyn."

"They definitely didn't look in Brooklyn," Julie said.

I shrugged. "I think if you really want to do something, you make it doable."

"That's probably true," said Julie.

"Well," said Will, "then the question is, do you really want to do it?"

"Maybe at some point the city will be too expensive," Dan said. "But we're not gonna say, 'Oh, the city's gonna be too expensive one day,' and move out now."

"There would have to be no other alternative," I said, annoyed at his theoretical approach. "We don't want to live in the suburbs."

By the late 1990s, everyone in this country—even the people who *lived* in the suburbs—seemed to have accepted the idea that suburbia was a homogeneous burial ground for creativity and thought. I was no exception. A mother pushing her baby in a stroller down Columbus Avenue seemed to have a rich interior life and her suburban, mall-strolling counterpart seemed to lack one. But there were two main things that made me want to avoid the suburbs, things that were, in my mind, both causes and effects of the suburban lack of people-in-your-neighborhoodness: car culture—obvious enough—and lawn Republicans—people who vote with one question in mind: how will this affect my lawn? and, inevitably, vote Republican. Capital gains tax? "I could use that money to put in a pool." Gun control? "I have to defend my property." People in the city might vote Republican, but it isn't because of their lawns.

"Oh come on, Rachel," Will said. "You want a house."

"Not really," I said.

"You know you'll be in the suburbs," he went on. "I give you guys three more years, tops."

And then it hit me. He wasn't just challenging me about the engagement. He was challenging me about New York! Will was implying that I wasn't a person who lived in New York because life was generally more interesting here—just regular life, not going to the hot new restaurant or club, or being the big macho Wall Street type or the "if I can make it there I'll make it anywhere" person, but just walking down the street and checking out the other animals in the zoo. He was trying to out me as a five-year tester, as a Nineties New Yorker! Dan's friend was calling me *Friends!*

I could overlook the pettiness about our engagement, but this was too much. This was *personal*. I looked over at Dan, who seemed, like everyone else, to be awaiting my response. Fine, I figured, they'll get it.

"This conversation has taken its usual turn for the ridiculous," I said, my voice rising more than *The Gypsy Kings* demanded. "We aren't leaving New York in the foreseeable future. And I would think that at this point you'd know how little impact your opinions have on our plans."

Five

$\mathcal{L}$ater that weekend, I had brunch with my friend Naomi at a diner near her apartment. Dan didn't come; he rarely came along when I went out with Naomi, citing the tendency we had to quote *Annie Hall* or *Hannah and Her Sisters* whenever something reminded us of *Annie Hall* or *Hannah and Her Sisters*. Lots of things reminded us of *Annie Hall* or *Hannah and Her Sisters*, I'd say three or four things a meal, and our voices would apparently become "loud" when we quoted, and then we'd laugh ("loud" again, I'm told), and all of this was, to Dan, annoying.

Normally, I didn't care that Dan didn't come along; Naomi was my friend and I had a better time with her one-on-one, when I could quote with abandon without Dan around to make me self-conscious. But riding the subway that particular Sunday, one question played itself over and over in my mind: "Why is it that I'm expected to put up with Dan's friends' hostility when Dan won't even deal with the odd 'annoying' 'very significantly, Wagner' and 'he's such an angry, he's such a depressive'?"

By the time I changed trains at Times Square, I was convinced that there were injustices going on. Inequities. As annoying as they may have been, *my* friends never gave Dan a hard time. And if they had, I would have stuck up for him, not held my tongue. The only reason I had to deal with stupid Will was that he was important to Dan, and Dan seemed to feel entitled to the effort without any obligation to make one in return. Had I unwittingly set up a pattern, a pattern where Dan was aloof and catered to while I was always malleable and scrambling, a pattern Dan and I would now live by *for the rest of our lives*?

The subway is a veritable petri dish for thoughts like these, especially when you have to transfer at Times Square. Times Square may have put on a tourist-friendly face, but its overhaul had yet to make it underground; the atmosphere at the 42nd Street stop, really more a web of connecting trains than a "station" in any true sense, was that of a huge maze of stadium restrooms minus the toilets, if not the smell. And my route that morning made it worse, because in order to get from our apartment on the Upper West Side to the diner near Naomi's off Union Square, I not only had to trudge through the Times Square subway station, but I also had to transfer to the N/R. The N/R line always lived up to its nickname—"the never and the rarely"—and picking it up at Times Square left you with plenty of quality platform time to pace back and forth and either listen to the would-be John Lennon singing "Imagine" off-key and think about the fact that the blackened dots on the ground beneath your feet were once pieces of gum in other people's mouths, or tune out such distractions by concentrating on one vexing question, a question like the one I was asking myself that morning, which was really a combination of "Am I a big sucker?" and "What have I gotten myself into?"

I had never been the girlfriend type. Before Dan, I'd only had one boyfriend whom I actually referred to as a "boyfriend"—

Seth Pollack—and the only reason I'd "gone out" with him was that it was the eighth grade, I was in a new school, and agreeing to be half of "Rachel plus Seth" had been the equivalent of a get-popular-free card. But it soon felt weirder and weirder to be half of "Rachel plus Seth" and still be me. I walked around with a sinking feeling in my stomach, and eventually, I just wanted that feeling to stop—popularity be damned!—and that was the end of "Rachel plus Seth," and of my desire to be a girlfriend.

Instead, I was a flail-arounder, a hooker-upper. I hadn't wanted a "boyfriend" until Dan and I started going out senior year of college. By then, I'd hooked up with enough guys who didn't let the lack of official commitment stop them from being liars, jerks, and all-around pains in my neck (and read enough Jane Austen) to think of Dan as the noble Mr. Darcy, saving my Elizabeth Bennet–like self from a world of charming but caddish Wickhams.

With Dan I'd never felt like a *girlfriend*, I'd always just felt like myself. I attributed this to two factors: Number one, the notions of "girlfriend" and "boyfriend" had changed a lot since eighth grade; number two, Dan had never been comfortable with those notions either, and, like me, had never been a person who had, or wanted, girlfriends.

Getting married was supposed to be about nothing more or less than the two of us deciding to spend our lives together. But as I settled into a booth at the diner near the Strand, I wondered if it was. I was back in eighth grade. Suddenly, there were these ideas of what I was supposed to do, these *expectations*. And Dan had done nothing to make it otherwise. My belly button felt like a drain. By getting married, was I agreeing to be something I didn't want to be—agreeing, in a sense, to become a girlfriend?

My thoughts were interrupted by Naomi's arrival.

"OhmygodI'msosorry," she said, throwing her bag, then herself, onto the seat across from me. "Just as I'm walking out the door, my phone rings, and it's my totally insane client."

Naomi was a real estate broker. She had become so fascinated by the intricacies of Manhattan real estate while buying her own apartment that she became a Realtor soon after her closing. Since then, she'd had one totally insane client after another, all of whom seemed to call just as she was walking out the door.

Naomi was also an actress—a pretty actressy actress, which was why Thomas referred to her not as "Naomi," but as "the actress," with the "actress" overpronounced the way you would overpronounce "theater" if you found it spelled with an "re." Naomi had wild curly hair, which she dyed red to make even wilder. She was a Bette girl, as opposed to a Barbra one, which I was too—though for me it was more in spirit than in practice. Being a Realtor was a great and flexible way for Naomi to make money while she waited to "come into type." "I'm a character actress," she'd say. "There's no real work 'til I'm thirty-five." In the meantime, she was deep into the improv comedy world, which meant she was constantly taking classes and attending shows, then going out to dinner somewhere in a big group afterward. It also meant dating a lot of "improvisers" in their mid-to-late thirties, urban costumeless cousins of the Renaissance Fair type. Naomi was one of those people who had a whole shtick, which meant in order to be friends with her you had to like her shtick in spite of its shtickiness. I did.

"So what's up?" she asked, settling into her seat. "Wedding madness? Insane florists? Psycho caterers from hell?"

"I wish the psychos in this wedding were people I could fire," I said.

"Not more Phyllis?"

"Nope," I said. "At dinner last night, the ever-charming Will Foster demanded to know when we were moving to the suburbs."

"The suburbs? Who said anything about leaving the city?"

I shrugged. "Not me. But apparently, I'm just kidding."

"What does he think Dan wants?"

"Good question."

"Well, what did he say?"

"He changed the subject," I lied.

"Probably a good move."

"Probably."

"Okay," Naomi said, waving her hands. "I've been waiting all weekend to tell you this one! Friday night, I'm at the Second Avenue Deli after class with a bunch of improvisers, and one of them has this friend in from Iowa or Wisconsin—somewhere totally great like that—who's there too. So we're chowing down on the complimentary health salad and the waiter comes over to take our order—standard stuff, I had the mushroom barley soup—and the friend says—"

"Pastrami on white with mayo, lettuce, and tomato!" We always said the punch line in unison.

And though I laughed, and high-fived, and was probably "loud," I was really wondering why I didn't tell Naomi the truth— that Dan had barely done or said shit and that up until the moment she'd entered the diner I'd been seething about it. There had been a time when I'd complain about Dan to Naomi, and she'd stick up for him by saying something like, "But he's so *menschy!*" Naomi liked Dan, but eventually talking to her about him seemed somehow disloyal—as if, by complaining about him to her, I was saying that she was more important to me than he was.

Or maybe I was being self-protective. Despite her enthusiasm and the party she threw just after our engagement, I knew that Naomi thought that, by marrying Dan, I was doing the "safe" thing. To her, getting married was somehow a cop-out. When I first told her I wanted to get engaged, Naomi had said "oh" in a way that sounded like "oh-hoa," as in "so *that's* the type of woman you are"—*that* being the type of woman who goes to Barnard to get the proverbial Mrs.—which pissed me off for a number of reasons, some more obvious than others.

The main one was her hypocrisy. Naomi prided herself on being a feminist, but she was really more like one of Charlie's Angels, running around in great outfits thinking she was so self-sufficient, her gutsy independence in fact handed down by a patriarch who remains conveniently invisible. You see, Naomi hadn't actually bought her apartment. Like other friends of mine from Barnard, she had Down Payment Parents—parents, typically, as Naomi's were, from Jersey—who knew how astronomical New York rents were and, after much agonizing about their children "flushing all that money down the toilet," gave them the money to buy an apartment so that instead of paying rent, they were paying carrying cost (mortgage and maintenance fees) and instead of "flushing money down the toilet," there would be "something to show for it." Naomi didn't like to say she had Down Payment Parents. She didn't like to mention her parents' hand in "her" apartment at all, but when pressed for specifics, she would present the whole thing as a fifty-fifty/win-win situation. "I get to live in the apartment, and they get a pied-à-terre in the city," she'd say, conveniently ignoring the fact that her parents, Doris and Doctor Mort, lived in Alpine, a ten-minute drive off the G.W., and had never once stayed overnight in her apartment, which meant that she was, in effect, pieding all over their terre.

So when she'd said "oh-hoa," instead of challenging her assumptions I'd thought, "I love you, Naomi, but you are so full of shit."

But she hadn't been entirely wrong. I did want the security of marriage, the settled-forever feeling that marrying Dan would bring. I wanted our apartment to feel like a *home*. Yes, I needed to be my own person, but I also needed to feel loved. And I knew that Naomi couldn't really understand that. She was a person who'd had so much safety in her life that she could never really know how important it was for me to feel protected, never really understand the deep desire I had, Cinderella-ish as it may have been, to be held in someone's palm like a lucky penny.

But that morning I didn't feel like Dan's lucky penny, I felt like a piece of change found in his pocket and left, not even in a bowl, but on the dresser. And not telling Naomi about it only made me angrier with him.

Dan didn't notice me enter the apartment. His back was to the door and he was singing "Billie Jean is not my girl / She's just a fox and / That's what I'm gonna be," complete with snapping and a signature dance move that combined a chugging of the right arm with a bending of the right knee, as if his whole right side was gathering momentum for blast-off. A pen was clenched Bob Dole–like in his blast-off hand, and his immunology textbook and notebook were strewn across the coffee table, along with an uncapped highlighter.

"Hey," he said, turning around after hearing the door close.

"Hey," I said, hanging my coat on the coat rack.

"How was brunch?"

"It was fine," I said, coming into the living room and sitting, stick-straight, on the far end of the couch, a seventies Danish modern relic with a few missing belts, which meant the cushions would fall through occasionally—another hand-me-down, like the coat rack, this one from his parents.

"Then what's the matter?" He was still standing.

"Why is it that I have to hang out with your friends and you don't have to hang out with mine?" I said.

Dan looked utterly confused. "I thought you didn't want me to come to brunch with Naomi. I thought I make you self-conscious."

"I didn't, and you do. But that's not the point."

"Then what is the point?"

"The point is that you seem to think that you spending time with my friends is optional, and me spending time with your friends is required, and I'm not setting myself up for a lifetime of being a dutiful little wifey who scratches your back while you never have to scratch mine."

"Okay," he said, looking at me as if I were just shy of insane.

"Yeah, now you say 'okay.' *Now* you say okay. All weekend you say nothing, and now you just say 'okay,' like I'm crazy."

"All weekend?"

"Yes, all weekend. All weekend when your friend has me driving carpools in the suburbs. All weekend when you do nothing to make him think otherwise!"

"Since when do you care what Will thinks?"

Good question. "It's not that I care what *he* thinks. It's that I care that you care what he thinks."

"So you think because Will thinks marriage means moving to the suburbs, that I'm going to suddenly think that's what marriage means? Weren't you the one who said it's just about the two of us spending the rest of our lives together?"

Do you notice anything about Dan here, like the fact that all he's done is ask questions? Do you see what I mean about the Socratic debate?

At moments like these, Dan really annoyed me, and not just because he was totally right. Dan annoyed me at moments like these because he reminded me more of Mr. Knightley than of Mr. Darcy, which meant that I was more like the spoiled brat–ish Emma Woodhouse than the near-perfect Elizabeth Bennet.

"That *is* all it's about. But the two of us have to agree on what the rest of our life is going to look like."

"And you don't think we do?"

"No," I said. "I do think we do. At least I think I think we do. But when people—*your* people—start saying these things that don't fit into that picture and you don't say anything at all to set the record straight, it makes me wonder."

"Well, just because I don't feel the need to challenge Will on his opinions doesn't necessarily mean I agree with him."

"It doesn't *necessarily* mean you agree with him. But it *could* mean that."

"Well in this case it doesn't."

"Then why didn't you feel the need to challenge him?"

"Because Will has already shown just how little he gets the whole idea of us getting married."

Dan was effectively saying that his not challenging Will's suburbs statement was a lot like me not challenging Naomi's "oh-hoa." But there was a difference.

"Okay," I said, "that all makes sense. But the problem is he wasn't saying all those things to *you*. He was saying them to *me*. And you did nothing!"

"You know, you really have a thing about me sticking up for you," he said, nodding aha, very-in-ter-est-ing style. All he needed to complete the look was a pipe and some taps to the chin. "Since when are you a person who needs someone else to stick up for her?"

"Since always," I replied, shocked and a little wounded.

"Trust me, Raych, you do a pretty good job on your own."

"Really?" I said, turning on a dime. I thought of that Jackie Mason joke: You call an Italian girl a whore and she'll slap you. You call a Jewish girl a whore and she'll ask, "How was I standing?"

"Yes," Dan said. "Believe me, if I ever thought you needed me to stick up for you, I would."

"You would?"

"Of course."

"You promise?"

"I promise."

I didn't know whether to believe this, and was still unsettled regardless.

"Why is it that people seem to think all these things about me and not you?" I asked.

"You don't think what they think about you means they think something about me? Like that I'm this typical suit who's gonna go out and bring home the bacon?"

"So I can fry it up in a pan?"

"Exactly."

"But I don't want pork in the house."

"Exactly."

"Yeah, but if it wasn't for me saying I don't want any pork in the house, you'd bring home bacon."

"Rachel, I was talking figuratively, which you know."

"Well, so am I. I'm extending your metaphor. I'm saying maybe if it wasn't for me, you'd be bringing home both kinds of bacon."

"Bringing home bacon to who?" Dan asked, switching back to the Socratic debate.

"Someone else."

"But I'm not with someone else, am I?"

"No."

"And do you think that's just by accident?"

The thing about Socratic debate mode is that it can transition into very cute mode very quickly. I turned my head to the side, tucked my chin into my neck, and gave him a little smile—an expression that Dan and I both made on occasion, one that we'd nicknamed "flirty."

"I guess not," I said.

"You *guess* not? You don't think I'm with you for a reason?"

"Well . . . what's your reason?" I asked, deepening my chin tuck.

"I have more than one," Dan said, joining me on the couch.

"Watch out!" I laughed, as a corner of his cushion fell through to the frame.

"Reasons, reasons, reasons," he said, ignoring the little gap between us. He kissed a different part of my face—forehead, left cheek, right cheek—as he said the word again and again. "I'm full of reasons. I am bursting with reasons. I am a reasons machine!"

What happened after that is none of your business, but suffice it to say, we made up.

Six

In the early phase of wedding planning, once-casual activities become oddly official.

Dan's parents lived in suburban Philadelphia, an hour and a half's drive away, conveniently close and far at the same time. The Gershons coming up for dinner wasn't crazy, it's just that they'd never done it before. They usually came up for a substantive reason—Dan's father had a conference or Dan's brother was in a play—known far in advance. Also, since both of Dan's brothers lived in New York, under normal circumstances, if we were meeting Dan's parents for dinner we'd be meeting them too. But, just from the tone of his father's voice on the other end of the line when he'd called to say, "Mom and I want to come up and have dinner with you and Rachel this weekend," Dan knew these were not normal circumstances. On this night, we were to discuss the Gershons' contribution to our wedding.

One of the advantages of dating someone for four years, two of them spent living together, is that you know your in-laws before you have to plan a wedding with them. The main thing I knew about Marty and Carol Gershon was that I was lucky to have them as in-laws. Lucky because they were not psycho, lucky because they were pretty laissez-faire, lucky because I genuinely liked them.

Marty and Carol Gershon were probably the most happily married couple I'd ever seen, and it made me think that the key to a happy marriage was having someone who would indulge your theories about how the rest of the world was missing the boat.

Marty was a professor of History at Temple—"a second-rate institution in a second-rate city," as he put it with jovial pride. Marty was very satisfied with his place on the academic slow track because he saw himself not as a great intellectual, but as a history buff who, through the gift of intelligence, had lucked into a career that allowed him to pursue his hobbies full-time, unencumbered, for the most part, by the tyrannical forces of the real working world. To Marty, those who lacked his mindset toward academic life weren't more ambitious or more rigorous; they were just plain spoiling the fun. It was as if he felt that the root of all evil was not money or religion but academic snobbery, with the departmental meeting running a close second.

Carol was also a paid buff, but her specialty was music. Once her sons were in high school and her carpooling skills were less in demand, she began giving piano lessons from home. Carol enjoyed her job, but every so often, she would sigh and shake her head and bemoan "overachiever" parents who "overschedule" their kids. Such sighs were usually brought on by a parent's complaint that the child wasn't practicing enough. Carol would then explain to the parent, in her calmest voice, that not every pupil "would be going on to the Philharmonic," and that she'd rather her students "enjoy the piano for one hour a week than feel burdened by it every day." It would quickly become clear to Carol that her explanation made no sense to the parent, and that's when Carol would sigh.

Before I'd ever met Carol and Marty, back when Dan was just the love of my life, I knew the Gershons would make great in-laws. That was because they had a family tattoo.

What had started as a typical wry Dan comment had led to a permanent body marking for him, his brothers, and, yes, his parents. Tattooing had become the thing to do around our sophomore year in college. The Gershons were discussing the phenomenon around the Seder table that year. (Gershon Seders were nuclear family events, and the Gershons were a nuclear family with the astonishing ability to have amicable discussions.) They were all basically in agreement that, rather than being "cool," sticking something permanent on your body in late adolescence was regret waiting to happen.

"In fifty years, you're going to have a bunch of senior citizens running around with names of rock bands written on their chests," Dan's father said with a laugh. "Forget about how stupid they'll look. What if they don't like the bands anymore?"

"What if instead of a band tattoo, you had your own name?" said Dan's older brother Adam, who would later become a lawyer.

"Something about actual words sort of ruins the whole effect," said Dan's younger brother Joel, who would later become involved in experimental theater and live in an industrial loft in Brooklyn with five other artist friends. "The best tattoos are the ones that are just designs."

"Oh, Joel," said Dan's mother, "not those big ones, I hope! - They're like big murals on skin!"

"No," said Joel, "not big multicolored ones. More like a really small funky design that you have to know to look for. That can be cool."

"Oh, that's not bad at all then," said Carol.

There were nods all around the table as the family processed this information.

"Well, then," said Dan, "if we're all in agreement on small tattoos, then I say we get one."

"A tattoo?" Adam asked.

"Yeah," said Dan. "A family tattoo." To this day, he is unsure whether he was kidding. His familial role was to stretch things to their most absurd, at which point his mother would say, "That's our Danny, *one step beyond*." But that night, she didn't say it.

Instead, Marty said, "A family crest." With his love of history, Marty was obviously intrigued by the idea. But that wasn't the only element that piqued his interest. A family tattoo would be the ace-in-the-hole that would prove his nonconformity to middle-aged suburban norms. And with a family tattoo, Marty Gershon would transcend the ordinary empty-nester and become the tribal leader of a branded flock.

"I could design it," Carol offered. For her the appeal was simple: Any demonstration of family unity, especially one with an artistic angle, was something she could get behind.

"I'm down with that," said Joel, who would applaud any step his terminally straight family took in the direction of funky.

"Me too," said Adam. Adam was a big sports fan (in the Jewish—heavy on the stats, low on the drinking and yelling—way), so a family tattoo appealed to his sense of team spirit.

So Carol drew up a sort-of star with five loops—one for each family member—with the largest loop on top to "symbolize the strength of the individual," and each of the Gershons tattooed it on a different spot. News of the tattoo and the story that accompanied it quickly circulated the Barnard/Columbia campuses; so, before I'd ever met Marty and Carol Gershon, I knew I liked them.

But Dan's parents were not without their downsides. For all of their quirks, their happy marriage was built on a strict Ozzie and Harriet foundation that occasionally made me bristle. I'd never seen Marty wash a dish, or Carol drive the car when Marty was in it. She knew as much about their stock portfolio as he did about cooking dinner, which is to say, nothing. At first I felt bad for Dan's mother, who, from my vantage point at the dinner table where she served while Marty complimented, seemed to have gotten the shorter end of their marital stick. But if Carol was happy, then who was I to judge? Dan's parents had a system that obviously worked for them, so the only real problem I had with that system was that they didn't seem to fully grasp that it wouldn't work for Dan and me.

Eating in Manhattan with the Gershons was not an easy task. Not because they were picky or, like many parents in from out of town, hungry less for dinner than for the name of a designer restaurant to drop to their friends back home. The Gershons were just the opposite; they were constantly going wide-eyed over diners and Chinese restaurants in proximity to their many hotels, not to mention Carol's ongoing love affair with Midtown salad bars ("They have just about everything, and it's all prepared! I told Marty, If we lived here, you couldn't tear me away!"). The other problem with dining with Dan's parents was that Marty was hard of hearing, which, while a great coping mechanism for his departmental meetings, was inconvenient for us when trying to find a restaurant with an acceptably low level of noise.

In New York that night, we opted for one of the overpriced, faintly Italian restaurants on Columbus right near our apartment, which, considering it was a Saturday, seemed as quiet as we could get. But at the table, Marty was still forced to play with the remote control on his hearing aid. We hadn't even opened our menus when he said, "You know what would be really nice the next time we come up? A home-cooked meal."

Even with their dynamics, this seemed a lot to ask of Carol. The logistics alone were a little nuts. Would they pack things in a cooler? I was about to suggest that, since the noise was bothering him, we go back to our place and order in, when Carol said, "Gee, Marty, that's a big undertaking for Rachel."

With my future in-laws gazing at me expectantly, I realized that Marty wasn't talking about noise or "a" home-cooked meal: He wanted a meal cooked in my home by me. The year before, he'd called each of his sons to say that his sixtieth birthday was coming up, and what he really wanted was for them to throw him a party "just for me and Mom and you guys." As Dan and I hung streamers around our apartment and waited for his brothers to arrive with the ice cream and cake, we laughed about Marty belonging to the Kiss My Ring school of fatherhood. Now I looked over at Dan, who was reading the menu.

"Actually, it would be more of an undertaking for Dan," I said, reminding them of something we'd told them many times. "My idea of cooking is boiling water, adding noodles, and heating up sauce. But Dan makes a mean stir-fry."

Just as I joined Dan in menu-reading, his parents pulled The Split. Marty turned to Dan and asked how school was going. Carol turned to me and said, "I love those earrings. Where did you get them?"

We had not always flowed into The Split this naturally; at first, Carol would fish me out of conversations. We would all be talking about politics. Marty would be holding forth on why he hates Clinton, and I would be listening, waiting to point out, as I always did, that the best thing about Clinton was that he wasn't in bed with the religious right, when out of nowhere, as Marty continued, Carol would turn to me and ask, "Rachel, what do you use to keep your lips from getting chapped?" or another question that could have been a tagline from *Ladies' Home Journal*. I would be dying to say something quick like, "Just plain old Chap Stick," and then turn back to the more interesting conversation, the one I thought was being had in general, by the whole group. But Carol never chimed in on political discussions. Guessing that Carol felt politics was "men's stuff," all of my Barnard antennae would go up, ready to defend the seriousness of my gender. But, thanks to the sweet, eager look on Carol's face, I didn't have the heart to tell her that I was much more interested in the president of the United States than beauty products. After years of silent annoyance, I thought about the fact that Carol and Marty were hardly social butterflies—she had one close friend, known as "Libby Becker, Mom's hippie friend," and spent a good 90 percent of her time in her house either alone, with Marty, or listening to seven-year-olds bang out "The Entertainer." Much as she adored her husband and three sons, to Carol, having another female around must have been akin to being handed a bottle of water in the desert. Now I just waited for The Split to happen, like a wave, and rode it out, no fishing required.

Once our pastas and piccatas had arrived, it was time to get down to the nitty-gritty.

"So," Marty said, leaning back in his chair, "we figured that we ought to let you guys know what our contribution to the wedding is going to be."

"Sounds good," Dan said in his best deep, man-to-man-talk voice.

"Have you ever heard of FLOP?" Carol asked us, emphasizing the word *Flop* as if it were the latest thing off the runway in Milan.

"I don't think we've heard of FLOP," I said.

"It stands for Flowers," Marty used his fingers to tick the letters off, "Liquor . . . O . . . what's O, Carol?"

"Flowers, Liquor . . . hmmm." Carol cocked her head and looked up at the ceiling. "Well, P is for photographer and one of the things was the band . . ."

"Orchestra?" I ventured.

"Orchestra! That's it!" Carol beamed.

"What was it?" Marty leaned inward and adjusted his hearing aid.

"It was 'orchestra'!" Carol told him.

"Orchestra! That's it!" Marty smiled. "But we're not gonna pay for a full one!" At this, he and his wife chuckled.

"I think we can live with that," Dan said.

"Yes," Marty continued. "We hear from our sources that that's the thing the groom's parents should do. Flowers, Liquor, Orchestra, Photographer. FLOP."

Unless I'd forgotten something, with Dan's parents providing the band, the alcohol, the flowers, and the photographer, my father had to cover the place, the caterer, the invitations, and the big question mark of my dress. Maybe the ten thousand dollars could work out after all.

"Sounds good," Dan said, as he squeezed my hand under the table.

"And we can go with you to find these things," Carol said. "I'm a little unsure of how to go about it in Washington, but we can always ask Jan Levy—she must have a list left over from Debra and Zhang's wedding, and they're so excited that you're having it at the Audubon Society! Oh, but I'm forgetting all about Phyllis. Maybe it's better to ask her . . ."

Dan and I made eye contact across the table. We both knew this would not be "better."

Dan's parents had met my father and stepmother the year before at a lunch at Jerry and Phyllis's condo. While no sparks had flown, it was clear from Carol's shocked expression the moment she stepped into Phyllis's blonde wood, bright art, Bloomingdale's furnished abode (which Thomas and I had dubbed "the model home," given its perpetual state of appearing uninhabited by actual people) that this was not a parental match made in heaven. But it didn't seem to matter, at least until now.

"Why don't we just ask Jan?" I suggested.

"Okay," said Carol, brightening. "I'll call her. I'm sure she'll be happy to help."

"Have you guys thought at all about the rabbi?" Dan's father asked. Religious observance was his realm. Even though Carol had converted before they married, Marty's mother had refused to see her as anything but a *shiksa*. Dan's grandma Sophie had been dead for fifteen years, but Carol remained tentative in all things Jewish, scarred because of her.

Marty's question had clearly been meant for me. Dan had gone to Hebrew School—the religious equivalent of "eat your Brussels sprouts." His father was well aware of the limitations of this upbringing—any discussion of synagogue "when you boys were home" inevitably led to grousing about Hebrew High School and fond memories of the time the family skipped services and went to a park for their own Yom Kippur retreat.

"I was thinking of asking one of my teachers from high school," I said. "But nothing definite yet."

"Well, I think our rabbi would be great." Marty had often spoken of their new rabbi, usually to say what a bright and dynamic guy he was and how much Marty wished this rabbi had been around when Dan was in Hebrew School, which would lead to the aforementioned grousing by Dan and his parents about the irrelevance of Hebrew School.

"We can certainly talk to him about it," I nodded.

"Great," said Marty. "You know, he's coming in for a conference or something in the next couple weeks. He said he'd have time to meet with you."

"Oh," I said, digesting the fact that Marty had already spoken to the rabbi about this. I looked over at Dan to see his reaction. He was winding pasta around his fork. Marty, meanwhile, was looking at me, waiting for my reply. "Well," I said, "that's definitely convenient."

"I wish he'd been around when you boys were in Hebrew School," Marty said.

"Oh," said Carol, "but then we wouldn't have had our Yom Kippur retreat! Remember that, Danny? You got so *intrigued* by that reading Dad brought."

"Martin Buber." Dan nodded. "From *I and Thou*, right, Dad?"

"That's the one," said Marty.

"You've heard about that retreat, right, Rachel?" Carol asked. Of course I had. The Gershons were parents who loved to reminisce, and I had always been conscious of the role I played in these trips down memory lane. They were Dan's Parents and I was Dan's Girlfriend, both the excuse for telling these tales and the reason they needed to do so. I smiled and nodded, right on cue. Carol turned to Dan. "How old were you, Danny, fifteen?"

"Sixteen, maybe? Or about to turn sixteen. I didn't have my license yet . . ."

As they continued their stroll down memory lane, I tuned out, smiling, thinking how nice it must be to have a nonpsycho set of parents. The sound of Dan and his parents laughing together snapped me back into focus. And though I hadn't heard the joke itself, I laughed along with them.

Seven

The next day, it was time to get serious about the wedding. I'd read that week's *Vows* column—featuring one of those "she's such a free spirit, she hosts these all-weekend parties at her ancestral retreat in Newport and everyone just crashes in sleeping bags on the floor!" brides and one of those "he's a gentleman in that Cary Grant way you don't find anymore" (unless you're a regular reader of the *Vows* column, in which case you find one every other month) grooms and a photo taken as the thirty-two (the number of months they'd been together) doves were released at their lavish four-hundred-person wedding at said ancestral retreat (no sleeping bags this time)—and decided we needed to get down to business. Dan and I sat side by side on the readjusted couch. Our wedding file lay on the coffee table, and, with a fresh legal pad and pen in his hands, a trusty copy of *Martha Stewart Weddings* in mine, we checked our progress against Martha's "Six Months or More Ahead" timeline.

"We have the date—June fourteenth."

"Check," said Dan.

"We have the budget—ten thousand dollars plus FLOP."

"Check."

"We have the place—the Audubon Society."

"Check."

"We have the caterer—Phyllis's friend Deena from the board."

"Check."

"We're working on the officiant—we meet your parents' rabbi this week." I raised my eyebrows.

"Check."

"We have the band, sort of. Maybe I should call Jonah again." Jonah was a friend of mine from summer camp who'd lived in Washington, working for a senator by day and playing upright bass in jazz clubs around the city at night. He was confident that, with a round or two of calling, he could put together a quartet for us. I left a message on his machine to check on his search.

"Check," said Dan when I hung up.

"I don't think that counts as a check. That or the rabbi. - They're not done deals, and a check is a done deal. You check things *off* your list—they're still *on* ours."

"I'm not checking anything off," Dan said, holding up his still-blank legal pad.

"Why not?"

"Because I'm waiting to write the to-do list."

"Then why are you saying 'check'?"

"What else am I supposed to do?"

I shot him a look.

"Lighten up," he said. "It's a party. It's supposed to be fun."

"The party itself will be fun," I said. "Planning it isn't."

I turned back to Martha, the only one around who understood that planning a wedding was serious business, a delicate juggling act where attention must be paid at all times to the numerous balls in the air. This is, after all, what women's magazines are made for, to alternately fuel and assuage our neuroses.

"'Compile guest list,'" I said with a groan. Well, it wasn't exactly six months yet. "I'm sure once my father hears about FLOP, he'll come to his senses and tell Phyllis they have to invite the cousins. But still, we'll worry about that later."

"Right," said Dan.

"Well, the florist and photographer don't need to be done until four to six months before, and we'll take care of them with your parents in Washington." Carol had suggested we use the Levy-Wu florist and photographer, so we were all going down in a month or so to meet with them. We could figure out the number of guests then too.

"'Order dress and accessories'—I'm working on that one."

Dan said, "That counts," and I nodded.

"Hey," I said, "while I have the magazine open, can I show you the dress I like?"

"Isn't that supposed to be bad luck?"

"Only if it's the actual dress on the actual bride."

"Okay then," he said, shrugging.

I turned to the Post-it–noted full-page ad for Josephine, the SoHo studio of an adorable little Vermont husband and wife team, right around the corner from Thomas's store. The ad featured the simple, elegant dress I'd been imagining myself in for weeks.

Dan wrinkled his nose. "Not bridey enough."

"What?" Who knew he'd have an opinion, much less this one?

"It's a really nice dress, but it doesn't look *bridey*."

I squinted back and forth from my fiancé to the picture. He was so matter-of-fact.

Unsure how to process this, I closed Martha and put her on the coffee table. "Okay, to-do list time. Ready to write?"

"Check."

We sat in silence for the next few minutes, me thinking and Dan waiting. It felt like there should have been a million things to do. But, sitting on the couch that afternoon, it was clear that anything that needed doing this far in advance was already pretty much under control. Anything, that was, except the one and only thing I could think to put on our list, the very thing I'd been dreading and avoiding this long: "Talk To Mom."

"And there it is in black and yellow," I said, "the reason that planning this wedding will never be 'fun.'"

"Come on, Raych. How bad can she be?"

"You have no idea."

He did, but only from me telling him. Because I deliberately kept her at arms' length, Dan might have met my mother, but he'd never seen the real Joyce. Whenever Dan was around she was sure to be on her best behavior, speaking only in The Sweet Voice, the saccharine tone she used weekly at Shabbat *Kiddushes* as she gobbled up the free whitefish salad and butter cookies, hoping all the while that no one realized she'd skipped the actual service. Joyce's great hope was to win Dan over, her fantasy was him saying, "Aw, come on, Raych, your mom's so nice. We really should see her more often," words strikingly close to the ones he was uttering just then.

"Joyce has been kissing your ass since the day she met you for this exact purpose," I said. "Don't let her fool you."

"True. But think about it. That works in our favor."

"Yeah, for a little while. But her Little Miss Sweet act is like balancing a book on her head. She can pull it off every so often for a minute or so, but eventually it drops with a big fat thud and smashes your toe underneath it."

"So she'll stop being sweet. Maybe she'll be a little nasty. So what?"

"You have no idea what she does. How she holds things hostage."

"Yes I do," Dan said. "You've told me. But she won't be able to this time because you won't let her. Right?"

"I'll try. But we're talking about Joyce here. I'm telling you, - she'll find a way."

Anyone who knew my mother knew she was a little wacky. But, like anyone who's a little off, she was like a pointillist painting—the closer you got, the harder it was to see anything other than a mess. The woman broke new ground in the field of indecisiveness. My brother went without a name for the first three months of his life because Joyce couldn't decide on one. She would walk through the supermarket aisles—the suburban equivalent of a town square—stopping people and asking, "Does he look like a Matthew or a David?" with a laugh that said, "Aren't I wacky?" This was Potomac, Maryland—like most affluent suburbs, not exactly a place where people were inclined to let their freak flags fly. Pretty soon, everyone who set foot in Safeway (and that was everyone) had been consulted. Even the cashiers knew us by his nonnames. "Hi, Matthew or David," they'd say as our groceries glided toward them. "Does your brother have a name yet?" "What do you call him?" my third-grade classmates would ask on the playground.

"Just decide!" I'd beg. I could have gone on calling my brother S (for Silverstein, the one name he did have) for the rest of his life (in fact, I still call him that), but every time my mother asked a new stranger's opinion I wanted to crawl into the freezer section and bury myself in a stack of Hungry Man dinners. Even worse than the embarrassment was the constant "Matthew or David?" "Matthew or David?" pounded into my head like Chinese water torture.

"Oooh, I don't know!" she'd say, again with that laugh that, as the months wore on, seemed less and less wacky and more and more maniacal. "Aunt Thelma says Matthew, but Uncle Stuart says David, and you and Grandpa Sol say either. How am I supposed to choose?"

Somebody had to do something. This was an innocent child! My fed-up father had started calling him Ralph.

"Here," I'd say, grabbing a quarter from my pocket. "Flip it!"

"But which name should be heads and which should be tails?"

In the end, it was Matthew—and when I say "the end" I mean it literally. The deadline to file a birth certificate is three months after the day of the baby's birth, and on my brother's three-month birthday, at five minutes to five (five minutes before the post office closed), I stood over my mother and yelled, "Just name him Matthew! We're not gonna make it!" and she said, "Oooh, okay!" and wrote "Matthew" and signed her name. We raced to the car where the newly named Matthew had been sleeping for the half-hour since I'd put him in his car seat. Minutes later, we sped into the post office lot. The clock on the dashboard read 4:59, so I said, "Give me the envelope," and ran out of the car, into the post office, and up to the window. Handing over the letter, I exhaled and said, "Thank God," and the lady behind the counter laughed at this combination of exhaustion and relief, coming as it did from a ponytailed eight-year-old.

I try to comfort myself and say Elizabeth Bennet had a problematic mother too, but the comparison once again leaves me falling short. No matter how crass or embarrassing her mother was, Elizabeth kept her cool.

I wanted a mother like Carole King, a mother who wrote "It's Too Late," who could say she was still "glad for what we had." No words were less likely to come from my own mother's mouth.

Every so often, one of those TV law shows will have a child custody episode. The parents will be fighting back and forth about some "issue" and there's always that scene where the lawyer sits the client down and asks him or her to "take a step back" and "look at the big picture." The lawyer says, "I know this is important to you. But I also know you love your daughter. Is having her parents constantly at war really what you want for her?" The parent always softens, looks sad, and compromises. "I just want what's best for little Suzie."

Needless to say, the show is absurd: Has one divorcing couple in history ever turned suddenly, reasonably amicable? But the premise works and is satisfying because the show has them act the way we'd like them to act. It works as a sort of prime time after-school special—an after-work special!—illustrating a moral example. Instead of instructing adolescents on what to do if their friends start drinking and "hanging out with The Wrong Crowd," the law show tells supposed grown-ups how to behave if their spouse becomes their mortal enemy.

Even before they separated, my parents could have used that instruction. Unlike the TV couple, my parents' battles had been as much a condition of their marriage as their divorce. Unlike the show, there was no hardworking lawyer trying to "do the right thing"; I had been cast in that role, first for myself and then for my brother. And neither of them could ever be convinced to take a step back.

As far back as I can remember, getting anything from my parents—money for a field trip, new clothes for school, a duffel bag for summer camp—had meant numerous rounds of walking back and forth between my father playing solitaire in the den and my mother puttering around in the kitchen, both of them hemming and hawing and making their case for why taking care of my request was really the other person's job, frustratedly asking me time and again why exactly that thing was needed, as if I were the one causing the problem. It would go on and on like this—sometimes for days, sometimes for weeks, sometimes for months—back and forth, tell your mother this, tell your father that, *why* do you need this again? Gradually, I'd become less a lawyer than a jack-in-the-box and each round would serve as another crank; the more it seemed that neither of them would budge, the closer I'd get to the inevitable burst.

In the end, I'd be hysterical and one of them would give in. With my father, it would be out of sheer exhaustion. He'd sigh, wanting to stop my crying, but still wanting to prove his point. "I will sign this permission slip and give you the money, but you tell your mother that next time field trip money comes out of her budget." With my mother, it would be in anger, her concession further proof of her point. "All right. I'll sign your permission slip and give you a check. But you remember who did this for you—me, not him!"

I knew that planning this wedding would mean a reprisal of my lawyer role and that, more than my mother herself, was what I dreaded the most.

On the couch that afternoon, it dawned on me that Dan and I were having the same conversation we'd had on the way down to Washington, only that time it had been about Phyllis and I had been the one waving the flag of reason to convince both of us that an insane person would act like someone other than herself.

But I told myself that Dan was right. Things were different now. I was no longer a child. I'd been living in New York for eight years without them. I was marrying Dan. I'd moved on, established my own life in my own place; it had been years since I asked them for anything. I was an adult, and this was kid stuff that didn't matter anymore.

Besides, it was their only daughter's wedding. Surely, in the spirit of the event, they'd put their differences aside.

But I wasn't taking any chances. I'd waited to get as many of my wedding ducks in a row as possible before involving my mother. And now I could see only one duck left waddling solo on the wedding planning horizon. I told Dan he had to stay on the couch and be encouraging while I made the call I needed to get it in place.

"Is this really necessary?" he asked.

I had some thoughts here, thoughts like, "And you don't depend on me to make conversation with your parents?" but all I said as I dialed was, "Yes."

"Hi, Dad."

"Hey there, Raych. How are you?"

"Good, good."

"You workin' on a book?" Since I'd graduated college, conversations with my father always began with him asking me about work. Until recently, he'd asked these questions Jerry-anally—"You gettin' any job leads?" "You still writin' those books?"—as if trying to fix a picture on his wall that, despite his many efforts, simply would not hang straight. His newfound casualness had coincided with my engagement. Coincided without being a coincidence.

"Yup."

"And that's still going well?"

"Work's good. How about you?"

"Fine, fine."

"That's good. You're just hanging out?"

"Yep. Phyllis had to return a few things to Nordstrom's, so she's out taking care of that. I'm trying to finish up the Sunday papers before she gets back." The newspaper was an ongoing "problem" in their marriage, an example that Phyllis liked to cite as further evidence that my father was "impossible." For as long as I could remember, Jerry had had both *The New York Times* and *The Washington Post* delivered every day. He'd read the papers over breakfast, before heading out to work. Phyllis did not read the paper ("It makes your hands filthy! Besides, I don't need it— I keep CNN on all day") and was driven to distraction by the "clutter" it caused. First, Jerry was given a cubbylike spot in the wall unit for storing his newspapers, but the "clutter" would still be "all over the table" as he read. Soon he was having his weekday papers delivered to the office, his paper spot storing only the weekend papers, which he still received at home. But, even in its spot, the sight of the "clutter" still drove his wife crazy. Eventually, newspapers had to be thrown out the day they arrived, regardless of whether they'd been read. "It's getting there, but I still have these heavy stacks of filth dropped on my doormat every weekend," Phyllis would say, exasperated. "Your father is just impossible." You had to pity the guy.

"Well, I'll make this quick so you can get back to your paper," I said. "I'm calling on wedding business."

"Okay," he said, rising to the mock-seriousness of my tone.

Figuring I'd start with the good news, I told him about the Gershons' FLOP contribution.

"That's very generous," he said, sounding pleased and a little surprised.

"Well, so, with Dan's parents doing all that stuff, we can probably have more people." This was my too-subtle way of raising the guest list question.

"Probably," my father said.

Deciding to give the news time to sink in, I refrained from pressing the cousins issue further. Besides, more important matters needed addressing. "So," I continued, dipping my toe in the water slowly, "now that things are sort of on their way, I was thinking I should give Joyce an update."

Dan gave me the thumbs-up. My father said, "Okay." So far so good.

"Good. So, now, I don't really want to get her all involved, but I know one of the first questions she's going to ask is if the wedding will be kosher."

A Jerry-anal huff made its way through the receiver. "Rachel, you know I want to stick to a budget here." FLOP or no FLOP, kosher catering still cost more, and, even when his role of father wasn't followed by the words "of the bride," it was always about the money.

"I know, Dad. But just listen to me for a second. I don't think you should have to pay for a kosher caterer."

"Well, that's good, because I'm not going to—"

"But I do think Joyce should be able to make the wedding kosher for Grandpa Sol's sake."

"You know, you brought this up at the Kosmos Club, and I didn't agree with it then. Your mother has always used Grandpa Sol as an excuse to get her way. She doesn't even really keep kosher. I'm not going to keep on accommodating her. She needs to know there are limits."

Here we go, I thought. Whether or not my mother used Grandpa Sol as an excuse didn't seem to matter. The fact that my mother kept kosher only in her house, and, even then, allowed my brother to keep McDonald's leftovers in the refrigerator and warm them up in the microwave as long as he did it on paper plates, seemed very much beside the point. This was for Grandpa Sol, not her. He was my grandfather; he kept kosher. What did it have to do with Joyce? Obviously, as usual, everything.

"But, Dad, I want to give her limits. That's the whole point. What I want to do is tell her it can be up to her, but if she wants the wedding kosher, she has to pay the difference."

Dan nodded encouragingly. I had run this idea by him on the train back from Washington.

"That seems totally reasonable," he'd said. "I can't imagine why your father wouldn't go for it."

"I can imagine," I'd told him. "But I hope you're right."

It was a fair deal, but I was annoyed at having to broker it. My father knew better than anyone that Joyce would be waiting for the slightest opening to turn my wedding into her federal case, so it seemed to me that he should have been trying his best not to make waves. My father was the one who'd married someone with an Orthodox parent. Why did I have to drag him into being the least bit accommodating?

"All I want to do is to give her the option," I said. "Come on, Dad. You know Joyce. It's not like she's gonna let this drop. If I don't say the wedding can be kosher up front she'll turn it into a whole big deal and we won't hear the end of it for months. Is that really what you want?"

Dan gave another thumbs-up, this time accompanied by a "yeah, baby" nod. I was laying out a firm case, making a reasonable argument without getting emotional or being argumentative. There was grumbling on my father's end of the line, but I knew I had him.

"Well," he said, "Phyllis has already spoken to Deena about doing the catering. Are you sure that she can do kosher?"

"No. But she's a big caterer in D.C. I imagine she can."

"Well, that's . . ." he stammered a bit as his foot came down, "that's top priority, Rachel. Deena is a friend of Phyllis's from the condo board. It's very important to Phyllis that she does the catering. I'm not gonna let your mother interfere with that."

This was what my father thought was important. I could always feel my blood pump faster at moments like these, moments when I could tell that a concept had come from Phyllis's mouth and gone straight into my father's ears and out his mouth without any evidence of involvement from his brain. My temples started throbbing.

"Hold your horses, Dad," I said, turning, as I often did in these situations, to the comfort of clichés. "If you give me her number, I'll call Deena and ask. I bet she can do kosher catering. And if she can't, we can cross that bridge if we get to it."

Dan nodded. There was a sigh on my father's end, but he said, "Hold on," and got Deena's numbers—both home and work—from Phyllis's electronic Rolodex.

"Just be sure to check with Deena before you call your mother," he said after giving them to me. "I'm not prepared to make your offer if she can't do kosher catering."

"Okay. I'll call her right now and check."

We exchanged good-byes and I wondered why, during any discussion of my wedding, my father seemed angry with me.

"See?" Dan said. "That wasn't so bad. You don't really need me to sit and hold your hand."

"Yes I do," I said. I couldn't tell whether he meant to encourage me or relieve himself of further duty. "Anyway, that was the easy parent."

I told Dan he could take an intermission while I called the caterer at home. Deena knew me by name and instantly launched into a description of the carpeting and wallpaper that she and Phyllis were proposing the condo board accept for the lobby's renovation.

"And I hear there's also a big project going on with you," she said.

"Yes," I said. "That's actually why I'm calling." I told her that Phyllis had been raving about her catering (in words I will not re-create here, but let's just say I decided if you can't beat 'em, join 'em and adopted the Phyllis style of making flattery the sincerest form of flattery). I told Deena I was looking forward to her doing the wedding. I just had one quick question: Could she do kosher? As I expected, she could, and we went on to discuss the merits of kosher versus kosher-style (the no pork, no shellfish, no mixing milk and meat option that wasn't strictly kosher but nonetheless retained the *kashrut* spirit, which was the way we'd go if my mother didn't want to pay the difference) and the relative costs of doing the wedding meat or dairy.

"All's clear with the caterer," I called out to Dan, who was making popcorn in the kitchen. When he returned with the popcorn, I said, "Even if my mother pays the extra for kosher, I think it might make sense to have a dairy wedding."

"A dairy wedding?"

"Yeah, as opposed to a meat wedding."

"A meat wedding?"

"Yeah, you know, *flaishig*. We'll just serve fish for the main course. Even if we do it kosher, it's a lot less expensive than meat."

"So you're saying no meat?"

"Well, no chicken or beef, or lamb or whatever." I couldn't believe he even cared about this. "But we'll have fish."

"So, no pigs in blankets?"

"Are you serious?"

"Yes." He was. "I love pigs in blankets. We're not gonna have pigs in blankets?"

"Who are you—the groom or the bar mitzvah boy?"

"I love pigs in blankets."

"Please don't be an obstacle," I said. He went back into the kitchen and I picked up the phone to call my aunt Annie for my usual pre-Joyce consult.

My relationship with Annie and her husband, my mother's younger brother Stuart, had always had that mutual life raft, "You guys think they're crazy too!" quality more common to siblings than uncles and aunts and nieces, a quality that tended to manifest itself in fortifying phone calls, end-of-table huddles, and closed-door kitchen chats. Over the years, with me in New York and my mother increasingly viewing us all as "the enemy," it had come to mean my spending the Jewish holidays with them in Teaneck, in a way becoming more a part of their family than my own.

I told Annie I was gearing up to fill my mother in on the wedding. She said, "Just get it over with."

"I know, I know. But I don't wanna call her."

"I don't blame you," she said. "I wouldn't want to call her either. But you have to, so just do it and get it over with."

"You're right, you're right." She always was. "I will."

"Good luck," she said. "You'll need it."

I hung up with Annie, and, still unfortified, dialed Matthew's Brown dorm room. As usual, I got the machine. I listened to his message—the first few bars of the *Sanford and Son* theme song—then heard the beep.

"S? S, if you're there, pick up." I gave him a few seconds to answer. Sure enough, he did.

"Hey, there."

"Screening?"

"As always. Sunday afternoon is prime Joyce phone call time. She's still up my ass about my major."

I groaned in sympathy.

For the past six months, Joyce had been trying to make sure that Matthew would major in Astrophysics, not Astronomy. Matthew, who intended to apply to Ph.D. programs after graduation, had found out that the distinction made little difference—except if he wanted to double-major in Philosophy, which he did. Since the Philosophy seminars conflicted with the Astrophysics labs—but not the Astronomy labs—he was leaning toward an Astronomy major. This was a source of endless worry for Joyce, who reasoned that Astrophysics "just sounds better." And an endless worry for Joyce meant endless nagging for Matthew, which was why he screened his phone calls.

"I have to call her today. About the wedding."

"Good," he said. "One less thing she'll complain to me about."

"She's already been complaining to you?"

"Not really," he said, "just the usual." He put on his best Joyce voice, complete with New Jersey accent. "'Your sister hasn't told me one thing about this wedding. What's going on? Do you know?'"

"Ugh." Fearing just such a POW inquisition, I'd deliberately kept Matthew out of the loop.

"Don't worry about it," he said. "Just get it over with."

"I know. I should. I will."

"Good luck."

I hung up with Matthew and said, "I'm dialing," loudly, to Dan.

This time he knew to take his seat. I always had Dan around

when I called my mother, for bolstering (the poignant eye roll), pinch hitting ("say hi to Dan"), or emergency exits ("Dan's really hungry; I have to go").

"Hello," said Joyce through the phone.

"Hi, Mom," I said, waiting for her usual greeting of, "Oh . . . well, look who's calling!"—not a greeting of so-nice-to-hear-from-you surprise, but an it's-about-fucking-time-you-called delivered in a low-register voice that set the general hostility-with-attempted-guilt-trip theme of the conversation from the beginning.

Instead, my mother said, "Hi, honey. What's up?" in The Sweet Voice. Perhaps she sensed Dan next to me, my own lucky charm.

I told her that I was calling with a wedding update (which she greeted with an "OOOOoooh!" as though it were a piece of candy), and told her that we were having it in Washington because New York was too expensive (no mention of my father, or Phyllis) and that we'd decided to do it in June. There was a pause.

Her voice dropped several octaves. "Have you picked the date?"

"Yes."

"You know what the twenty-third is, don't you?"

How could I not? "Yes, Mom. I know that the twenty-third was your and Dad's anniversary."

"Is. Just because we're no longer married, doesn't mean the date—"

"Don't worry, Mom, I have no intention of getting married on the twenty-third," *which you would know if you let me tell you the date*. But the date of my wedding was of course not her point. My mother was fighting a war; anyone not firmly on her side had to be declared a traitor.

"It would be very hard for me if you did," she said.

I looked at the VCR clock. Less than a minute. Impressive, though hardly a record. I looked at Dan with raised, told-you-so eyebrows.

"Well, you don't have to worry about it—"

"Of course I do!" Ah, the indignation! The frail martyr soldiering on in a world that was out to get her! The real Joyce Silverstein had come to the phone! Next up, the therapy-speak gone wrong. "It's important for me to stick up for myself and tell you what I can and can't do"—punctuated by the dagger—"I can hardly count on *you* to look out for my interests, can I?"

"I guess not," I said. "But since the twenty-third is a Tuesday, I don't think you have anything to worry about."

"Oh," she said.

Silence. Rachel: one. Dan was looking at me and shaking his head. The small smile in the corner of his mouth reminded me that this could in fact be funny. I made a mental note to pass this one on to Annie.

"The date is June fourteenth," I said, picking up on Dan's mood and rolling my eyes.

"Oh," she said. "So, have you started thinking about what you're gonna do yet? The flowers, the bridesmaid dresses?" The Sweet Voice was back in full force, the clear blue sky after a sudden downpour.

"Not really," I faked, glancing toward the coffee table where the pile of wedding magazines sat stacked, a Hansel-and-Gretel trail of Post-it notes marking my way.

"Do you want some of those bridal magazines? I could pick you up some, but I guess you can get them anywhere in New York."

Her comment hit me, as any bit of real kindness from my

mother did, right in the gut. *She is trying*, I thought, snapping myself like a rubber band back to familiar, guilty terrain. Maybe she really did want to help. Maybe I was being too hard on her. Maybe I always had been. Despite the saccharin in her tone, or maybe because of it, my stomach turned a bit marshmallow.

"Yeah," I answered, "you don't have to. I already have a bunch." Then I remembered that positive feedback was important and added, "But if you see something you really like . . ."

"Okay," she said. "So, do you have a place yet?"

"Actually—"

"Beth Zion has that nice social hall, remember?"

Congregation Beth Zion was Joyce's synagogue, a place of supreme importance in her mind. My mother was born in 1944, technically not a baby boomer, but really on the cusp. Strangely, she managed to combine the negative stereotypes of two different generations: boomer selfishness and irresponsibility when it came to her divorce, *alter kacker* provincialism and machetelike guilt-wielding when it came to matters of *shul*. In addition to teaching at the Beth Zion Hebrew School, Joyce was part of a core group of people in the synagogue whose main form of religious observance was to buzz around kissing the rabbi's ass. There were all sorts of petty politics involved—"Sandy Grossbard nominated Rabbi Siegel for Rabbi of the Year," my mother would say, eyes narrowing. "She's such a phony." "Norman Hirsch had the rabbi over for *yontif* lunch," she'd report. "He's always kissing up." No Sisterhood brunch or Purim carnival could pass without some minor intrigue. It was as if the rabbi was a father, and all his little children were fighting amongst themselves for the coveted position of favorite. Need I remind you that Grandpa Sol, my mother's father, was seriously Orthodox? I think you can connect the dots.

"We're not getting married at Beth Zion," I said, rolling my eyes at Dan yet again. "We already have a place."

"But what about Rabbi Siegel?"

There was no way I would have ever let Rabbi Siegel officiate my wedding. I never liked Rabbi Siegel, and found much of his behavior suspect. There was, of course, the childishness of his core group of sycophants, childishness he fostered. But that was the least of it. Rabbis were supposed to be learned, and being learned was supposed to make you wise. Rabbi Siegel was not my idea of wise. During Shabbat morning services, he would take the microphone and go around asking questions about that week's Torah portion, a bearded Phil Donahue minus the empathy, shouting "Correct!" or "That was *Moses*, not Abraham" into the mic.

My mother knew my feelings about Rabbi Siegel, and she knew full well there was no way I'd want him to marry us. Which was, of course, why she brought it up in the first place. For Joyce, asking for things she knew she wouldn't get was a win-win situation in which she'd either get the thing itself, or the chance to play the victim. She was up to her usual Joyce tricks, but this time I wasn't going to fall for them. I would not let this drag on so she could cry to my brother and who knows who else about her coldhearted daughter. I wouldn't explain my dislike of Rabbi Siegel for the hundredth time just to have her call me "fresh." This was my decision, this was my wedding, and I was an adult. The end.

Better yet, why not use a trump card?

"We can't have Rabbi Siegel," I said. "I already told Dan's parents we would use their rabbi." The fact that we hadn't met the Gershons' rabbi suddenly meant nothing. I could trust their judgment. Dan raised his eyebrows as he nodded and gave a thumbs-up for creativity. The officiant was a check off the list after all.

"But Beth Zion just did all of those renovations—"

"Mom," I was firm, "we're not getting married at Beth Zion."

"But Rabbi Siegel will be hurt—"

Oh please, I thought.

"I'm sorry, Mom," I said, looking at Dan, my banister, to keep an even tone. "But it's Dan's wedding too and I have to accommodate my in-laws." She'd have to let it drop. I loved Dan. I loved my in-laws. I loved their rabbi.

"But you're sure you don't want to do it at Beth Zion?"

"Yes. We want to do it outside at the Audubon Society. We already put down the deposit." Look how well I was doing! Dan was nodding "good job."

"You want it outside? But what if it rains?" I'd made her nervous, no great feat.

"We're not going to worry about things we can't do anything about," I said, heady with use of the first-person plural. We-we-we-we-we. "Besides, the building has a tented patio, so there's a backup option."

"If you say so . . ."

"You can check it out for yourself. I'll give you their number."

"What difference would it make? It's obvious you don't want my opinion."

"So you won't be worried about the rain."

"You can't control the weather. You always think I worry too much, but you'll see. I hope I'm wrong . . ."

Yeah, right, I thought.

"Mom, it's not that big a deal. As I said, there's a backup option. And it doesn't even rain that much in June."

"But it could be really humid here in June."

With my mother in Maryland and my father in Virginia, my brother and I liked to say they needed separate states.

"It could be," I said, as in, yes, I know, and, no, I don't care. I looked back at Dan, who continued to find this exchange amusing.

"Well, what about their kitchen?" she asked. "Can you even do a kosher wedding there?"

I gave myself a mental pat on the back for having worked out the bone to throw her. "You use an outside caterer, so you can just get a kosher one."

"And I suppose your father doesn't want to do it kosher because it costs more."

"True. But—"

"Well, what about Grandpa Sol? You don't want him to eat at his own granddaughter's wedding?"

"Don't worry. Grandpa Sol will eat. I talked to Dad about it, and to the caterer we're going to use, and both of them say it's fine to do it kosher if you pay the difference."

"If *I* pay the difference! Isn't that a surprise!"

"Well," I said, again the lawyer, "you do want it."

"Well, I don't know," she said in a huff. "I'll just have to see."

"Have to see what?"

"How much it costs, for one thing. Why should I spend an arm and a leg on a wedding I'm barely consulted on?"

So much for Grandpa Sol.

I wanted to say: You should spend the money because your daughter is getting married to a guy you claim to love and you want to show you're happy for her. I wanted to say: You can't make decisions, you want me to trust my wedding ceremony to a guy you know I hate, and you try to guilt-trip me at every turn. For what possible reason, other than sheer masochism, would I want to consult you? I wanted to say: Just this once, do you think it could be about something other than the money? But I was starting to get a headache and I looked at Dan, still noddingly proud of me, and let it drop. Instead, I gave my mother the caterer's work number.

"So," she said, switching her tone along with the subject, "do you know how big you want it? Should I start making up a guest list?"

I said, "It's up in the air."

"Right," she said. "Well, let me know."

"I will."

"And let me know if there's anything you want me to do . . ." My mother's speech was crawling, the way everything in a movie slows down right before the big action.

What *did* I want her to do, other than not torture me? Any responsibility I gave her meant another chance for Joyce to hold the wedding hostage. But she *was* being nice. And I *had* gone ahead and made all of these plans without consulting her. Maybe she could do it. Maybe Dan was right. Maybe her nuttiness was just funny now. Maybe—

No way, the rational voice inside me said. *Give Joyce an inch, and she'll make you walk a mile down a gravel road without shoes.*

"I'm so happy for you, honey," she was saying. "Dan's such a nice guy . . ."

My mother was one of the few remaining people for whom "Jewish Doctor" still trumped "Internet Millionaire." But flattery will get you everywhere. "You know, Mom, there is something I'd like you to do. If you want. Remember when I was little, how you used to make those birthday cakes with the homemade icing?"

"Of course! Like the hot-air balloon one with the licorice for the ropes?"

"Yeah," I said. "That was my favorite."

"I know. I think you were four. Or was it five?"

"I can't remember. Anyway, I was thinking it would be nice if you made the wedding cake. If it's not too much." It was the perfect solution: something meaningful and nice, and easy enough to replace at the last minute if Joyce freaked out.

"I don't know if I can make a cake that's pretty enough. Wedding cakes have to be so pretty."

"I'm sure whatever you did would be great," I said, meaning it. "But if you don't want to make it, you can be in charge of picking it out and buying it. Think about it and let me know."

"I will, honey."

"Well, I'd better go," I said, knowing with Joyce it was best to end on a high note, rather than press your luck.

"Okay," she said. "Tell Dan I say 'hi.' "

"I will."

"See?" said Dan, when I hung up the phone. "That wasn't so bad."

"You're right," I said. "It wasn't."

But I knew we were still far from a check.

Eight

*A*ny lingering doubts I may have had about the Gershons' rabbi had started to fade when he'd suggested we meet over lunch at Barney Greengrass. "I can't be in New York and not eat there," he said, "so this way I'll kill two birds with one stone."

But, walking uptown to the restaurant, they were replaced with a new, stranger anxiety. "This feels like a date," I told Dan.

"Because we're meeting in a restaurant?"

"That's one thing—"

"Over a less-of-a-commitment lunch?"

"Yes! And, don't forget, your parents fixed us up with him."

Dan nodded. "True."

"This is a Rabbi Blind Date!"

Dan laughed, but I grew more serious.

"Actually, thanks to my move to keep Joyce at bay, it's really more like an arranged marriage."

"Relax," Dan said. "They really thought we'd be right for each other."

He was already there when we arrived, seated in the so-early-sixties-heinous-it's-now-retro dining area, looking over the menu and smiling. We spotted him easily—in part because, as it was mid-week, the restaurant wasn't crowded, but mostly because Rabbi David Tannenbaum couldn't have looked more the young *menschy* rabbinical part. If the dark hair, trimmed beard, and wire-rimmed glasses hadn't given him away, the navy blue, hand-crocheted, Yankees insignia–patterned "Rabbi David" *kippah* would have.

Apparently, we looked our part too, because the moment we entered he was up on his feet, smiling, extending his hand and saying, "You must be Rachel and Dan."

"You must be Rabbi Tannenbaum," Dan said, shaking his hand.

"We've heard so many great things about you," I said, smiling. "Dan's parents are big fans." Could I have been any more date-y? Not that I'd ever been on an actual date.

Rabbi David Tannenbaum flashed a small, self-deprecating smile and, as we all sat down, said, "They speak very highly of both of you too—which is something I'd expect where Dan's concerned, but I take extra notice when parents say great things about a future daughter-in-law." It was my turn to offer a modest smile. "But, really, you guys, just call me David."

"You might want to rethink the *kippah* then," I joked, breaking the ice.

"Oh that," he nodded and motioned toward the back of his head. "A gift from my wife. It's great to be able to wear it completely unselfconsciously. Normally, I'm surrounded by Phillies fans. Don't worry, I'm not planning on wearing it to the wedding."

"Hey, don't hold off on our account," I said.

"It'll be a New York–heavy crowd," said Dan.

"Hmmm," he nodded, smiling. "Well, I'll take that under consideration."

We turned to our menus, and the rabbi said, "I'm sorry, but I just have to ask—did you know they opened one of these in Los Angeles?"

"A Barney Greengrass?" Dan and I looked at each other and shook our heads.

"Not just that—it's in the Barney's!" Our faces registered the shock. "I know! They told me just now. I couldn't believe it! I mean, I guess, *Barney* and *Barney's*—"

"But still—" I said. How could I ever have had any doubts about this man?

"Not really the same . . . *tone*," said Dan.

Rabbi David looked relieved. "At least I know I'm not the only one."

A middle-aged waiter came to take our orders of bagels and nova.

"I'm sorry," Rabbi David said to the waiter, handing him his menu. "I'm trying, but I still can't get over the idea of a Barney Greengrass in a Barney's."

The waiter shrugged. "I look at it this way—over there, it's fancy-schmancy. Here, we're just schmancy."

There were satisfied nods all around. Clearly, our threesome had bonded.

"So." Now that the pressure was off, Rabbi David "just call me David" Tannenbaum folded his hands and rested them on the table. "Down-to-business time, huh?" Dan and I smiled, and he continued. "I guess what I'd like to do first is get a sense from you guys about what you envision for this wedding. What do you want this day to be?"

I looked at Dan, waiting, out of a completely ludicrous sense of egalitarianism, to see if he'd like to field this one, then realized that this was, of course, a question for me.

"Well, I mean, there's so much that goes into this—obviously—but I think the short answer is we want it to be meaningful." I looked at Dan. "Wouldn't you agree?"

"Definitely," Dan said, nodding.

"Well, that's good." The rabbi smiled. "Because I can do meaningful."

We all laughed—*huh-huh-huh*.

"What we need to talk about, then, is how to go about getting to that. I'm sure I don't need to tell the two of you that we're living in an era where a lot of emphasis is put on weddings." His comments were met with the appropriate mixture of groans, nods, eye-rolls, and smiles. Then the rabbi went on, "For the most part, I actually applaud this—" he raised a crossing-guard qualifying hand "—at least as an impulse. Unfortunately, however, it often translates into worrying about things like menus and flowers and seating arrangements, which, I think, completely misses the point. Don't get me wrong—I think it's great to have a big celebration and Judaism puts lots of value in rejoicing at a wedding—*kol sasson v'kol simcha*—"

"*Kol chatan v'kol kallah*." We were finishing each other's Hebrew sentences!

The rabbi smiled. "The Gershons told me you went to day school."

"And Ramah." Between school and camp, I had all the Jewish bona fides.

Dan was looking at me as if I'd spoken in tongues. "It means 'the voice of joy and the voice of gladness, the voice of the groom and the voice of the bride,' " I told him. "It's from the seven wedding blessings."

"Couldn't have said it better myself." The rabbi smiled. "So, obviously, celebration is an important part of our tradition. But it's important to remember that a wedding is much more than an excuse for a party. It's a *mitzvah* so important it's allegorically linked to some incredibly sacred things—the coming of Shabbat, for one, even receiving the Torah at Sinai. In other words, Jewishly speaking, this is a big deal."

"As it should be," Dan said, and I nodded my deep agreement. This was, of course, what I'd been thinking all along—all of my sessions with Martha had, obviously, at all times, been in service of these ideals.

"So, I know, you're having it in Washington at the Audubon Society—which your parents, Dan, said was like an old private home with grounds?"

"Yup." Dan nodded. "That pretty much describes it."

"So, it'll be an outdoor ceremony then?"

"As long as Mother Nature cooperates," I said. Mother Nature, the parent I was least worried about.

"That's great," the rabbi said. "I so much prefer outdoor ceremonies. Even if it rains—which I'm sure it won't—I just think it's the most appropriate place to have a wedding ceremony. For an event that's all about continuity and the cycles of life—it just, you know, *fits*."

"That was our operating principle," I said.

"Plus, having it outdoors, it can never get *too* over the top."

"Not fancy," I said, "just schmancy."

"Exactly." The rabbi laughed.

Why had I ever cared about Dan's father's pushiness? This guy was great; I would have been pushy too. Chuck Woolery would have been beaming: This was a total rabbinical love connection.

The waiter returned with our food, and as we schmeared our cream cheese, the rabbi continued.

"Since we don't really know each other," he said, "I thought it might be a good idea to tell you why it is I'm doing this—why I became a rabbi." Dan and I nodded, chewing. "Like any nice Reform, bar mitzvahed but for the most part secular Jewish boy from Westchester, I made my mother proud and went to Yale Law School. But in my third year, I realized practicing law was not what I wanted to do with my life. What I wanted was to be with people at the most important times of their lives, to try to help them, and myself, wrestle and come to terms with the questions that, it seems to me, we were put on this earth and given the power of thought to try to answer. So I took remedial Hebrew, applied to rabbinical school, and basically gave my mother a heart attack. And now, fifteen years later, here I am, sitting with you guys, doing exactly the kind of thing I wanted to do. Because—" he smiled "—no matter what anyone tells you— the caterer, the florist, your mother, whoever—that wrestling, that grappling, really is what a wedding is about."

Hold the fucking phone.

Need we discuss how much I loved Rabbi David "just call me David" Tannenbaum?

I looked over at Dan, balancing red onion and tomato on his nova-heavy bagel as he took a bite that left a gob of cream cheese in the corner of his mouth. He nodded, winked at me, and chewed, smiling that smile of his.

I had my ideal man, I had my ideal rabbi, I had an onion bagel with possibly the world's best smoked salmon. Who could ask for anything more?

We ate and Rabbi David asked us how we met, why we decided to do what we do professionally (in the wake of his speech, my standard answer, "I've always wanted to write," had never felt more hollow), whether we planned to keep kosher (no for now, but maybe when we had kids—I was still working on

Dan with this one, but the rabbi just nodded, whatever-works-for-you, giving me no ammo). We then moved on to the nitty-gritty.

"Now, Dan," he said, "I've heard horrible things—mostly from your father actually—about the state of B'nai Shalom Hebrew School in the years before I got there, so I assume you won't mind if I give you the whole *schpiel*. But Rachel, with that day school education, some of this might be a repeat."

"Yes," I said, faux-haughtily. "Well, I think I could stand a refresher."

"Okay, then. But stop me if I get too—I don't know what—or if you have any questions, comments, objections, whatever. Feel free."

"Okay," said Dan.

"Basically," he began, "according to Jewish law, a wedding is incredibly simple: The bride accepts an object worth more than a dime from the groom, the groom recites the ritual formula of acquisition and consecration, and these two acts are observed by witnesses. That's it. The truth is, you don't even need a rabbi to perform the ceremony. So," he smiled, "if after today . . ."

We all smiled, each of us knowing how well this date was going, each sure there'd be another.

The rabbi continued, "The rest of what constitutes a Jewish wedding—the *huppah*, the seven blessings, the breaking of the glass—isn't legally required. They're *minhagim*—customs—and customs change over time. Now, you said you wanted your wedding to be meaningful. Well, that makes it extra important for you to think about which of these customs have meaning for you, and how you might want to take those customs and add something personal to them. Things like choosing the design and wording of your *ketubah*, choosing or even making your *huppah*, choosing your own translation of the seven wedding blessings and having special friends or family members read them during the ceremony. I keep saying 'choosing'—that's because a modern Jewish wedding really does offer a lot of choice. There's really no 'right' or 'wrong' way to do these things, despite what people—relatives especially—might have to say to the contrary." We laughed and he said, "No, it's really true. Especially these days, when people's levels of religious observance can be all over the map, every Jewish marriage is an intermarriage."

Dan laughed, and I thought about my parents. Only later did I realize he must have been thinking of his too.

"I don't think that's much of a problem between the two of us," I said.

"No," Dan said, "me neither. I mean, Rachel has more of a background, but we agree about most things, at least in principle."

"Well, that's good," said the rabbi. "And, from what little sense I've gotten here, you seem to be on the same page."

I took this as a compliment and beamed.

He went on to say that he only performed ceremonies with egalitarian *ketubot*, meaning the traditional Aramaic groom "acquires" bride with two hundred zuzim marriage contract was out—which, we said, was more than fine. He then mentioned the tradition of "circling," where, upon stepping under the *huppah,* the bride walks around the groom seven times. Some couples, he said, circle each other, but since this is only a tradition and not legal requirement for the ceremony, it was up to us. He mentioned the *mikvah,* the ritual bath, and the *auf-ruf,* the week-before-the-wedding honor where, during Shabbat services, the bride and groom get called to the Torah for an *aliyah*—which we'd do in Philadelphia.

"Do they throw candy at us when we're done like a bar mitz-vah?" Dan smiled.

"If you'd like them to . . ."

I raised a hand and said, "Don't listen to him. This falls into the 'can we have pigs in blankets' category."

"What?" Dan said. "I love pigs in blankets."

"If we have a meat wedding, we'll have them. If we have a dairy wedding, we can't."

He faked a grumble, and the rabbi laughed, then continued.

"So," said the rabbi, "back to the ceremony. One thing we haven't touched on is the procession. Traditionally, the groom is escorted by his parents and the bride is escorted by hers. Rachel, I understand from your in-laws that your parents are on less than amicable terms."

"That's the very diplomatic way of putting it."

"A certain amount of diplomacy is required in this line of work." He smiled. "Look, I'm not in a position to make this deci-sion for you. You know the particulars, and I can only offer to be here to help you weigh them. What I can tell you is that this is another one of those things that's not an obligation, just a tradi-tion. From the perspective of Jewish law, you're free to do what-ever you want. But, that said, I'd like to say that nothing's 'just' tradition—traditions became what they are for a reason, and, in this particular case, I personally think the reason's still a pretty good one. The idea behind the Jewish wedding procession is that it mirrors the life passage that's taking place. Both the bride and groom are leaving their family of origin and joining together to form a new family of their own. This really is serious business— for everyone involved—and, in my opinion, the tradition has great psychological and symbolic value."

"I couldn't agree with you more," I said. "I mean, I love the tradition and everything it stands for, and Dan's parents will definitely walk him down the aisle." I turned to Dan. "I mean, I assume you want it that way . . ." and he nodded. "For them, the tradition totally makes sense. But Dan has a nuclear family. I have a nuclear event."

Both Dan and the rabbi laughed.

"Seriously, though. You don't know my parents. My mother didn't come to my college graduation dinner because she refused to sit at a table with my father." I rolled my eyes and let out a snort-laugh, isn't that absurd? "Even if they'd agree to both walk me down together, I don't know if that's what I'd want. I want to feel like a bride, not a wishbone."

Rabbi David Tannenbaum nodded his Yankee-*kippah*-ed head.

"And in all honesty," I continued, "that act of leaving them behind, starting something fresh and on your own adult terms, I feel like that's something I did years ago out of sheer mental health necessity."

The rabbi smiled, then sighed. "There's no way the people who thought up these customs could have envisioned the complications we face in our lives today. To me, that's why it's all the more amazing that these traditions still have relevance. I don't think you should do anything that you're not comfortable with, or that will in any way detract from the joy of that day for the two of you. Just think about it," he said, reaching for his bagel. "Eventually, something will feel right."

Nine

The first thing my aunt Natalie had said when I told her that Dan and I were engaged was, "You have to start thinking about your dress."

Aunt Natalie loved Dan, and had always been his most vocal supporter. The first time she'd met him, at a dinner she'd taken us out to just two months into our relationship, she'd leaned in and told me he was "a keeper." "He's like the men in our family," she said. "Smart and solid and good-natured."

But to aunt Natalie, an outfit is the nucleus of any event. When her granddaughters were bat mitzvahed it was Aunt Natalie, not their mothers, who dragged them around Saks and Bloomingdale's to find the appropriate young lady suits for the services and their something-special-but-age-appropriate outfits for the evenings' receptions. On learning our wedding preparations were getting into serious gear she'd said, "Come over next week and we'll talk about the plan for your dress." Tonight was the night. Dan had a study group, so Aunt Natalie and I were having a girls-only dinner where she would, no doubt, lay out her dress strategy. Taking the M66 across the park, I wondered what she had in mind.

Aunt Natalie and I had a bond that went beyond aunt and niece, a bond that was similar to one she'd had with her own aunt, my aunt Lilly. When Aunt Natalie was a girl, Aunt Lilly had taken her under her wing—buying her clothes, fixing her hair, urging her to attend her alma mater, paving the way for her to join her sorority, setting her up with the wealthy sons of Uncle Joe's business colleagues (which was how she'd met my uncle Walter). Aunt Natalie liked to say that Aunt Lilly, whose philosophy of relationships was that "the woman should be a diamond and the man should be a setting," had taught her "all the womanly things," things Aunt Natalie tried to pass on to a niece who didn't want an engagement ring.

Though I didn't always take her advice, I loved that Aunt Natalie gave it. I was part of a family tradition, I belonged. When I was four, I had a favorite book called *The Sky Was Blue*. In it, a little girl looks through a photo album with her mother. She sees pictures of her great-grandmother, grandmother, and mother at her age—what kind of clothes each wore, what kind of car each drove, what kind of house each grew up in—and asks, "What was it like? How did she feel?" The mother tells the girl that they felt a lot like she does now. "The sky was blue. The grass was green. The sun was warm and yellow. Just as they all are now." And while their clothes, their cars, and their houses all typified each girl's era, like the enduring sky, the girls themselves all had the same dark hair, the same blue eyes. When I was six, Aunt Natalie sat me down at her kitchen table and told me about her special friendship with Aunt Lilly. She told me that she wanted us to be special friends, too, and I remember thinking I had my own version of *The Sky Was Blue*, not just because of our multigenerational connection, but because we all looked alike.

I realize I haven't given much in the way of physical description, and I guess that's because I've always sort of taken my looks—which are good enough to charm supers with smiles, but plain enough not to turn heads—for granted. People often tell me I "don't look Jewish," a backhanded compliment to which I've never found a satisfactory response. But it's true—with my pale skin and stick-straight blondish-brown hair, I do not fit the Semitic stereotype. My mother "looks Jewish"; her hair is dark brown and curly and her olive complexion can tan. But I take after my father's fair, fine-boned Hungarian side of the family, specifically my aunt Natalie, who took after her mother's afore-mentioned sister, Aunt Lilly. I'd be reminded of the resemblance at the cousins' events, and each time someone would say, "You look more and more like Natalie," or, "Lilly's looks went to Ida's children," I'd take it as the compliment it was. My mother would remark on the resemblance too, but from her it was a rueful piece of evidence, further proof of my ties to the enemy camp.

Aunt Natalie and I had always been close, but our relationship solidified once I moved to the city. When I was at Barnard, we'd go out to dinner at least once a month, always preceded by drinks at her place, and always ending with her handing me a twenty for the cab "and incidentals." She'd moved into the city from Long Island a few years before I did, after my uncle Walter died, and at these wine-heavy dinners in chic East Side bistros we'd both feel like the incredibly glamorous New York City gals we now were. I'd even stayed with her one summer, meeting her various suitors—the wealthy widowers from her Long Island country club or her lectures at the Ninety-second Street Y, "penniless mad geniuses" from her Midtown bridge club—while she campaigned for me to wear makeup, get highlights, and use purses, in other words, trying to teach me "all the womanly things" in the Aunt Lilly tradition.

I was eager not only to hear Aunt Natalie's wedding dress strategy, but also to learn if my father's ten thousand dollars figured into it. When it came to her brother and his wife, Aunt Natalie had a tendency to minimize or ignore certain less-than-pleasant facts. This made sense; it had been Natalie's idea to fix up her recently divorced brother with her recently widowed decorator. From the beginning, she'd let her role as matchmaker morph into that of cheerleader—which was fine, except for the odd occasion when Aunt Natalie would try to convince me that the moon was the sun.

It was dark by the time I got to her building, a modern high-rise on Sixty-first and Third. I entered the marbled lobby, greeted Aunt Natalie's doorman and concierge, and exchanged mmm-hmms about how short the days were getting.

Once on the thirty-fourth floor, I was met at the door by Macy.

Macy was a Queens-bred cabaret singer in her early forties with pinkish-orange hair, a slight limp, and the smallest teeth I'd ever seen. She was also Aunt Natalie's manicurist. Over the years, Macy had become a fixture, making weekly manicure house calls and tending to other Aunt Natalie odds and ends—"Macy's help-ing out with the break-fast" type of thing—an almost-member of the family who came to brises and baby showers and introduced Aunt Natalie to new recordings of "The Girl from Ipanema" and concoctions made with Alizé.

"How've you been?" she said, embracing me as I entered. "Long time no see."

"Yeah," I said. "It's been a while. How are things?"

She shrugged. "I don't know. Same old. Can't complain. You still seein' Dr. Chen?"

Dr. Chen was my acupuncturist. Macy had turned me on to him the summer I'd lived with Aunt Natalie. I'd been suffering from mono and migraine headaches, and she'd told me that her cousin Sylvia worked as a receptionist for an acupuncturist in Chinatown. "He's *everybody's* acupuncturist," she'd said. "Madonna,

Miles Davis, Phil Donahue. He's supposed to work miracles. Woody Allen's a patient. So was Mia Farrow, before—you know. He based a character on him."

"The Chinese doctor in *Alice*?" I asked.

"That's the one where she goes to an acupuncturist?"

I nodded.

"Then that's it."

That, of course, had been all I'd needed to hear.

"I haven't been in years," I told her as I hung my coat in the closet. "He totally cured me."

"How about that." She shook her head.

"Your cousin Sylvia's not still there, is she?"

"She's with an ophthalmologists in Forest Hills. Not as glamorous, but a better commute."

Macy's cousin Sylvia had been an integral part of the Dr. Chen experience. She had hair even pinker than Macy's, wore big blue-framed glasses, and always chomped her gum—not exactly a natural Chinatown fit. Since I was a friend of Macy's, Sylvia would always give me an extra-special greeting, filling me in on which celebrities had been in that day. "Com'ere." She'd lean in, her accent thick even when whispering. "You just missed De Niro." Then she'd raise her eyebrows and violate doctor-patient privilege. "Lower-back pain."

Macy and I headed out of the entryway. "So I hear you and Dan are finally makin' it official," she said.

"You hear correctly." I smiled.

"Well, if you want me to do your nails, consider it a wedding gift."

"Thanks," I said. "That's sweet of you."

"Rachel, honey," called Aunt Natalie, "come in here, I'm still drying."

I made my way to the frosted-glass dining room table where

Aunt Natalie sat in pearls and a studied casual outfit—wine-colored cashmere twinset and matching wool pants—her blonde bob perfectly coiffed, hands splayed under the nail dryer, toes under the frosted-glass table in little foam holders. The lights of the city shone through floor-to-ceiling windows behind her, a view of the twinkling Fifty-ninth Street Bridge that, no matter how many times you saw it, refused to be anything less than spectacular.

"Hi, honey," she said, big smile, as I knelt to give and get a kiss on the cheek.

Aunt Natalie gave her usual quick up and down scan and said, "You look great." If I'd been wearing something with extra "personality," a "Look at those pants/boots/sneakers!" would have followed, with a smile and a laugh, as if I'd delivered a bon mot. But, coming as I was on business, I was dressed in the no-nonsense basics—black turtleneck and jeans—so she moved on to highballs instead. "What are you drinking, honey? Macy'll make it for you, won't you, Mace?"

Any Aunt Natalie evening began with highballs and some form of hors d'oeuvres, proving that you could take the early sixties housewife away from the country club, but you couldn't take the country club away from her. I loved this little ritual, but often found myself wondering if any non-Reform Jews performed it. Tonight it took on a different tone. Aunt Natalie was Queen Elizabeth, Macy her lady-in-waiting, I her trusted deputy, preparing for a summit.

I told Macy not to bother and headed to the bar for a vodka and ginger ale. "What can I get you, Aunt Natalie?" I asked, looking for the ice cube tongs.

She tested her nails and said, "I'll take a vodka tonic, honey, thanks."

Macy asked if she should bring out the cheese plate, and Natalie said that would be great.

I brought over the drinks as Macy laid the plate on the dining room table. Normally, this setup centered on the couch, but between its silk upholstery and the drying manicure, at the table we'd stay.

"Can I get you one too, Macy?" I asked.

"Oh, no thanks, sweetheart. I'm leaving in a sec. I got a hot date."

"Oh yeah?" I asked, sitting down at the table.

"Yeah," said Aunt Natalie, taking her feet out of the foam holders and sliding them into toe-exposing terrycloth slippers. "With her new boyfriend! A *fire*man! Tell her how you met him, Macy."

Macy told me about her fireman while packing up her things. They'd met the week before, when Macy's stove had a suspicious smell. "I knew it was gas," she said, "but I'm rent controlled, so of course my landlord wants nothing to do with it. So finally I say, This is it, and call the fire department. I told them it was no emergency—yet. So they send a couple guys over, and sure enough it's a leak. I said, It's a good thing I quit smoking, and one of the guys—he was real cute—said, Yeah, good thing. He'd just quit too and he offered me some Nicorette, which I thought was real sweet. So they fixed it all up and he asked me out before he left."

"Isn't that a great story?" Aunt Natalie asked. "As soon as Macy told me I said, There's a story for Rachel. Just the kind of thing you love."

"It is," I said. "All the makings of a great New York romance."

"I'm not so sure," Macy said. "You gotta figure the guy gets a lot of damsels in distress. For all I know he hits on all of them." In spite of herself, she smiled and said, "I guess we'll see!"

"Have fun," I said.

"Yeah," she said, kissing Aunt Natalie's cheek, "you guys too."

"Thank you, Macy," Aunt Natalie called as Macy showed herself out. "I'll see you next week. Have a wonderful time." Once the door closed, she sighed and said, "I hope this one works out. Poor Macy. I've never seen anyone with worse luck with men." Aunt Natalie was always bemoaning some aspect of Macy's "hard life"; it was a reason she'd cite for her skepticism about my writing. "I see what Macy goes through as a creative person," she'd say. "It's a very hard life." Now, of course, this was no longer a worry.

"A fireman," I said. "That could be promising."

Aunt Natalie nodded. "They are brave."

"And they cook."

"Yes," she said. "But they do drink."

We reached for our highballs.

"So how's it going, honey, huh? How's work?"

"Good," I said, slipping off my shoes and tucking my feet underneath me. "I'm finishing up a book. Should be done next week."

"Terrific," she said, sipping. "And the wedding?"

"It's coming along. We met the rabbi yesterday, and he was great—"

"Uh-huh—" This kind of news she could give two shits about.

"Oh—and I finally got my father to agree to give Joyce the option to make it kosher, so there's a step in the right direction."

Aunt Natalie sighed. "Well, you know, your mother's never been the best at making decisions . . ."

"Believe me, I know," I grumbled, cutting off a hunk of port cheese.

"Well, why worry about that now?" she said, rings clinking as she planted both hands on the table. "We're here to talk about your dress."

"Right."

"Have either of your parents mentioned anything about it?"

"Nope," I said.

Aunt Natalie pursed her lips. I remembered that look from a Passover seder I'd gone to at her house with my father. She and I were poring over the contents of my suitcase and she'd said, "What kind of mother forgets to buy an eight-year-old dress shoes to go with her outfit?"

"Well," she said now, with deliberate brightness, "do you have any ideas?"

I had ideas, but I was here to hear hers. "I don't know," I said. "What do you think?"

"You want to hear my plan?" Aunt Natalie had been through this three times, with each of her own daughters; any plan of hers was one perfected in the trenches.

I nodded.

"Now you don't have to do it this way . . ."

She was trying to be "good."

"I know," I said. "I want your advice."

"Well, okay, then." Any sign of hesitation vanished. "First, you look through the bridal magazines," she said, General Schwarzkopf minus the fatigues. "Then you go around town and try on everything. Now, I'm not going to tell you what kind of dress to get. That has to be your decision. But you must keep in mind that you're not looking for the style you like the most."

"Then what am I looking for?" I asked. Nothing scared me more than a pouffy, sequined bridal gown. Then there was Dan's "not bridey enough" comment. The idea that he'd actually care about the style of my dress was something I was still digesting.

"You want the one that looks best on you," said Aunt Natalie.

I nodded, a quick study.

"You are planning on wearing a white one, aren't you?"

"Yeah," I said. "Why wouldn't I?"

"Oh, good, sweetheart," she said, patting her heart. "I didn't think you'd do something like that, but then you hear things like 'color is in' and you see these Vera Wang ads with these dresses—*green* ones, for God's sake. Green—can you imagine? Anyway, I know you don't always like to do things by the book," she said in an I-get-a-*kick*-out-of-you tone, "so I couldn't help but worry."

"Why futz around? Either you're wearing a wedding dress or not."

"That's exactly right. Good. So, then, you'll see which shade of white best suits your coloring and narrow it down to a few basic shapes. Then we'll go to Kleinfeld's."

"Kleinfeld's?"

I already knew what I wanted, and I didn't think it was Kleinfeld's. Kleinfeld's, the Brooklyn bridal gown store to end all bridal gown stores, seemed the mouth of the pouffy bridal beast. I wanted to breeze into some downtown boutique that looked like a fantasy version of your grandmother's attic and pick out something sophisticated, elegant, and sequinless. I wanted to get my dress at Josephine, the adorable husband-and-wife SoHo atelier. I didn't want to be drip-dried through the bridal machine.

"Yes, Kleinfeld's," she said. "I know, I know. I thought the same thing at first. But your cousin Lynn got her dress there and they were leaps and bounds over Vera Wang and Bergdorf's."

"I don't know . . ."

"Listen, go to all the other places you want, then we'll go to Kleinfeld's. If you don't like anything there, fine, you get the dress at one of the other places. Just so long as you go there—I only say this because they really and truly are a *great* operation."

"Fine," I said, figuring I'd humor her by going to Kleinfeld's but get the actual gown in SoHo where, I was convinced, the dress of my dreams awaited.

Provided, of course, I had the money to pay for it.

"You realize, of course, that this whole discussion could be moot."

"What do you mean?" she asked.

"I mean I'm not sure if I can even afford to shop for a dress like this. I might have to go to a sample sale or buy a used one or something." I sipped my drink.

"A *used* one?" Aunt Natalie looked horrified. "Why on earth would you have to do that?"

Denial, just as I'd suspected.

I set my glass on the table. "Because I have no idea if my dress is included in my dad's ten-thousand-dollar budget."

"Oh, that," said Aunt Natalie, promptly shooing the thought away. "Ten thousand is a number pulled out of the sky. What your father is saying is that he wants to keep the costs down, which he will certainly be able to do now that Dan's parents have been so generous. Forget the ten thousand dollars. Don't worry about your dress."

Would she have been this nonchalant if I'd told her about the possible cousins blow-off? Figuring my dad would come to his senses, I hadn't yet wanted to make waves. "How can I forget the ten thousand dollars? That's the budget. And how can I not worry about the dress when I don't know if it's included in it?"

"Rachel, honey, you're getting yourself upset over nothing. Whatever this ten thousand thing is, it has nothing to do with your dress."

"You know this for sure?" The only way Aunt Natalie could be truly certain I could get the kind of dress we were discussing was if she were paying for it herself, and even if she'd wanted to be that generous, she'd never think she'd need to be. Her Lexus-driving brother had the money; he would, of course, come through. To Aunt Natalie, this was a given.

"Yes." She was firm.

"Then you've talked to them about it?"

"No . . ."

I threw up my hands—see?

"Rachel," she said. "You need to understand something. Every parent dreams of seeing their daughter walk down the aisle in a wedding dress—it's one of the great joys of having a daughter. Especially when you have a daughter as beautiful and wonderful and special as you, who couldn't be marrying a more terrific guy than Dan." She pressed her hands to my cheeks, fingers splayed and pointing outward, nails avoiding contact. "This is a parent's fantasy! Why are you worrying?"

I felt my eyes tear, and not just from the nice things Aunt Natalie was saying. This wasn't "a" parent's fantasy, it was hers.

"Oh, sweetheart," she said, removing her hands. "Now, look, we've gotten ourselves all emotional. But you see my point."

"I do," I said, still lacking luster. "There just hasn't been any sign that they feel that way."

"Only because they haven't realized it yet."

"And you're confident they will."

"Yes, I am." She nodded.

"Why?"

"Because Phyllis will come with us to Kleinfeld's."

Right then, I stopped worrying. I wasn't sure Aunt Natalie was right, but I did know one thing for certain: Phyllis kissed Aunt Natalie's ass.

This particular dynamic, no doubt a holdover from their client/decorator relationship, could be very annoying at, say, a dinner, when Phyllis would fall all over herself complimenting Aunt Natalie and agreeing with everything she said. But it served a utilitarian purpose when combined with Aunt Natalie's Henry Higgins act. While I was in college, Aunt Natalie became disturbed about my "stringy, unstyled" hair. "You and I have the same hair," she'd say, gathering it in her hands and making a disappointed face. "It's so fine, we really need a good cut." She voiced her concern one time at dinner when my father and Phyllis were in town. "Natalie, you are right. Absolutely," Phyllis said. "Rachel's hair is a disaster." For the next two years, until I graduated, Aunt Natalie and I had back-to-back appointments with Nino, her Madison Avenue hairdresser, and, without a word of protest from my father, he and Phyllis footed the seventy-five-dollar-a-cut bill.

Not that Aunt Natalie realized the power she had over her sister-in-law. She wouldn't be trying to get Phyllis to pay for my wedding dress any more than she'd tried to convince her to comp my haircuts. In her mind, she was doing Phyllis a favor, showing her the light, and when Phyllis invariably jumped to get with her program it was only because her program was so obviously right.

The fog of my doubts had lifted.

"I'll call her tomorrow and invite her along," Aunt Natalie was saying. "We can have lunch afterward—really make a day of it."

"I think that's a great idea," I said. "Thank you, Aunt Natalie."

"Of course, sweetheart," Aunt Natalie said. "You see? No problem. So, now, no more worrying, right? A bride shouldn't worry so much. Especially you. You furrow your eyebrows," she said, motioning toward the zone of my third eye. "It'll give you lines."

I smiled, neglecting to point out that this too would give me lines.

"Now where should we have dinner, huh? I was thinking Fiorello's. They have that black linguine with seafood sauce that's always so good . . ."

"Whatever you say," I said, kissing her cheek.

Ten

When the phone rang the next morning, I was towel-drying my hair.

"Hiya, honey," Phyllis's voice boomed.

"Hey—"

"I wasn't sure I'd find you there," she said.

"No, I'm home," I said, resting the towel on my shoulder.

"Well, I'm glad I caught you! I just got off the phone with Aunt Natalie, and she told me about her Kleinfeld's idea."

"Oh, she did," I said, wondering why Phyllis always referred to Aunt Natalie as "Aunt Natalie" to me. Was this condescending or chummy?

"Yes!" Phyllis continued. "And I think it's great!"

"You do?" My fake surprise was coated with real excitement. I would be getting my dress!

"Yes! It'll be so fun, just us girls. I'll fly in on a morning shuttle and meet you there straight from the airport. Aunt Natalie told me about her idea to have you look at other places before, which I think sounds great. So we can do Kleinfeld's, then grab some lunch and then head into the city if you found something spectacular somewhere else. I'll catch an evening shuttle and be back in time for dinner with Dad."

"Sounds like a plan."

"I can't wait to see you in all those dresses!" she said. "It's so great to have a daughter to do this with!"

Phyllis's words hit me like a punch in the gut. Maybe she wasn't just doing this to kiss Aunt Natalie's ass. Maybe she really was excited. Maybe I was a selfish, manipulative bitch.

How had I become such a stepmother cynic?

I was in my first year at Barnard when Phyllis moved to D.C. She made jokes about being a "stepmonster," a term she'd picked up from one of her "all-time favorite" movies, *St. Elmo's Fire*. (I found these jokes funny, not because they were funny, but because when I was twelve, my father had taken me to see *St. Elmo's Fire*, and when the projector broke halfway through the movie, he'd quipped that it was proof of the existence of God.) In those early days, Phyllis and I had one big thing in common: We both wanted to be friends. Phyllis didn't want Jerry's daughter to hate her, and I didn't want to hate her either. Stepmothers were supposed to be wicked, stepmothers were supposed to torment you—just ask Snow White and Cinderella. The word stepmother comes with a built-in eye-roll, not "this is my stepmother," but "this is my *stepmother*." But most people with stepmothers want their original family back, and a Joyce and Jerry reunion was the last thing I wanted. When my parents finally divorced, I'd been relieved. I saw Phyllis's arrival as more concrete proof that the war was finally over, so, when she first came, I was there with a band and bunting, just as Aunt Natalie had hoped for, more than ready to usher in the new peace.

But, by my first winter vacation, it was clear this attitude did not play well with Joyce. "Where were you?" she'd bark like a jealous lover, and I'd tell her I'd been to the movies or lunch or both with Phyllis. Why not? In my mind, I was an adult, or at the very least, a person who was in college and didn't live at home anymore. What could Joyce possibly do? As it turned out, quite a bit. First she could hide the keys to the beat-up Nissan Sentra that I'd used since getting my license, a car whose cost (twenty-four hundred dollars—four hundred dollars more than a dress I'd wear once, thank you) she, my father, and I had split, but, citing her name on the registration, one that Joyce now referred to as her own. When I found the keys and went off to meet Phyllis, she could threaten to call the police and report the car stolen. She could, in other words, do enough to make me decide that from then on, I'd gladly be spending my vacations either in the dorm or with my father and Phyllis.

Phyllis was thrilled to be, as she put it, my "home base." In her mind, I was now some sort of political figure, a suburban daughter-of-divorce Che Guevara fighting for her stepmother's cause, and I was happy to let her think that I'd been fighting for her instead of my own freedom. For a while, we were buddies. We were family. I decided I had a stepmother who wasn't a *stepmother* and Phyllis went around telling everyone that she wasn't a "stepmonster," that we had a great relationship, that there were "no stepchildren in our house, only love."

The hollowness of this statement revealed itself when I came down with mono my junior year. It was late March, about five weeks until the end of the semester, and, on doctor's orders, I needed to take incompletes in my courses and go home and rest. I was at Jerry and Phyllis's for about a month, sleeping eighteen hours a day, eating the dinner they'd order to go from whichever restaurant they'd gone to that night as I sat in the den with my father watching whichever *Godfather* was on HBO, the two of us shaking our heads and saying, "That Santino, what a hothead," and, "Freido, Freido, what are you doing?" But by the end of April, Phyllis decided I'd "done enough lying around the house." "Really, Raych," she said, nodding her head and speaking in a sympathetic, stepmonster-knows-best tone, "it's been enough already. Besides, you'll never get better if you don't push yourself."

Only I wasn't the one doing the pushing.

I ended up back in New York at Aunt Natalie's, where I spent the bulk of the summer asleep in her spare bedroom, making the occasional appearance when one of her suitors came by, and heading to Chinatown twice a week for acupuncture treatments.

Aunt Natalie told me not to be hurt, that Phyllis "meant well" but my relationship with my father made her feel like "an outsider." I told myself that was true. "It's not as if you're out in the cold," she'd say. "You're here with me!"

Phyllis still told people that there were "no stepchildren in our house, only love," but now when she did, I made a little joke about it: "She means the 'no stepchildren in our house' part literally!" If she was really annoying me, I'd say it out loud. And if Natalie was around, she'd say, "Now, *Ray*-chul."

But maybe Aunt Natalie was right. Maybe "there are no stepchildren in our house" was more than just a platitude. Maybe the mono incident had been an anomaly, not a true-stripes revelation. Maybe Phyllis wasn't a *stepmother*. She wanted to buy me my wedding dress. She'd called me her daughter.

"So, I'll see you in a week or so then?" she was saying.

"Yeah." I smiled. "I'm looking forward to it."

With things thus settled, I was ready to enter the next phase of Operation Wedding Gown: research. Knowing this was something not to be done on one's own, I enlisted the help of the greatest shopper of all time, Naomi.

"Feel free to say no," I said, clipping my toenails in front of the mute TV. "This is so not mandatory."

"Are you kidding?" she said. She was on her cell phone walking east, fresh from showing a loft on Seventeenth Street. "Shopping for a wedding dress? This is my fantasy."

"I'm so happy you said yes. All this wedding stuff is so emotional. It'll be great to have you with me. Do you want to pick a time and place? I should probably do this sooner rather than later . . ."

"I'm about to get to Crunch. Later this week is fine for me. Just call me tomorrow with the details. I'm really psyched."

"Me, too," I said, meaning it.

Eleven

A few days later, Naomi and I walked up Madison, coffees in hand, ready to take on wedding dress shopping. Deciding it best to round all of my pre-Kleinfeld's bridal gown bases in one day, I'd made appointments uptown at Vera Wang and Yumi Katsura, at Josephine in SoHo and at Bella, a tiny shop in Alphabet City that was, according to Naomi, "the place where all the hip brides go."

"You're still swimming, right?" she asked me.

"Yeah. Why?"

"Well, when I told my trainer we were going wedding dress shopping, he said arms are the biggest problem area for brides. But then I told him you swam and he was like, oh, that's great, don't worry about it."

Up until that point, I hadn't been. "You have a trainer?"

"Yeah, only twice a week. Someone in my improv class said I should try the Alexander technique."

"Hmmm." She had a trainer?

"Look!" Naomi cried, pointing her chin across the street toward our destination, "Vera Wang, the Tiffany's of wedding gowns!"

"I'm thinking if I find a style I like, I can get it for half price at their sample sale." I figured Naomi, bargain shopper extraordinaire, would appreciate this kind of logic.

Instead, she said, "Rachel, this is your *wedding dress*. Phyllis already said they'd pay for it."

The light changed and we started crossing.

"True," I said. "But she never mentioned how much they'd spend."

And I was determined to keep the cost down regardless. The gowns in *Martha Stewart* cost three to seven thousand dollars apiece, and even if my father would pay for one of them (which I still very much doubted), I couldn't justify spending more than two thousand dollars on a wedding dress. (I couldn't really justify spending two thousand dollars, except by reminding myself that that's how much wedding gowns cost.)

But price was not my only concern. Whenever I thought about wedding dresses, it was as if two parts of me sprang up, one behind each shoulder. The first was the pragmatic I-don't-style-my-hair part. She looked Scandinavian—blonde hair pulled back in a bun—and wore a well-tailored, untrendy black outfit. She'd say, "I don't need a gown, I could be happy walking down the aisle in a simple white dress." But the other part of me was the little-girl-who-wants-to-play-princess part. She wore a frilly dress and black patent leather Mary Janes. She'd pout and say, "A plain white dress! What a bummer!" And then there was Dan. He apparently wanted a *bride;* I wasn't going to let him down.

From the minute we walked into the tasteful cream-colored Vera Wang lobby—me in no makeup and Naomi in her vintage leopard print overcoat—and the receptionist said, "Can I *help* you?" it was clear: We'd been pegged as bridal impostors.

"We have an appointment," I said, though it came out sounding like a question.

"And which one of you is the bride?" asked our saleswoman, the suit- and scarf-accessorized Tara, peering over a lucite clipboard.

"That's me," I said, grinning goofily.

Both she and the receptionist did instant scans of my ringless left hand, which no doubt served to reinforce their skepticism. I fought back the impulse to justify myself: This was not a milieu where "I'm not a big jewelry person" would have gone over well.

"Oh," she said, her up-and-down look-over now flagrant. Clearly, I was still a Before. "And your wedding is in June?"

"That's right," I said. "The fourteenth."

"So it says on your card." I caught Naomi's eye. What was that supposed to mean? That June was the most obvious wedding month? I was almost too fascinated to be offended. I'd seen *Muriel's Wedding*, but did people really try on wedding gowns just for kicks?

"We are here to learn," Naomi reminded me as Tara disdainfully led the way to the samples from their spring collection.

In spite of the continued frosty looks, I learned many things at Vera Wang:

1. Trying on a wedding gown is *intense*. Standing there in this gown, on a box with mirrors catching you at all angles, the little girl part of you starts cheering, and you get hit, hit with the full weight of the fact that *you are a bride*, a weight you had agreed to bear, but also hadn't realized until this very moment, this moment of pomp and circumstantial truth, was quite so heavy. You may be on Madison Avenue and it may be a five-thousand-

dollar designer dress, but there is no doubt that this is ceremonial garb and that ceremonial garb is worn when something really big is taking place. And at that moment, the moment when you first see yourself transformed by a wedding gown, all of your thoughts of the million things you have to do, all of your worries about this event coming off, all of your ambivalence about the decadent amount of money you're spending, all of your concerns about the people in your life being pains in your ass, even—I'm sad to say—all thoughts of your fiancé, are replaced by one single notion, a notion that registers not in your head, but in your gut: *Holy shit, I am getting married.*

Standing in the Vera Wang salon in my first wedding dress, I was struck dumb.

"Oh, my God! You look so beautiful!" Naomi exclaimed, bringing me back to planet Earth.

"It's a beautiful gown," said Tara, who was pinning the dress to fit.

I looked in the mirror again and wished for the millionth time that I was taller, and that my hair was thicker, then reminded myself that these were not real problems.

Once over the initial shock and following self-flagellation, I was able to continue the mission Aunt Natalie had sent me to accomplish:

2. With my pale skin, I needed a *white* white dress.

3. Big tulle skirts made me look like a loofah with a head.

4. Sample sale or not, I did not want a Vera Wang dress.

(The Scandinavian blonde-bunned me was proud.)
Much as I admired their elegant, architectural lines,
they all looked a bit too much like Vera Wang gowns.

5. Naomi had no critical eye. No matter how atrocious a
dress looked, when I left the dressing room to show her,
she'd gasp, bite her lower lip, and exclaim either, "Oh,
my God!" or "I am so *verklempt!,*" neither of which went
over well with straight-from-*Town-and-Country* Tara.

As I changed back to civilian clothes in the wood-paneled
dressing room, I heard voices from the other side of the wall.

"Moth-er," someone was saying. "Stop being so puritanical!
There is nothing wrong with a strapless gown!"

"Well, I don't know. It seems a bit unorthodox . . ."

"Walter!" boomed the bride. "Tell her!"

"Believe it or not, Mrs. Hutchinson, strapless bridal gowns
are very in vogue . . ." It could have been Thomas in full fabric
butler mode.

"Thank you, Walter," the bride said. "See, Mother?"

"Well," trilled the mother, "Walter *is* the best dress consultant
in the city. If you say so . . ."

A wedding dress consultant? Did people really have this much
money? On the street below, ladies who lunched roamed the
sidewalks. Stupid, stupid question.

"I think these are all no-gos," I told Naomi as we made to
leave and she asked Tara for her card.

Yumi Katsura turned me off mermaid shapes and lace and on
to exposed clavicles, "the most feminine part of a woman's body,"
the sleek Asian saleswoman told a nodding Naomi, who asked
for her card.

After a diner lunch (tuna melt for Naomi, turkey burger for me), we headed downtown to Josephine.

With its freestanding wooden mirrors, yellowed old-time dress figures, and faded oriental rugs, the Josephine studio was the embodiment of my grandma's attic fantasy. Instead of fussy saleswomen, the wife end of the husband-and-wife team helped me in and out of their simple, elegant dresses, always sure to note that since each dress is individually made, any of the styles could be modified to suit my tastes. I asked if they had samples, and was told they did have some, which I could buy at two-thirds the price. Naomi sat in a rocking chair while I modeled different dresses, covering her mouth and shaking her head as if to stem a ready tide of emotion with each one, but, as much as I'd wanted to fall in love with a three-thousand-dollar Josephine dress that I could get for two thousand, I couldn't. They all just seemed so *plain*. As I looked into the mirror with each dress, the practical side of me appeared over my right shoulder. She cocked her head and said, "You could get a regular white dress just like this for five hundred tops." And the little-girl side appeared on my left. She folded her arms across her chest and said, "*Bor*-ring." As nice as their simple organza gowns were, I could see what Dan meant: The Josephine dresses weren't bridey enough. Once we left the store (with Naomi adding their card to her now-growing collection) and sat drinking some much-needed coffees, I wished I could somehow wear the studio instead of the dresses it showcased.

"You're going to love Bella," Naomi said. "Remember when I played Rosencrantz in that all-women *Hamlet* two years ago? Four of the women in that cast have gotten married since, and all of them got their dresses at Bella."

We soon found ourselves off Avenue B at Bella, the small

storefront that was our final destination. The place was unlike any other we'd visited; its narrow walls were dingy, its carpeting frayed, and the samples of tops and bottoms—none of them white or even a full dress—hung from a side wall without care. The only possible nod to décor was a large Art Deco ashtray, thick with butts, which sat in the middle of the floor. Toto was not at Vera Wang anymore.

The place was empty, so I called out, "Hello?"

There was rustling from the back, behind the piece of fabric that hung over a wooden bar, which I assumed was the dressing room. Soon a woman emerged from behind the curtain, smoking. She was rake-thin and wore a 1930s-esque black silk blouse and a tailored black skirt with a slip hanging below the hemline. Her thick brown hair was cut in a chic bob, but her skin was the same ashen color as the carpet. The overall effect was that of fine crystal, smashed. She had to be European.

"You are here for bride or bridesmaids?" she asked, blowing smoke in our faces, in an accent that sounded French.

"For the bride," I said. "That's me."

The woman (I assume she was Bella, she neither told us her name nor asked us ours) eyed me up and down, lifted my arm, took another drag off her cigarette, and said, "Go to the back and take off your clothes."

I made to lift the makeshift curtain and she said, "No. You don't go there," then fanned a black screen around the corner where I stood. Did she moonlight as a dominatrix?

Moments later, I was swathed in muslin, trying to balance on the beat-up six-inch Prada heels I'd been ordered to don ("You need the height"). I looked in the mirror and saw a Christo on stilts.

"For you, the neck is open, and the skirt cut on the bias."

"What kind of material?" I dared to ask.

The woman who ate cigarettes shrugged. "Silk shantung."

"What color?"

"What color you like?"

"White. White-white."

She shrugged again, and exhaled. "Okay, so white-white."

She told me there would be two fittings and that the dress would cost two thousand dollars. "You call and let me know," she said, handing me her card. Then she disappeared behind the curtain, leaving only smoke.

"You *have* to get your dress here!" Naomi said, taking the card from my hands once we were out on the street.

"But I have no idea what the dress is going to look like."

"That's the point. Bella is a genius. I mean, there were some gorgeous dresses at those other places, but she is an *artist*."

"I'm not interested in an artist. I'm interested in a painting and whether or not it'll look good hanging on me."

"But this is so *cool*," she said. "Don't you want to be a cool bride?"

A cool bride. There was an oxymoron. The Scandinavian, the little girl, and I shook our heads in unison and said, "No."

We were ready for Kleinfeld's.

Twelve

$\mathcal{T}$he day we went to Kleinfeld's was one of those bitter, rainy early December days whose rawness reminds you of the whole, long winter you have ahead of you. Aunt Natalie and I took the subway out to Bay Ridge. We used one of my favorite meet-up tricks. I stood at the back of the N/R Times Square platform and she rode in one of the last two cars. When her train arrived, Aunt Natalie popped her head out the door and, seeing me a few feet away, cheered.

"All right!" she said, kissing my cheek as I entered the car. "What a great system!" She told me that Phyllis, who was meeting us there, had been "shocked" she was taking the subway. "People who don't live in the city just don't understand."

Almost an hour later, we found ourselves in Bay Ridge, Brooklyn, walking down a street lined with travel agents, produce shops, and Italian butchers. The ethnic working-class feel reminded me of Grandpa Sol's Bayonne, New Jersey, neighborhood. A block or so down, tuxedo stores began springing up, then jewelry stores, then veil stores. On the corner stood the Mecca, a building whose Italianate façade looked as if it belonged in the hoity-toity suburban enclave of a warm-weather city. There it was: Kleinfeld's.

We pulled the gold handle and stepped inside the lobby. With its marble floors and large flower arrangements, you might have mistaken Kleinfeld's waiting room for Elizabeth Arden's, until you noticed that the women inside were clustered for the most part in pairs, that most of them looked like an older and younger version of the same person, and that all of them were too giddy to be getting facials. Phyllis hadn't arrived yet, but it was still about five to twelve, so, though we were told our salesperson was ready, we figured we'd take a seat and wait. Settling in on the plushly upholstered bench that lined the waiting room wall, I wondered if people mistook Aunt Natalie and me for mother and daughter. We too were giddy, but less so as time wore on and we sat there, watching our bench compatriots head into the store and get replaced by more people who weren't Phyllis. The more brides got up to go back with their mothers, the less I felt anything like them.

Aunt Natalie said, "I'm sure she's stuck in traffic."

"Yeah," I nodded, pushing aside a creeping melancholy and following her lead. "Especially with this weather."

You could always make excuses for Phyllis, especially with Aunt Natalie around.

At twelve-thirty, our saleswoman, Judith, came out to meet us. Perhaps it was the bifocals dangling across her chest on a gold chain, but something about her gave the impression of a beloved high school guidance counselor who'd let you skip class to hang out in her office and listen to her very definite ideas about where you should and shouldn't apply to college. We shook hands and I apologized, explaining that my stepmother was flying up from Washington "just for this," and asked if we could give her a little more time.

"Of course we can, darling," she said, adding her second hand to better hold mine. "But why don't you give me an idea of what kind of dress you'd like, so I can get a head start on looking?"

I gave her the list: white-white dress, exposed clavicles, no tulle, no lace, no mermaid, no beads, no sequins. "And, if possible, two thousand dollars or less?"

There was a twinkle in Judith's eye. "I think I know just what I can do for you," she said. "Give me a minute."

Aunt Natalie asked if I could have the same fitter, "the wonderful Rosella," who had done my cousin Lynn's dress. Judith said, "I don't see why not," and ushered her to the alterations area to double-check. Alone, I picked up a Kleinfeld's brochure and learned that they'd been "turning wishes into wedding dresses since 1941," and that they attributed their success to their unique "philosophy": On her wedding day, every bride is a princess. The little girl inside me cheered.

At one o'clock, there was still no sign of Phyllis. We decided to get started. "It'll take a while for you to get in and out of the dresses," Aunt Natalie reasoned. "She'll be able to find us in back."

As Judith led us through the tasteful mother-of-the-bride gown and shoe salon areas, we heard gasps, followed by a round of "you look so beautiful!"s. Forget Bella, I thought, Naomi would fit right in here.

We entered the bridal dress area, a veritable hive of activity that brought to mind the place where Dorothy got her made-it-to-Oz makeover—though here, little Brooklyn ladies buzzed around instead of Munchkins. It soon became clear that most of the clamor was emanating from an area in the center of the room where a cluster of at least ten onlookers watched as an elevated bride stood admiring herself from the many angles afforded by the multiple mirrors in front of her.

"Isn't this something?" Aunt Natalie asked. "And this is a weekday! You should have seen it the Saturday I came in with Lynn!"

"Normally, we take our brides on a walk through various closets," Judith said, commandeering us to a dressing room. "And, if you want to do that later, we can—though, frankly, with your budget, I don't have much to offer. But I don't think it's going to be necessary."

She unlocked the door and hung up the gown in her hand with a flourish.

"This," she said, "is your dress. The minute I saw you and heard what you wanted, I knew this was the dress for you. My only concern: the cost. It retails for five thousand, but I checked with my manager, and I do have a sample I can sell you for two."

"That includes alterations?" asked Aunt Natalie.

"Alterations are included. Two thousand dollars—and if you ship it outside New York you don't have to pay tax," Judith continued as she made for the door. "Call me when you have it on, and I'll come back in and pin it. Your aunt will come with me to the twirling area. I don't want either of you to see it without the whole picture."

They called it "the twirling area." The place was genius.

Once the dress was on and pinned, Judith led me from the dressing room to the mirrored area. Per her orders, my eyes were closed. I stepped up on the box and Judith said, "Okay, open up!"

There I was, the bride. You could blame it on Judith's master saleswomanship, on the brilliance of Kleinfeld's public parade (the reason a small crowd now stood behind me gasping), or the tears in Aunt Natalie's eyes, but it took only a moment to register: This was my dress. The white-white dress had no beads or sequins but its design made it anything but plain: The off-the-shoulder sleeves were made of roses, the corsetlike bodice fitted, the skirt draped flatteringly in front, giving shape without pouffi-ness. It was simple, it was elegant, it was timeless, it was bridey. It was also unlike anything I would have originally imagined. You could have stuck me on top of a cake. But the little girl was jumping up and down, and the Scandinavian was saying, "Beau-tiful material. Two thousand for this is a good deal." I knew Dan would be happy.

"I love it," I said.

"Oh, goody!" said a beaming Aunt Natalie. "I love it too! But I wanted to be good and wait for your opinion!"

"It's stunning," said Judith.

"Stunning," a customer behind her repeated. "I wonder if that would look good on my daughter?"

"I have not seen your daughter," said a solemn Judith. "But this is a dress not every figure can pull off."

"You know what it looks like?" I said. "Cinderella at the ball!"

Aunt Natalie chuckled and the others around nodded agree-ment.

"Does that make me the fairy godmother?" she asked.

Before I could answer, in rushed Phyllis, still wearing her fur. She kissed Aunt Natalie's cheek, offered her apologies, and launched into a convoluted monologue about her cab driver and traffic lights.

"Well, you're just in time," Aunt Natalie said, ignoring the implausibility of a cab driver bearing sole responsibility for an hour and a half delay. "Rachel has found her dress." She turned Phyllis to face the mirrors. I smiled and waved from my perch.

"Rachel," she said. "You look . . . beautiful." I told myself that the disappointment in her tone came from the fact that I'd made the decision without her. "So that's it?" she asked. "I don't get to see you in more dresses?"

"This is the dress," said Judith. "For what she wants, for this price, I can't show you anything better. Forget the price—just look at this," she said, motioning to me. "This is *magical*. I wish I could do this for every bride who walks in here—discount or no discount! Listen, if it were just my opinion, I'd be happy to show you more dresses. But given how late we started," the clock behind her now read one-thirty, "and how much the bride seems to like the dress . . ."

"Well, Rachel, are you sure about the dress?" asked Aunt Natalie.

"I think so," I said. "Yeah."

"Well, then." Aunt Natalie shrugged. "If it weren't so wonderful, I'd say we should keep going, but it's clear that this *is* the dress. Don't you think so, Phyllis?"

"It's a beautiful dress . . ." Phyllis sounded skeptical.

"I'm happy to try on more," I said, putting the twirling in the twirling area.

"I can bring you some more," Judith said, "but they'll be more expensive, and, frankly, not even in the same *league*. Look at this material!"

"Well, how much is this one?" Phyllis asked.

Judith explained the pricing to her.

"Two thousand?" Phyllis seemed to be balking.

"Isn't it fabulous?" Aunt Natalie asked, beaming. "Leave it to Rachel to get a five-thousand-dollar dress for two thousand dollars!"

"Yes," said my stepmother, looking up at me in my gown. "Rachel is very good at getting what she wants."

"Shall I bring out more dresses?" Judith asked.

"Well, I guess if you like this one there's really no point . . ."

I looked at myself, the bride in the mirror. "I really do."

"Then, hey, we've got the dress!" Aunt Natalie cheered. Phyllis handed Judith her gold card and I hopped off the twirling platform.

"We do," I said, hugging both Natalie and Phyllis with as much relief as gratitude.

Phyllis asked Judith for a restaurant "a bit more high-class than the neighborhood." On the walk there, Aunt Natalie and I were too busy gushing about every little detail of the dress to press Phyllis for further explanation of her lateness. She seemed happy to let the subject drop. After we ordered, she and Aunt Natalie chatted about the "exquisite" new condo their mutual friend Beverly had bought in Boca Raton. But once lunch arrived, Aunt Natalie changed the subject back to the wedding.

"It really is great how much your in-laws are contributing," she said.

"Yeah, I know," I said, ready to seize my great cousins' opportunity, keeping my eyes on the plate. "It really makes things doable—the Audubon Society, the cousins . . ."

I looked up, eyes only, to catch Phyllis's nod. We were out of the woods.

"Dad's Scranton friends . . ."

"We're still working on that," she said, biting into her chicken piccata.

"Oh, I'm sure the numbers will work out," I said, looking up at her. "They can fit up to one-sixty . . ."

"I know." Phyllis gave one of her double-nods. "It'll be fine. Dad and I just have to do some finessing."

"Okay," I said, reaching for my water, content to hear no evil. Leaning over her plate, Aunt Natalie clapped her hands to a clasp and said, "So terrific, huh? Everything's moving right along . . ."

I smiled and sipped.

Phyllis sighed and said, "*Al*most everything."

"What?" I asked, putting my glass back on the table. I didn't really want to hear the answer.

"We've gotta take care of something here, Raych," she said, shaking her head in "it's just so impossible" mode. "I know you wanted to give your mother the kosher option, Raych, but I don't think that's gonna work out."

"Why not?" I asked, sitting back in my chair. Phyllis's use of the word "Raych" was never a good thing, but I was still post-dress euphoric.

"Your mother has been calling Deena and asking strange questions about using new dishes."

I laughed. "It might seem ridiculous, but the only thing that would make an all-dairy wedding nonkosher would be if the pots and dishes had been used at some point to serve meat." I shrugged, leaning back in and splitting a spinach ravioli with my fork. "She's just trying to figure out if she can have a technically kosher wedding, but avoid the extra cost by doing it dairy."

"Well, be that as it may," said Phyllis, shooing the explanation away with her French-manicured fingers, "I can't have your mother calling up Deena with these bizarre requests."

"Why not? Deena's a caterer. That's her job."

Phyllis sighed and shot Aunt Natalie a see-how-much-I-have-to-put-up-with look.

"Deena is not complaining. Deena is perfectly lovely. But when you work with people on affairs you have to have a *relationship*." She enunciated this last word like a dictionary entry: re LAY shun-shipp (n.), an interaction between my stepmother and a person who is helping her spend money, replete with much mutual ass-kissing. "Deena and I have a *relationship*. And when your mother calls her up, it interferes with that *relationship*. And, I wasn't even going to mention it, but you *did* call her up at home."

"Dad gave me the number." I shrugged again. "I assumed since you were friends it was fine to call her there. Deena didn't seem to mind at all at the time. She also seemed very aware of all the ins and outs of kosher versus kosher-style catering."

Phyllis looked at Aunt Natalie, who was twisting her linguine into her spoon unperturbed, then back to me. She exhaled loudly. "I'm not saying Deena minded. I'm saying *I* minded. There are delicate things going on here."

"What delicate things? She's the caterer."

"Yes. And she's also a member of the condo board! It's very important to have allies."

I wish I could tell you that, in my postdress bliss, I found it in my heart to be sympathetic to Phyllis then, to remember that, like her incessant shopping and organizing, her making a mountain out of the condo board molehill was a manifestation of her need for control; to remind myself, as I so often did with my stepmother, that if she didn't cling so tightly she might—God forbid!—lose her grip and have to digest the fact that one day without warning, her first husband dropped dead on a racquetball court. But how could I show that kind of compassion to someone who didn't make the slightest effort to reciprocate? Even now I'm not sure whether it would have made me a saint or a doormat. I could justify Phyllis's need to arrange things, but couldn't tolerate her treating me like one of them. So much for my postdress bliss.

"What are you saying? That Deena is *your* friend so you don't want my mother playing with her on the jungle gym at recess?"

Aunt Natalie said, "Rachel—"

Phyllis said, "Do you see how impossible she is?"

Aunt Natalie gave me a look that said, "Don't make a scene."

"I just don't understand," I said, turning down my own heat. "It's already been agreed that my mother can have the option to make this wedding kosher, so she called the caterer to ask about it. You want to renege on the offer because of *that*? Even a reasonable person would be pissed about this, and you know Joyce is not a reasonable person. Are you doing this just to make me crazy?"

"Rachel," my stepmother said slowly, donning her cloak of supreme condescension, "this is about things you don't understand."

"Like what?" The condo board? I didn't know what to react to first: the content of what she'd said or the you-are-so-young-and-I-am-so-wise way she'd said it.

"Phyllis," said Aunt Natalie gently, "I know Joyce is difficult, but it really isn't right to tell her one thing and then change your mind . . ."

"Change my mind!" my stepmother wailed. "I was never consulted about this! I think the whole idea of a kosher wedding in this day and age is absurd! Rachel was the one who brought it up to begin with, and we were doing our best to try to accommodate her. But I'm not going to sacrifice my position in the building—in my *home*—for some show of religiousness for a person who'd eat in this restaurant just like you or me."

"Grandpa Sol has never eaten in a nonkosher restaurant," I said. That wasn't actually true—he'd eaten a salad at my uncle Stuart's law school graduation celebration in Austin when he'd had no choice, but the fact that I knew the one and only exception served to reinforce the rule. "And this isn't just some random party—it's a religious ceremony. It's his granddaughter's wedding. It's not like anyone's asking you to pay for it." I was fourteen all over again, begging my father despite his belief that "the public school system is the greatest progressive achievement of this country" to let me go to Jewish Day School, an education that Grandpa Sol was funding, as he did my summer camp. School and camp, the twin pillars of my adolescence. The only things I always knew would be taken care of, because a person I could count on was taking care of them.

"Well," Phyllis said, breaking it to me with her hand on mine, "Dad and I do feel that Grandpa Sol is truly religious. However—"

"I'm sure Grandpa Sol will be glad to know he gets the seal of approval from a woman who doesn't know the laws of *kashrut* and made her first husband change his name from Markowitz to Marks," I said dryly, removing my hand from under hers to reach for my water.

"Rachel, please," said Aunt Natalie. "Is that really necessary?" It probably shouldn't have been, but, at the time, yes, it kind of was.

"Do you see this?" Phyllis asked her. "What I have to put up with? I fly in here, for not even three hours—"

"Could have been more than four if you hadn't come an hour and a half late," I muttered, and Natalie shot me a just-be-quiet look.

"For what? For a person who's *completely* unappreciative." She turned to me, and in a breaking-it-down-for-your-benefit-missy tone, continued, "We are spending *a lot* of money on this wedding, *a lot* of money on a dress you'll wear once, *a lot* of money on a party where your dad gets to invite all his friends and I get to invite hardly any of mine!"

Was *this* what they were finessing? "Do you think maybe that's because I'm his daughter and these are people who've known me my whole life?"

"Perfect," she said. "It's always you, you, you, isn't it, Rachel?"

Aunt Natalie tried to intervene. "That's a bit unfair, Phyllis, don't you think?"

But Phyllis was on a roll. "*Your* dress, *your* wedding! Does it ever get to be about *me*?"

Only then was it too obvious to deny: I *was* Cinderella. She was, and had always been, a *stepmother*.

I don't know which upset me more, the hollowness of her platitudes—"this is the great thing about having a daughter!"—or my own pathetic need to believe them.

I wanted to scream, but my voice was quiet.

"Why would my wedding be about you?"

Aunt Natalie was shaking her head, looking up toward the ceiling, as if someone up there might pay attention to her. "Oh, dear . . . I thought this would be such a fun day, the three of us, the dress . . . now look what it's turned into . . ."

"Why? Because you want *my* money! Gregory and Thomas didn't ask for a cent—"

"Gregory and Thomas?"

"Yes—"

It took all my strength to keep from blurting out the truth: that the reason they hadn't asked her for a cent for their wedding was that Thomas's parents had financed the whole thing.

"Would you rather Dan and I wore his-and-his Armanis also?" I asked in the new dry tone that was fast becoming my specialty.

"Phyllis," Aunt Natalie said sharply, "I'm not sure that's a fair comparison."

"The point is," my stepmother said, cutting into her meat, "*they* acted like *adults*."

"And I'm acting like a child." I shook my throbbing head. I could have laughed. "*I* am acting like a child."

I felt Aunt Natalie's hand on my knee, trying to keep this from going any further.

"Well," Phyllis said, "when it comes to this wedding, you haven't exactly been *independent*."

I nodded slowly, gave Aunt Natalie a not-to-worry look. I was letting this one sink.

"Well, I'm sorry to be such an inconvenience," I said, choking back tears I was surprised had sprung up. "Excuse me."

I rose and made for the sanctuary of the one-person bathroom I'd spotted on the way to the table, thinking it plausible that Elizabeth Bennet would have done the same.

But Phyllis's indignant voice carried.

"Do you see what I have to put up with?"

Thirteen

After lunch, Aunt Natalie and I took the subway back into Manhattan.

"You know how Phyllis is, honey," she said, patting my knee. "She means well, but she can get very threatened."

I said, "I know how Phyllis is."

She put her arm around me. "Wanna come home with me? We can sit and unwind, have a drink, talk about how beautiful you looked in that dress . . ."

My first-choice activity would have been to crawl into bed.

"I appreciate the thought." I smiled. "But I can't. I'm meeting Dan for a movie."

Sitting in a darkened theater for two hours was probably the next best thing.

I arrived early at the Lincoln Plaza theater, but instead of wandering around the little square reading poster-sized *Times* reviews, I headed downstairs to the mauve lobby and used a pay phone to call Thomas at work. The theme of the conversation was one of our favorites: Can you believe what Phyllis just did? I told him about her hour-and-a-half-late Kleinfeld's arrival ("No way!"), about her grudging, it's-a-beautiful-dress compliment ("Just like the Vera Wang bitch!"). I told him about her reneging on the kosher ("Unbelievable!") and her demand for an equal number of guests ("You're kidding!"). Then I delivered what I knew would be the pièce de résistance, her comment about us "being children" by not paying for our own wedding, unlike Gregory and Thomas, the "independent adults."

"I can't believe she actually still thinks that," he said. "One of these days someone has to tell her that Alice and Clyde footed the whole bill. It'd be worth it just to see her try to do damage control with them."

"But enough about Phyllis," Thomas went on, "I want to hear about the dress."

Too drained to do it justice, I gave him a hairline sketch.

"You'll have to come with me to a fitting," I said.

"Oh, goody!"

We hung up just as Dan arrived.

"How'd it go?" he asked, kissing my cheek.

"Depends on what you mean by 'it.'" I gave him the same update I'd given Thomas.

But Dan was not incredulous. He shook his head from side to side. "What did you expect? She's Phyllis."

"Thanks a lot," I said. "It's always nice to hear, I told you so."

"The important thing is, did you find a dress?"

"Yes," I said.

"And you're happy with it."

"Yeah." I smiled. "I think you're gonna like it."

"Then who cares about Phyllis?"

"Right," I said. I had a dress I loved—that was the important thing. Why let a stepmother overshadow it? "You're right."

People were walking past us, going to wait on the ticket line.

He kissed my head and said, "Did you buy the tickets yet?"

"Yeah. You hungry?" We usually split one of their smoked salmon sandwiches, but I barely had an appetite.

"No," he said. "But it sounds like you could use some rugelach."

"Very true."

"Should we divide and conquer?" he asked.

I nodded. "You get on line, I'll get the rugelach."

"Okay," he said, turning to go. "Oh, and a Diet Coke?"

"Regular," I said. We always split drinks at the movies.

"We already have sugar with the rugelach . . ."

"Come on," I said. "I had a rough day."

He smiled, conceding my choice of concessions. "Okay," he said. "And I also have some news." He was smiling devilishly.

"What?" It wasn't often Dan had gossip.

"I'll tell you when you come back."

We met up again on line.

"So what's the news?" I said. Nothing like dish to clear up a headache.

"You're gonna like this," he said, smiling.

"What?" My eyes were wide.

"It's a goodie . . ."

"Come on," I pleaded, "I'm not in the mood for suspense."

"Okay," he said. "You know that movie Lisa was in L.A. auditioning for?"

"The one with Sean O'Malley?" He nodded and I said, "She got it."

"Yup," he said. "But that's not all."

"What's the rest?" I asked.

"She and Will are moving to L.A."

My eyes went even wider, my mouth dropped open. Then I smiled. "After all of his crap, look who's the one leaving New York."

Dan nodded. "I thought you might get a kick out of that."

"I do," I said, and not just because I felt vindicated. Will's move reinforced our Seventies New Yorkerdom—Seventies New Yorkers had friends who moved to L.A., Nineties New Yorkers had friends who moved to San Francisco.

"So when are they leaving?" I asked.

"Right away. Will's packing up the apartment and flying out next week."

"That's quick," I said, wondering what they were doing with their apartment, then quickly remembering that their rent was no deal.

"So we're meeting up tomorrow night to say good-bye—"

I nodded; this was to be expected. The line started moving.

"And I figured it'd be a good occasion to tell people about the wedding party. You know, make it more festive—"

"Wait a minute," I said, as we neared the theater entrance. "We haven't even talked about a wedding party yet."

"Well, let's talk about it now, then," Dan said.

"Now?" I motioned toward the theater in front of us and the crowd all around.

"I mean, once we sit down."

"Fine," I said.

"Work your magic, baby," he said, hanging back as we entered the quickly filling theater.

We were suddenly, purposefully silent. I scanned the near-packed room for seats. Then, spotting an opening, I made for the row, ready to do the dance.

"Excuse me," I said, leaning over to address the professorial-looking man four seats in. "Is there anyone sitting there?" I motioned toward the seat to his left, which held coats I assumed were his and his female companion's.

"No," he said.

"Excuse me, ma'am?" I asked, craning toward the woman in an ethnic-printed scarf seated next to the coat chair. "Is there someone sitting on the other side of the woman next to you?"

"No," she said. I smiled, and, without further ado, the man moved his coats and the woman and her companion shifted over and Dan and I made our way through the row and sat down—the Manhattan Movie Theater Shuffle.

We took off our coats, turning to either side and thanking everyone involved. The man smiled and the woman said, "Don't mention it."

Thus settled, I faced Dan and said, "I don't think I want a wedding party. It's cheesy."

"What do you mean it's cheesy? It's a *wedding*."

"It's just—weird. It's like you're seven years old and you're having your birthday party at the Ice Capades and you can only bring four friends. I hate that kind of birthday party. It's too complicated. It's a small-scale *Sophie's Choice*."

"Come on, Raych," he said as people filed in around us. "What's so hard about choosing bridesmaids?"

"Is this really an avenue you want to go down?"

"You have Naomi."

"Right. I have Naomi. But then do I branch out from Naomi to the whole college suitemates thing, even though I'm not such good friends with Erin or Andrea anymore, or do I not do the whole college suitemates thing, thereby making the official state-ment that I'm not such good friends with Erin or Andrea any-more? And do I ask Julie, who I am actually good friends with? But she's like a couple-friend, and that's like a whole different phase of life I'm not sure we've really entered yet. Like, what if, for some unforeseen reason, she and Connor break up? And now that the cousins are invited, I really should have my second cousin Melissa. Oh, and Jodi Grunthal. I have to have Jodi Grunthal."

"Who is Jodi Grunthal?"

"My best friend from childhood. Known her since kindergarten."

"What? I've never even met her."

"I know. But in fourth grade we made a promise that we'd be each other's bridesmaids."

"Isn't there a statute of limitations on that kind of thing?"

I shrugged. "How should I know? I've never had bridesmaids before."

"Okay," he said, shaking his head. "I grant you it's complicated. But I still want a wedding party."

"Okay," I said, deciding to come at it from a different angle. "Who's gonna be your best man? Are you gonna pick one of your brothers?"

"No," he said. "That, to me, is Ice Capades. I don't really get the purpose of a best man anyway. What does he actually *do*?"

"I have no idea. But you realize that you're basically saying that because you have friends you want in your wedding party, I have to be Ice Capades, right?"

Dan shrugged. "Don't have a wedding party if you don't want one."

"Oh, yeah, right. You have people standing on your side and I have nobody on mine. Nice loser bride. If you're having a wedding party, I have to have one too."

"So have one too."

"But I don't want one."

"But I do."

Strike up the mariachis.

It had been a long day. I reached for the rugelach.

The lights were dimming, the previews about to begin. I sighed and took a moment to think. Part of me was saying, "Don't be Bridezilla—this is a bigger deal to him than it is to you, just suck it up and have a wedding party." I had to admit, I agreed with that part. But as soon as I did, I felt that old rake in my gut, dredging the swamp.

"Fine," I said, changing my voice to a whisper to adapt to the now-beginning preview, "you win. Wedding party it is." He smiled, and I held up a not-so-fast finger. "But I want it acknowledged that not only am I having a wedding party when I don't want one, but I am also having a wedding party consisting of people who didn't even want the wedding to happen in the first place," I added, mumbling.

"Ray-chul—"

"I know, I know. He'll come around! He may even smile for the pictures!"

"You know, you're not the only one with a reason to be angry about that," he said, making sure his whisper carried over both the preview narrator's voice and the other people talking over it.

"What does that mean?"

"Do you think I like the fact that when I told one of my supposedly closest friends I was getting engaged he could only think about himself? That he couldn't put aside his own bullshit for one fucking second and be happy for me? You think that I like that I went to the bar that night to share something important and positive and meaningful with him and left thinking about Nietzsche and how truly alone we all are in this world?"

I wish I could say that, upon hearing this, I thought, "Wow, I've been really selfish. I haven't considered Dan's feelings at all." That would make me a better heroine and a better person. But what I actually thought was, "Leave it to Dan to bring Nietzsche into a conversation about bridesmaids."

"I wouldn't think you'd like it," I said. A lovely Greek village was up on the screen. "But all you do is defend him. You seem to want to stuff the whole episode in a little box, throw it in the back of the closet, and pretend it never happened."

"I don't want to walk around thinking that my friend is an asshole."

"But he *is* an asshole!"

"He's not an asshole. He's an idiot. You know that. Why can't you just let it go?"

"You know what I really hate? The way you put this all on me. It's not as if I'm sitting here saying I don't want Will in the wedding party. He's your friend and it's your decision."

"Then why do you grumble every time he comes up?"

A gorgeous woman was hanging her laundry while wearing the skimpiest housedress on the Mediterranean.

"How can you ask me that? You know exactly why."

"I have a hunch, but I'd like to hear it from you anyway."

"Fine. Because, in case you've forgotten, that whole episode really hurt my feelings. Is that even a factor in your mind when we have these conversations?"

"Let me ask you a question," Dan said calmly. "If Will had said all the same things that night, but I hadn't gotten up in the morning and said what I did to you, would you still be this pissed?"

I narrowed my eyes as his point came into focus. "No," I said.

"Then it's not really him you're this angry with, is it?"

"No," I said. I looked up at the screen and bit the inside of my mouth. The Greek goddess was accepting an olive from the shy farmer who'd loved her from afar. The deep-voiced preview narrator was saying, "This spring, fall in love all over again."

"Listen," Dan said, turning me to face him. "I am really, really sorry I said those things. You thought the case was closed, and I should have thought about how much it would hurt you to reopen it. But we're different. When you feel something strongly, that's the way you feel and you don't need to second-guess it."

"That's not true. I'm always thinking, 'Am I right?' 'Am I doing the right thing?'"

"But you don't doubt the feeling itself." I shrugged, and he continued. "Rachel, a person who meets someone once and goes around calling him the love of her life doesn't second-guess her feelings."

He had me there.

"The point is," Dan continued, "I don't trust my emotions the same way you do. And you'd been so patient with me up until then that I guess I sort of took advantage."

"That's how it felt." I was tearing up during the previews at Lincoln Plaza Cinema. It had been an emotional day. "Like you took advantage."

"I didn't mean to," he said. "I really didn't." We sat there for a moment, looking up at the preview, transported for half a second to Greece. A woman behind us said, "Irving, I can't hear what he's saying. Get them to fix the sound." Then a man said, "What do you care? This is just the commercials. The movie's in Polish with subtitles."

Another preview came on and Dan continued, "I know you're not gonna like this, but I'm kind of glad the whole thing happened."

"I thought this was an apology," I said, turning to look at him with suspicion.

"It is. I'm sorry for the way I handled it. Truly. But I'm not sorry the whole thing came up."

"Oh yeah?"

"Yeah. Getting engaged is a big decision. It's an important thing. And having to sort through all of Will's crap actually made me even surer about my decision."

I tucked my chin, flirty-style. "It did?"

"Yup," he nodded. "You know, come to think of it, you should be thanking Will."

I untucked my chin. "Don't push it, buddy."

He reached for the soda and took a sip.

"You got Diet?" He smiled, touched.

I rolled my eyes and settled back into my seat. "Of course."

On the walk home that night, we completed our wedding party plan. Our brothers (Dan's two, Matthew, and Gregory) would hold the *chuppah*. Dan's attendants would be Will, Connor, Rob, and Andrew (two other friends from his Columbia posse). My attendants would be Thomas and Naomi and former suite-mates Erin and Andrea (despite the lack of current closeness).

The next night, we found ourselves at the Blue and the Gold, an East Village bar, for Will's going-away party. The usual suspects were there, along with some peripheral fellow Columbia/ Barnard grads. Dan, Will, Connor, Rob, and Andrew toasted themselves as the newly anointed wedding party (at which point I smiled at Julie, hoping to mask my guilt and uncertainty over not making her a bridesmaid). Will spent the better part of the evening verbal-Rumpelstiltskining about "it all" being "about connections out there," and how, now that Lisa was on her way, there was no doubt he too would soon get his break. "All I know," he said, "is that all roads lead to the bicoastal Susan Sarandon–Tim Robbins life."

Toasts were made, but I doubted my nausea stemmed from excess alcohol.

Fourteen

The following Sunday, I lounged on the sofa, reading the most important part of the paper, the *Vows* column, again. This week's featured a couple who'd met at Wesleyan—he a sculptor, she an avant-garde theater director. Their wedding took place in their DUMBO live/work loft space, and they'd filled it with thousands of brightly colored origami figurines.

"Lois Smith Brady is starting to bug me," I told Dan. He was sitting at the dining room table, finishing up some work before meeting with his study group.

"Ummm," he responded.

I put down the paper. "Mind if I turn on the TV?"

"Long as it's not one of those yelly political shows," he said without looking up.

I flicked the remote and headed straight for Lifetime. Sho' nuf, figure skating. Pairs. A couple in the most heinous gold and black outfits imaginable was gliding across the ice. Jackpot.

A male announcer said, "We've seen a lot of energy and athleticism from this Israeli team."

"They're part of this whole new field of competitors, who've really been changing the face of ice dancing," said his female counterpart.

It slowly became clear that they were skating to "Chava Nagi-lah" and that the hideous things on their shoulders, holding up their ensembles, togalike, were huge Jewish stars.

"Dan," I said, as the music changed to "Hevenu Shalom Alechem," "come over here. You've gotta see this."

He looked up, but was stopped from responding by the phone, which, at that moment, rang. Dan reached in front of him and answered. "Hello? Oh, hi . . . Good, just doin' a little work here. Sure," he said, rising, "I'll put her on." He walked over to the couch and handed me the phone. The Israeli pair took their bows.

"You missed the good part," I said, muting the TV.

He shrugged and went back to the table, leaving me on the couch with the phone and my father, to have a tête-à-tête I'd been expecting for the past few days, ever since Kleinfeld's day.

"Hey, Dad," I said. "What's up?"

"Not too much. I'm calling about the wedding—"

"I figured."

"Now, Rachel," he said, stammering, "Phyllis told me about the conversation you had when she went up there for your dress—"

"Uh-huh—" I wondered about her version.

"—and it's clear to me that nothing with this wedding's gonna run smoothly until we get things straight with your mother—"

So that's where the emphasis had lain. I turned to the screen and watched the marks for artistic merit come in—5.6's, 5.7's, and a 5.4 from the Ukrainians, perhaps anti-Semitism?

"Probably a reasonable conclusion—"

"Now," here he gained momentum, "I can think of three areas she's responsible for—a guest list of thirty-five people, this business with the kosher food, and, since you left it up to her, the cake."

"Okay . . ." Curious to see where this was going, I shut off the TV.

"Now, these are things you've already told her, so they stay on the table—"

"What do you mean, 'on the table'?"

"Rachel, I'm trying to resolve things here. Will you let me finish?"

"Fine."

"What I want to do is give her a deadline. Tell her she has until February 28 to give us her guest list, the check for her guests' catering, and the additional charge for kosher catering—if that's what she decides she wants—and a written agreement to provide the cake."

"A *written agreement* to provide the *cake*?" I sat up and looked at Dan, who, on hearing this, rolled his eyes as he loaded his backpack. "Don't you think that's pushing it, Dad?"

"No I don't," my father said firmly, maybe even angrily. "I figure she'll do two out of three, and that one's easily expendable."

It was my turn to roll eyes. "She hasn't even done anything crazy yet. All she did was call the caterer—"

"The point is not what she's done. The point is what she *can* do. The way it stands, you're giving her free rein to sit on these things until the very last minute. We need to have things *settled*."

Dan said, "I've gotta go."

"Hold on a sec, Dad," I said, covering the receiver. I cast a pleading look at Dan. "Should I tell him I have to call him back?"

"Rachel," Dan said in a give-me-a-break tone, heading toward the couch to say farewell. "This is your father. The reasonable parent. You're a big girl. You can handle him without me."

Everything Dan was saying was right, but I really didn't want him to go. Why was I suddenly such a wimp?

"Have a good study group," I said, getting up to kiss him good-bye.

As soon as the door closed behind him, my heartbeat started to quicken. I told myself to stop being a baby; Dan was right, I could handle my father on my own. I took a seat on the couch, readjusted the sunken corner of a cushion, and tried to do the diaphragmatic breathing I'd learned from Dr. Chen.

"No one wants this wedding settled more than I do, Dad."

"Well, then, good. That's why we put this deadline in place."

"I don't know, Dad, I think this is asking for trouble. Joyce has been totally under control so far. I don't want to set her off."

"Now, Rachel, we can't—that cannot be a factor here. Your mother is a very volatile person, but only when she wants to be." He went on to spout the same logic I'd heard so many times before—that Joyce's selective volatility was her means of strong-arming people into giving her what she wanted. "Once you start tiptoeing around her, she's won."

My father's tone was not Jerry-anal, it was definitive. It was a tone I knew well from discussions like these, one he used to convey the good, sound reasons why my mother was taking advantage of a situation and why he would not go along with it—"Rachel, I will pay a portion of your wisdom teeth bill, but only half. Your mother needs to learn that the money I give her to support you kids is all the money she's gonna get."

Matthew and I had no nickname for this tone. Neither of us

found it funny. But if I had to come up with a name, I would have called it the flattening-the-tires tone, because whenever I heard it, the air would slowly seep out of mine. I was deflating.

Sitting here now with Hindsight and Clarity, I see that I should have been angry. I know I should have picked up on the "she's won" the way I had the "on the table" and told my father right then and there that this was not a war, this was not a negotiation, this was my wedding and he was giving me a headache. But there was truth to what my father was saying; he had a point. I see now that I should have thought, "No shit, he has a point. It's the same point he's been making your entire life!" But I didn't. I didn't because it seemed as if I'd spent the bulk of my early life trying to "handle" ticking time bomb Joyce only to have her blow up in my face. So, while I did have a headache, while I was annoyed, all I could think was: "Will I ever learn my lesson?"

Which is why, after hearing my father out, I said, "All right, Dad, I admit you have a point."

I felt like shit, but my father was relieved.

"Good," he said. "I'm glad you think so, because I want you to be the one who tells her about the deadline. That way she knows it's coming from you, too."

This was a tune I recognized: Rachel Back and Forth in the Middle, in the familiar key of migraine. The jack-in-the-box theme song. Suddenly my tire had a lot more air.

"No way, Dad," I said, I Won't Dance, Don't Ask Me. "It's *your* idea. It's not coming from me, too."

"Rachel, you're the one who made this kosher thing an issue the day you first came down here to plan this wedding—"

"I what?"

"You made this kosher business an issue."

"I *what?*"

"You heard me," he said. "We've been trying from the beginning to accommodate you here and you don't reciprocate—"

"You're accommodating *me*?"

"Yes."

I wanted to say: "Dad, let me remind you of something. Many years ago, you married someone with an Orthodox parent. I have no idea why you married this person, you had nothing whatsoever in common with her, but I wasn't alive and I wasn't consulted so you can hardly blame me for your decision!"

But I was desperate to remain calm and collected. So instead I said, "I'm not doing this for myself. I'm happy to have the wedding all-dairy kosher-style. I'm doing it for Grandpa Sol, who is not volatile, who is not manipulative, who has done absolutely *nothing* to you, and who I think, at *my* wedding, deserves some respect."

My father sighed. "I knew I never should have let you go to a Jewish school and a Jewish camp. This was exactly what your grandfather wanted, another person who'd agree with his views."

This, while true, was utterly beside the point.

"What are you talking about?" I'm afraid I may have sounded as pissed off and frustrated as I was. "I don't agree with his views! I'm not *Ortho*dox! But I respect the fact that Grandpa Sol is. And I also don't want my wedding to be yet another cause for yet another big fight, which is exactly what you seem determined to turn it into!"

"The point of this is not to create a fight, Rachel," he said sharply. "The point is to keep your mother from pulling the strings."

"She's not—"

"Let me finish here, Rachel—"

"Fine—"

"Now," the Jerry-anal tone was back in full force, "I am spending an awful lot of money on this wedding. And I think that gives me the right to have some say. I don't want to see things getting out of control, which is why it's important that we give your mother a deadline. And she's much more likely to go along with it if it comes from you. Do you want these things settled or not?"

His voice was sharp—"Do you want dessert or not, young lady?"—and I wonder now why I didn't say, "Who do you think you're talking to?" instead of making it okay by answering.

"Of course I want things settled. But I don't think giving Joyce a deadline is the best way to get that done."

"Well," he was strictly air-out-of-tire now, "I do."

I was dizzy. Where was my pump? I knew the answer: on the One or the Nine subway line, probably around Eighty-sixth Street, on his way to study group.

Now, I remember thinking that I should stand my ground, I should tell my father once and for all that his deadline idea was incendiary, that the only reason he was doing this at all was that Phyllis was making yet another of her self-centered, controlling demands and that it was totally inappropriate for him to go along with her treating my wedding like his newspapers and there was no way I was going along with it.

But just thinking about it was exhausting. What about maintaining my sanity? My father was sticking to his position, and my head was pounding. I had already made my point—the lawyer, as always. If I continued, wouldn't I just be taking one more step down the road to a jack-in-the-box explosion? Wasn't avoiding the same old traps more important than debating some stupid deadline?

So instead of arguing with him any further, I sighed and said,

"Are you saying that if Joyce agrees to your terms by your deadline, then that will be it, this will be over, the wedding will either be kosher or kosher-style, no further discussion?"

"Yes," he said.

At least *that* was in my interest. I took a deep breath and exhaled hard. "Fine," I said. "I will back you up on this—"

"Good—"

"But I will *not* be the messenger. If you want to give Joyce a deadline you have to tell her yourself."

There was sighing on his end of the phone, but, eventually, my father said, "Fine."

We hung up and I clutched my pounding head, trying to find acupressure points. But I already felt a little better.

You see, I thought I'd held firm, stood my ground, remembered all those things I'd told myself about being a grown-up in my own place with my own life with Dan, about not being the jack-in-the-box anymore.

What I didn't realize, what I couldn't see, was that none of it was any different. I was already the jack-in-the-box. All I'd really done was let my father give me yet another crank.

Wedding Timeline:

Four to Six Months Ahead

- Book florist and choose arrangements
- Book band for reception/musicians for ceremony
- Book photographer and videographer
- Order stationery, including invitations and thank-you notes
- Register for gifts
- Order wedding cake

Fifteen

$\mathcal{N}$ow that we had a wedding party, it was time to clothe them.

This was easy enough, for the guys; they'd wear white oxford shirts, navy blue blazers, and Banana Republic plain-front khakis and a tie we'd provide. Since they wear basically the same uniform to any occasion anyway, when we informed them of their wedding wardrobe, they either had no reaction (our brothers and Rob), expressed relief at being somewhat informal (Connor, Will, and Andrew), or informed us that we had to make sure everyone wore the same color shoes and belts, and that they had to be brown—"black and navy, I don't think so" (Gregory and Thomas).

But when it came to the women, things got trickier. I thought I had to pick out a dress, a dress that I wanted them to like, a dress that wasn't the least bit "bridesmaidy," but a—as in *one*—dress nonetheless.

For all my thinking that I wanted a wedding to reflect Dan and me, that it was important to do things traditionally but not reflexively, etc., etc., I am somewhat surprised that the idea that the bridesmaids wear the same dress was so fixed in my mind. If

I had to do it over again, I think I would have told them to just wear whatever they wanted. Or maybe I would have said something like "wear a light blue dress" and then let them figure out which light blue dress they wanted to wear. Or maybe I wouldn't have; maybe I would have done the exact same thing I did. Who knows? The point is: I would have handled this differently. But I was the very first of my friends to get married, and having the bridesmaids wear the same dress was, to me, automatic.

Silly or not, this was my mindset. So, in the name of "I want them to like the dress," I told Naomi I didn't want something bridesmaidy and suggested that she and I pick out the dress together.

"Omigod!" she said, dropping a forkful of cheese blintz. We were having lunch at Veselka, the East Village Eastern European diner and hangout for low-key hipsters. We had just finished deciding to ditch the shower for a "kick-ass" (as she put it) Girls' Night Out. "I'm so happy you asked. I knew you wouldn't be one of those mint green taffeta types, but still. You know what would be really cool? Something *sexy*."

"Sexy?"

With the overall outside, afternoon, jazz quartet, people-who'd-invite-you-to-brunch effect I was going for, sexy was not what I had in mind.

"Yeah. I mean, we're in an ideal situation here. Not everyone's this lucky. Usually there's at least a chunky cousin to contend with. But, if I do say so myself, all of your bridesmaids are hot."

"True," I nodded.

"So I was thinking of a corset-type of thing on top. I saw the greatest corsets at that lingerie shop on lower Fifth, and all I could think was these would be so cool to wear with a red peasant skirt . . ."

A picture flashed in my mind of Naomi, Erin, and Andrea walking down the aisle, red feathers in their messily upswept hair, rouge circles on their overly made-up cheeks, cleavage up to their fake-birthmarked chins.

"This is my wedding, Naomi, not a Toulouse-Lautrec."

"Oh, don't be so uptight—"

Was that what I was being? I felt bad. I'd asked for her ideas, and now I was shooting them down. "I don't want to be uptight, Nome," I stabbed at a sweet potato pierogi and searched for something not-uptight to tell her. "It's just—not everyone is as comfortable as you are with putting themselves out there. Do you really think Erin could deal with a corset? She's in vet school."

"Hmmm. You're probably right." Relief! "But—I know! Let's get the dresses from Bella! I asked her about it while you were getting changed."

I saw Naomi, Erin, and Andrea walking down the aisle in burlap sacks.

"I don't know . . ."

"It'll be so cool! Everyone'll be comfortable. She'll do all sorts of funky things so they're similar, but not really the same."

Okay, burlap sacks that were similar, but with an obvious difference: Naomi's bore one hell of a lot of Wonderbraed cleavage.

A miniature Martha Stewart appeared on my shoulder, my wedding Jiminy Cricket. She leaned into my ear and whispered, "Think about the whole picture."

"I don't know," I said. "I mean, it would be really cool to get the dresses from Bella. But don't you think it'll be weird if all the guys are dressed the same and the girls are dressed similar but not the same?"

"No," she said, wrinkling her nose in disdain. "They're *guys*. Supporting players. No one notices them."

"Isn't the whole wedding party supporting players?"

"Oh, God, Rachel, don't tell me you've turned into one of those my-bridesmaids-can't-outshine-me brides. You're the last person I would have expected *that* from."

Was that what I was doing?

"This isn't about outshining," I said. "I want you guys to look good. And I'm gonna be wearing a big white *gown*. In case you've forgotten, it's pretty hard to look away. I just don't know if I want to leave the bridesmaids' dresses up to a dominatrix who eats cigarettes."

"*Whatever*," she said, sighing.

Worried that I was indeed being a controlling bitch, I decided to try to open my mind. "Well, how much do Bella bridesmaids' dresses cost?"

Naomi brightened. "It depends on the fabric, but she said around four hundred."

"*Four hundred?*"

"Please," she said. "I don't mind."

"Yeah, well—it's great that you don't mind—I mean, I appreciate that—but I don't think I can ask people to cough up four hundred bucks for a bridesmaid's dress. It seems—I don't know—*wrong*."

"Come on, Rachel," Naomi said. "It's not *that* much."

"Yeah it is," I said. "If someone expected me to spend that kind of money I would not be happy."

"Fine," Naomi sighed, clearly not happy.

"I'm just doing unto others—"

"Fine. I get it."

We sat in silence for a minute and I wondered what I had done wrong. Was Naomi pissed because she couldn't get exactly what she wanted? Or was I turning into Bridezilla?

"You know how much I appreciated you coming with me to look for wedding gowns, right? I mean, if I haven't thanked you enough . . . it was really, truly—"

"Don't be silly," she said. "It was fun."

"Okay." There was another pause.

"You know what?" Naomi broke the silence with a throw-in-the-towel tone. "You should just pick out the dress and tell me where to buy it."

"Is that really what you want?" I asked her.

"It's fine," she said. "It's easier that way. When you ask for my input, I think about the dress I'd want to wear. But you have all these other things you have to factor in."

"Are you sure?" I asked again.

"Yeah," she said. "I'm sure. Just pick the dress."

Then, saying she had to go—she was out of Pineapple Papaya Facial Scrub and needed to pick some up at Kiehl's before showing an apartment—Naomi motioned for the check. I had to get uptown and do work anyway.

I emerged from the Seventy-second Street subway station with a deep need for procrastination, so I headed for Timothy's on Columbus. I had a feeling some friends of mine might be there.

"Rachel, *mammilah!*" Frieda called from the window seat she occupied when not at the Y. "How is the *vedding* coming, *sveetie?*"

"It's coming," I nodded, weary at the thought of it.

"*Vhat's* a-matter, *sveetie?*"

I sighed. I told them about Naomi. "I thought I was being *nice,*" I said.

"You were." Esther nodded firmly. "You wanted her input. That's a very considerate bride."

"*Vhat* I *tink*," said Frieda, "she is jealous. She *vants* a man of her own."

"Trust me, Frieda, my friend Naomi does not lack for boyfriends."

"Boyfriends and husbands are not the same thing," Esther said, underscoring her point with a quick dash of the finger.

"She's not *von* of the *vons vit*," Frieda did a sharp survey of the half-empty coffee shop, then leaned in, "*zee* fake you-know-*vhats*."

"No," I said. "Hers are real."

"Well," said Esther, "at least that's something."

Once home, I called Thomas for his take.

He said, "It doesn't matter how nice you're being. No woman wants another woman picking out her clothes."

I said, "That's not true. If I were a bridesmaid, I'd rather the bride picked out a dress and told me to buy it. It would save me the hassle of shopping and worrying whether it was right. I'd just want it to be a dress I liked, which is why I asked her in the first place."

"Then you're the exception," he said. "I'm just saying the situation lends itself to complications."

"So what do I do?"

"You either say, 'Fuck it, I'm the bride and you're my bitch,' and pick out something really ugly—"

"Ha-ha."

"Or you try and find something that'll work, but you know she'll like."

Deciding to go with the latter, the next day I went back downtown to Jane Patterson, a little boutique on Ninth Street run by a funky (bleached blonde, flapperesque banged bob) but down-to-earth (her golden retriever, Sneaker, had a daybed in the corner of the store) designer named—surprise, surprise—Jane Patterson. Her cool but not in-your-face style was exactly the kind of thing I'd had in mind, and I knew Naomi bought a lot of things there—in fact, the light green Jane Patterson sundress Naomi had worn to a Mount Sinai luncheon where her father got some kind of eye doctor award would work perfectly. It would be a perfect her taste/my wedding compromise.

Ten minutes later, I had my bridesmaids' dresses. Jane said she'd make three light blue dresses just like the one Naomi had in green and, even though it was a custom order, charge only what she would in the store—a very reasonable $150.

As soon as I got home, I called Naomi to tell her I'd found the dress, certain she'd be thrilled with my choice.

She said: "But I already *have* that dress."

I knew I hadn't wanted a wedding party.

Sixteen

The call I'd been expecting came later that week. I was just returning from a postwriting swim and, knowing Dan was up at school, scrambled to pick up the phone before the machine did.

"Hello?" I said, beating it.

"Do you *know* what your *father* is *doing*?" my mother yelled.

"What?" I asked, bracing myself. Why hadn't I just let the machine answer?

"I just went to the mailbox and found a *typed* letter from your father saying that I have until February twenty-eighth to give him the money for my thirty-five guests, the additional charge for kosher food, and an agreement *in writing* to provide the cake. This is *outrageous!* I have never, ever heard of *anyone* doing *anything* like this! Did you know about this?"

I took a deep breath and thought about endorphins. "Yeah."

"And you think this is *right*—"

"I don't know if I think it's *right*—"

"You don't *know!* You don't—this is *insulting!* This is *incredible!* I've never in my life heard of *anyone* being treated this way—"

"I know it's bullshit, Mom. But, if you just do what he wants—"

"If I *what?*"

"If you just go along with his deadline, everything will be resolved and we can all just focus on the happy event taking place."

"Oh, yeah, sure! Go ahead! Have your party on my back! I should have known you'd take his side. You always do. Your *wonderful* father! You don't give a shit about me and you never have—"

"Mom, that's not true—"

"Oh, that's not true? That's not true? What kind of daughter allows her mother to be treated this way—"

"Mom, I agree with you. It's ridiculous. But just—please. There are a million and one things that have to get done for this wedding. Can't we just get some of them resolved?"

"You think this is *my* fault?"

"It's not about fault, Mom. It's not about fault. It's just about having things squared away once and for all—"

"That's right. Drag your mother through the gutter so you can get everything all neat and clean for your precious wedding—"

"Come on, Mom. No one's dragging you through a gutter. Just forget about his deadline and his bullshit way of going about it for a second. All of this is stuff you'd have to do eventually anyway, right?"

"A *written agreement* to provide the *cake?*"

"Okay, not that. That, I agree, is absurd. But the rest—"

"I have *never*—"

"Mom—"

"*Ever*—"

"Mom! I'm saying I *agree* with you. I think it's crazy. But if you just do the stupid things he's asked for—"

"And what about what happens if I don't make his cockamamie deadline? If I don't do what he wants when he wants it, he'll cut my guest list!"

"What?" He never said anything to me about cutting the guest list. I felt the first signs of losing my cool. I realized I was still in my coat and began struggling out of it.

"If I don't meet his deadline, he is going to start cutting my guest list. The first week, it goes down to thirty guests. The second week it's twenty-five. The third week it's twenty. He has a *chart*, Rachel! A *typed letter* and a *chart!*"

"Unbelievable," I muttered, though it really wasn't. A move like this had Phyllis's what-about-*my*-guests fingerprints all over it. My voice went flat, my stomach sour. I hung my now-off coat on the rack and took a seat at the table. Was I supposed to back him up on *this?*

"This is blackmail, Rachel! It's *disgusting!* I've never *heard* of another person—"

"Mom, I had no idea he was gonna do that."

"Well, he's done it. Are you going to let your wonderful father get away with this?"

Was I?

Right on cue, my temples began throbbing.

My father deserved to be called on this, but what about me? Did I really deserve another headache?

"Listen, Mom, I agree with you. The way he's going about this is absurd. But, when you think about it, none of his stupid threats amounts to anything if you just do the stuff—"

"So he gets to do whatever he wants! He can threaten me, give me deadlines, *humiliate* me—"

"Mom—"

"—and I'm just supposed to suck it up, tough luck?"

"You don't have to look at it that way—"

"And for what? For a wedding I'm barely consulted on, for a daughter who doesn't give a flying shit about me—"

"That's not fair, Mom—"

"Fair? *Fair?* Now you want to talk about what's *fair?* Of course you do! When it's about *me*, it's, 'Aw, c'mon, Mom, suck it up.' When it's about *you* it's about what's fair! How did I end up with such an ungrateful spoiled brat for a daughter?"

I thought: "The same way I ended up with a mother who refuses to go to her daughter's graduation dinner because her ex-husband is throwing it."

I said: "I don't know, Mom."

"Just as I thought. Looking out for number one as always." Joyce's voice was low and menacing. "Well, maybe I should start looking out for number one, too!"

I heard the phone slam down.

I hung up my end and headed for the couch, lifting my ass to readjust the cushion as I lay on it. I didn't feel satisfied at having held firm, or angry at my mother's selfishness, or even guilt-ridden as she had wanted. I felt stupid—what had I been thinking? Why had I gone along with my father's plan? And, more than anything, I felt like I was ten years old and I'd just walked out of the kitchen—"Do you hear what he's saying? I have to pay for your camp clothes or else you won't get them? I'm the one who pays, and he's the one you side with! Well forget it, missy, forget it! The two of you aren't making a fool of me this time!"

I reached for my temples and squeezed my eyes shut. I may have been twenty-six years old, I may have been in my own apartment in New York, I may have been engaged, but I was still standing outside that kitchen door. It was still the same. Nothing would be resolved until I felt like complete shit.

And as bad as I felt then, I knew it wouldn't be the last of it.

Seventeen

Dan returned home to find me lying on the couch with a cold compress over my eyes.

"What happened?" he asked. I could hear the thud of his dropped backpack.

"My mother called." Sitting up and removing the compress, I told him about the conversation and its unceremonious end.

He said, "Your father said *what?*"

"He said if she doesn't make the deadline she loses her guests."

"What the fuck?"

"Believe me, I asked myself the same question."

"Well, it's not gonna matter anyway. She's gonna make the stupid deadline, and it'll all be moot."

"I wouldn't be so certain," I said. "You didn't hear her screaming about what an ungrateful bitch I am, then slamming down the receiver."

"That's all bark, no bite," he said, shooing the thought away and making me feel foolish for having spent the past half-hour on the couch with a cold compress over my eyes. "She'll make the deadline. It'll be at the last possible second, but in the end she'll come through."

"I'm glad you're so sure," I grumbled.

"I am," he said. "Now put on some shoes or we're gonna miss the movie." He'd gotten us tickets for some mindless fare at the Sony.

Walking down to the theater, Dan told me his parents had called that morning. They wanted to have a more in-depth pow-wow soon, but he'd had a preliminary discussion with them about the upcoming D.C. FLOP weekend. He told them my father and stepmother would be in Florida, but that, rather than postpone the trip until they returned, we'd rather just get things done that weekend. He told me his mother seemed almost relieved (she'd said, "Oh, good, then you'll stay at the hotel with us"), and that they figured we'd have a meal with my mother— did Saturday night sound okay?

"Hmmm," I said, as we rode up the escalator. "You know, with this whole deadline thing in the air, I'm thinking dinner with my mother might not be such a good idea."

"Raych," he said, "you know she'll be on her best behavior with my parents there. Who knows? We might even get her psyched enough about the wedding to meet the deadline in advance."

I ignored this fantasy-land conjecture. "I know she won't scream and call me a spoiled brat. But you can bet she'll bring up the whole deadline thing to get them to think she's a martyr and my dad's an asshole."

"So what if she does?" Dan asked, as our tickets were ripped and we turned right into the big theater's minilobby. "Your dad *is* being an asshole."

"I know that," I said, stopping and stepping out of the flow of traffic. I had to get this all out before trying to find seats. "This is not me worrying about my father's image. This is me worrying about their crap affecting the entire wedding. It's bad enough I have to deal with him. And with her. And with Phyllis. But at least it's contained. It's like the wedding is a room and right now, with this kosher thing and this deadline thing and this Phyllis-needs-her-friends-there-too thing, there's a mess in the room. But it's only in one little corner. Once my mother sucks it up and makes the stupid deadline, we can just run into the corner and clean it up, no permanent damage. But if Joyce tells your parents—which you know she'll do if we have dinner with her—she'll bring the mess into their corner too. It will have *spread*. And before you know it, the entire wedding room will be a pigsty and I'll be spending all my time on my hands and knees cleaning it up."

Dan sighed. "Are we going main floor or balcony?"

"Main," I said.

"Okay," he said. "I'll go get popcorn. You work your magic."

We split and I headed into the big, red theater. Being a weekend it was, of course, nearly full. I walked down the aisle and scanned the optimal center section. Soon enough, I saw my opening.

"Excuse me," I asked a guy roughly my age in a button-down shirt and khakis about six seats in, "are the seats on either side of you taken?"

"This one is," he said, motioning to the seat on his right. "But that one isn't."

"And is that one taken?" I asked the slightly older woman sitting to the right of his "taken" chair.

"Nope," she said, smiling.

The theater continued to fill around us. The guy in khakis sat facing the screen, oblivious to standard protocol.

"Um, sir?" I said. "Would you mind moving down one seat, one way or the other, so I can get two together?"

He looked shocked. "You mean you want me to move my seat?"

"If you don't mind . . ."

"Well, yes, I do mind," he said. "This is my friend's seat."

I was stunned. Who didn't move seats? Having never encountered his species before, I had no idea what to say.

Luckily, I didn't have to say anything. The Arthur Miller lookalike in the row behind him leaned forward and said, "What? It has your name on it?"

The woman to Arthur Miller's left said, "It's a sold-out show. You can't cooperate?"

A younger woman turned around and said, "*Everyone* moves down."

A heavy man down our aisle chimed in, "Just move. Give the lady her seat."

Mr. Casual Friday was cornered. He was being stoned in Sony Lincoln Square.

"All right, all right," he said, moving down. "Have your damn seat."

"Thanks," I said, making my way in to sympathetic murmurs all around. "And thank you all as well," I said, waving as I reached my seat.

Mrs. Arthur Miller shook her head. "I just don't know about people these days."

Soon, Dan joined me, bearing popcorn and drink.

"Listen," he said, once he was settled, "there's no point in having dinner with your mother if it's gonna stress you out."

"Thank you."

"But I do think you're freaking out for no reason," he said.

"Excuse me?"

"Not about your parents—they're insane. I totally grant you that. But my parents are not insane. And you're lumping them in together. It's like you hear 'parents' and 'wedding' and you're like 'oh, no!' But there's nothing to be 'oh, no' about with my parents."

I stared up at the screen and unscrambled LILW TMSHI to Will Smith. Was that what I was doing? Letting the conflict with my parents spill over onto his? It was true—I was like "oh, no" whenever I heard the words "parents" and "wedding," but these days, the word "wedding" alone was enough to inspire nervous dread.

"You *like* my parents, Rachel."

That was true.

"Right," I said, turning back to him. "I do like your parents. Which is why I'm not lumping them together with mine. Your parents are sane—I don't think they're going to act like my parents in any way. That's not what I'm worried about."

"Then what are you worried about?"

"When your parents came up here for the FLOP dinner, you agreed we shouldn't tell them about my father's ten thousand dollars. Why?"

"Because we thought they'd take it like a dog with a bone and hatch a million theories about your parents."

"And we'd never hear the end of it."

"Okay," he said. "I see your point. But you can't control this thing forever. Besides, they already think they're having dinner with your mother. What reason do we give for why it's off?"

"You'll just say something vague but true—like that some details about the wedding are still up in the air and we don't think it's a good idea to get together with my mother until they're more resolved."

"*I'll* say?"

"Yeah," I said, annoyed. "They're *your* parents."

I took a sip of the soda. Diet, of course.

Later in the weekend, Dan's parents called.

"Hi there, Rachel," said Marty.

"I'm here too," Carol added. "You've got stereo in-laws!"

"Oh, no." Marty laughed. "That sounds awful!" I could hear Carol chuckling along.

"No, no," I said, "not at all."

"We're here in the kitchen on the speakerphone," Carol explained.

"Great," I said. I had known this already from the shouting-across-the-wires tone of their voices. Dan's parents would often call on speakerphone, and the conversations would have the *jeepers!* quality of astronauts checking in en route to the moon.

"We're calling for a pre-Washington FLOP status update," Marty said.

"Just a second, Dan'll pick up too."

A minute later, Dan and I sat catty-corner in the living room, he on the couch and me in the Ikea chair, he on the cordless phone and me on the long-corded one from the bedroom. After a minute or two of small talk—Dan's classes were fine, as were my teen novels; the Gershons were shopping for a new car—we got down to business.

"We were so sorry to hear we'd be missing your father and stepmother when we went down to D.C.," Carol said.

"Yeah, that's too bad," I faked.

"But we called them."

"You did?"

"Yes, so we got a chance to discuss some things."

I thought "Uh-oh," but said only, "Oh?"

"Yeah. You know, Jan Levy's made the generous offer to host a sort of night before the wedding gathering—"

"That's really nice of her," I said.

"And we figured," Marty continued, "with the bulk of the guests coming in from out of town—"

"That instead of each having our own events, maybe we could all get together and have one big party."

"What a nice idea," I said, hoping my parents would see it that way—inclined, however, to doubt it.

"So we ran that by your father and Phyllis, and they seemed very pleased about it," Carol continued. "Jan Levy had suggested using a market near her called the Sutton Place Gourmet— which Phyllis seemed to know well and think was very, you know, *high-quality*—and, since they charge, per head, we'll just each be responsible for our own guests and divide yours up between us."

"They agreed to that plan?" I asked.

"Yes," said Marty, "in fact, they suggested it."

Dan and I exchanged across-the-room looks of pleasant surprise. Maybe I should have had the Gershons deal with them all along.

"So now we just have to run it by your mother," Carol said.

"Great," I said. There, no doubt, would be the rub.

"But for now," Marty continued, "let's have a FLOP status report."

"Sounds like a good idea," said Dan.

First, we established that L and O were pretty much handled—Marty had talked to the caterer, who had put him in touch with a liquor wholesaler and things in that area were well under control; my friend Jonah had rounded up a jazz quartet for the reception, and two of the musicians (the keyboardist and alto sax player) could play at the ceremony, all for twenty-five hundred dollars ("Wow," said Marty, "that's really a bargain").

"So that leaves the florist and the photographer for us to take care of in Washington," Carol said.

"Okay," I said.

"Now the thing is," Carol continued, "I spoke to Jan Levy about using the same people she had at Debra and Zhang's and they're both available on our date. But the photographer will not be able to meet with us the week after next, so I don't know how that will work."

Dan and I had already discussed the photography. We'd seen the Levy-Wu album already and liked the all-candids, photojournalistic bent of the pictures. We wanted the same thing, but in black and white—maybe a few posed pictures before the ceremony, but no "table shots," just candids at the actual event. I looked at Dan, who had taken more of an interest in the photo area than I had, and shrugged. "She said she could do the candids in black and white, right?" I asked.

"Yes," said Carol. "And the posed pictures in two sets—black and white and color. But she needs a list of pictures we want, and any other kind of special details."

"That can all be done on the phone, right?" Dan asked. "Are we really missing anything by not meeting with her in person?"

"I can't think of anything," Carol said. There was a pause. "So, okay, then—phee-yoo, there's a problem averted."

In Gershonland, this was a phee-yoo problem averted. Once again, I found myself relieved to have a set of sane parents involved in this wedding.

"So then there's just the florist to meet with down there," Carol continued. "So, now, Rachel, would you mind driving? If you don't want to, that's fine, but I figured we'll be on your old stomping ground . . ."

"I wouldn't mind at all." This was the truth. Despite years of suburban carpool-duty living, Carol was the most skittish driver I knew. She was constantly tightening and loosening her grip on the wheel, and sinking back into her seat at every traffic light stop, then jutting forward at attention when the light turned green. She was the only person I'd ever seen who used one foot for the gas and one for the brake.

But I was confused. I looked over at Dan, who seemed untroubled.

"But—are you and I the only ones going?"

Marty laughed. "I don't think Dan and I'll be of much help in the flower department. Happy Marriage Rule Number One: Don't step on each other's toes."

I fought back the impulse to say, "Well, thanks, Mr. Expert, but who said I wanted your marriage?"

In a way, it made sense that Carol and I go alone—Dan didn't care at all about the flowers; this was certainly the kind of wedding detail that would cause his eyes to glaze over. (In truth, this was the kind of wedding detail that could cause my eyes to glaze over, too, but I did have things in mind and the idea of letting Carol choose the flowers herself didn't occur to me.) Maybe there was no point in Dan coming along. But, even if a paved road might be nice, you don't want to be hit by a steamroller.

I hoped a compliment might help make my U-turn. "That sounds like sage advice. But my toes aren't really in the line of fire on this one. I think I'm a little less passionate about flowers than Carol is."

"Well, then it'll be a nice opportunity for some father-son

bonding time," Marty said. Dan flashed a wry half-smile at the use of the words "bonding time."

"Yeah." Carol perked up. "I can't think of a better girl-time activity than picking out wedding flowers!"

"No, yeah, that would be nice," I said, trying to break through the thicket of their enthusiasm to say: "Wait a minute, just because you assume something doesn't mean it's what we want!" I said. "But, I don't know, it's just that we'll all be down there *together*, so I just sort of thought . . . I mean, Dan, did you think you were coming, too?"

"Well, I assumed so." He shrugged. "But I can go either way."

"We thought you'd want to do it this way," Marty said. "That it would be nice to split up."

Of course: The Split!

"Well, if Dan is *coming*," Carol said, worried, "then that sort of leaves Marty out in the cold. What would you do all by yourself all afternoon?"

"Why don't we all just go together?" I suggested.

"Marty's not going to come with us to a *florist's* house to pick out *flowers*," Carol said, as if I'd suggested he perform *Swan Lake* in a pink tutu.

I wanted to say: "Why does everything have to orbit around Marty?" But I didn't.

"Is it important to you that I come, Raych?" Dan asked straight into the phone.

Was it? If the question was about Dan coming to pick out flowers, the answer was definitely "No." If the question was about Dan's parents' assumptions dictating our plans, the answer was definitely "Yes." The problem was, I couldn't tell which question I was answering.

What was happening here? Why were the Gershons, whom

I'd always liked, suddenly on my nerves? Everyone else was acting so nonplussed. Was I being hypersensitive, turning minor annoyances into major flaws? Was I guilty of the very thing Dan had suggested at the movies, of letting the conflict with my parents turn into a conflict with his? Was bride anxiety making me look at my in-laws through funhouse-mirror glasses?

I reminded myself that, even if his parents were being a little pushy, Dan had made it clear that he'd do whatever I wanted, no big deal. So, figuring I was overreacting, I decided to treat the cigar like a cigar.

"It's not important to me," I said, smiling at Dan. "Hang out with your dad. Your mom and I can handle the flowers."

"Great!" said Carol. "So, then we'll take care of the flowers and see your mother. Maybe we should have dinner one night? We figured we could talk to her about the night-before party then."

I shot Dan a pleading look.

"Actually," he said, "it might work better that weekend if it was just the four of us."

"*Vhat?* No *machetunim* dinner?" Marty asked in the exaggerated *Fiddler on the Roof* voice he used for Yiddish idioms. He thought this voice was funny. I thought it was vaguely offensive.

"We're not meeting with either of your parents, Rachel?" his mother asked. I could feel her eyebrows rising.

I shook my head no, and pointed—You answer!—at Dan.

"Well," he began, "you know, I mean, it's not as if you haven't met before—"

"Well, yes, that's true. That one time in the city. But that was be*fore*. Back when you guys were just, you know, *da*ting."

"Well," he continued, "it's just—there's been some back-and-forth on things with the wedding and they're not quite resolved, so—"

"What kinds of things?" Carol asked.

I looked at him, eyes wide, and shook my head again.

"It's really not worth getting into," Dan said, making it sound as if the conflict itself couldn't bear the weight of the long, convoluted story required to tell it. I wondered if this was actually the case.

"Oh," Carol said. "Well . . ."

"So then we're just going down there so you two can meet with the florists?" The *what?* in Marty's voice came through. It did seem a little silly.

"You know," I said, thinking I'd had enough wedding planning to last a lifetime, "come to think of it, we could probably just do the flowers by phone too. Especially when it's just me and Carol going, we don't all really need a whole weekend down there."

"Oh, no!" Carol cried, as if struck. "We can't just do all this stuff by *phone!* That's not right . . . it's so *impersonal!* And part of the whole fun of doing FLOP was to, you know, be *involved . . .*"

Here was Dan's sweet mother, the only parent genuinely excited about this wedding and, sure enough, thanks to my exhaustion with my own parents' crap, I'd managed to hurt her feelings. Dan was the first of her sons to get married; this was a big event for Carol too.

I looked at Dan—*yikes!*—and immediately started tripping over myself with damage control. "No, no, I was just saying, I mean, yeah, it's great to have you doing FLOP and we love—and really appreciate—your involvement. I just meant—you know, if we're *only* going to Washington to meet the florist—I mean—I didn't want you to feel like we *had* to go down there—"

"Oh, but we were just so looking forward to having this wedding weekend—"

"No, no, I wasn't saying I didn't want to go." When you're digging yourself out of a hole, every word is a shovelful. "I just meant—you know, with the expense of taking the train and staying in a hotel and everything, I didn't want you to feel *obligated*. But if you *want* to go, I mean, you know, by all means—let's go!"

"Oh, I'm not concerned about the expense," Marty said. "I'm just surprised there's not more to do. It'll be nice just to see you guys, to spend some time together before the big event."

Dan's mother continued, "But we don't want to *drag* you guys down there—"

"No, no, it's not dragging," I said, pleading with Dan with my eyes.

"We're psyched to go," he said.

"Are you sure?" Carol asked.

"Yes, absolutely," I said.

"Yeah," Dan said. "It'll be fun."

"And Rachel," Dan's mother said, "you're sure? All of this conflict with your parents—whatever it is—hasn't gotten you sort of *weddinged-out?*"

Even a vague bone was apparently something for them to seize on. I looked at Dan with I-think-you-see-my-point eyes. Though she was right—weddinged-out was exactly what I was—this was the last thing I could tell Carol.

"Are you kidding?" I said in my brightest voice. "What kind of bride gets sick of her own wedding?"

Eighteen

The next weekend, we took the train down to Washington for the FLOP weekend, minus the LOP. Marty and Carol, who drove down that afternoon, were picking us up at Union Station. We stepped out into the first signs of spring air and saw Carol standing on a curb in the distance, waving her hands excitedly, beaming.

"Dan! Rachel! Over here!"

She always greeted us this way, as if we'd just returned from a Jamesian stay abroad and porters were handling our steamer trunks. You couldn't help but be touched by the enthusiasm.

We smiled and waved back in acknowledgment. "That must be the new car," Dan said as we headed toward his mother and the forest green minivan behind her.

"Greetings!" she said when we approached. She always greeted us that way, too—with the word "greetings." She said it with childlike gaiety; at the second syllable, she was practically on tiptoes.

We exchanged hugs and kisses, established that we'd all had good trips down, put our stuff in the back, then got in.

"How do ya like the new car?" Marty asked from the driver's seat.

"Very nice," said Dan.

"I like the color," I chimed in.

"Thank you," said Carol. "I thought it looked more *robust* than the silver."

"I can understand that," I said, nodding.

"So is this the same model as the old minivan?" Dan asked.

"No," said his father. "That one was a Pontiac. This one's a Chrysler. *Consumer Reports* gave it a higher rating."

"I see." Dan nodded.

"The Millstones were shocked we'd gotten another minivan," Carol said. "You know, like, 'All of your kids are out of the house, why on earth would you get a minivan?' and we told them we just really liked the old one. We could have gone right along with it forever, but it just started dying on us."

I nodded and Dan said, "Ah, yes."

"Well, I'm glad you like it," said his mother. "You know, I got the feeling the Millstones really thought we were strange. We were out to dinner with them the other night and they just couldn't quite fathom the idea that we'd actually replace a *minivan* with *another minivan*. You know, like minivans are for carpools and here we're supposed to be in *empty-nester* mode." The drama in her tone made both Dan and me laugh. "Well, it's true. Isn't that what they thought?"

"That's certainly what it seemed like," Marty agreed.

"But, you know, it's really convenient to have a bigger car. None of you boys has a car in the city. With the van, we can just round everybody up and we'll all fit comfortably."

I was thinking that her explanation sort of proved the Millstones' point, but I nodded and kept my mouth firmly shut.

"Makes sense," said Dan. I couldn't tell if he meant to agree or placate.

"And, you know, we just really liked the old van," said Carol.

"It really was a great car," said Marty. "Without a doubt the most successful Gershon family vehicle."

"Many years of faithful service," Dan said.

"Oh, yeah, that van was a real trouper." Carol smiled and sighed, as if remembering an old friend. Then, laughing, she turned to Dan and said, "Remember when we came up with Joel and picked you up at Columbia to watch the odometer flip to one hundred thousand?"

"Yup. I also remember that we were driving to Atlantic City, where Joel and I won fifty bucks at the blackjack table."

"Did you ever hear about that, Rachel?" Carol asked. "It was so much fun!"

"Yup," I said. "I think I have."

I was tempted to say *at least ten times*. But I didn't. There was still something sweet about a family that got excited by an odometer, but that day, in their new minivan, I realized I'd outgrown my captive listener role. I was no longer Dan's Girlfriend; I was Dan's Fiancée, preparing for the role of Dan's Wife. It was time for a new production.

But I didn't want it to be "Move Over Folks, There's a New Sheriff in Town."

I looked at Dan. He was lifting and lowering his armrest.

"You know where this car really steps it up?" he asked. "The bucket backseats. Much classier than the bench. And very comfortable."

"Did you see that panel next to you?" Carol turned to point it out. "You can control your own volume on the radio and your own temperature on the vents!"

Just like a big boy!

"Whoa," said Dan, fiddling with the vents. "Why couldn't they have had this a few years ago?"

"That's exactly what I said!" Marty chortled, looking back at Dan in the rearview mirror. "Can you imagine all the fighting we would have saved with one of you guys occupied with that thing?"

"You probably wouldn't have saved any," I said. "They - would've just fought over who got the seat."

Marty laughed. "Actually, you're probably right."

"You must not have experienced that kind of thing at all, Rachel," said Carol, "with your brother so much younger."

"That's true. The only kind of fighting Matthew and I ever did over seats was when I'd drive his soccer carpool and he didn't want to put his seat belt on."

"Oh, that's not a real sibling fight," said Carol. "We could have shown her a few of those, right, Dan?"

"You bet," Dan said, smiling.

Just as I decided to spend the rest of the car ride pretending that navigational duties required my full eyes-on-the-road attention, Carol said "ooooh," then turned herself around as best she could to face me.

"Rachel," she said. "The Millstones asked if you were changing your name to Gershon, and I told them I hadn't thought to ask. Is that what you're planning on?"

I told myself this was just a simple, practical question.

"It hadn't really occurred to me to change it," I said, shrugging. "Maybe because of writing. I'd want anything I'd write to be under the name Rachel Silverstein, so—"

"Well, yes, sure," she said. "That makes sense. And, so then, what are you planning on doing about children? Are you going to *hyphenate* both names?"

Dan was looking out the window. He wasn't even the naviga-tor! Then again, *he* didn't need an excuse.

"We haven't really discussed it yet," I said, telling the truth in a tone I hoped would squelch any further discussion. "We're not quite crossing that bridge at the moment."

Apparently, it worked.

"Oh," my future mother-in-law said, slowly, turning back around.

The next day, I drove through deepest Arlington with Carol in the passenger seat. "Now, I want you to know I'm only here to help," she said. "You're the bride, the flowers should be your deci-sion."

"Well, thanks, Carol," I said. "That's really nice of you. But you know much more about flowers than I do, so I'm gonna need your help!" Grateful, self-deprecating, and peppy all rolled into one. Who the hell was this person and what had she done with me? Again, I found myself wondering why, after years of being comfortable around Dan's mother, I'd suddenly become so self-conscious.

We soon found ourselves in the living room of Sharon Shelby, freelance flower designer. Aside from the floral-printed fabric on her couch and chairs, and the small arrangements on her coffee and end tables—"Those are fresh, not fake!" she told us on our way in—sitting in her living room, you would not have known that Sharon Shelby was a freelance flower designer. You would, however, have known that Sharon Shelby was fond of parrots. There were parrots everywhere—parrots in needlepoint on the pillow cushions, parrots in watercolor in paintings on the walls, parrots in porcelain on every surface available, including the piano, with its parrot bench cushion. And those were the inanimate ones. "I have five parrots," Sharon Shelby offered, unasked, as we walked in. "But I keep 'em out of the front room when people come by. You're not afraid of birds, are you?"

As Carol and I took seats on the flowered sofa, squawking began in the kitchen. "I won't be a second," Sharon Shelby said. "Take a look through these, and I'll be right back."

"Now I know why Jan Levy called her the *parrot woman*," Carol whispered as we started thumbing through the sample books she'd handed us.

"Not much mystery there, huh?"

We laughed a little. Maybe I didn't have to be so self-conscious.

"If this is a little too out there for you, Rachel, I'm sure we can find someone else . . ."

"Nah," I said, wondering if Dan had been right, if I'd unfairly thrown his mother into some kind of stressful parent stew. "I like a little eccentricity."

I do like a little eccentricity, and I didn't mind. But I would have had visions of the parrot lady taking my wedding for a Long John Silver turn if she hadn't done the flowers for the Levy-Wu wedding. I remembered those flowers only vaguely, which made the parrot lady eccentric rather than frightening. As far as I was concerned, it also made her a great flower designer. The way I saw it, if people came away from your wedding talking about how great the flowers were, you'd done something wrong. The same held true for the food, the band, or the cake. Those were all things that you hired people for, things that would be the same for anyone who hired the same people and told them to do the same things. That wasn't what I wanted our wedding to be like. I wanted people to go home saying, "What a great wedding," without really being able to put their finger on why.

Even though I hadn't touched a wedding magazine since the day I bought my dress, I still remembered my Martha Stewart mantra, "Think about the whole picture."

Which is why, when Sharon Shelby returned with a parrot on her shoulder, sat down, and said, "Now what kind of flowers did you have in mind?" I said, "Well, we're going for a sort of casual elegance, so since it's going to be outside, I thought some kind of wildflower thing would be nice."

Carol nearly leaped from her seat. "Oh, Rachel! That's just what I was hoping you'd say! It just seems a *waste* to have stuffy table arrangements when you're out there with the trees and the grass."

The parrot lady pulled out another book. "We can look through these and pick out the ones you like. The first thing I tell all my clients is that flowers in season are much less expensive, so you can pick out what you like and I'll tell you if it's in season."

"Okay," I said. I started thumbing through the spiral-bound book she gave me. Carol looked over my shoulder. "I don't know. They all look pretty. I'm just not sure I know how they'll look together. Maybe if I told you the general idea, we could go from there."

"That sounds good," said the parrot lady.

"Good, good," said the parrot.

Carol and I jerked back a bit, startled.

"Sorry. He likes that word."

"The word 'good'?" I asked.

"Good, good," squawked the parrot.

"Yes," said Sharon Shelby. "Don't pay him any mind."

There was a parrot on her shoulder saying "good." But I was a New Yorker; I could go with the flow.

"Okay," I said, reminding myself that I liked eccentricity.

"Well, I wanted something with a wildflower, just-picked-from-the-garden look. I was thinking we could even put the flowers in Mason jars—"

"*Mason* jars?" My mother-in-law looked stricken.

"Or not. We don't have to. Just something that looks informal."

Sharon Shelby nodded. "And bouquets?"

"I'd like them to have the stems still showing, you know—so it almost looks like they picked them."

"The stems," said Carol. An eyebrow was raised, perhaps involuntarily. "Well, that's certainly unique."

Was this, in her mind, helpful?

"Well, I just thought with it *outside*, it would all go together."

"I've never really seen bridal bouquets done that way, but—" Both of her eyebrows were now raised, but Carol nodded slowly, as if reminding herself that it was in fact my wedding. "But I can see the appeal of your reasoning."

Instead of annoyance, I felt a twinge of satisfaction. I was not the one making this difficult.

"Okay," said the flower lady with a parrot on her shoulder, "so we want a very natural, just-picked wildflower feel. Did you have any specific flowers in mind?"

"Well, my dress has roses on it, so I thought maybe I'd carry roses. And Gerber daisies are my favorite flowers, so I'd like to have them."

"Roses *and* Gerber daisies?" Carol fell off the wagon. "Are you sure that won't be a little *overwhelming?*"

That's when it became official: The problem was not in my head.

Of course I wasn't sure, I didn't know shit about flowers. Yes, Martha Stewart covered flowers and yes, I'd looked at those articles a million times. But to me, seeing all those flower names and combinations was like coming across the names of Eastern European leaders in the *Times;* I knew I should probably focus and learn how to pronounce them, but really, as long as you knew what it was when you saw it, what was the point?

"There are smaller Gerber daisies that should be fine with the roses," the flower lady offered.

I would (and probably should) have boned up before the trip, but, at this point, the thought of opening a *Martha Stewart* exhausted me.

"Maybe I'll just carry roses, but everyone else can have Gerber daisies in their bouquets. And there'll be Gerber daisies and wild-flowers on the tables." I shrugged. "That's it."

"Okay," flower/parrot lady nodded. "Sounds good."

"Good, good," said the parrot.

"So then we just need to figure out what the other flowers will be—"

"So wait," said Carol. "I'm sorry. Are you sure you want to carry a bouquet of roses with the stems still on them?"

"Oh," said Sharon Shelby, "well, I'll cut off the thorns, of course."

Carol looked as if she were trying hard to swallow a particularly untasty bit of food in a way least likely to offend her host.

"Well," I offered, "maybe not the stems on the roses, on my bouquet that is, but I'd like the other bouquets to have stems, maybe with a ribbon tied around them or something."

"Oh," said Carol, brightening, "I see. And you're sure you want *Gerber daisies.* Not something more *weddingy*, like freesia or stephanotis."

I didn't know what freesia or stephanotis were, much less why either one was more *weddingy* than a Gerber daisy. But I did know that Gerber daisies were my favorite so I said, "Yeah."

Carol took a deep breath. "Well, okay then."

We started looking through the book again.

"These are good for filling in a wildflower arrangement," said the parrot lady, pointing to delphinium.

"You could do those," Carol nodded. "Or larkspur."

"What's larkspur?" I asked and Carol turned the page and pointed it out to me. Frankly, it looked a lot like delphinium.

"I've had lots of success with larkspur in the garden," she said.

I took the hint and said, "Larkspur seems good."

"Good, good," said the parrot.

"Have you given any thought to aster?" Carol asked. "I don't know how they'll work with Gerber daisies, but they're a really nice arrangement flower . . ."

"I hadn't, actually—"

"And then of course there's Queen Anne's lace, but you have to give some thought to the color palette. If the roses are white it might be too much . . ."

My eyes began to glaze over. Carol was off and running, and this room had enough parrots already. Whether or not she knew it, this was beyond helpful. I started to wonder how much of this was Carol being much more interested and knowledgeable about flowers and how much was her thinking I'd want to do things her way, but soon grew tired of the question. Did it really matter? The issue at hand was flowers, and aside from a few details, flowers mattered very little to me. To Carol, however, they obviously meant a lot. As long as I got the things I wanted, why not let her have her way? And, if that was my strategy, why not just put it out there?

"You know what, Carol?" I said. "The things I mentioned are the only things I really care about. You know much more about flowers than I do. If you'd like to, I'm happy to let you decide the rest of the details."

"Really?" she said.

"Yeah."

"Well, thank you, Rachel, that's very nice of you. But I want you to be happy, you know, it's your wedding. So—just a wild-flower look, right?"

"Yep."

"And you don't need Mason jars."

"No."

"And you're really certain about those Gerber daisies?"

"Yes."

"But the smaller ones are okay?"

"Yes. As long as there are Gerber daisies, I don't care about the size."

"Okay. And you still want the stems showing on the brides-maids' bouquets?"

"Yes," I said.

"Well, all right," Carol said brightly. "I'll just work with that then."

See? I told myself. *There doesn't have to be a problem with your in-laws.*

"Sounds—great," I said, remembering the parrot just in time.

"Well, that went well," Carol said as I drove the new minivan back to the hotel. "I was worried for a minute there, when she first came back with that parrot!"

"Me too," I said, as if the parrot had been what worried me. "But I think it'll work out fine."

"I'm glad we came down. It's nice to have some together-time with you guys."

"Yeah," I said.

"Oh! And I brought the pictures you wanted," Carol said.

"Great," I said.

"Now, you said they were for the tables?"

"Yeah," I said. "We thought we'd do something creative with the place cards."

A cloud descended upon her brow. "With the place cards?"

"Yeah," I said. Figuring it would give our wedding a "personal touch," we were collecting old pictures of ourselves and planned to use them instead of table numbers. Guests would get a card with their name on it and, instead of a number, there would be a minipicture inside. They'd match the photo on their card to a larger, laminated version on the table. All of the pictures would be of one or the other of us, from a different stage of our lives, except the one at our table, which would be a shot of us together. I explained the concept to Carol.

She said, "But, are people going to be able to read them?" She looked scared. A cartoon thought bubble above her head would have read: "First the Mason jars, now this!"

"Well," I said, figuring I'd try some humor, "they are place cards. That's sort of their point, right?"

She laughed a little—good sign!—and said, "Of course, of course. And it's nice to be creative. You just don't want to be *too* creative!"

"Right," I said. Disaster, it seemed, had been averted.

We rode in silence for a beat. Then Carol said, "It's too bad things didn't work out with seeing your mother."

I couldn't tell if she was fishing, and didn't want to inadvertently take any bait, so I said, "Yeah, it's too bad. But it's probably best to hold off on asking her about the night-before party until this wedding stuff's squared away. And now, you know, we'll have a lifetime of opportunities for family dinners." Part of me sprang up and said *Are you crazy?* but I told that part I was just being polite.

"Oh, I didn't mean for *our* sake," Carol said. "I mean, it must be hard for you, not having a close relationship with your mom."

I shrugged. "Maybe when I was younger," I said. "But I now think it actually has benefits. I think it's made me a much stronger person."

"That's probably true," Carol nodded, then waited a beat. "Well, that's one nice thing about having kids of your own. You get the chance to be the kind of parent you didn't have."

Here we were again! Would Carol be worming the topic of children into every conversation we had until I bore her an heir? Maybe I needed to take a lesson from the flower situation. Perhaps it was time to say something firmer, something more direct.

"You know, Carol," I said, keeping my tone even and my eyes on the road, "I am looking forward to having kids one day, but I'd really like to feel more established professionally first."

"You know," she said, "Marty and I were married in the summer, and I had a job lined up for that fall. I was going to teach music at a Friends' school—Philadelphia has some top ones. I was really excited about it. I'd just finished my master's in music education."

"What happened?"

"Well, you know, Marty was against it—he didn't want it to seem like his professor's salary couldn't support a family—but I told him I'd do it for a year, just for the credential, in case I wanted to go back when the children were grown."

"Sounds reasonable."

"Yeah, that was the plan. But then we were married and I thought, What am I doing? I've made a commitment to build a family. That's my job, not running off to the outside world. So, when we came back from our honeymoon, I turned down the position. And, you know, Rachel, not for a moment have I ever regretted it."

I nodded, waiting a beat. "That's great, Carol. I'm glad you realized what was right for you and did it."

"That seems like a nice thing about writing—you can take some time away and raise a family, then get back to it if you really want to."

At that moment, the only thing I wanted to take time away from was Dan's mother. Suddenly, the Gershons' marriage seemed less an anomaly than a threat—a setup that, without real vigilance, Dan would fall into as easily as bad posture. Determined to remain composed, I reminded myself that Carol was coming from a different place, a different era. Maybe the idea that I really, truly wanted to be a working writer was a concept so foreign to her that she couldn't accept it. Still, Carol's presumptuousness was on a steady course toward pushy; we were getting dangerously close to a Boundary Issue.

"Carol," I said, thinking she needed a reminder, "neither Dan nor I wants to have children right away."

"Well," she said, her voice as sweet as ever, "given your childhood, it's only natural you'd have some ambivalence."

"What makes you think I'm ambivalent?" I thought I'd sounded very, very bivalent.

"I'm not saying you shouldn't be," she clarified. "I think it makes sense. I mean, with your family situation. Why wouldn't a person who had to take on the responsible, parental role in her own childhood be reluctant to jump right into having kids? But I think once you have some more positive mother associations," she patted my knee, all sympathy, "you'll be more comfortable with the idea."

What was Carol saying, that something was wrong with me because I wanted a career? That having goals beyond being a wife and mother meant I needed *rehabilitation*? That I was some abused pound puppy she'd been kind enough to adopt who, through the shining light of her example, would learn to love again?

Even without details, Dan's mother had managed to spin my broken family into something for her to fix.

Is this what she thought the new production would be? That my new role was to be her fourth child, another "kid" for her to "round up," who'd fit comfortably in the backseat of the new and improved Gershon minivan? Getting married was supposed to be an adult step. How had it become an excuse for people to treat me like a child?

And she was hitting below the belt. I considered telling her that not needing to rush into motherhood was not the same thing as ambivalence toward it, but decided to come at the subject from a different angle, the "positive mother" angle she'd been so quick to bring up.

"You know, Carol," I said. "I'm surprised that you'd want Dan tied down with kids while he's so young. He hasn't even decided on a specialty yet. I'd think you'd be happy that he'll have the time and space to take risks and figure out what he really wants to do."

"Oh, I'm sure Daniel will be successful at whatever specialty he puts his mind to," she said, smoothing her skirt. "Success is all that really matters to a man."

Aarrgh! So many responses came to my mind simultaneously—A) Maybe it's important to some women too! B) Don't people define success differently? C) How would you know what Dan's goals are when he deliberately avoids telling you what he thinks? D) Haven't you ever heard of *Free to Be You and Me?*

Which to say first?

Of course, I chose E) None of the above, opting instead to keep my eyes on the road while giving my future mother-in-law a slow nod with pursed lips and an arched eyebrow, a neutral vanilla with a skeptical cherry on top.

But here is what I wanted to say most of all: "Ever since I can remember, I've wanted to be a writer, and ever since I met your son I knew I wanted to spend my life with him. There is no reason why those two things should be mutually exclusive! I am not you and you are not me! Leave me alone already!"

Instead, I kept on driving.

"Okay," I said when I got back to our room, "we need to talk."

Dan was lying on the bed reading V. S. Naipaul, an activity that fell under the ever-broadening umbrella of "planning for the honeymoon." He rested the yellowed paperback on his stomach and said, "Okay."

"Not here," I said. "Let's go for a walk. I feel like I've been sitting on my ass all day."

Whenever I left New York, I worried that my legs were atrophying. The only use they seemed to get was walking to and from automobiles that were always parked in the best spots possible, "best" of course meaning the ones that required the least amount of walking. Twenty-four hours away from N.Y.C. and I'd start thinking about gangrene.

Two minutes out the door and I'd realize: You can't go for a walk outside of New York City. You can go to a park and go for a walk on a nice paved trail or something, but it's totally inorganic. You have to *drive* to get there. All spontaneity, all hope of the walk evolving into crossing the park or seeing a movie or grabbing something to eat or browsing the sales racks at Banana

Republic—dead. Most suburbs don't even have sidewalks, and when they do, everything's static and dull; aside from stray passing cars, there's no action, no activity, nothing to look at but houses, nothing to listen to but lawn sprinklers, nothing to do but walk. There, you are not going for *a walk*. You are just walking. That is all. Minutes pass like hours. It *sucks*.

That afternoon, I thought it would be different. We were staying in Roslyn, a minicity just a short trip over the Key Bridge from Georgetown, where buildings could be built taller than the Washington Monument and, in the eighties, had been. I'd failed to consider that those buildings were offices and it was a weekend and the only place worse to walk in than a suburb is a deserted, work-only city. Cars would pass, but needless to say, we were the only people hoofing it in Roslyn that day.

"You obviously didn't bring me out here for the people-watching," Dan said as we passed the first of many closed lunch shops.

I smiled. Why Can't You Walk Anywhere Outside New York? was one of our favorite Toto-we're-not-in-New-York-anymore questions.

"Okay," I said. "In the interest of fairness, I will begin this conversation by saying that I know this wedding has me wound a little tight, and I know that I'm probably extra-sensitive to parents in general since mine in specific are driving me crazy."

"Okay . . ."

"But—"

"How'd I know that word was coming next?"

"*But* just because I'm paranoid does not mean they're not out to get me. Your mother totally freaked me out in the car just now."

"What happened?" he asked.

I told him about my "understandable ambivalence." I told him about my need for "positive mother associations." I told him about success being the only thing that matters "to a man."

He said, "Why does this still bother you? You know she doesn't get it."

"You honestly don't know why this bothers me? I just told you that your mother suggested I had *psychological problems* because I see no reason to have kids before I'm thirty. Are you going to stand there and tell me she's just a kind old granny?"

We'd been down this road before, but it had never felt this urgent.

"I'm not saying it's okay," Dan said. "I just don't think you should let it get to you."

"I shouldn't let it get to me? That's convenient. Nobody's bothering *you* about anything. My father's not coming up to *you* and saying something equally retro and annoying like, 'You need to choose a specialty that makes real money. You know all women want to be provided for.' And if he was, I'd be telling him to get off your back, not telling you it's your problem. Maybe the next time your mother asks me about our children's names I should take my cue from you and just stare straight out the window."

"You know my parents are in a time warp. You've known that for the past five years. The first time you met them you said, 'They're really great, but they're in a time warp.'"

"And what did you say?"

"I said, 'I know.'"

"Right. So *I* know you know. But the problem is, *they* don't know you know! They think you're in the time warp with them! Right there, saying nothing, in the backseat of their brand-new minivan!"

"So what do you want me to do? Go knock on my parents'

door and say, 'Mom, you're in a time warp. Leave Rachel alone'?"

"No," I said. "Not literally. But your mother is only doing this because she thinks she knows how you feel, and that it's exactly the way she does. So if—we're obviously past the point of if here—*when* the topic comes up again, instead of sitting there silently avoiding the subject, it would be helpful if you'd say something like, 'Neither of us wants kids right away,' or, 'Hold your horses, there, Mom'—anything that would show her it's not all me. That you are living *with* me in the year *1998* and you actually have an opinion that differs from hers."

"So we're back to me not sticking up for you."

"No way," I said, waving my hands. "While that technically may be true, this is so not about me. Let me ask you a question: Why are you so reluctant to tell her what you think?"

"I don't know," he said.

"In her mind, it's like you're either in complete agreement with her or you're the generic little man symbol on the restroom door. How does this not bother you?" Two could play the Socratic game.

Dan nodded, genuinely considering this for a minute while a car or two went by, then said, "I think you can't relate to this because you have such contentious relationships with your parents—"

"Unh-uh. Sorry. I am not the one with the problem here—"

"No, no, no, no, no," Dan shook his head, "that's not what I was saying. That's not what I meant to imply."

"Then what did you mean to imply?"

"Just that it's nice to have a relationship with someone where there's no conflict, where you can exist in this bubble where everything's just positive."

"And you don't think you pay a price for that bubble?"

"Of course I do."

"Like what?"

"Truthfulness, for one thing."

"Then it's a false positive, isn't it?"

"Hmmm." Dan seemed almost amused. "Lemme think about this for a minute." He motioned his chin up ahead, toward a 7-Eleven, the closest not-in-New-York equivalent of a deli. "Wanna go in and get Slurpees?"

"Okay," I said, brightening. Something spontaneous was happening, legitimizing our walk. Besides, we'd spent our whole adult lives in New York. Maybe the only way we knew how to act outside it was like teenagers.

We emerged from the *Sleven*—as my high school classmates had dubbed it—with Slurpees in hand and tongues well on their way to turning blue. Freed from the burden of just plain walking in a ghost city, we headed back toward the hotel, pleasantly slurping.

"So, I have a theory on the not-letting-my-mother-know-my-opinion front."

"I'm eager to hear it," I said, biting my straw.

"Now that I think about it, I guess it really comes down to not wanting to think three-dimensionally about my mother. To keep the flat childhood ideal of Mommy who loves and takes care of me. Which you could say really boils down to not wanting to grow up. Pretty interesting, when you think about it."

"Or pretty annoying," I countered, sticking my blue tongue out at him.

"Point taken."

The next morning, on our way back to Union Station, where Dan and I would catch a train back home, the four of us sat in the minivan and talked about what a successful trip it had been. We had our florist, we had our liquor, we had our orchestra, we had our photographer—the F, the L, the O, and the P. Everything, we all agreed, was really coming together. Someone remarked that the next time we'd all be in Washington together would be for the wedding itself. We were all excited.

Carol looked over her shoulder. "Oh, Rachel," she said, "I meant to ask—I hadn't even thought of this, but the Millstones asked us if you were getting the tattoo. Is that something you're considering?"

Carol's face was bright. Her tone was full of sweetness and excitement.

"I don't see how that would work," I said matter-of-factly. "The tattoo only has five rings. That's the way you designed it, right?"

"That's true!" she gasped. "One loop for each of us—oh *dear*! I guess that was a little shortsighted, huh? You know, at the time, the concept of a *daughter*-in-law—I mean, the idea that one of the boys would be getting *married*—I guess I just didn't think that through. We just weren't in that *mode* yet, you know? Oh, dear! But, well, you know, if you wanted to get the tattoo, we could stick a little loop on the side or something . . . I'm sure that Adam and Joel wouldn't mind . . ."

I did not want another loop stuck on the side. I did not want a tattoo. Yes, tattooing was against Jewish law, and the thought of getting one did remind me of the numbers on the arms of people like Frieda and certain friends' grandparents in a blurry sort of way. But I didn't think having a tattoo was *wrong*, it just wasn't something I'd want to do. Which is why, when Carol started going on and on, I felt a little mean. Mean, but not unjustified. I could have pointed out that, at the time they had gotten the Gershon family tattoo, two of her three sons were away at college, the last one in his senior year of high school, and I could have wondered aloud if the concept of them going off and starting their own lives had in fact fueled the tattooing in the first place.

But I didn't, and it wasn't because Carol was sweet, and it wasn't because I felt mean. It was because the tattoo was something I had always liked about the Gershons, and, as long as they saw that things were changing and respected what those changes meant, I didn't need to ruin their tattoo, for them or for myself.

"Don't worry about it, Carol," I smiled. "I don't really think I'm a tattoo person."

"Are you sure?" she asked. "Because we really could change it."

"Yeah," I said. "It's fine. Really."

"And if you change your mind," Dan said, "we can always get our own."

A great, happy "we can handle anything" surge seemed to power us all the way back to New York and into our apartment, where the answering machine light blinked like an eager puppy, welcoming us home.

I hit Play and heard my uncle Stuart's voice.

"I hate to have to leave this on your machine, Rachel," he said. "But Grandpa Sol is dead."

Nineteen

The service took place in Grandpa Sol's Bayonne synagogue. This was an honor only two other people—the rabbi and the cantor—had ever been given. "He was a wonderful man," a bearded man in thick, taped glasses and a tattered wool sweater told members of the family as we entered the building. Xeroxed pages of *mishnah* poked out of the faded ShopRite plastic bags he was carrying. My uncle Stuart would later identify him as Rabbi Sapperstein's son. "Sol Lefkowitz kept this *shul* going," the son said with pride and awe as I passed.

"Thank you," I said, patting Rabbi Sapperstein's son on the hand, one of the few places on him not covered in dandruff.

He was right. For people like Grandpa Sol, Bayonne was a place your children moved up and out of, either taking you with them or installing you in Florida—unless you *were* Grandpa Sol, in which case you said, "Why should I move? I like it here," and your children bought you Sharper Image massage chairs instead.

At the entrance to the sanctuary, Aunt Minnie, Grandpa Sol's sister, leaned in and whispered, "For once, the women aren't relegated to the balcony."

I smiled and kissed her cheek.

Dan and I made our way toward the bench in front where my brother Matthew had saved us a spot. The floor of the sanctuary had that kind of chipped porcelain tile you find in prewar apartment bathrooms.

I looked up at cracks in the baby blue ceiling where all the tribes of Israel were represented in gold. When I was little, I thought they were the constellations my father would point out in the sky. I had never been relegated to the balcony here. The only memories I had of this *shul* were of being downstairs, standing on Grandpa Sol's shoes, holding his fingers, looking up at the ceiling for Cassiopeia the W, safe under the tent of his *tallis*.

"This place is incredible," Dan said, taking in Congregation *Beth Tzedek* in all its faded glory.

"Stuart says they have less than twenty members now."

Once at our row, I leaned in and asked my brother, "Are you sure this is where we should sit?"

He shrugged. "I figured Mom would sit with Aunt Thelma in front."

"And this way we don't have to sit with them."

"Ding-ding-ding."

"Good thinking."

Even under normal circumstances, we would want to avoid my mother and Thelma, sisters who fed off each other like a bad fungus. But since Joyce had, unsurprisingly, taken up her role of grieving daughter with maximum wailing, this was doubly true today.

I turned back to find her, hunched and leaning on her cousin Irene. "It's so, so awful. Such a shock." She stopped, swallowed, sobbed, "He was my *daddy*," then turned to Rabbi Sapperstein's son, held up a white head-covering doily, and asked, "Are there any of these in black?"

"Has she come up for air?" I asked Matthew, sliding into the row.

"Only to harangue me about my major."

Dan and I took our seats but kept our coats on. Honor or not, the *shul* was freezing. Matthew was doing the same. He slid his hand into a pocket. It looked chapped and raw. At least he was wearing a hat, even if it was one of those tasselly, ear-flappy, I-go-to-Phish-shows ones. Noticing me noticing, he said, "Left my gloves in my dorm room." A few ripe pimples dotted his chin.

Taking off my gloves, I reached for Matthew's hand, pressing it in between mine to warm it. I turned to Dan and said, "Let S wear your gloves for the service," and he passed them over.

"I can't believe Grandpa Sol is dead," Matthew whispered to me as people filed in around us. "He just didn't seem like the dying type, you know?"

I nodded.

Leaning over me, Dan said, "A guy who drops dead changing a lightbulb at eighty-nine definitely does not seem like the dying type."

"He wasn't even sick or anything," Matthew said. "Aren't grandparents supposed to get sick?"

Dan said, "Mine did."

"They said it was a massive stroke," Matthew continued. "That he probably felt nothing."

I shrugged. "They always say stuff like that to people they know will refer to them as 'they.'"

I was having trouble buying the "it was all so peaceful" party line. At the very least, he had to have been scared to fall off the ladder. But I'd been (unsuccessfully) trying not to picture that, so I sighed and repeated my own positive-spin platitude/mantra.

"But we should all be so lucky to be his age and have everyone so shocked."

Matthew leaned in even farther, and, in an even lower voice, whispered, "Do you think it was all the praying?"

I was stopped from answering by a tap on my shoulder. I turned to find a youngish guy with a receding hairline and tan and black blazer/black pants ensemble straight out of a suburban office park. He looked like a ten-years-older version of my cousin Kenny. Then I realized this actually was my cousin Kenny, whom I hadn't seen in about ten years.

"Kenny," I said, turning to give him a kiss. He was how many years older than me—five, six, twenty? "It's good to see you." He and Matthew did that goofy man half-hug/half-handshake and I said, "This is my fiancé, Dan. Dan, this is my cousin Kenny—"

"Kenneth now, thanks, Rachel." He gave Dan's hand a firm shake. "Good to meet you. And this," he said, his arm engulfing the slightly hard-looking, big-boned but not unattractive blonde to his right, "is my wife, Silka."

"Your *wife?*" I asked, detecting Matthew and Dan's eye contact above me.

"Yup," said Kenny-now-Kenneth. "Did it in December."

"Just the two of us," Silka said in a surprisingly thick accent. *Zee* two *off zem* had gotten married.

"On the beach in Hawaii," Kenny continued. "Only way to go. Resort took care of everything. Just showed up, said the I do's, and it was back to piña coladas on the chaise longue."

"Wow," I nodded. Was he *bragging?* "I hadn't even heard."

"Yeah, well, Thelma's not too thrilled, of course." My aunt Thelma was his mother, poor guy. "The whole non-Jew thing is one thing, but, add the German thing into the mix"—he said this with pride, like he was some kind of badass—"and, well, you can imagine . . ."

"I can," I said.

When we sat back down, I leaned toward my brother. "Did you *know* about that, S?"

He was cracking up, though with a bit more subtlety than Dan. "Mom told me, of course," then, in his best quiver-lipped Joyce, added, "'*You* would never do that to your mother, would you?'"

"Why didn't you tell me?"

"I don't know," he shrugged. "I guess I kinda forgot."

I shook my head and looked up at the ceiling.

"Wait a minute," I said. "Did *Grandpa* know?"

"He didn't know." Aunt Thelma shook her head, dabbing at her eyes. She stood in one corner of the dining room, a lampshade's tassel threatening to graze her shoulder at any moment. "I was just going to tell him *that very day. That very day.* I was picking up the phone, and thought, No, maybe I'll wait until after he's had his dinner. Maybe, I don't know," her voice trailed off. "The Lord works in mysterious ways."

We had put Grandpa Sol in the ground in Staten Island and were now at his semidecrepit, old-man-who-lived-through-the-Depression-then-alone-as-a-widower-for-twelve-years Bayonne house, smelling the smell I was reminded of whenever I visited friends' apartments in Brooklyn brownstones with carpeted stairways. Stuart and Annie had brought platters down from Teaneck and laid them out on a lace tablecloth on Grandpa's dining room table. The guests, and there were quite a few of them (mostly extended family), were filling up on standard *Kiddush* fare—bagels and nova and whitefish and herring with onion in cream and whitefish salad and herring salad and tuna salad and egg salad and pasta salad and rugelach and minibrownies and assorted cookies, some of which involved unnecessary layers of jelly undetectable until you actually bit into the cookie and thought, "Why is there *jelly* in here?" Aunt Thelma was busy justifying herself to some older relatives at the dessert end.

Hearing her, I caught Stuart's eye and he shook his head. Even from his sister, "the most *chutzpadik* woman in the world," this was unbelievable. We rendezvoused at the cream cheese. "She waits *three months?*" Stuart said. "Until that very day? We're supposed to believe that?"

"She's Thelma." I shrugged.

"I mean," Stuart continued, "it's too bad she didn't want to convert, but—whatever. It's too bad, but she seems like a nice person, and if Kenny's happy . . . so she's German. It's two generations already. Who cares? What gets me is she can't just tell the truth. It has to be this whole big, pathetic story where everyone's supposed to be gasping—'The Lord works in mysterious ways.'"

"She's Thelma."

"I know," he sighed. "My sister, the most *chutzpadik* woman in the world."

My uncle and I dispersed and I went to find Dan. He was in the living room, on the plastic-covered sofa talking to Kenny (sorry, you'll never be Kenneth to me) and Silka about the pharmaceutical industry. They worked for the same in-one-ear-out-the-other company, where Kenny was apparently a salesman and Silka did research of some kind—that's how they'd met. They had just bought a house and were installing a fishpond. The rest of the conversation was blah, blah, blah to me, so I figured Dan was fine on his own and moved on to other relatives.

In another corner, Joyce had temporarily shelved her designated mourner persona. Instead, she was torturing Matthew about his major, trying to enlist her cousin Roger the urologist in the campaign.

"Don't you just think astrophysics *sounds* better?" she was saying. Matthew shot me a pleading look and I made my way over.

"Mom, do you really think this is the time to get into—"

"What? I'm asking! Roger's a doctor. He knows about these things!"

Roger said, "This is a little out of my field. . . ."

Matthew said, "Mom!"

I said, "Come on, Mom. Is this really necessary?"

"I just want to ask his opinion about what Aunt Thelma said."

"I don't care about what Aunt Thelma said." Matthew's face was reddening. "You're the only person in the world who thinks Aunt Thelma knows what she's talking about."

"No," I corrected. "There are two people in the world who think Aunt Thelma knows what she's talking about: Joyce and Aunt Thelma."

Roger tried to suppress a snicker.

Everyone knew about "the sisters," and the hold Thelma had over my mother.

In addition to being the most *chutzpadik* woman in the world, Aunt Thelma was my mother's older sister, prime counselor, and, though Joyce didn't realize it, worst enemy. Up until the year I left for college, when my uncle Larry's acceptance of a position at California University necessitated their West Coast relocation, Thelma had lived a too-short ten minutes away from Joyce in the neighboring town of Bethesda. Thelma always offered her opinions, opinions that were like lighter fluid to the flame of Joyce's insecurities. Her California move had turned half the family into avid fans of the San Andreas Fault.

"Why do you listen to her?" both Matthew and I had asked Joyce many times. We'd point out that Thelma's own family was hardly a model for emulation—now we had the fuel of Kenny's elopement to add to our fire. We'd mention the little speeches Aunt Thelma would make at family gatherings about Joyce "always being Daddy's favorite" and note the eerie resemblance she'd bear at those times to an evil villain rubbing his hands together as he justifies his plan to take over the world.

"She's my *sister*," Joyce would say. "She loves me."

"She's my *sister*," Joyce said then. "And she does know about this stuff. Uncle Larry is a big shot! They meet all sorts of important people!" She then turned to Roger. "You know Larry was promoted to dean at Cal U, right? Well, Thelma says anything with physics is much, much better. She says everyone in all the other departments looks up to physics. That it's the most respected of the sciences."

Matthew shook his head. His jaw was beating at the sides of his chinline.

"Besides," she continued, "you say ast*ronomy* and people think ast*rology*. They think I'm paying Brown tuition for him to study the zodiac!"

"Why would I care about what a person who doesn't know the difference between astronomy and astrology thinks?" Matthew's tone was the aural equivalent of a fist clenching.

"Listen to him!" Joyce said. "Mister big shot! You're *young*. You don't understand that the decisions you make now will affect you for the rest of your life!"

"How?" I asked. "He's gonna apply to the same graduate programs either way."

"But astrophysics *sounds* better!" Joyce insisted, adding her little I'm-so-wacky laugh.

"To people who don't know what they're talking about!" Matthew said, squeezing his fork. I gave him a let-me-handle-this look.

"Leave him alone, Mom."

"But Aunt Thelma says—"

"Aunt Thelma doesn't know what she's talking about!"

Joyce turned to Roger. "Are your kids this fresh?"

After that, I headed for the place I always headed during gatherings of my mother's side of the family: the kitchen. I knew my aunt Annie would be there as she always was, taking care of things. I walked in to find her wiping a counter. Out the window behind her, her fifteen-year-old twin sons, Eric and Jeremy, were playing one-on-one basketball.

"What can I do to help?"

"Nothing," she said. "Sit and keep me company."

I sat. The upholstery sighed.

"Why don't you sit, too?" I asked her.

"Why don't I sit? Because if I sit, I'll fall asleep. Between running around after three-year-olds all day, dealing with all the crap from the *shul*, then getting this whole thing together all of a sudden, I'm too exhausted to be exhausted."

Annie taught nursery school and had recently become the president of her synagogue, a time-consuming, unpaid position for which she was constantly dealing with "crises" and "emergencies," all of which involved what she grumblingly referred to as "*shul* politics." "It's just like nursery school," she'd say. "I deal with three-year-olds all day."

I nodded. Annie never sat down anyway.

People who met Annie Lefkowitz tended to make the same two comments about her. The first was that she looked "like a teenager." Even at forty-five, with a son in college, she was asked to show ID on the rare occasions when she ordered a drink. She wore no makeup, had dark wavy hair that frizzed in humid weather, and a smattering of freckles that increased with exposure to the sun. Though on close inspection you could see the little lines spreading around her eyes, you were more likely to remember the thing that caused them, the wholehearted, crinkle-eyed laugh that tumbled out of Aunt Annie, often as involuntarily as a sneeze.

She also dressed young. Even when she wasn't working, Annie's style was "nursery school comfortable," jeans—either long and slim-fitting or cut off into shorts—and sneakers, with T-shirts or turtlenecks depending on the season. If it was really cold, she'd add hooded sweatshirts or checkered flannel shirts.

The second comment people made about Annie was that she was an "*ayshet chayil*"—a woman of valor whose value, according to the book of Proverbs, is a price above rubies.

In response to the comparison, Aunt Annie would say, "I hate that *ayshet chayil* crap."

But it was true. Whether she liked it or not, Annie was my personal *ayshet chayil*—she and Stuart were my personal *anashim chayillim*. In my mind, they could do no wrong. They could not only speak with solemn reverence about Tom Hanks dramas, but also come into the city with the twins for a musical, then top it off with dinner at the Hard Rock Café, and I wouldn't even mind. In fact, they did all of those things, and, aside from an occasional nails-on-chalkboardiness ("You really *like* Times Square on New Year's?"), for the most part, I didn't.

I had always loved Stuart and Annie, but they had won my

undying devotion at my college graduation dinner, a dinner that my father was hosting in the city, to which he'd invited my mother, Grandpa Sol, and Stuart and Annie.

My mother refused to go. At first, it was on Grandpa Sol kosher grounds. When I got my father to agree to a kosher restaurant, my mother still refused to attend, citing something absurd about Grandpa Sol's salt intake. We went back to the nonkosher restaurant plan, and Annie and Stuart joined us, and they and Jerry and Phyllis and Gregory and Thomas and Aunt Natalie sat at a round table in Shun Lee and toasted my Barnard degree. Glasses clinked all around and Annie's laugh tumbled out of her as she said, "You know Joyce is gonna kill us."

She didn't, at least not technically. What she technically did was call Annie and Stuart up and scream for half an hour that they were "traitors." They tried to explain that "the dinner was for *Rachel*, not Jerry." She, of course, would hear none of it, and, saying she didn't need people like them in her life, slammed down the phone. Things had remained icy in the five years since.

I knew it wasn't my fault, but I still felt guilty for the rift. When I'd tell them that, Annie and Stuart would both say, "It's not your fault." They both blamed my mother and Thelma, feeder of all bad impulses, for the cold war.

Stuart would say, "My sisters were always crazy."

Annie would say, "It's fine with me. Actually," she'd laugh, "I like it better this way."

"Can you believe this Kenny business?" Annie now laughed as she wiped the sink. Today she was dressed in *"shul* clothes"— black turtleneck, black cardigan, long flowered skirt.

"I know," I said.

"Actually," she stopped and turned to face me, "I *can* believe it. I can believe he married someone not Jewish. Even the German thing." She shrugged. "It's a different day and age. What I *can't* believe is that Thelma. The woman is nearly sixty years old and she still doesn't have the guts to tell her father."

"Yeah, but you know how they are." We both knew "they" meant both Thelma and Joyce. "It's like reverse dog years. They're in their fifties but they're actually seven."

Annie laughed. "Do you remember all the hoops they'd jump through to put on a show for him?"

"Remember that time with the McDonald's bag in the car?"

"Yes. Thelma's yelling and screaming—*Get that bag outta here before Grandpa sees it! Get that bag outta here!* Joyce is saying—*Ooh, ooh, Daddy'll see!* Like it's such a shock you don't keep kosher? Do you think the man doesn't realize it's *Shabbos* and we've just picked you guys up from the train? So ridiculous."

"They're insane."

"You're right." She nodded. "Actually," she said, dropping the sponge, "I *can* believe it. I can believe the whole thing. I can believe it because the two of them are so unbelievable."

I laughed.

"But this Silka seems like a sweet person," she said, picking the sponge up again. In Aunt Annie's nursery-school–sharpened worldview, there were only two kinds of people, "a sweet person" and "not a sweet person." Aunt Thelma was "not a sweet person." My mother was "a sweet person, she's just nuts."

"I guess," I said. I was tired of thinking about Kenny and Silka, tired of thinking about my crazy mother and her crazy sister. It seemed unfair to Grandpa Sol. "I can't believe he's not gonna be at my wedding."

"I know." Annie took a break from assembling the coffee-maker to shake her head along with me. "Just—boom, like that. Who would have thought?"

"Not me," I said, resting an elbow on the table and my cheek on my hand. "All this time, with all this back-and-forth about the kosher business, I never once thought the whole thing would be moot." I felt my eyes well up.

"You're a sweet person, Rachel, sticking up for your grand-father like that."

Sweet was the last thing I felt like. "I never imagined Grandpa Sol wouldn't be there."

Annie leaned against the counter and sighed. I shifted in my chair and the vinyl sighed too.

"A wedding without any grandparents. Doesn't that just seem *depressing?*"

"That's life." Annie shrugged. "Sometimes it's pretty depress-ing."

I nodded, and Annie went back to the coffee. She headed for the refrigerator, an enormous relic with a heavy silver lever you had to really pull to open and a freezer below with a pedal you had to stomp on.

"How old do you think that thing is?" I asked her. About five years before, Grandpa Sol had painted everything—the refrigera-tor, the washer/dryer, the metal on the chairs, the wooden cabi-nets—white, his idea of a renovation.

"As old as I am," she said, laughing and looking at it. "God, am I *that* old?"

"What, you don't think the paint job spruced it up?" Annie and I were both laughing.

"You know," she said, "Old Grandpa Sol was really a weird person. A sweet person, but a weird one."

"Wanna know the weirdest thing about him?"

"What, that since it was just him living here he decided he didn't need to use dishwashing soap? I already know that one. I had to remember to bring some down and wash everything before everyone got here. The glasses were all filmy and disgusting."

"No." I giggled. "Not the soap. That's not being weird, that's just the whole Depression thing. Do you know what Grandpa Sol's favorite TV show was?"

"Well, I know his favorite movie was *It's a Wonderful Life*. At least until we got him the tape of *Mr. Holland's Opus*."

"Yeah, then he went around asking everyone he encountered if they'd seen it, without ever using the correct title." I put on my best Grandpa Sol Bayonne brogue, "'*Have ya seen that movie*, Mr. Holland the Music Teacher?' '*That music teacher movie*, Mr. Holland, *d'you see it?*' *Mr. Holland's Opus*—it's just three words. He always made it so much more complicated. Must've been something about the word 'opus.'"

"You know, when you do that voice, you really almost sound like him."

"Anyway, I'm not talking about movies. I'm talking TV show here. I'll give you a hint: It was a sitcom."

"I don't know—*All in the Family*?"

"Good guess, but no. *Small Wonder*."

"*Small Wonder*? What's *Small Wonder*?"

"It was like the dumbest nonhit eighties sitcom about a girl who was a robot. The father was an inventor and they couldn't let the neighbors catch on for some reason."

"*Small Wonder*?"

"Yes! He would set the timer so he could watch it on *Shabbos*."

Annie's eyes widened. "Really? He set a *timer* to watch TV on *Shabbos*?"

"Yes! That's how much he loved this show. I was like,

Grandpa, you're setting a timer to watch *Small Wonder?* And he was like, *'The little girl's really a robot! They have to hide it from the neighbor!'* and then he'd crack himself up."

Annie and I now cracked up at the thought of it.

We were in various stages of postlaugh sigh when Dan entered the kitchen. Annie said, "Speaking of sweet guys . . ."

Dan said, "How'd I know I'd find the two of you in here?" then patted my hand and took a seat at the table. His chair let out the usual sound effect. "These things are like built-in whoopee cushions. Who knew Grandpa Sol was such a prankster?"

"A prankster—no," Aunt Annie said, closing the freezer, Shop-Rite nondairy topping in hand. Sarcasm was often lost on her.

"Mmmm, maybe not." Dan nodded, smiling at me.

"So you were out there chatting with the happy couple," I said.

"Yup," Dan said. "Got all their marital advice."

"Any news we can use?"

"Not unless we're planning on spending a lot more time with your aunt Thelma."

"Nothing of any value at all then, huh?"

"Nope."

"Poor Silka," Annie half-laughed. "She must be givin' her a real hard time." Then Annie turned to face us, suddenly serious with a hand on her hip. "But you know what?" she said. "I don't worry about you two."

"Thanks," I said.

"No, really, I mean it. I never worried about you, Rachel. Not that you're not a great guy, Dan, because you are—"

"Well, thanks—"

"But even with all the statistics and how they say kids from divorce are real screwed up, I never once worried about you. You wanna know why?"

We nodded.

"Because of something you once said to me at a Seder. You were keeping me company in the kitchen. You must have been seven, eight years old—you couldn't have been any older because Matthew wasn't born yet. You asked me if I knew why your parents got married."

"What did you say?"

"I said I wasn't sure, so you asked if I wanted to hear what you thought, and I said yeah. You told me that your father had had a girlfriend that he couldn't marry because she wasn't Jewish and that your mom was twenty-six, which was really old—I remember that part 'cause I was twenty-seven or something at the time and was thinking, thanks a lot, kid—and that Thelma fixed her up and she always did whatever Aunt Thelma said. Now that was all stuff I already knew, but I couldn't believe that you knew it and had thought it all through and put it all together like that— you were a little kid, remember. And then you said, and I'll never forget this, you said they didn't really want to marry each other, they just wanted to get married."

"Wow," Dan said.

"I know," said Annie. "See why I remembered it?"

"I said that?"

"Yeah." Annie nodded, then turned back to whatever it was she'd been doing. "You were always a smart kid."

A few hours and many "Next time we see you, it'll be a happy occasion"s later, I made my way over to Joyce.

"So I think we're going home now," I said, leaning in to give her a hug. Matthew had left a little while before—Kenny and

Silka had given him a ride to Newark to catch his train back to Providence.

"All right, honey," she said in The Sweet Voice. "But you'll be back, right? You know Thelma and I are staying here for the *shivah*."

"I think so," I said, disentangling. "Dan's parents said something about maybe coming up and paying a *shivah* call."

"That would be nice of them."

I nodded.

Then she said, "Oooh, wait. How're you getting back?"

"Annie's giving us a ride back into the city."

"Oh." My mother's eyes narrowed. The Sweet Voice was gone. "She is, is she?"

"Yup," I said, neutral. "She is."

Joyce nodded slowly, as if to say, "I see."

But I wasn't taking the bait. Instead I said, "I was thinking about something. Something for the wedding."

"You know what?" she said, her lips pursing and unpursing and the sad, frail voice back in place. "I think I might do the wedding kosher," here her voice caught, "in honor of Grandpa Sol. It seems even more important now."

I nodded and patted her shoulder. Whatever got her through the day. "So should I call the caterer and tell Dad to expect your check?"

"I didn't say I'd decided." She'd gone from designated mourner to low-voiced hisser, zero to sixty in less than three seconds. "I don't want your father to think he can bully me with these strong-arm tactics."

"I thought you wanted to honor Grandpa Sol."

"I do!" She drew the handkerchief to her face, the return of the mourner martyr. "He would be sick about this whole thing.

Sick! Sick about the way your father is treating me! Sick about you going along with it! Just sick!"

I held back an eye-roll.

Grandpa Sol would not have been sick over this. If he would have been, I might have called him earlier—either to ask him to pay for the kosher himself or to help convince my mother to settle the issue. But I hadn't called Grandpa Sol, because I knew he wouldn't have done either of those things. Even when I'd gotten my father to agree to change my graduation dinner to a kosher restaurant, Grandpa Sol hadn't said, "Come on, Joyce, Rachel's your daughter, she's my granddaughter, we're going to her graduation dinner." He hadn't said anything at all.

Grandpa Sol did not get sick over things—not graduation dinners, not cars driving up to his house on *Shabbos* (with or without McDonald's french fry containers), not even (I would bet) his grandson marrying a non-Jewish German. If he'd heard the news, he would have sighed, maybe shrugged, probably said, "I don't like it, it's not right, but what am I gonna do?" then promptly turned on the TV or left for *minyan*, doing his best to avoid thinking about it ever again.

Grandpa Sol lived his life doing exactly what he wanted—following the Torah to the letter of the law, while finding a loophole on rare occasions when he really liked a show about a girl who was a robot. He saw only what he wanted to see, ignoring or avoiding anything he didn't.

That, I suspected, is how you die at eighty-nine changing a lightbulb and leave everyone shocked.

But this was not the issue I'd come to discuss.

"I don't care about the kosher thing. That wasn't what I meant. What I was thinking—I know he was buried in one, but I was wondering if maybe Grandpa had another *tallis* around—"

"Why?" Aunt Thelma had materialized next to me.

"I was thinking it would be nice to use it for the *huppah*. That way," I swallowed, refusing to get emotional in front of them, "it can feel like he's there."

My mother's face crumbled. "There's still his high holiday *tallis*. The one we got him in Israel."

"Great," I said. "That's perfect."

"Not so fast," said Thelma. "If we give it to you, I want to make sure it's coming back."

"Coming back?"

"Yes. So *all* of the grandchildren can use it."

I thought about saying, "Like who, Kenny?" but managed to keep myself in check. "I'm not trying to *steal* it. I just want it for the *huppah*."

"Then you'll give it back when you're done?" Thelma was eyeing me.

"Yes," I said, confused. What about this was suspicious?

"Back to *us*," said my mother. "Not to Stuart for the twins."

So *that's* what this was about. "Why shouldn't Stuart have it? You just said you wanted everyone to be able to use it."

"*We* were the ones who bought it in Israel," Thelma said.

"Oh, come *on*." I rolled my eyes and rubbed my forehead.

"Those are the conditions," my mother said, no trace of her frailty in evidence. "Do you want the *tallis* or not?"

I did want the *tallis*. I wanted it badly and I wanted it now, as if it were Grandpa Sol himself, and I could wrap myself in him and stand on his toes and look up at a ceiling I thought was the sky.

"Fine," I told them. "Whatever you want."

Twenty

$\mathcal{B}$ack in the kitchen, *tallis* in hand, Dan, Annie, and I put on our coats, preparing to leave through the back door.

"So, are things with the wedding pretty much under control?" she asked.

"Pretty much would be the accurate assessment," I answered.

"You get the invitations yet?"

I knew I'd been forgetting something. "No." My mind raced to Martha's calendar. "Shit. We have to do that this week."

"I can't do it this week. I have that Histology thing due Friday."

"We have to do them this week. We have to send them out in three weeks, and it'll take two for them to print them—"

"Relax," Annie said, taking an address book from her purse. "Bryna Finkel from the *shul* does them out of her house. I'll call her up. We can go over there right now and order them before I take you back into the city."

"Annie," I said, "you rock."

"Yeah, Annie," Dan said. "Thanks so much."

Like most compliments, Annie shooed these away. "It's nothing. It'll take two minutes."

"I can't believe I'm doing this after my grandfather's funeral," I said as she dialed.

She shrugged. "Life goes on."

Forty-five minutes later, Dan, Annie, and I found ourselves in the eighties-mauve living room of Bryna Finkel's Teaneck split-level. We'd been asked to "try and keep it down" because "Jonathan is upstairs doing a practice SAT." Parental college board neuroses—the Sisterhood version of parrot collecting. Two huge binders sprawled on the glass coffee table, their contents sample invitations of the silver-bordered variety, many of which featured swans and/or doves prominently.

"We were just thinking of something really, really simple," I said, hoping I was keeping "it" sufficiently down. Frightened by the invitations in front of him, Dan nodded along. "Like maybe even just a white card with black lettering."

Bryna Finkel's eyebrows lifted toward her highlighted hairline. "That'll be very *plain*," she said, pushing her glasses up the bridge of her nose and sucking in her cheeks.

"Well, maybe if we had a Hebrew quote along the top . . ."

"We could do that," she nodded.

"And then just real simple."

"Well, then, pick your card stock first," she said. In what looked like a wrestling move, she flipped the shiny black notebook swiftly onto its back.

I peered over the page. "Do you have any thoughts?" I asked Dan.

"They all look nice." Translation: It's been a long day and I don't give a shit.

"How 'bout that one?" I said, pointing to one with a little framelike raised border. "What do you think, Annie?"

She nodded. "Looks nice."

"And you want white-white, not off?" Bryna Finkel asked.

"Yeah," I said. "White-white."

"Fine," she said. She made a note on her pad, then gave the book another brisk flip. "Choose your lettering," she said, then rose to leave. "I'll go get the Hebrew lettering sample."

Annie leaned in and whispered, "I think she's a little pissed about meeting on such short notice." She shrugged. "No one says no to the *shul* president. Isn't it stupid? Suddenly I'm a big *macher*." She shook her head. "People are nuts. But, hey, it means she'll give you a deal."

Soon enough, Bryna was back, and I was looking down at the paper she'd brought—a sort of mini-Aleph-Bet seeing-eye chart. I leaned in toward Dan.

He said, "It's all you, babe."

I looked back and forth, back and forth from sheet to the binder, trying to suss out the right lettering combination.

"I think this one and this one," I said, pointing.

Bryna Finkel raised her eyebrows again. "You don't want script? For a wedding? It's more romantic . . ."

"Hmmm, yeah. Well, I think we'll let the quote be romantic and the lettering be more, you know, classic."

She shrugged, pushed up her glasses again, and noted the fonts I'd chosen. "It's your life."

I stole a look at Aunt Annie, who, I could tell, was avoiding my eyes and the giggling that would ruin her big *macher* façade.

"So," Bryna continued, "all that's left is the wording. What were you thinking for the Hebrew?"

"I was thinking the basic *kol sasson v'kol simcha, kol chatan v'kol kallah*," the voice of joy and the voice of gladness, the voice of groom and bride, taken from one of the seven wedding blessings.

"Fine," said Bryna Finkel in a been-there-done-that tone, noting this on her pad. "You want the translation with a dash?"

"No," I said. "Just the Hebrew. The people who know the quote will know the quote, and the people who don't will either ask us or think it's decorative."

"Have it your way." I felt Dan shake back a laugh next to me. "Now the English."

I had toyed with this in the car ride up. I took the piece of paper with my notes out from my pocket. "We have a sort of nontraditional family arrangement," I said. "So I thought we'd put our names first."

"Fine." Bryna clearly hadn't got time for my pain.

"So which—"

"Bride goes first," she said. "Always."

"Okay. So, Rachel Beth Silverstein and Daniel Joseph Gershon, together with our parents, invite you to share the joy of our wedding—"

"Just lemme see the paper," Bryna said, reaching. "It's easier that way."

I handed it over to her.

"You want the line breaks like this?"

"Yeah," I said. I'd written it up in invitation verse.

"Oh, wait," she said. "Before I write this all down, lemme get the return address for the response cards and the envelope."

I looked at Dan. "Should we just do ours?"

"That's probably easiest," he said.

Annie nodded. "Do yours."

So I gave Bryna Finkel our address.

"Now, back to the wording," she said, looking again at the paper I'd given her. "What's this question mark?"

"Oh," I said. "It's for the name of the place. We're getting married at the Audubon Society headquarters, but it's an old mansion called Woodend, so I just need to double-check how to refer to it."

"Well, I can't put in an incomplete order." She shot an I-thought-this-would-be-fast look at Annie.

"Just a quick call and I can resolve this. Do you mind if I use your phone?" I asked.

Bryna Finkel sighed and led me to the phone in her wall-papered, immaculate kitchen, no doubt pissed this was going to be long-distance.

"This'll be really quick," I said, picking up the receiver as she left and praying Phyllis would be home. She was.

"Hi, Phyllis," I said when she answered.

"Rachel, honey, how *are* you? The funeral was today, right? Dad thought about going but didn't want to make a scene."

I was Rachel honey again. "I'm fine. Really. Fine. I'm actually at a friend of Annie's ordering the wedding invitations."

"Oh?"

"Yeah, I realized we hadn't done anything about them and with the ordering time and everything—"

"Sure."

"Well, so, I had a quick question. We're figuring out the wording—"

"Uh-huh—"

"And I wanted to know—you have all the Audubon Society stuff from when you made the deposit, right?"

"Yup."

"Well, how do I refer to them on the invitation? Woodend, or the Audubon Society, or what? Do you know?"

"Hold on a sec, I'll get the brochure." Here was a great thing about hyperorganized Phyllis—she kept everything in files, so it really would just take a second. Sure enough, a few moments later, she was back. "The brochure says 'Woodend, The Audubon Naturalist Society,' so I'd just put that."

"And Audubon is A-U-D-U-B-O-N."

"Uh-huh."

"Okay," I said. Visualizing Woodend on one line, the rest on the next, I turned to hang up. "Great. Thanks so much, Phyllis."

"Hang on a sec," she said. "What are you doing about the rest of it?"

"Huh?"

"The rest of the invitation."

"Oh. We're having the response cards sent to us, so you don't have to deal with all that."

"Well, that's good. But I meant how are you *wording* it?"

"Oh. Rachel Beth Silverstein and Daniel Joseph Gershon, together with our parents, invite you to share—"

"'Together with our parents'?"

"Yeah. I thought it would be a nice way of putting it—"

"It's nice," she said. "No, it's nice. It's not that. It just doesn't include me."

Huh?

"I think it does," I said. "To me, you're a parent."

"Well, to you maybe. But not to *people*."

People: a species of which I was not.

"I don't think—"

"Listen," she said, "do it however you want. It's fine. I don't want to be a problem." I had to stifle myself at that one. "I just don't think it's *right* that an invitation your dad and I pay for doesn't even *include* me. But if *you* think that's okay—"

I was so far from wanting to deal with this. "How about 'together with our families'?"

She thought about it for a moment. "That's better," she said. "It implies something more than just your mother and your dad."

"Fine," I said. "'Together with our families' it is."

"Great, honey."

I was honey again. I rolled my eyes.

"Thanks again," I said, hanging up.

Back in the living room, I explained the Woodend/Naturalist Society setup. "And one more change. Instead of 'together with our parents,' we'll have it say 'together with our families.'"

Bryna nodded and made a note.

Annie said, "Why?"

"Phyllis felt that 'parents' did not include her," I said with an anchorwoman's delivery.

Dan laughed.

"Oh, please," said Annie.

"Well," I said, thick with the faux-cheer of a Disney World tour guide, "after all, she and my dad *are* paying for these invitations."

"But you're putting down the deposit now," Bryna said, looking up from her notes.

I nodded. "Oh, yeah," I said. "Not to worry."

Annie shook her head. "People are nuts."

Twenty-one

Two weeks later, Dan and I were having coffee at the table in our pajamas.

"You know what today is?" I asked him.

"Saturday," he said, not looking up from the *Times Magazine*.

"The kosher deadline," I said.

"We have to get this registering thing over with before I go into exam seclusion," Dan said. "My mother's still on me about it."

"Did you hear what I said?" More and more it seemed as if he was a person with a rich, full life and I was a person with a wedding.

"I heard what you said. I just don't think you should worry about it. Your mother's gonna do what she always does, wait until the last possible second and then decide to do it. Besides, it's between your mother and your father. Why should you be in the middle of it?"

I said, "Do you not know anything at all about my entire life?"

He said, "I'm getting in the shower, and then we're gonna go register."

As the water went on in the bathroom, the phone rang.

"Hello?" I said, answering it.

"Do you know what today is?" It was my mother. She was not speaking in The Sweet Voice.

"Saturday?"

"That is *not* what I meant, and you know it. Today is your wonderful father's deadline."

"Oh," I said. Why had I answered the phone? I made Dan's advice my mantra: Do not engage, do not engage.

"Is that all you're gonna say?"

Why couldn't I just say "yes"? "I don't see what the big deal is now. Grandpa Sol isn't even gonna be there."

"All the more reason why the kosher is important. To honor his memory."

"Fine," I said flatly. "Then do it kosher."

"And go along with your father's insensitive, humiliating demands?"

"Then don't do it kosher." My tone was still dead.

"That's right! I forgot! You don't care. You don't give a shit about me. Why should you? I'm just your mother."

"You know that isn't true, Mom—"

"All you want is your precious wedding! All you care about is yourself!"

I told myself that she was being ridiculous, that she was being manipulative, that I would not fall for the oldest Jewish mother martyr trick in the book. But part of me still felt like an ogre. The deadline really was bullshit, and I really had gone along with it. Did that mean I cared about my wedding more than I cared about my mother?

"That's not true, Mom."

"How is that not true? How? You let your father do whatever he wants to me. You don't care—"

"That's not true," I said, snapping. "Why do you think there's a kosher option to begin with? Because I fought for it, that's why!"

"Well, bully for you! Pin a medal on that girl's chest! How wonderful she is to stick up for her grandfather! He only paid for your school and your camp! You do the least you can to repay him, and you want *applause!* He was," here her voice caught, "the kindest, gentlest person. And look what's going on in his name. He would be sick, *sick* about this . . ."

"I don't know what to tell you, Mom. It's really a simple question. Do you want to do it kosher or not?"

"A simple question—that's right. Simple for *you*. How did I end up with such a spoiled brat for a daughter? No, no, don't even say it—it's my own fault. I *never* should have paid that money for Barnard. You and your father with your hoo-ha schools. I should have stuck to my guns and made him pay for the whole damn thing. Every year, the same thing. 'Mom, I need your half of the tuition.' 'Mom, school's already started.' 'Mom, I'm already in the dorm.' And now I'm stuck shelling out the same money for your brother, all because all you ever cared about was you, you, you!"

At times like these, it was hard to tell who my mother really hated, my father or me.

"It's a simple question, Mom. Kosher or not, your decision."

"You're damn right it's my decision," she said, slamming down the receiver.

A moment later, Dan emerged from the bathroom in a towel.

"That was my mother," I told him. "I am an ungrateful spoiled brat who doesn't give a shit about her own mother. She hung up on me again."

He said, "Get dressed. We've got stuff to take care of."

*   *   *

Since they were both national, Dan and I had decided to register at Bloomingdale's and Crate and Barrel. The plan was to hit Crate and Barrel first because it was closer, then walk to Bloomingdale's and finish the task in one day. We set out at the crack of eleven.

The air was crisp that Saturday, and the park wasn't crowded. An Asian wedding party posed for pictures near Bethesda Fountain. The bride wore a black down jacket over her gown and held a big bouquet of red roses. Her hair framed her face in hot-off-the-curling-iron tendrils.

"Is it just me, or is it impossible to set foot in this park these days without seeing an Asian wedding party?"

"There do seem to be a lot of them," Dan said. "But maybe there always were and you're only just noticing them now."

I was about to mutter something about it being the winter of my wedding discontent, when it struck me that Dan was walking rather peppily.

"Are you excited about this?"

"Why not?" he asked. "It's presents."

"You mean there's stuff you actually *want?*"

"Well, yeah," he shrugged. "I'd like to get some good knives, and maybe a Cuisinart. Oh, and you know what else? Do you think Bloomingdale's would have lightweight binoculars?"

"Lightweight bi*noc*ulars?"

"We can use them on the honeymoon. They'll be great for this place in Sumatra where you go trekking with orangutans in the wild."

"There's a place where I do what with who?"

"Nevermind, nevermind," Dan said, half-patting, half-massaging the top of my back. "Forget the honeymoon. I want to start getting into bird-watching."

"Bird-watching?"

"Yeah. Central Park is supposedly this great place to watch birds. New York City is on the migratory path for all these different kinds. You might think they'd say, 'Hey wait, it's a city, why not just tweak it out to Long Island or something?' but the birds are just like, 'This is my migratory path and I'll find whatever greenery I need to get the job done'—and this is the obvious place for a stopover. I heard it on Leonard Lopate."

I gave him a look and kept walking, trying to keep warm.

Not long afterward, armed with the metal clipboard-folder given to us when we checked in at the gift registry counter, Dan and I made our way through Crate and Barrel. Dan headed purposefully for the knives, and I wandered bewildered behind him. All around us were couples with metal clipboard-folders, roughly our age, wearing roughly the same jeans and baseball caps we were, looking earnestly at wooden salad bowls and woks—an army of Banana Republicans on medical rounds. Nineties New York Jupiter had aligned with Wedding Magazine Mars; it was the dawning of the Age of Crate and Barrel.

Dan used the word "serrated" in a sentence.

"I need a pause here," I said.

He looked up and said, "Okay."

"Remember how all that Generation X stuff was okay because it was bullshit? Just look at Dustin Hoffman in *The Graduate*?"

"Yeah?"

"So, how is this okay?"

"What?"

"This," I said, gesturing broadly. "Us. Them. Look at this place! You could conduct market research in here. We're a *demographic*."

"Of course we're a demographic," he said. "We're registering for wedding presents."

"Why are we doing this?"

"Ray-chul—"

"I'm serious. It's just—I mean, what are we saying here? It's like the rest of our lives is just about the accumulation of *stuff*."

"You don't want wedding presents?"

"I don't want *stuff*. I just want money."

Dan laughed.

"We can tell people to either give us money or make a donation to our favorite charity," I said, brightening with my bright idea.

"We don't have a favorite charity."

"We'll pick one! How 'bout the Fresh Air Fund?"

"Who are you—Caroline Kennedy? Coming from us, that's self-righteous and pretentious."

"No, it isn't," I said.

"Yes, it is," he said. "Look at the Talmud. The highest form of giving is the one where everything's anonymous. You're suggesting we do the exact opposite of that. It's like yelling, 'We're good people,' at the top of our lungs."

"All right," I said. "You have a point. And I applaud your use of the Talmud. But it also says that any kind of giving is better than none at all."

"So we'll give a percentage of the gifts we get to charity without announcing it to the world. I'm down with that. I think it's a nice idea." He kissed my cheek. "Now, let's get this registering business done with so my mother will stop harassing me."

Dan bent back over the knife case and said, "I think this one, this one, and this one." I said, "Fine," and he added the details to our list. We moved on to flatware, where we lifted forks and spoons to test their heft. Dan feigned eating a three-course meal while I lifted and lowered absently, staring straight ahead. He said, "I like these." I said, "Fine," and we ordered that set. We then went on to the "dinnerware" section.

"I assume 'dinnerware' means everyday dishes," Dan said, staring at the rows of place settings on display.

"As opposed to what?"

"I don't know—formal stuff?"

"We're going to register for *china*?"

"No way." Dan shooed the thought away with his hand. "That's the biggest ripoff. If we want that stuff, we can get it so cheap at auction."

"Well, we already have everyday dishes. We use them every day. What do we need these for?"

"I don't know. I guess for casual dinner parties."

"Casual dinner parties?" My hands rose to my temples. I was nervous in a way I sometimes was when buying things with a credit card—as if my signature on the receipt wouldn't look like my signature on the card and nobody would believe that I'm me. "Do we really have to do this? All I need to feel like a real married lady is one of those Good Seasons salad dressing shakers. They're free when you buy two packets."

"I know you're nervous about this deadline stuff with your parents—"

"I'm also nervous about *this*! Why do we need these dishes? Since when do we throw casual dinner parties?"

"Well, when we want to start throwing casual dinner parties, we'll have them ready to go."

"What do you mean *when*? If! *If* we want to start throwing casual dinner parties, then we can go out and buy casual dinner party dishes. Why do we need them now?"

"Why do you have to second-guess everything? Look at everyone else in this place. This is what people getting married *do*."

"Exactly! I don't want to spend the rest of my life doing what people do!"

"You're the one who wanted this."

"I did not! *This* is not what I wanted! I wanted to get engaged, and that was because we loved each other and we were already building our life together so why not make it official. It was *organic*. Casual dinner party plates are not organic."

"Rachel—"

"No, I mean it. I mean, look around this place," I said, gaining momentum. "It's like by getting married you're fated to walk down this road of fancy blenders and houses in the suburbs and midlife crises and *Men Are from Mars, Women Are from Venus*."

"They're just picking out plates."

"No they're not!" I said. "They're walking around thinking, 'This is what you do when you get married,' thinking that deciding between this set of silverware or that one is a choice that makes them *different*, when it really just proves how exactly the same they all are by buying into the whole system hook, line, and sinker. They're putting themselves on an escalator and telling themselves they're walking. It's *fucked up*."

"You're talking about reification." He nodded. "Consumerism as the opiate of the capitalist masses. Walter Benjamin—"

"Fuck Walter Benjamin!" My boulder was rolling downhill; there was no stopping it now. "I'm talking about *unthinkingness*! The 'oh-this-is-just-what-I'm-supposed-to-do' of registering for casual dinner party plates is the same *unthinking* reason lots of people get married in the first place. Like my parents. Thinking 'this-is-what-I'm-supposed-to-do' was the only thing they ever had in common. You know the story! My mother was—oh, my God!" My eyes went wide and both hands reflexively flew up to cover my open mouth. My boulder had hit flat land. "Oh, my God," I whispered. "She was *twenty-six!* What the hell am I doing?"

"You're freaking out in the middle of Crate and Barrel," Dan said, putting a kiss on my forehead and a leading arm around my shoulder.

The good thing about freaking out in the middle of Crate and Barrel is that there are plenty of couches to collapse onto. Dan led me up the escalator and onto one, then told me he'd be right back. Once he returned, bearing a cone-shaped cup of water, I'd had a chance to calm down a bit.

"Tell me I'm not my mother," I said as he took a seat beside me.

"You're not your mother," he said.

"Tell me we're not doing the same exact thing as my parents."

"We're not doing the same exact thing as your parents."

"How do you know?"

"Because we're having this conversation, for one thing."

"Good point."

"There are a million differences between us and them, but the major one is we like each other."

"You like me?"

He nodded. "A lot."

That made me teary. "Even though I freaked out in the middle of Crate and Barrel?"

"Are you kidding me? I think it's great you freaked out in the middle of Crate and Barrel. I'd be worried if you were into all this stuff."

"You would?"

"Of course! This is the stuff that made me so nervous about getting engaged in the first place. But remember what you told me?"

"What?"

"You said that getting married didn't mean we'd decided all the terms of our life, it meant we'd decided to figure them out together."

"I agree with me," I said.

"Me too."

I felt better, much better, and I told him so. "It's like the rain came down and washed out all the humidity."

"See what I mean?" he said. "Freaking out is good."

He leaned in to put his arm around me and was poked by the metal clipboard, a physical reminder that registering was still the task at hand. Dan said, "We need to think through our strategy."

"I think we should only register for things that are organic— things we either really need or want or know for sure we'll have some use for."

"Sounds good to me."

"It's too bad we can't just register for this couch," I said. "It's comfortable and we need one."

"Why can't we?" Dan asked. The world was now our oyster. If life were a musical, he would've burst into song.

"Because no one is going to buy us a twenty-two-hundred-dollar couch," I said.

"Aha," he said. "But they might buy us twenty-two hundred dollars' worth of other stuff that we can then exchange for a couch."

"Now that kind of thinking is the reason I'm marrying you," I said, grabbing the clipboard.

Twenty-two

A few hours later, we recrossed the park with a new sense of buoyancy and accomplishment. We had conquered the bridal registry world.

"You know what?" Dan said. "I'm gonna make the Silver Palate Lasagna for dinner tonight."

"Wow," I said. "You're really feeling bold." The only other time he'd made this dish, which contained roughly four hundred ingredients, it had taken three hours and two trips to Zabar's for obscure kitchen utensils. "Are you sure you're up for it?"

"Yup. I'll go to Fairway and get the stuff. You go home and dig up the nutmeg grater."

Fairway on a Saturday afternoon. There was bravado.

I entered the apartment to find the answering machine light blinking like a beating pulse. There was, no doubt, a message from either one or both of my parents on it. With our registering battle won, I'd managed to forget all about the deadline passing. And now Dan was at Fairway.

"Fuck," I said, hitting Play.

I had two new messages.

Message one, 11:33 A.M.:

"Rachel, this is your mother. I wanted to let you know that even though neither you nor your father seem to give a damn about treating me with anything *approaching* respect, I have given in to his demands and made his deadline. I have paid for my guests for the amount of the kosher-style all-dairy wedding. It doesn't really matter to anyone else, and having it kosher would—" she gulped, "would just be a reminder that Grandpa wasn't there." She sniffled, then changed her tone. "Just remember," she said, and I could tell her jaw was clenching, "I did this for you, against my better judgment. You got what you wanted, as always. I hope you're satisfied."

I was. It was over.

Message two, 1:17 P.M.:

"Rachel, this is your mother! Pick up if you're there, goddammit! Do you know what your wonderful father is doing now? I'm sure you do, and I'm sure you're gonna stick right behind him as always—you don't give a flying shit! Is it enough that I met his deadline and gave him his lousy fucking check? No! He put it back in my mailbox, *ripped up,* with another one of his asshole typed letters saying I have a week to give him another check for ten less guests, all because I forgot his stupid written agreement to provide the cake! This is *humiliating,* Rachel. This is *indecent!* How much more of this am I supposed to take? You know, I'm tempted to say fuck your father, fuck you, fuck this whole wedding, just like Aunt Thelma says. You don't give a shit about me—"

I hit the stop button. My head was pounding. I should have waited for Dan, but some still-stupid part of me thought I had one reasonable parent. I picked up the phone and dialed.

"Hello?" my father answered, normal as ever.

"Hi, Dad. Listen, I just got home to a real doozie of a message from Joyce. Please tell me that she's somehow gone nuts and you didn't actually return her check?"

"I can't tell you that, Rachel, because it's not true. I did return your mother's check. I also let her know that she now has ten less guests, and that she has two weeks to meet the new deadline." He said all of this calmly, reasonably, as if it were actually reasonable, as if he actually was the reasonable parent he was supposed to be.

"Dad, what are you thinking? Why are you doing this? She gave you the money, she settled the kosher business, why have this drag on and on?"

"Because she did not meet the terms of the deadline," he said, as if this was the obvious course of action. "She was supposed to give me an agreement in writing to provide the cake." He was being Jerry-anal, but this was not funny.

I wanted to say: "You were supposed to be my sane parent! I was supposed to *have* a sane parent," but instead I said, "Do you really expect me to back you on this?"

"Yes," he sounded almost indignant, "I do."

"Well, then, at the very least, why didn't you consult me first?"

"Because I knew you'd try and talk me out of it, and I was determined that"—here he stammered—"I was determined that this was what I was going to do."

"Dad—" I said sharply, my postregistering tires still full.

"Rachel," my father was saying, his air-out-of-tires tone slow and firm—You need to understand this, young lady. "I have let your mother get away with too much for too long. Now I finally have the chance to teach her a lesson—"

"Since when is my wedding about teaching her a lesson?"

"Since I'm the one paying the lion's share," he roared. "You know, you could have taken a page from Gregory and Thomas's book and taken care of this wedding on your own."

"A page from Gregory and Thomas's book?" Now I was really annoyed.

"That's right."

"Yeah. Well, Dad, if you took your blinders off for two seconds, you might be able to see that Thomas's *parents* paid for their whole wedding."

Did I have the go-ahead from Thomas to say this? He had said *someday* they'd have to know. . . .

"What?" my father said. Any misgivings I had about spilling the beans were replaced by a thrill at his shock. "Is that true?"

"How else could they have afforded it? They flew the Florida State Champion synchronized swimmers in from Tampa Bay."

I could tell from the silence that I'd thrown him off his game. "We—we didn't realize that," he stammered.

"Obviously," I said. (Uch! So not Elizabeth Bennet!)

My sarcasm helped him regain his footing. "Well, be that as it may," he said, air-out-of-tires tone back in full force, "ever since that first day at the Kosmos Club, you've been nothing but difficult and unappreciative."

"I've been nothing but *what?*"

"You've been stubborn and uncooperative."

"What?" My temples were throbbing.

"You heard me, Rachel." He was stern and angry—not Spencer Tracy and definitely not Steve Martin. "I am spending *ten* thousand *dollars,* ten *thousand dollars* on your wedding. Your mother, your in-laws—no one is spending more than I am. Do you think that's fair?"

Did I? "I don't know," I said. I was six years old.

"And, despite what you seem to think, I don't just have that kind of money lying around. We have to make sacrifices to give you this wedding. Do you appreciate that at all?"

What kind of sacrifices? I guess I didn't . . .

"Right from the start, you've been making all sorts of demands. You want the Audubon Society. You want the cousins. You want kosher. You want an elaborate dress. You came in with a chip on your shoulder!"

Did I? I had wanted everything he said. But was any of it so wrong? Was it wrong to want a wedding in a place that felt like you? Was it wrong to want your family there? Was it wrong to accommodate your eighty-nine-year-old grandfather? Was it wrong to want a wedding dress? Was this the stuff of chips on shoulders?

Weren't these all things *parents* were supposed to want, too?

I wanted to say: "Why do I have to *fight* you for everything? Why has my whole life been such a *battle?*"

But my father went on. "You know your mother always tries to get away with something, and this time I'm not allowing it. We've got very tight numbers here, Rachel, and we can use the extra guests."

Of course! Phyllis and her guests! I should have known she put him up to this.

"Let me talk to Phyllis," I said, tires replenished. This time, the gloves were coming off.

"She isn't here," he said.

"Well, when she gets back—"

"She's in Florida. With her friend Beverly in Boca Raton."

"Well, fine, then," I said, reaching for a pencil, "what's the number there?"

"Why do you want to talk to Phyllis?"

"To tell her how stupid this plan of hers is."

"Phyllis had nothing to do with this," my father said. Did I detect a note of pride? "She doesn't even know about it. I haven't spoken to her since last night."

"What?"

How could this be possible? The stepmother was supposed to be the wicked one. All this time, had I been fingering the wrong man? Come to think of it, where was Cinderella's father? Why doesn't anyone bother to ask about *him?*

I sat down at the table, elbow bent, hand on aching forehead.

"Dad," I was almost afraid to say the words and tears sprang to my eyes as I did, "do you care about this wedding? I mean, not the guest list or the catering or whatever—but the actual *wedding?* Are you happy that Dan and I are getting married?"

"Well," he stammered, "yes, yes I am."

"Then why are you doing this?" I sniffled as the tears rolled down my cheeks.

"I—I—I'm trying to do what's best, Rachel." His voice was softer and he sighed. But then his tone grew firm. "There are other things I need to consider."

"Right," I said, gulping, wiping away the tears. There always were.

It seems like such a stupid thing, such an obvious point, something you could see from a mile away, from the very beginning—divorced father with new Nordstrom's-loving Long Island interior decorator wife drives a Lexus and doesn't want to spend money on his daughter's wedding because she's not very high on his priority list—of course! It's a cliché really, a stereotype. But stereotypes were bad! They were flat, they were reductive—they weren't *true.* And yet here I was, smacked in the face by a punch I'd told myself couldn't be coming.

He was no better than Joyce. Like everything from duffel bags to college tuition to mono convalescence, my wedding had been, first and foremost, about their ongoing battle with each other.

I wasn't a pawn in their game—you have to actually *see* a pawn to move it. I was Gettysburg, the earth they'd scorch with their battles. But what soldier thinks about the grass? What warrior bothers to reseed?

What's King Solomon to do when neither parent cares about cutting apart the baby? What happens when the baby is supposed to be King Solomon?

I'll tell you what happens, she gets a headache.

I suppose I should come up with some snappy new way to say I felt like I'd been hit by a Mack truck, something emotional and physical and psychologically astute. But the truth is I just felt hurt. Hurt for this and a lifetime of lawyering.

But that would end now. I was too tired, or maybe too old.

"Do whatever you want, Dad," I said. Clearly, he would anyway.

The pain I felt after hanging up was like that of a stubbed toe—you're hopping around the apartment going "ow, ow, ow" and thinking, "It's so stupid that this hurts so much," simultaneously, but it really, truly, *kills*. And you just have to keep hopping until it feels better.

My version of hopping was lying in bed with a cold compress on my head, crying.

What had happened to me? Here I was, this supposed adult, making it in the city you were supposed to be able to make it anywhere after, and I couldn't even handle planning a wedding. All I'd managed to do was stick myself back in the same black hole I thought I'd crawled out of years ago, while giving myself the worst migraine since mono to boot. My parents were the

Mafia—just when I think I'm out they suck me back in. They were the undead Glenn Close popping out of the bathtub.

Why had I ever involved them in this wedding?

Had I needed something from them that I knew they couldn't provide, or had I needed them, once and for all, not to provide it?

This was what I was wondering when Dan returned from Fairway and found me on the bed, looking and feeling like shit.

"Uh-oh," he said, sitting at the edge. "What happened?"

I tried not to cry. I told him my father had returned Joyce's check. I told him he wanted to teach Joyce a lesson once and for all. I told him I tried to protest, but, after all, I was the one who wanted this wedding. I told him my father was happy about this wedding, but he had other things to consider. I told Dan I couldn't fight anymore.

"This is insane," he said. "Our wedding is not his personal battlefield. Look at what it's doing to you!"

"I don't . . ." I was sobby and hiccupy, "I don't . . . know . . . what . . . else . . . to do . . ."

"Well, I do," Dan said. He got up, grabbed the phone, and hit Redial.

"Jerry?" he said a moment later. "This is Dan . . . not too well, actually. I'm hoping there's been some kind of misunderstanding. Rachel tells me that despite the fact that Joyce gave you her check and said the kosher-style was fine, you still want to keep this going. She seems to think you've already taken action on this that she and I are supposed to go along with it, even though you did it without consulting us first."

Throughout this speech, I was stuck on one thought: Had Dan ever before addressed my father as "Jerry"?

There were "umm-humm"s here and there on Dan's end as he

nodded along, shifting his weight from one side to the other, listening.

"Well," Dan said after a moment, lifting his chin to make eye contact with the ceiling. "I can see why it would be frustrating to have Joyce do only two of the three things. But wasn't the cake stuff supposed to be a negotiating point?"

One "umm-hmm," some pacing, and then, "Well, it's really too bad you did that without asking us first. . . . Well, if that was deliberate, you knew it was a risk, then . . . so you knew there was a chance we wouldn't go along with it? Okay, because that's what's happening now. We're not going along with this."

There was silence for a moment. Dan was no longer pacing, he was standing still, looking down, massaging his brow.

"Yes, Jerry, I do realize that you're paying more than the other parties for this wedding, and I do appreciate that fact, and am very grateful for it, as I know Rachel is. But what I don't think you appreciate is that this is our wedding, not the latest round in a fight you're having with Joyce—"

I was amazed at Dan's calm demeanor. He was so man-to-man.

"Well, again," he continued, "I am very appreciative of your monetary contribution, Jerry. I do appreciate that. But I don't appreciate you using our wedding this way. You should take a minute to think about that and decide whether or not you want to change your course of action with Joyce."

Right before my eyes, Clark Kent had turned into Superman. But it wasn't over yet.

"Well," Dan continued in his same strong, firm tone, "I'm sorry to hear you say that, because this can't keep going on. If you insist on pursuing this with Joyce, we can't have you involved in the wedding anymore. Let's just say you have the same number of guests as you would have if Joyce had met your terms, and you send us a check for whatever amount of money you want—given what you expected to be spending, or however you want to do it. Or you can not send anything at all, whatever you want. But from now on, you and Phyllis are out of the planning."

Then he said the magic words: "I'm not going to let you put Rachel through this anymore."

He had slain my dragons! And at the risk of sounding juvenile, at the risk of sounding weak, at the risk of letting my distress turn me into a damsel, I will tell you that never in my life have I felt so truly loved. And if that makes me a princess, I'll wear the crown.

Dan finished up the conversation in the same reasoned tone he'd used throughout. "Well, just let us know your contribution and we'll figure things out from there." He said his good-byes, then came over and joined me on the bed.

"Well," Dan sighed. "I guess that's that."

"You're my hero!" I cried, covering him in kisses.

"Really?" he said, making the flirty face.

"Yes," I said, nodding my sore head. "So, so, yes!"

"But I could've just completely screwed us." He laughed. "What if he doesn't give us a cent?"

"Then we'll go to the park with everyone we like and just get married! Rabbi David will go with the flow. We've got the *tallis*, and they already paid for my dress."

He shrugged, said, "Sounds good to me," then, turning flirty again said, "so I'm really your hero?"

"Yes," I said. "Definitely."

Twenty-three

$\mathcal{D}$an wasn't only my hero; he was Joyce's as well.

Later that evening, as the lasagna baked in the oven, we called to tell her to ignore Jerry's last missive and resend us her check.

"He took it too far," I said, and Dan nodded. "From now on, you're no longer dealing with him."

"Oh, thank you, honey, thank you," she said, the dying patient refusing a sip of water—no, no, you take it. "I tried. I wanted to give you what you wanted, to make this day special for you. But he wouldn't even let me. I tried to tell you, but you wouldn't listen, you never do—but, better late than never. The important thing is that you saw what he was doing to me and put a stop to it."

Fortunately, we hadn't eaten yet; after this monologue, it would have been hard to keep food down.

"Actually, I didn't. Dan did." And actually, the point was what he was doing to *our wedding*.

"Oh! He did! Really? I always knew he was such a great guy. Please, put him on. Let me thank him."

"Bette Davis on the line. Wants to present you with your Oscar."

I handed over the phone and headed for the kitchen to get the stuff to set the table.

"Hey there, Joyce," Dan said, readjusting the dishtowel on his shoulder. "Well, you're very welcome. . . . No, no. . . . Well, thanks. . . . Oh, really? That might be nice . . . yeah, I'll ask her . . . I'm sure it will. . . . You're welcome again—" He looked up at me and asked with his eyebrows if I wanted the phone back. I immediately shook my head no and he said, "All right then, Joyce . . . no, no, I'm sure you will . . . you, too . . . 'bye."

"Your mother couldn't have asked for a better son-in-law," he reported. I shook my head, spare me. "And she hopes the two of you can be close someday."

"Oh, does she?" I folded a napkin and rolled my eyes.

"She's sure the wedding will be beautiful, she's sending the pictures for the place cards, and she wants to know if you want her to hire a videographer."

"You mean, like for a wedding video?"

"Yeah."

I sighed and considered this. "What do you think?"

"I don't care," he said, "as long as it's not obtrusive."

"Well," I said, setting down a fork, "it's all gonna be outside in the daylight, so there's no risk of a big light shining in people's faces." He nodded, considering. "And I'm sure if you tell them you want unobtrusive—no interviewing people or anything— they'll stay in the background."

Dan shrugged. "If we don't even notice them, it might be nice to have later."

"All right," I said, switching to the other side of the table. "I'll call her back at some point and tell her yes, but with the un-obtrusive ground rules."

"Good," Dan said. "Out of curiosity, what do videographers run you?"

I stopped and looked up at him. "At least as much as making a wedding kosher."

"Mmmm." He laughed. "Just what I was thinking."

*   *   *

The next morning, I got a call from Aunt Natalie.

"We have a real problem here," she said, no hellos. It was barely eleven and Dan and I were still in bed, sipping coffee and reading the paper. That week, I'd decided to skip the *Vows* section and head straight for Maureen Dowd. Dan had the rest of the Week in Review. I shot up, worried that word of Dan's action had gotten to her and some further problem with my father had come up—could we be back to not inviting the cousins?

"What's wrong?" I asked, dreading the answer.

"I went to Bloomingdale's first thing this morning to check out your registry," she said. "This is just not going to fly."

I should have known. This was more her type of emergency. "Oh," I said, relieved, sinking back down.

"I am serious about this, Rachel. You've gotta fix this thing before people see it."

I was in Registry ER and she was doing triage.

"What's the matter with it?"

"What's the *matter* with it? Rachel, sweetheart, what is this stuff? Where's the china? Where are the vases? Where are the decorative platters? Nobody wants to buy what you have here."

"It's the stuff we want," I said. "We don't want things that aren't *us*. You get all that stuff, then you're forced to live a life that incorporates it. We want it to be more *organic*—"

"Rachel, sweetheart, I know you're young and a little bohemian, and most of the time I think that's great. But Dan is in *medicine*. There's gonna come a time in your life when you're gonna have to *entertain*. And when that time comes—"

"*If* that time comes, we'll go out and buy the stuff then. That's what I mean by *organic*."

"Fine," she said, clearly not in the mood to fight this kind of battle while there was work to be done. "But, be that as it may, nobody's going to *buy* you the things you have on this list. I mean—comforters, pillows, *bedding?* This isn't *Poland*, Rachel."

"But it's stuff we actually *need*," I said, proving my point by trying to fluff one of our flattened-out down pillows, then settling for folding it over.

"I'm not saying you shouldn't want those things, honey," though that sort of was what she was saying, "I'm saying you shouldn't—no, you *can't*—*register* for them. Binoculars—who wants to buy you that?"

"I appreciate what you're trying to do, but I can't deal with another day of registering. Yesterday was very exhausting—"

"Well, you have to. You keep this list this way, and you'll end up with a bunch of hideous platters from Judaica shops from here to Osh Kosh you can never return. You'll still get something like that from Murray and Florence—you should have seen what they got Lynn, some kind of Native American–themed menorah—just horrible! You know what they're like in Scottsdale, nothing's worth buying if it hasn't got turquoise or a leather fringe. The point is: You don't want people imposing too much of their tastes. You have to give them something to work with."

"Hmmm." Visions of Boca Raton *mezuzahs* fresh off the set of *The Golden Girls* were popping into my mind.

"Listen," she said, East Side Colonel Schwarzkopf mode in full effect, "you fix the list, and then, if you really don't want the gifts, you can bring them back for credit. I'll meet you at Bloomingdale's and we'll go through the department together. Who knows, maybe we'll find some things you like . . ."

Fat chance.

"Meet you there in a hour."

*   *   *

Once at Bloomingdale's, Aunt Natalie and I waded around in a sea of crystal, surrounded by couples holding purple folders. These couples were no cause for alarm. They were older than the ones at Crate and Barrel, and more expensively, though less fashionably, dressed. They looked as if they'd met at Jewish singles events. When they bumped into people they knew who had come in "to complete," they would shriek and say, "I can't believe we're seeing you here! What a coincidence!" and talk about honeymoon hotels on the Amalfi coast or in the south of France and say, "Oh yeah, we've heard of that, friends of ours stayed there last year."

"How 'bout these champagne glasses?" I asked calmly, a mercenary on completely foreign, nothing-to-do-with-me, Eighties New York soil.

"For a girl who wants to be so practical, you sure seem to like Orrefors." Aunt Natalie smiled. "They're fifty dollars apiece, you know."

"You said that was a good price point."

Aunt Natalie nodded. "It is. And they're cute with the polka dots." She giggled.

"Sure," I said, thinking they were hideous.

She added four to our list and we headed for the Nambe.

"So I heard what happened with Dan and your father yesterday," she said, looking for the price tag on the bottom of a vase.

"You did?" I'd been wondering what, if anything, to tell her.

"Phyllis called and told me the news." I raised my eyebrows, bracing myself, but Aunt Natalie kept looking for the price tag. "I think it's great."

"You do?"

"Yeah. You know you probably should have done it this way all along. You know how your father is, how your mother can push all his buttons."

I said, "I know how my father is."

"With so much bad blood between them, best to let each of them stay in their corners, no mixing."

So this was going to be the spin. Dan had called my father with a plan, one that everyone agreed was eminently reasonable. That was what had happened—sort of. Had my father even noticed anything else?

At least it meant he'd probably give us the ten thousand dollars he'd offered all along.

"I think this is nice," Aunt Natalie said, holding the vase forward for my inspection. "It's one hundred twenty dollars."

"It's great," I said, barely glancing.

Noting the SKU, she said, "And did you hear their news?"

"What news?"

"Your father and Phyllis are buying a condo in Boca."

"They're *what?*"

"Buying a condo in Boca Raton. Isn't it great? Now we can all go down and visit. It's in a full-service building, right on the beach with views of the ocean. Phyllis is disappointed they couldn't afford a higher floor, but the way the stock market's taking off, who knows, in a few years . . ."

Her words swirled around me in a Bloomingdale's haze. Was *this* the sacrifice my father had mentioned? A lower floor for their beachfront-condo second home in Boca?

I shook my head, which, for once, wasn't pounding.

Aunt Natalie said, "What about Costa Boda?"

And I said, "Lead the way."

Wedding Timeline:

Two to Four Months Ahead

- Discuss details of menu with caterer
- Mail invitations
- Plan rehearsal dinner

Twenty-four

A little more than eight weeks before the wedding, with checks in hand from both my parents (ten thousand exactly from my father, deadline amount exactly from my mother), it seemed everything was on track. I called the caterer to double-check and found that, for a kosher-style dairy wedding of 160 people, we were safe.

"Just out of curiosity," I said. "What if we do it with kosher meat?"

"Hmmm," I could hear her punching numbers. "That's an extra fourteen hundred, minimum."

I held the phone to my chin and called out to Dan, who was preparing to leave for the library. For the past few weeks, he'd been in near-seclusion, studying for intensive end-of-second-year exams. "Fourteen hundred dollars for pigs in blankets."

He looked up from his backpack and said, "I don't like them that much anyway."

He left, and I returned to the phone. "Kosher-style dairy it is."

We settled on tablecloths (just plain white, like restaurant cloths), wooden chairs (included in the price she'd quoted), and buffet instead of seated dinner.

As I wound up for good-bye, Deena gasped. "Wait a minute!" she said. "You haven't picked a menu!"

She was right. I leafed through some papers, then scanned the choices she'd faxed months ago, which were, thanks to my wedding file, still on hand. They all looked good (and sort of the same) to me, so I did the thing I do when deciding between entrees at a restaurant.

"If you were me," I said, pretending Deena was my waiter, "what would you go with?"

"The Chilean Sea Bass," she said without hesitation. "We'll do an orzo and wild rice with haricots verts and a mesclun salad and a pasta primavera in cream sauce for people who don't like fish. Then for dessert we'll have wedding cake and assorted mini-pastries, served at the table. It's the best menu, I think."

"Fine," I said. "We'll take it."

Almost a second after I hung up with Deena, the phone rang again. Muttering something about knowing it had all been too easy, I picked up the phone again. But it wasn't Deena, it was Naomi.

"Hey, bride," she said. "What's up?"

"Not much," I said. "Assorted wedding chores. I just got off the phone with the caterer and am now making up a packet of invitations for my mother-in-law-to-be to send out to her guests."

"Wouldn't it be easier for her to just send you their addresses?"

"Yes, it would. But then I would be addressing them, along with all the other invitations, on my aunt Annie's laser printer. And my mother-in-law feels that is 'too impersonal' for her guests."

"You've got to be kidding me."

"Nope."

"That's ridiculous."

"At this point, Nome, words cannot describe how little I care."

"Very Zen of you."

"Perhaps."

"Well, I assume you've heard the news, right?" The excitement in Naomi's tone meant this had to be a goodie.

"Heard what news?" I couldn't imagine what she meant.

"You haven't seen the tabloids?"

"Seen the tabloids about what?"

"About Lisa Stevenson!"

"Will's Lisa?" What would she be doing in the tabloids?

"Well, if Page Six is right, I don't think you can call her *Will's* Lisa anymore. Apparently, Lisa Stevenson has run off with her costar . . ."

"Run off with Sean O'Malley? To where?"

"Well, to nowhere, really. They're still in Los Angeles. No one actually runs off anywhere when they run off with someone anymore. It's just an expression now."

With or without any actual running, I wasn't buying it. "Will just moved out there."

"I know," she said. "Did they give up their lease?"

"Yeah," I said.

"Mmm," she said. "Sucks for Will. The market's really tight."

"But Sean O'Malley is like a million years old. My *mom* had a crush on him."

"I know," said Naomi. "So did mine. Can you believe it? But, you know, when you think about it, Sean O'Malley does kinda look like an older version of Will . . ."

"Yeah, a *much* older version." We had taken a turn toward some very un-Zen fun. "I always pegged Lisa for a Daddy's-girl type, but I never thought she'd be so *literal* . . ."

"Well, honey, she is literal now. You know what else I was thinking? Remember how she gave Trevor that book?"

Trevor Pasternak had been a particularly crush-worthy member of the Barnard theater department faculty. Lisa had been in his acting class and had given him an end-of-semester present.

"Yes!" I shrieked. "It was Proust—*Proust,* for God's sake!"

"Does that not shed light?"

Hmmm . . . maybe it did. Lisa and Will had always seemed not, for lack of a better word, *normal* . . . there were those weird facial angles and the whole diorama thing. Maybe Naomi was right. If so, that meant someone I knew was responsible for a celebrity break-up. How bizarre and oddly thrilling—a front-row seat to a sideshow event!

But there was no way she was right.

"What about Mara Austin?" I asked.

"Supposedly, she's back in rehab. The cover of the *Enquirer* has the most unflattering picture of her."

"Wait a minute," I said, fun and games now over. "Do you *honestly* think this is true? How do you know it isn't just a way to get free publicity for their movie?"

"Possible," Naomi said. "But there's an actual quote from Lisa, saying how sorry she is that Mara got hurt. It also says she's playing Mary Ann in the *Gilligan's Island* movie. Did you know that?"

I was trying to process this information—that the words Will, Lisa, Sean O'Malley, and Mara Austin could be strung together in sentences with the words *National Enquirer*—not just *with,* but *in;* that instead of being Tim Robbins to Lisa's Susan Sarandon, in the eyes of the checkout-line public, Will would now be the nameless dumped boyfriend. And the fact that was hardest to grasp: that this was *real*, that Will had *really* moved out there, and, despite any verbal Rumpelstiltskinning, was probably terribly hurt. But I was stuck on one thing.

"Lisa's gonna play Mary Ann in the *Gilligan's Island* movie?"

The next week, invitations addressed and in the mail (and one person fewer on the guest list), we found ourselves back down at the Blue and Gold. It was one of those early spring nights where you find yourself tempted to not wear a jacket.

"Well, at least you're taking a break from exams," I said to a shrugging Dan as we entered.

It was a Tuesday and the place was dead. Will slumped in the corner of a booth, alternating shots of Maker's Mark with glasses of beer from his own personal pitcher. The *Globe*, the *Star*, and the *Enquirer* were sprawled across the table in front of him, each with its own version of a "Sean O'Malley Dumps Mara Austin For Young Starlet" headline and its own blurry "caught on film" shot of Lisa and the washed-up movie star who could have been her father in front of a black Lexus, kissing. Forget Rumpelstiltskin, Will was barely verbal. I'd never seen him look so small.

"Are you sure you want to be looking at those?" Dan asked as Connor made room for us on his side of the booth.

"They're actually pretty amusing," Will said.

"The *Star* calls Lisa 'the next Gwyneth Paltrow,'" Connor said.

I made a face. "I don't think so."

"I'll drink to that," Will said, downing a shot.

Connor said, "He'll drink to anything."

"Yes, I will." Will nodded. "And hey, hey, hey," he said,

looking at Dan, "now I don't have to fly in for your bachelor party."

"True," Dan agreed. "Or, as I prefer to see it, my exams-are-over party."

"I'll drink to that," Will slurred.

"And," I offered, "now you don't have to live in Los Angeles."

"That's right," Will said. "'Sgood to be back in New York. It's Sodom and Gomorrah out there. Trust me, I've seen it firsthand. Dance with the devil, the devil don't change—devil changes *you*."

So L.A. was the culprit. I found myself smiling at this, thinking (to my surprise) that it was nice to see a flash of Will's old self.

Here I was, sitting with Dan and the very same person who a year ago had sat at a similar bar trying to talk Dan out of our engagement. Six months ago, part of me probably would have been sitting there thinking, "Serves Will right for all his bullshit." But no I-told-you-so flame burned inside me. There was nothing to dredge, no swamp in my gut. It was funny how far away it all seemed. I poured myself a beer from the pitcher.

Twenty-five

About a month before the wedding, exams over, response cards rolling in, we made the final preparations for our honeymoon. Dan bought the round-the-world tickets, arranged for a summer intern from Harvard Business School to sublet our apartment (this alone covered a third of our trip expenses), and made our one-and-only hotel reservation for the first week, at a sit-on-the-beach-and-do-nothing place in Bali.

We went to EMS to buy backpacks.

"Everything here's so *outdoorsy*," I said. "I'm indoorsy. You realize that, right?"

"I think we should get this too," Dan said. He held a gray, minibicycle-pump–looking object up in his hand.

I said, "What is that?"

He said, "It's a water purifier."

I said, "What's in your other hand?"

He said, "Mosquito netting."

"Mosquito netting?"

He shook his head, Don't worry. "Just a precaution."

I said, "Where are we going again?"

We went to a travel doctor to get shots.

She said, "What an adventurous way to spend a honeymoon!"

Dan said, "I think the six weeks in India will be the high-light."

I stared at the thick wad of prescriptions she'd written us.

As we left her East Seventies townhouse office, I said, "Where are we going again?"

Later that week, I sat at my computer, going over the edits on my most recent manuscript with Laura on the phone.

"I would maybe add Jake to the scene where we first hear about the down-on-her-luck cousin," she was saying. "It sort of sets up the idea of her trying to steal him from Chloe, without really setting it up."

"Okay," I said. "Should be easy enough to stick him in there."

"And then I'd say, more descriptions of the dresses at the junior prom—"

"Gotcha."

"And, other than that—"

"Just wait for my Pulitzer?"

She gave a little laugh, but it was more like an exhalation.

"Charlie," I said, "is something wrong?"

"You mean other than the utter silliness that constitutes my professional life?"

"Other than that."

She sighed. "You remember Bryce, right?"

"Film school guy you weren't sure you had chemistry with?"

"Exactly," she said. "Well, the verdict is in. Apparently, he has chemistry with someone else. She works in advertising. Part of me thinks he just wants to direct commercials."

"You're so better off without him."

"Yeah, but it's still kind of a bummer. Even when you're not that into 'them, you don't want them to be into someone else."

"That's true," I nodded.

"Anyway," she said, sighing the thought away. "Forget my sad forays into the dating world. I also have some potentially good news."

"Tell me, tell me."

"We-ell," she said. I could hear the squeak of her chair as she swiveled. "I got a call from someone at Scholastic. They're looking for someone to edit children's books."

"That's great," I said, leaning forward. "Full-time?"

"Yup. A *real* job. In an office. Working on *educational* books."

"Charlie, that's great!" I said. "I'll miss you, but it's great. It's exactly the kind of thing you've been wanting to do!"

"I can't even think about it," she said. "We have to talk about something else. I want to hear about the wedding! What's going on? It's coming up so soon!"

"There's not much to tell. Tonight I have—wait a minute," I said, sitting back. "What are you doing tonight?"

"Stir-fry for one and a video. Why?"

It was time to break the work-friend barrier.

"Wanna come to my Girls' Night Out?"

"I don't know . . ."

"Please, Charlie?" I was looking forward to a wedding-related event that was plain, uncomplicated fun. "I'd so love for you to be there . . ."

Laura let out a small groan. "But everyone will know everyone—"

"Nuh-uh," I said. "My bridesmaids all know each other from college, but only two of them will be there. My aunt Annie's coming in from Jersey. And, hey, wait—you know Thomas! Now you can meet in the flesh!"

In the second's silence, I could tell her mind was ripe for changing. "Are you sure no one'll mind?"

"Positive," I nodded. "Besides, I think a Girls' Night Out is just what you need."

"You've got me there," she said, warming.

"C'mon," I said. "It'll be fun. I promise."

Twenty-six

My Girls' Night Out dinner took place at Tootsie Tang's, the East Village Chinese restaurant known for its drag queen waitresses. The location had been Thomas's idea, and it was perfect—and not just because Dan took considerably less pleasure in drag queens than I did; serious camp tended to fall under the same not-as-much-fun-with-him umbrella as quoting Woody Allen movies. When Tootsie Tang's first opened, it was the ultimate spot for downtown tongue-in-cheek hipness, but in the five years since, it had become a parody of itself. In the beginning, Tootsie Tang's was the best kitschy place for a New Yorker to have her Girls' Night Out. In the years since, it had become the best kitschy place for a non–New Yorker—especially a non–New Yorker of the Bridge and Tunnel persuasion—to have a Girls' Night Out. What was once *Priscilla, Queen of the Desert* was now *To Wong Foo, Thanks for Everything, Julie Newmar*—which meant it was now the perfect place for a New Yorker to have an *ironic* Girls' Night Out.

Sure enough, the place was packed with other girls, all of

them clustered in gaggles, many with big hair, some (one per gaggle) wearing plastic tiaras.

They wouldn't seat us until our full party had arrived, so Laura, Aunt Annie, Thomas, and I waited for Andrea and the chronically late Naomi in the crowded red-and-gold bar area (Erin, the missing bridesmaid, was at Cornell vet school and couldn't make it in from Ithaca, and I'd made the editorial decision that Tootsie Tang's was not Aunt Natalie's scene).

Laura said, "I think your first drink should be on *Turnerville*, Charlie," and ordered us both vodka ginger ales. Yelling over the noise, I introduced her to Annie, explaining why we called each other Charlie.

"You know," Annie yelled back, "when you think about it, your job's really strange."

"I know," Laura and I yelled in unison, then looked at each other, laughed, and clinked drinks.

"So tonight's Dan's bachelor party, too?" Annie continued. I nodded, and she said, "Uh-oh."

"No," I said. "It's rated PG. We decided anything X-rated would degrade the sanctity of the marital event. They're going to Peter Luger's, then a Russian nightclub in Brighton Beach."

"Anyone but Dan," she said, as a cheer erupted from a nearby group of bachelorettes, "and I'd be thinkin', 'Yeah, right. And I have a bridge to sell you.'"

Soon enough, Naomi and Andrea arrived together.

"Sorry we're late," Andrea said, kissing my cheek.

"Andrea's looking to buy a co-op, and I have an exclusive in my building!" Naomi's voice had no trouble carrying.

"My parents are hooking me up with a down payment," Andrea explained.

"Great," I shouted. "You guys know Thomas and my aunt

Annie, and this is my friend Laura from work. This is Naomi and Andrea—two of my bridesmaids—we were all roommates at Barnard."

Once the "hi's" and "nice to meet you's" were yelled all around, Naomi said, "Before I forget, I have to give you these." She reached into her fake zebra fur purse and pulled out two penis-shaped ring pops, one red and one yellow. "Piña colada and strawberry," she explained. "One for each hand."

"Put 'em on!" said Andrea.

"If I must . . ." I said, putting one on each middle finger.

"They have little ridges and everything," Thomas said, impressed.

"For the record," I said, "I much prefer these to a tiara."

Annie said, "I hope they don't interfere with the sanctity of the marital event."

"Nah." I sucked each one, then raised my arms in triumph. Everyone cheered. Annie volunteered to push her way to the hostess and see about our table and Thomas said he'd join her.

"Speaking of penis," said Naomi as conspiratorially as possible at the necessary decibel level, "you'll never guess who I saw last night, Rachel."

"Who?" I asked.

"Max Ulrich!"

"Max Ulrich," I said, surprised by the sourness the name elicited. I hadn't seen or thought of him in almost six years.

"Who's Max Ulrich?" Laura asked.

"Boyfriend before Dan," Andrea explained. Laura nodded.

"He was not my boyfriend."

"Fine." Naomi rolled her eyes. "The guy she was with for three months second semester junior year. An actor," she added. Laura nodded again.

"An asshole," I said.

"That too," said Andrea.

"I know all about assholes," Laura said.

"Laura just broke up with a guy who wasn't good enough for her anyway," I explained.

Andrea said, "Most of them aren't."

"Can you believe I saw Max Ulrich?" Naomi asked, excited.

"No," I said, not. "Where was he? Didn't he move back to Minneapolis after graduation? I thought he'd at least done me the favor of crawling under a rock and dying."

"He did. But he came back a couple years ago. He's doing really well. He's in the second company of Gotham Improv Brigade. That's how I saw him—a friend of mine just joined so I went to see the show. He lives in Williamsburg."

"Another good reason to avoid Williamsburg," I said, sipping.

"Actually," Andrea said, a hint of mischief in her voice, "Williamsburg might not be your problem."

"What do you mean?" I asked.

"Well, for one thing," Andrea said, "he just did a *Law and Order*."

"Yeah," nodded Naomi. "And not just a walk-on as a cop or a bailiff. He's an actual defendant. A publisher who killed his writer-slash-mistress."

"Lemme guess," I said. "He gets off."

"Of course," said Naomi.

"Figures."

"That's exactly what I said!" Andrea laughed.

"Oh, well," I said. "There are worse places to see an ex than on TV standing trial for murder with the rabbi from *Crimes and Misdemeanors* giving him the evil eye."

Naomi's eyes brightened and I prepared for a *Crimes and Mis-*

demeanors quote. But instead, she said, "Actually, you might be seeing him before that . . ."

It took a second to register. "You didn't tell him about tonight?"

"Well—"

"You didn't *invite* him—"

"No." She shook her head. "I just told him if he wanted to stop by—"

So much for uncomplicated fun. "Tell me you're kidding."

Andrea said, "I told you she wouldn't think it was funny."

"Oh, relax," Naomi said. "He won't come. He has a show."

I was about to ask her how Max Ulrich showing up at my Girls' Night Out was funny—funny for whom? and why?—but, just as my mouth began to move, Aunt Annie came back.

"Table's ready," she said. Behind her, Thomas waved from the hostess stand.

As we made our way out of the crowded, cheer-filled bar, I leaned in to Laura and said, "Why would she do that?"

"I don't know her," she said. "Maybe she thought it went with those," pointing to my penis-ringed fingers.

Max Ulrich was not my idea of a Girls' Night Out accessory, but I chalked it up to Naomi's strange sense of sexual humor and decided to let it drop. By the time I took my seat, I was ready for the fun to begin.

A waitress waved her boa in Thomas's face. "What's a Girls' Night Out without drag queens?" he said.

"I thought this party was supposed to be for *me*."

"Oh, come on," he pouted, jokingly. "The rest of you have liquor." I explained that Thomas was a recovering recovering alcoholic—off both drinking and AA meetings.

And have liquor we did; by the time the fortune cookies

came, everyone but Thomas and Annie (who had to drive home to Jersey) was pretty hammered.

"Now," Andrea said, passing an envelope across the table to me, "even though you wouldn't let us throw you a shower, we still got you a gift. It's from Erin too."

I looked at her and Naomi as I opened it. "You guys so did not have to do this."

"Shut up with that already," Naomi said.

I looked at the certificate inside, which entitled the bearer, one Rachel Silverstein, to a Mango Sugar Body Buffing at a day spa called Oasis. "Thank you, guys," I said, leaning over to kiss them.

"The spa is in Washington," Andrea explained. "According to *Vogue*, it's the best in town. We figured you could do it the day before the wedding."

"That's so nice of you," I said. "Fun!"

I thought this was a sign that our night was winding down, but a moment later, our waitress appeared with a tray full of shot glasses and began lining them up one by one in front of me.

"Somebody better brace herself," the waitress said, batting glitter-heavy false eyelashes.

"Oh, no," I said in the faux-grumble the situation warranted. "What is this?"

"This," said the waitress, waving her elaborately manicured hand, "is a Tootsie Tang's tradition. Now's the time for you to say sayonara to all the men you've loved before."

"One shot for every ex-boyfriend," said Naomi.

"I didn't *have* any other real boyfriends—"

"No way, honey," said Andrea. "Spare us that shit."

"You mean you don't buy Rachel's little way of maintaining emotional distance any more than I do?" Thomas teased.

I gave him a penis-ringed finger, which he leaned in and licked. "Mmmm," he said. "Strawberry."

"Forget the semantics," said Naomi. "One shot for every guy you've slept with. In order. And with details."

Everyone cheered. Aunt Annie laughed and said, "Now comes the juicy part!"

"Oh, god." This time the grumble was real. "I should have known I was in for something like this the minute you brought up Max Ulrich."

"Drinky-drinky," Naomi said.

"Fine," I said. "But before I do, you have to promise me he's not showing up."

"Rachel," she said. "Of course he's not showing up. I mean, I told him, but there's no way."

I knew she was right—there was no way Max Ulrich would come to my Girls' Night Out. He had nerve, but not that much—so again I pushed aside my annoyance and considered the task at hand. In front of me was a sea of kamikaze shots—at least fifteen of them.

"Well, far be it from me to mess with tradition," I said, batting my eyes at the waitress. There were cheers from the table, and the waitress departed.

"Okay, first of all," I said, raising my penis-ringed fingers, "I want it known that I do not need this many shots. I am not even in double digits." Awareness of this stat was part of what propelled me to say "enough's enough, time to make something happen with the love of my life Dan Gershon" at the beginning of our senior year. "I," I said, laying a hand over my heart dramatically, "am a *lady*."

"Stop qualifyin'," Thomas said. "Start drinkin'."

"Is there a form to this or—"

"Say their name, do the shot, then give us the details," Naomi ordered.

"I don't remember all the details—"

"Not about the sex," Andrea said. "About the guy."

"Okay," I said, warming to the idea. I lifted the first shot glass, said "David Gottlieb," and downed it. I looked at Andrea. "What can I say about David Gottlieb?" I asked, sucking the piña colada ring. She knew him from the Jewish Geography world of summer camp.

"How old were you?" Laura asked.

"Seventeen. He was my boyfriend senior year of high school."

Annie said, "Wow. You were older than me."

Laura said, "I thought you didn't have any boyfriends in high school."

"I didn't really. He wasn't in high school. He was a freshman at Cornell. He'd been in the class a year ahead of mine. We didn't start going out 'til he graduated, so it was a long-distance relationship. That's how people put it—'You're having a *long-distance relationship*'—like there was serious drama and danger involved in the undertaking. To me it was perfect—no boyfriend hanging around every day, plus the untold glamour of dating someone in college. But it was not—as they say—all that."

"What about the sex?" asked Naomi.

Thomas said, "Inquiring minds want to know . . ."

I rolled my eyes. "Aye, there's the rub. We only did it once and I had to mount this whole campaign to convince him."

"Why?" asked Thomas. "Was he gay?"

"No, unfortunately—that at least would have added some spice. He was just too much of a nice Jewish boy. Neither of us had done it—listen to me with the 'done it,' I can't even talk about it without sounding like I'm in high school! The thing was, he had this whole theory that you should have sex with someone only if you're either totally in love or totally not in love with them. And since we were somewhere in between, he wouldn't do it with me."

"Whoa," said Laura. "Mature for a college freshman."

I shrugged. "He was prelaw. Since birth."

"So how'd you convince him?"

"Well, for a while we were doing everything but—*everything but*, I love this!"

"Remember *everything but*?" Andrea said to everyone and no one.

"Suck that lolly!" Thomas said, so I did.

"On with the story!" Naomi demanded.

"Okay," I continued. "Well, I'd made up my mind that I really didn't want to be a virgin anymore, so I kept trying to convince him that it was fine, we should just go ahead and do it. But he wouldn't budge. Finally, at the end of his winter break, I told him I didn't see any future for us so there was no point in keeping up *a long-distance relationship*. Once we were breaking up anyway, he said he didn't see the harm. So we drove fifteen minutes to 7-Eleven to get condoms, and did it in about ten minutes in the backseat of his Volvo station wagon. All in all, about half an hour later, he dropped the no-longer-a-virgin me off at my house and I wished him a good semester. The end." Everyone laughed.

Thomas said, "You lost your *virginity* in a *Volvo*?"

I nodded, pained. "Station wagon." There were shrieks. I shut my eyes. "It used to be his mother's!" There was laughter all around. "The whole thing was absurd. But that's the risk you run when you pick an eighteen-year-old *mensch* to deflower you."

"Next!" Naomi demanded.

I raised another shot, said "Andy Hess," made a face as much for the alcohol as the memory, and drank.

"Andy Hess. Made up for lost time in the passion department. Very Heathcliff and Catherine. Sex, sex, sex and drama, drama, drama. The pendulum swung from good boy to bad boy, but ultimately did not stray from nice Jewish boy. Hmmm," I said, tapping my index fingers together. "Never thought of it quite that way. You know this little exercise," I said, pointing to the shots, "is really giving me a whole new perspective."

"Back to Andy Hess," Naomi said, fist on the table. "Too vague."

"Yeah," said Thomas, pounding his fist as well.

"It's true," Annie said. "I don't have a clear picture."

"Ahright, ahright, ahright. Andy Hess. Soccer player—a good one, too. He had all these colleges recruiting him. We spent the better part of the last semester of high school screwing our brains out in his parents' den after repeated screenings of *9 1/2 Weeks* and *Dangerous Liaisons*. You know, everyone makes this whole big deal about teenagers and movies and copycat violence—what about the copycat sex? Huh?"

"I'd like to state for the record," said Thomas, "that this is only after two shots."

"I had a head start with all the wine at dinner. And my vodka and ginger ale."

"Even better."

"How'd it end?" asked Laura.

"Uggh," I said. "Badly. Pregnancy scare and another girl. Bad behavior left, right, and center. Drama, drama, drama." I sighed, and shrugged. "We were young. Now we're a version of friends that proves how truly malleable the term is."

"Next shot!" Andrea called out.

"Yes, indeed." I lifted a glass. "I don't even know who's next."

"I do," said Andrea. "Eric Lorch."

"Oh, that doesn't count!"

"How can that not count? You slept with him."

"Yeah, but only once and not on purpose. And even then, I'm not sure there was actual sex. He claimed there was," I explained to the others, "but it was all really blurry—I'd had too many of these."

"It counts," said Naomi.

"Fine," I said, and drank. "Eric Lorch. From him I learned not to drink so much—a lesson that I've managed to unlearn this evening."

There were shouts of "hear, hear."

"Next one," I said, raising a glass. "Where are we now chronologically? Sophomore year?"

"You hooked up with other guys freshman year," Andrea said.

"Yes, but I did not have sex with them."

"Fair enough."

"Okay, so sophomore year. There was that guy Alex from my Politics and Mass Media class—what was his last name? Something WASPy with a G . . ."

"Not Jewish?" asked Annie.

"No," I said. "We're firmly in the *trayf* section now. But he was circumcised."

"Well," she said, "that's something."

There were nods all around, but I was distracted.

"What was his last name? We hooked up all first semester. I really should remember . . . I'm starting to feel pathetic—he's only the fourth guy. Really only the third, in my opinion."

"Forget it," Naomi said. "Just do the shot."

"But I can see his face . . . What the hell was it? G-r, g-r,

Grant, Granville! Alex Granville," I said, triumphant, and downed the shot. "Not much more to say."

"On to the next one."

"Okay, next one, next one. Oh, oh, oh, Jesse Malden," I said with four shots' worth of sloppy melancholy. I raised the glass and downed my fifth. "Jesse Malden. Summer camp oldie but goodie. He was a younger man." There were yelps from around the table. "Yes, yes. And he was cute. A crunchy little hacky-sacky hippie guy. Total summer fling. Tasty little morsel. Uncomplicated. *Loved* him. Fond, fond memories. But then," I sighed, "I ruined it."

"How?" asked Laura.

"It's like Paul Simon, Charlie." I started singing. "*Kodachro-woa-woam.*"

"What is she talking about?"

"I think that's supposed to be singing," said Thomas.

I put a little shake in it, waving my penis fingers. I stopped singing, remembering something that seemed important. "You know, Paul Simon lives in my neighborhood. I saw him walking around with his kid."

"I wanna hear about the ex-boyfriend," Laura said.

"He wasn't my boyfriend, Charlie! He was a *summer fling!*"

"I don't really understand the difference," Annie said.

"There is none," said Naomi.

"Not now. But there was one at the time," I insisted, the drunken lawyer.

"Fine," Laura said. "He wasn't your boyfriend. I just wanna hear what happened to sour you on him."

"Okay," I said. "Two years ago, Dan and I drove down the Pacific Coast Highway and we stopped in Santa Cruz."

"He's not Unabomber Guy?" Thomas asked.

"Yes, yes," I said, bringing my forehead to the table with a bit too much force. "My tasty morsel turned into the yucky Una-bomber!"

"Not literally," Naomi explained.

"No, not literally," I said, lifting. "Just grooming-wise. The Unabomber had a lot more ambition."

Aunt Annie was cracking up.

"I want to hear the story," Laura said. "So you and Dan were in Santa Cruz."

"Right. We were in Santa Cruz and I'd heard Jesse Malden lived in the mountains near there. I thought it would be fun to see him all these years later and Dan said why not, we had nothing better to do anyway. So I called information and, sure enough, Jesse Malden was listed and at home when I called, sitting on his couch doing bong hits and grieving over Jerry Garcia or something. So we set up a dinner with him. So we're at the total bean sprout Birkenstock restaurant he picked and he shows up, completely stoned—which, who cares—but with an over-grown, skanky, crumb-filled beard—which, *yuck*. He could've been the Unabomber."

"Hence the name Unabomber Guy," said Thomas.

"Right," I said. "It was like he'd just come out of hibernation or something. It was gross. And then he spent the whole dinner talking about how the problem with our society is that women expect men to do women's work. He was this yucky dirty hippie hostile sexist pig. I mean, if you're gonna have a skanky beard and smoke a lot of pot, you should at least be peaceful and mellow. Dan was like, 'You *liked* that guy.' He thought it was really funny. And I was like, 'It was a *summer fling* and he did *not* have that beard.' Then I had to say things like, 'I swear, that was not *my* Jesse Malden!' all the way to San Simeon. Oh, man," I said, sighing. "It's depressing."

Naomi said, "On to number six!"

"Number six. You know who number six is, Nome. Patrick Hamilton," I said. The shot went down and an alcohol/sesame-chicken–flavored burp came up. "Patrick Hamilton. First semester junior year. We were friends. Ran in the same posse. He'd been on my case since, I don't know, sophomore year? He'd say things like, 'Oh, Rachel, you dance so sexy,' and I'd say, 'Does that mean you're breaking up with your girlfriend?'" I threw my head back and laughed and the head—was it really mine?—rolled back onto my shoulder. "He was cute, in a WASPy tennis-player way. Tennis-player body. Tennis-player legs."

"He *was* cute," said Naomi.

"I know it. That's why junior year, when he didn't have a girl-friend, he finally wore me down."

"And then what happened?" Annie asked.

"I don't know," I said, suddenly blue.

"Do you think he was gay?" Thomas asked.

"Noooo. Why do you have to make everyone closeted?"

Thomas shrugged. "Just checking."

"Well, Patrick Hamilton was not gay. He was just pretty. And clean. He was from *Bos*ton."

"Okay. So then what happened?"

"I don't know what happened." This seemed really, urgently, frustrating. Andrea had been in the aforementioned crowd, so I turned to her and said, "Andi, you remember."

"I remember you being really stubborn about it just being sex between friends."

"I was, I was, that's true. And that's 'cause it was. Patrick didn't really wanna be my boyfriend. Nah. He wanted to have sex, and we had sex. A few times. All very nice. But then we kept getting into these *spats* about *every*thing, and then he went to Ireland to study Joyce. He was really pretentious about *Finnegan's Wake*. But he sat in the emergency room with me for four hours one time when I broke my toe even though we were in a fight." I sighed. "That was nice." I could have cried. I'm sure I was slurring. "I like Patrick. Of all of these boys," I said, waving a penis ring at the empty shot glasses, "Patrick is my favorite. He wins the prize. Is there a prize? 'Cause if there is, he wins it."

Thomas said, "Next!"

"I don't wanna do next. I already thought about him enough for one night."

"Max Ulrich," Naomi sing-songed. I narrowed my eyes at her.

"Oh, goody," said Laura. "This is the one I've been waiting to hear."

"Oh, yeah?" Annie asked.

"You missed it before," Laura told her. "He's gonna be on *Law and Order*."

"As a criminal," I said. "Perfect casting."

"*Law and Order*, huh?" Aunt Annie said. "That's pretty good."

"Let's hear it," Laura said. "I've been waiting all night for an ex to hate. Misery loves company."

"Fair enough," I said, downing shot number seven. "Max Ulrich. Actor. Theatre type, and I mean with an *r-e*. Looked like Hugh Grant. Same untrustworthy hair."

"That is totally true," Andrea said.

Thomas said, "You never liked Hugh Grant. Not even in *Four Weddings and a Funeral*."

I nodded sagely.

"He still looks good," Naomi said. "Max, that is."

"Thanks," I said. "Just what I wanted to hear."

"I wanna hear the story!" Laura said.

"It's not that interesting," I said. "Basically, in a nutshell, for a few months he was the most over-the-top charming guy in the world, then he started acting confusing and weird and mind-gamey, then I listened to his answering machine messages and found out he'd been sleeping with this icky girl he was in a play with and I told him I never ever wanted to see him ever again."

"You're leaving out so much stuff, Rachel," Andrea admonished. "You have to tell about the valentine."

"I'm too drunk," I said. "I don't want to get maudlin."

"We want the gory details," Thomas said.

"Fine," I said, sighing. "We had this great flirtation involving prank phone calls—not worth getting into. Suffice it to say, when we finally did hook up, there'd been a lot of buildup, which I thought was *soooo* fun at the time. But in hindsight it was obvious he was just a total game-player. One night, we were studying in the library and he passed me a note that said 'It's late. If you want you can stay over.' And I wrote back 'Are you asking me— underline—to stay over? For what, a slumber party?' And he wrote back, 'You don't let me get away with my usual shit.' The next day I came home from class and found an envelope taped to my door, with this note he had gotten *professionally calligraphied* requesting the honor of my presence at a slumber party for two."

"Cute," said Laura.

"Yeah, too cute. But it worked, of course. I stayed over. We had a great time together for a couple of months, and then Valentine's Day rolled around."

"I'm sorry," said Laura, "but has anyone anywhere ever actually *enjoyed* Valentine's Day?"

"Exactly," I said, lifting a finger then flopping it down. "And *that's* why we decided we didn't want to do some big romantic thing. So we went to a cheap Sixth Street Indian dinner and I gave him some kind of joke present—I don't even remember what it was. Then he was *so mean* to me for the rest of the night. He made me so mad. Finally I was like, 'What's your problem?' and he accused me of secretly trying to get him to be my boyfriend, and I told him I didn't want him to be my boyfriend, I just wanted him to be nice and fun and not a big jerk and if that was too much for him to handle, we should just stop doing whatever it was we were doing. But no, no, no, no, no—he didn't want that. So I told him he had the rest of the weekend to make it up to me or forget it—over."

"Good for you, Raych," Aunt Annie said.

"Thank you. Well, the next day, there was a knock on my door." I simulated this knock on the table. "I answered it but there was no one there—just a big envelope."

"He was really into envelopes and your door," said Laura.

"Yes," I said, eyes narrowing as if envelopes and my door were in and of themselves nefarious, "he was, wasn't he? Well, inside was this twenty-page illustrated handmade comic book that told the story of him being an asshole on Valentine's Day and then going around to all the characters from *90210* and asking each one what he should do to make it up to me."

"This was in the heyday of her *90210* column," Andrea explained.

"Wow," said Annie. "Pretty elaborate."

"Yeah," I said. "He'd stayed up all night doing it. And it was really good. He got the characters just right in what they said and everything. The last person he asked was Kelly—my favorite— and she told him to just come to my door with one red rose, so I went back out and sure enough he was standing there with a rose looking all sheepish."

"That's sweet," Laura said.

"Yeah, too sweet. But it worked, of course. A few weeks later he started having all these rehearsals for his play. Well, long story short, five elaborate lies later, my lesbian buddy told me she'd heard he'd been hooking up with his costar, a fact I confirmed by checking his answering machine messages. He came over and I confronted him and he said, 'I told you all along I wasn't your boyfriend,' and I said, 'Right. I'm not your girlfriend, which is why I'm extra baffled by you sneaking around and lying to me.' Then he returned to his favorite theme, my covert, sneaky CIA mission to turn him into my boyfriend and make everything *serious*, and I was so fed up with him that I said the worst thing I ever said to a guy, which was, 'I do not want to make everything serious. You aren't even *Jewish*.'" I put my hand on my head. "It makes me sick just thinking about it."

"Why?" asked Laura. "That's not so bad."

"I don't know, it's just—maybe it's that I was so mad when I said it, or maybe it's because I'd never really thought about it, but the second it came out I knew it was true. And the weirdest thing was, he didn't even want to stop seeing me! *I* had to break up with *him*. He was like, 'If I'd told you about what's-her-name'— he didn't say what's-her-name, I just can't remember it—'if I'd told you about what's-her-name from the beginning would you have stopped seeing me?' And I said, 'Yes.' And he said, 'See. There's no difference. Either way you'd break up with me.' And I said, 'No. The difference is that if you'd told the truth I might have some respect for you.' He was unbelievable. I mean, who had *time* for all his crap—I had *homework* to do and *TV* to watch, and I don't know—why did I have to spend my time deciphering all his little mixed Max messages? So, I avoided him for the rest of the semester and then he graduated and I never saw him ever again." Finished, I sighed and said, "I can't believe you'd ask him here, Nome."

"Come on, Rachel," she said. "There was no way he was coming. I think he still feels bad. He asked about you right away. He really did like you."

"I don't care if he liked me!" I said. "I'm getting married!"

"I know," she said, eyebrows moving up and down. "He seemed sort of bummed out about it."

"Why are you trying to make drama?" I asked.

"You really liked him," said Thomas.

"Yeah," I said, "I did. And then I really, really didn't. He was a mindfucker. Very charming, but a real snake."

"You were tough, though," Laura said.

"I'd reread *Pride and Prejudice* for a seminar and decided he was my Mr. Wickham."

"Aha."

"Everyone has to date one guy like that," Annie said. "They make you appreciate the nice guys."

"That's right," I agreed, smiling. "Which is why the first thing I did when I came back senior year was head straight for Dan, whom I'd been calling the love of my life since freshman year."

Everyone said, "Awwww . . ."

Except Andrea, who said, "It wasn't the first thing. First you wrote an article about answering machine warfare for the newspaper. I edited it."

"Right," I said. "It was the second thing. But the point is: That was it! The End! Which means no more of these," I gestured to the shot glasses and somehow knocked one over. "Whoops!"

"Just in the nick of time," said Thomas.

"So," Laura said, "eight total, including Dan?"

"I never count Eric Lorch, but, yeah."

Laura raised her eyebrows.

"Eight's a lot?" I asked.

"Considering you stopped at age twenty-one."

"Eight is not a lot!" I said. "You wouldn't say that to a guy."

Laura tilted her head. "I might."

"Do you think it's a lot, Annie?"

She shrugged. "I fooled around plenty when I was young—don't forget, it was the sixties. I don't think eight's that many. I'm more surprised by all the frivolous dating."

"What do you mean, 'frivolous dating'?"

"Well, you keep saying none of these guys was your boyfriend, which I take to mean you were never serious about them."

"Exactly," I said, though it sounded more like "Igggg-zackly."

"Well, then it was frivolous." She turned a palm upward. "It's not really a negative. I mean, guys have been foolin' around like that forever."

"Still," I said, frowning, "it wasn't frivolous." Something about the word didn't seem right; maybe it was all the alcohol, but I couldn't put my finger on why.

"You used to be so wild," Naomi sighed. "But now, no more."

"What do you mean?" I said. "I've been with Dan for five years already."

"Well, the *possibility*," she said. "Come on, Rachel, aren't you even the teeny-weeniest bit sad that that's it—eight."

"N-O, no," I said. "I like the way they all fit on two hands."

"If you could do it with one more person, who would it be?" Laura asked.

"Hmmm. Maybe some anonymous guy I'd pick up at MOMA. He'd be really well-dressed, and we wouldn't even speak, we'd just look at each other and head downstairs to the darkened cinema."

"A well-dressed guy at MOMA?" Thomas said. "I'm sorry, honey, but the best you can hope for there is bi. Or, okay," he raised a finger, "maybe foreign."

"I still think eight is a lot," Laura said. "I only have five."

"That's 'cause you had long-term boyfriends. Eight isn't really a lot, is it?" I turned to Andrea. "You have at least ten."

"I do not!" she said. "I have seven!"

"Like a year from now you won't have eight!"

"Good point."

"And you," I said, pointing to Naomi. "You have more than fifteen!" She nodded proudly. "And you," I said, pointing to Thomas, "you're a *gay man*!"

He threw up his hands. "Hey, Betty Buckley, I think eight is *enough*."

"Right," I said. "Eight is enough." I did another shot for emphasis. It quickly became apparent this was not such a good idea.

"Oh, my god, I'm gonna be sick," I said, using my penis-ringed hands to push past drag queens and clusters of laughing bachelorettes as I made for the bathroom—an appropriate ending to a trip down old nonboyfriends' lane.

Looking back now in sobriety, I see why "frivolous" irked me. When it came to sex, I had been, or at least had thought of myself as being, methodical. All the "not a girlfriend" stuff might have been my way of playing it emotionally safe as Thomas suggested or the outright bullshit Andrea thought it was. But I'd been so adamant about it because I liked my relationships black or white, terms defined, not my boyfriend, just a fling. Problems arose when things moved into gray areas.

Which meant that, strangely enough, I'd been just like David Gottlieb all along.

Twenty-seven

*J*ust when we thought it was safe to have a wedding, the next morning, we got a speakerphone call from Dan's parents.

"There's been a bit of a problem," Marty said, once Dan and I, each equally hungover, had each picked up extensions.

"We called your father and Phyllis this morning, just to check on some last-minute details about the night-before party," Carol began, her determination to remain calm, cool, and collected apparent. "And he was very—"

"He seemed put out by the phone call," Marty said.

Dan and I looked at each other. Apparently, there was another shoe, and it was dropping.

"Put out how?" Dan asked.

No trace of calm was left in Carol's reply. "He expects *you* to pay for this party! To pay for *his* guests out of your own pocket! Where are you supposed to get that kind of money? Dan's in school! You're the bride and groom, you're *young people!*"

"Well," I said, trying to plug up the dam, "we had this agreement where he gave us a lump sum of money and—"

"But you said that just covers the wedding!" Dan's mother was incredulous.

Dan and I looked at each other, the same thought occurring to us both: It did.

Marty said, "When we spoke to your father months ago, we agreed to split the costs of the night-before party. That was between the two of us and the two of them. There's no reason it should involve you two."

The mess was clearly seeping out of the corner. My already hangover-weary temples were making themselves known. I looked at Dan.

"There's obviously been a misunderstanding," Dan said, his not-to-worry tone as much for my benefit as his parents'.

"Well, I *certainly* hope so," said his mother.

"But, you know, Rachel," said Marty, "your father sounded very inflexible. I was honestly taken aback—"

"Give us a few minutes, guys," Dan said, at the reins. "We'll call you back."

We looked at each other and shook our heads. Neither of us said, "I can't believe this," because, at this point, we both could.

We hung up our phones and Dan said, "You just sit there. I'm calling," then picked the phone back up and said, "What's the number again?"

"Don't bother," I said, reaching for the phone. "They won't budge."

"Then what do we do?" he asked.

I put my hungover head in my hands. "Well, with the Levys hosting it, all we're really talking about is the food cost per head for his guests—and they're getting the food from a supermarket, a fancy supermarket, but a supermarket nonetheless. This thing can't cost more than a thousand bucks, can it?"

"If that," he said.

I sighed. My father's ten thousand just barely covered the wedding. Paying for anything else meant dipping into our almost-nonexistent, med-school–indebted pocket.

"I think it's worth it," I said.

Dan said, "So do I." Then he called his parents, told them we'd cleared up the "miscommunication" with my father, and that, from now on, they should just deal with us.

Wedding Timeline:

One to Two Weeks Ahead

- Have final dress fitting
- Arrange seating plan and write place cards
- Write toasts
- Break in wedding shoes at home
- Have facial or other beauty treatment

Twenty-eight

The weekend before the wedding, we went down to Philadelphia for the *auf-ruf*. Rabbi David called us to the Torah and we sang *barchu et adoshem hamvorach* in unison. He wrapped us in Grandpa Sol's *tallis* and said another blessing. The congregation threw candy at us. Most of the women wore *kippahs*. Dan's parents and brothers were there, as were my mother and Matthew (my father hadn't asked, and I hadn't told).

At lunch afterward, my mother turned to Marty. "You're a professor. Tell me, isn't astrophysics much more respected than astronomy?"

Matthew said, "Mom!"

I said, "I don't think this is the place."

Joyce said, "What? He's a *professor*!"

Matthew and I both said, "Mom!"

Joyce turned to Carol and said, "Are your kids this fresh?"

We went back to New York to take care of "last-minute things." Sunday night we packed up our apartment for the subletters.

"Now that we've done all that registering," I said, "I don't have to get skanked out by strangers using our towels and sleeping on our sheets!"

As Dan nodded, Good point, our buzzer rang. Dan reached for the receiver.

"It's Connor and Julie," he said, buzzing them in.

"What's up?"

Dan shrugged, and went to unlock the door.

"Hi guys!" and hugs were exchanged all around.

"Sorry to just drop by like this," Connor said. "But we've got some news we wanted to tell you in person."

"Okay . . ." I said, smiling. We already knew they'd both gotten into Yale. Julie's hands were behind her back.

"We're engaged!" she said and, with a little jump, produced her left hand. A diamond ring in a platinum 1940s setting glinted in the light.

There were more hugs, and they told us their engagement story. Connor had asked Julie to take a walk over the Brooklyn Bridge, where he'd planned to give Julie the ring. But as they strolled along, he looked down at the wooden slats that give the bridge its character. It seemed to Connor that those slats were pretty far apart, far enough apart for a diamond ring in a 1940s setting to slip through if someone with shaky hands were to drop it. Right then, Connor's hands got shaky. Abruptly, he said, "I think we should turn around. Now." Once back on Manhattan terra firma, he got down on one knee and popped the question.

"You have no idea how wide those slats are, man," he told us now.

While everyone was excited, no one was really surprised. The two of them had already signed a lease on an apartment together for the fall, and Julie had always said she'd never live with someone "until we were at least engaged."

When they left a while later, I said, "I *knew* I should have made Julie a bridesmaid!"

On Monday we completed the seating arrangement (a task that we found surprisingly easy) and began the twelve-hour odyssey known as "our place cards project" (surprisingly hard).

To make a long, convoluted, and frustrating story short, Dan had decided that the best way to go about the arts and crafts element of this task was to scan the photos into a computer up at Columbia, then use the color printer to print them out. Eight grueling hours later, we said, "Fuck it," and headed for the color Xerox machine at (bless you for being open twenty-four hours) Kinko's. We then cut and pasted and gluesticked and (I) wrote guests' names into the wee hours of Tuesday morning.

Tuesday I went to Kleinfeld's with Thomas for a final fitting, then to Aunt Natalie's colorist for highlights.

Wednesday I went to a townhouse on Seventy-seventh Street, right next to Stand Up New York, with a subtle ground-floor buzzer that read "Mikvah." It was time to do what brides had done for centuries before me, immerse myself in the purifying ritual bath. Aunt Natalie thought going to a *mikvah* was insanely old-world, but I found the prospect electrifying.

I showered and cut off any hangnails in its marble bathroom, then went through a back door to a nicely tiled little room that contained what could have been an enormous Jacuzzi. A well-dressed woman in a blonde wig smiled and inspected me for any loose skin. Then, holding on to the handrail, I stepped in. I waded out to the center, said the *schecheanu*—thank you, Lord, for bringing me to this day—and dunked, making sure not to touch anything.

Thursday, we practiced the wedding surprise no one knew about, then packed our rented Toyota Camry with all of our wedding and honeymoon stuff, set to relocate for the next few days to the Bethesda Marriott.

"So we have everything?" I asked for the thirtieth time as we entered the double-parked car.

"Yes."

"Passports?"

"Yes."

"Airline tickets?"

"Yes."

"All the place card things?"

"Yes."

"My dress?"

"Yes."

"Your suit?"

"Yes."

"And Annie's bringing the *kippahs* and the stuff for the welcome baskets down with her tomorrow."

"Yes. And if we realize we forgot anything, she has a key and can come back and get it."

"Right," I said.

"And if we realize we forgot anything else, Will or Naomi can get it."

"Right."

"So then, we're ready?" he asked.

"I guess so," I said, and, knowing the next time we'd be back here—back home—we'd be married, we rode off over the G.W. Bridge.

Wedding Timeline:

One Day Ahead

- Finish seating chart
- Assign different responsibilities to members of the bridal party
- Give each member of the bridal party his or her gift
- Hold rehearsal dinner

Twenty-nine

The Levys lived in the Foxhall section of Northwest D.C., blocks from Sutton Place Gourmet and the office of my pediatrician. Their house was a brick colonial filled with rugs and tribal masks. Nostalgic for their own Audubon Society wedding, Debra and Zhang Levy-Wu had decorated the exterior with Chinese paper lanterns—small ones laced around the back patio, large ones staked along the front walk.

Dan and I made our way inside, and thanked Jan and Richard so much for hosting the party. We'd spent the past two days running last-minute errands. (How could we have forgotten the welcome goody-bags—complete with directions to the events, just in case someone forgot theirs at home, that guests staying in the hotel receive at check-in—until the night before most of our guests were set to arrive???) But now, in my little black dress and glowing from the mango sugar spa treatment I'd gotten at Oasis that day, I was more than ready to switch from "getting ready for it" to "actually enjoying it."

Carol, who'd come early to help the Levys set up, greeted me with a stunned "Ray-chul!," causing me to look in fright for a huge stain or some other horrible blunder, until she said, "You look so—*glamorous*!" Just as I started to wonder: Could I just not take a compliment, or was this really not a cause for shock? Dan asked if I wanted a drink.

"Yes," I said, as if thrown a life raft.

Before I knew it, the party started, and we were Greeting Our Public.

I stood on the Levys' front lawn welcoming guests and giving my all to my duties as hostess/guest of honor—hugging, kissing, smiling wide and permanently, thanking people so much for coming, telling them how glad "we" were they'd "made it" (as if the journey to D.C. was fraught with unknown dangers), letting them wipe lipstick off my cheeks, sneaking in sips of vodka and ginger ale from the sweaty glass I was holding, and grabbing the odd pig in blanket (I'd called Jan Levy with the special request) as it passed on a tray.

It was *work*, but it was genuine. I really was "happy" and "touched" that so many people had come "all the way to Washington" to "celebrate our big day"—especially these people, who were close enough to us to come and "share our joy," but far enough from us to have never caused any headaches. I loved my guests the way a pop star loves her fans—they were the ones I did it all for, the ones who made it all worthwhile. And now it was time to give something back by being the bright and beaming bride they all wanted, the bright and beaming bride I wanted to be for them—and, of course, for me.

Less was required of Dan, but less was far from nothing. His job was to appear jovial and untroubled, mature and wise, to smile at the phrase "ball and chain" and respond to the comments "last night of freedom" and "gettin' cold feet?" with unambivalent hahaha-I'm-one-of-the-guys laughter. The best he could hope for was a question about the honeymoon. Not that I knew this at the time, mind you. Though he'd been standing in close proximity, the "Thank you" I'd said when he'd returned with my drink is the only thing I can remember saying to Dan the whole party.

I was telling some friends of Dan's parents how great it was they could make it when I felt a tap on my shoulder. I turned to find Naomi and Andrea standing behind me in low-cut sundresses and shades. They had driven down with Erin and Jill, another Barnard friend who'd become close with Andrea since graduation.

"You look gorgeous!" Naomi said, hugging me. She'd gotten her hair blown out straight for the occasion.

"Thank you!" I said, hugging back.

"You're glowing!" said Andrea.

"It's all thanks to you guys and that sugar rub," I said, hugging each of them.

I gave them my standard line—food and drinks are in the dining room, inside to the right, help yourself, enjoy!—and told them that the wedding party was assembling out on the patio after dessert.

"Cool," Naomi said. "You *have* to hear what we decided on the way down."

"You're gonna love this," Andrea said.

"You know what we are?" Naomi said.

"No . . ."

"The Jewish Spice Girls!"

Andrea broke it down. "Naomi is Scary because of her hair, I'm Ginger because of my boobs and henna highlights, Jill is Posh because she's in law school, and Erin is Sporty because she's gonna be a vet, can ride a horse, and has a new pair of Nikes that she wears all the time."

"Which means you're Baby Spice!" Naomi said.

"*I* am *Baby* Spice?" Baby Spice was clearly the lamest Spice Girl. I thought about protesting—I was the one getting married, surely the furthest from a baby in the bunch. But, at the moment, I was Hostess Spice, so I smiled and said, "What makes me Baby?"

"Because you have straight hair," said Andrea.

"Because that's the one nobody else wanted to be," Naomi said, laughing.

"Ah," I said.

"Can we get the band to play Spice Girls tomorrow?" Andrea asked.

"The jazz quartet?"

"Oh, that's right," Naomi said. "Damn."

"So they're not even playing Madonna?" Andrea asked, shocked.

"Doubtful."

"Ew. Then you have to run around and sing with us now." Naomi grabbed my hand and began to skip. "We can pretend we're in the 'Tell Me What You Want, What You Really Really Want' video."

"It's called 'Wannabe,'" I said, putting the brakes on the skipping. "And I can't sing the Spice Girls. Look around." I gestured with an unhooked arm. "I have about a million relatives and in-laws to deal with."

"Well, catch up with us later," they said, undaunted, skipping off arm in arm.

I was standing talking to one of my father's cousins, when I turned to the sound of a familiar voice.

"Rachel, *mammilah, conkrachulaychuns!*"

"Rachel, honey," said Esther, "you look to die for."

"I am so, so glad you guys could make it," I said, truly touched. "It really means a lot to me. Washington's a ways for you to travel."

"*Vee* took *zee* train, *mammilah*," said Frieda, "*zee* Metroliner. Very fast. No problems."

"Besides," said Esther, shooing with her hand, "once you leave the West Side, you might as well leave New York."

Laura arrived and hugged me. "Congratulations!" she said. "I can't believe the big day's finally here!"

"I know." I did my exaggerated gulp.

"Guess what," she said, a sly smile forming at the corners of her mouth.

I smiled too. "You got the job!"

She nodded, bursting. "I gave notice with *Turnerville* yesterday!"

"Congratulations!" I said, hugging her again. "I'm so happy for you, Laura! I knew it would work out."

"Thanks," she said. "I'm pretty psyched."

"And rightfully so," I said. I linked my arm in hers and moved through the crowd. "You know, just because you're not gonna be my editor, it doesn't mean we have to stop our Charlie phone calls."

"I wouldn't have taken the job if it did," she said.

The party went on as parties like it do. In the beginning, people bounced around and off one another like heated-up molecules in a chemistry class filmstrip. Then they got their food and found the people they knew, cooling down and becoming solids as they settled down in their own little territories together. My dad's people—assorted cousins, Aunt Natalie, Gregory and Thomas, Thomas's parents, him and Phyllis—occupied the far corner of the living room. The Gershons and their family and friends sat on and around the sofas. My mother and her side of the family (except Aunt Annie, who was helping Jan Levy in the kitchen) sat at the tables set up just beyond the foyer. As far as I knew, my mother and father had not exchanged a word.

But I tried not to know very much. Being gracious took concentration, and I was deliberately avoiding the living room. Our friends dominated outside ("the kids' tables are out here," at least ten people had joked) and the everyone-feeds-at-the-trough dining room made the latter part easy enough.

The evening was a blur of honeymoon talk ("Around the world in four months with just one tiny backpack! I never knew you were so *brave!*" "Six weeks in India—don't drink the water!"), Clinton-scandal chatter (me as adamant about it "blowing over" as I had been about O.J.'s conviction), and I-remember-when-you-were-this-high reminiscences. I noticed Laura and Dan's friend Rob huddled in conversation near the bar and hoped I'd seated them at the same table. Throughout it all, I remember thinking, "Where is Dan?" and how odd it was that, at a party to celebrate our relationship, he'd be the one person I didn't get to see. But, in the course of speaking to all of these relatives and family friends, something unexpected happened. People kept mentioning my *Turnerville* books and wanting to know what I was writing next. Maybe Laura's new job had inspired me, but midway through telling the umpteenth person, it hit me: People were taking me seriously. I was a writer. Whatever it was I'd been seeking since college—permission? legitimacy? steady, income-producing writing gigs?—I had. There was no excuse: Once I returned from my honeymoon, I would sit down and write something serious—well, maybe not *serious*, but something that felt real.

As the party wound down, it was time to assemble the wedding party, say a few words, and give them their gifts. Thomas had already grabbed his; he and Gregory had left to have damage-control drinks with Thomas's parents at Jerry and Phyllis's. I made my way through the house to the back patio, where a group of our friends—Connor, Julie, and Will among them—were gathered, laughing, around a table. The Chinese lanterns were swaying in a seemingly-from-nowhere breeze I hoped did not mean rain. I paused and looked back into the house—should I go back in and find the groom and the bridesmaids?—then felt a hand on my back and turned abruptly.

"Oh, Will," I said. "You scared me."

"Sorry," he said.

"No, no. It's me—it's the first time all night I could actually hear myself think. I guess I just got caught up in it," I said, laughing.

"Well, Dan's mom grabbed him to say good-bye to an aunt or something—I figured I had a sec to run in and get a glass of water—"

"Oh, yeah, sure, go ahead—"

"You want anything?"

"No, no. I'm fine, thanks." I looked to where he'd been sitting. "Do you by any chance know where Naomi is?"

"Yeah," he said. "She took off with the other bridesmaids about half an hour ago. Said something about finding a Spice Girls CD before the record stores closed."

"Tell me you're kidding," I said.

" 'Fraid not," he said with a laugh, as if my disappointment stemmed from their musical taste.

"Truly amazing." I looked up at the starless, possibly ominous sky. For the first time all night, I felt like myself. I turned to face Will, met his eyes, and said, "What is her *deal?*"

"Naomi?" He laughed. "Simple. Easy as pie."

"Lay it on me."

"You want the long version, or the short one?"

"Start with the short."

Will sat down on the stoop, took a cigarette from the pack in his pocket, and offered me one. I'm not a smoker, but the cigarette sure was appealing. I took it and sat down beside him on the concrete.

"She's an actress, and you're the center of attention," he said, offering me a light.

That actually may have been right. But I exhaled and said, "What's the long answer?"

"Okay," he said. "Long version. Why's she here by herself? Have any of her relationships lasted more than a few months?"

Who was he—Esther? "Uh-uh," I said. "Don't even *try* to make this about her not having a boyfriend. It's sexist and it's retro and I'm not buying it."

"It's not *just* about a guy, but a guy is part of it. It's about her whole life! What is Naomi doing with herself? Selling real estate? Performing in some second-tier improv group with a bunch of people who'll never make it to *Saturday Night Live?*"

"Hey," I said, thinking this was unfair. "She's waiting to come into type. In the meantime at least she's out there, putting herself on the line or whatever. *Trying.*"

"Exactly. She's waiting. She's *trying*. You're *doing*."

"Getting married is doing?"

"Yes!" he said. "Of course! And before you say it's sexist, it's doing for Dan too. It's about being a legitimate grown-up instead of an overgrown kid."

"It is about that," I conceded.

"Of course it is! And do you have any idea how hard it is to look around you and see your friends moving on to the next phase while you're still figuring out the last one?"

"But why be so competitive? They're supposed to be your friends."

"How can you not? You feel like a loser, it means you lost."

"Lost what? Life isn't a race, Will."

"Oh, it's not? Take a look around you. Things are happening. People's lives are clicking into place. They're going to grad school, they're moving to L.A., they're getting married. People are moving on. We've entered the era of the Phase One wedding."

"The Phase One wedding?"

"Yes," he said. "The phase of we-met-before-we-were-fully-formed-and-we're-gonna-make-our-way-through-the-world-as-a-team-together couples. The innocent phase. The romantic phase. The phase where everyone says, 'Oh, they were made for each other.' The phase of true life partners. After Phase One, it's all downhill. Phase Two will be the we're-already-thirty-it's-time-to-get-married couples, and everyone will talk about how great it is they *found* each other, because everyone knows they were looking, and instead of saying, 'They're made for each other,' everyone will be taking bets on how long it'll last. Then there's Phase Three, which'll be the it's-about-fucking-time couples. The Phase One people will already be on their third kid. The Phase Two people will be separated or, at the very least, in counseling. Everyone will have been to so many weddings they won't even be thinking about the couples anymore. They'll be thinking the centerpieces are lovely or the band's too loud. Trust me, it will not be pretty. And as a single person, that's what's starin' you down at the other end of the barrel. You go to a Phase One wedding, you're thinkin', Which am I, Phase Two or Phase Three?'"

"So the Ghost of Weddings Future makes the single person Scrooge."

"Exactly."

"Uh-huh," I said. I waited a second, then turned to look at him. "Are we still talking about Naomi?"

"Were we ever?"

The next thing out of Will's mouth was a self-deprecating laugh. It was contagious.

Just then, a cheer of "Groom! Groom! Groom!" erupted from the others. Dan was making his way around the side of the house. He puffed out his chest and raised his hands magisterially. "Indeed," he said, the Buddha returning from the mount. "It is I." I smiled an involuntary, nonhostess smile.

Will looked at me. "You don't give a shit about immature bridesmaids. All you're thinking is, 'I'm marrying that guy tomorrow.'"

My smile widened. He was right.

Thirty

On the morning of my wedding, at 8:03 exactly (if the hotel clock was right), I bolted awake and headed for the window. I yanked open the polyester Marriott curtains. The wet trees and darkened parking lot pavement made it clear it had rained overnight. The sky was still a blanket of gray.

"Oh, my god," I said to Annie. "Mother Nature was the only parent I thought I didn't have to worry about. I'm so fucked."

"No, you are not." Annie grabbed my shoulders and, in one deft move, turned me around and shut the curtains. "It's gonna clear up. You just worry about getting ready."

A few hours later, Macy, whom Aunt Natalie had brought down with her as part of my wedding present, had already finished with my natural, "it's-you-just-'popped'" makeup and was working on my hair. I was wearing a bathrobe. We were still in my hotel room. The heavy layer of curtain was now opened, but the white, sheerish, let-in-some-natural-light layer remained closed. It let in very little light. Aunt Natalie and Aunt Annie sat facing each other on upholstered hotel chairs, going over the list of portrait groupings for the photographer. We were Not Discussing the Weather.

"So your fireman's coming to the wedding, huh?" I asked Macy.

"Yup." She smiled, rolling a section of my hair out with a round brush. "After six months, I think we can safely call him *my* fireman."

"Well, it makes me feel so good to have you here," I said. "Really. I mean it."

"Thanks, sweetheart," she said. "I'd kiss ya, but frankly, right now, the hair's more important."

"It makes me feel good too," said Aunt Natalie. I could see her and Annie behind me in the mirror, solidifying the game plan.

"So you'll supervise the photographer and I'll supervise the *huppah* construction."

"Right," said Aunt Natalie. Then, placing her hands on her knees with extra mission-accomplished vigor, she added, "Well, it looks like everything's pretty much set."

"Not everything," Annie said, catching my eye in the mirror.

I looked back at her, lips scrunching. This was the moment I'd been dreading. "I know," I said. "The processional."

Annie raised her eyebrows and nodded. "It's not just gonna go away . . ."

I exhaled loudly.

"Oh," said Aunt Natalie, reaching for the pad. "This shouldn't be hard. First you have the *huppah* bearers. Then you have the groom's side—do you want his attendants to walk down one by one?"

"Yeah."

"In any order?"

"I don't think it matters. Will's carrying the rings, so I guess he should be last, since that'll leave him closest to the action."

"Fine. So Will's last. Who's first? This is important. We need someone responsible who'll be a good pace-setter."

"Connor," I said without hesitation. "Connor, Andrew, Rob, Will."

"Fine," said Aunt Natalie, noting this down.

"Then Dan and his parents," I said.

"Oh, Rachel." Aunt Natalie's shoulders sank. "You're not doing that parents-on-either-side thing, are you? I can't stand that. Everyone in the world's gotta walk down the aisle together—all at once. It's so . . . *messy*. It's like the *hora*, people running around in circles, lifting themselves onto chairs. It's a mish-mosh. We're not in the Old Country anymore."

Annie shrugged. "I love the *hora*."

"And I like it that the bride and groom get escorted by both parents," I said. "It reflects the life cycle event. You're moving from one family to another. It's very psychologically astute."

Aunt Natalie sighed. "Fine, then. Have it your way." She noted this down on her list, then said, "Okay, your side."

I said, "Naomi first, then Erin, then Andrea, then Thomas," for no particular reason.

"And what about your parents?"

Annie and I caught each other's eyes in the mirror. "Aye," I said. "There's the rub."

But then I thought back to what the rabbi had said that day at Barney Greengrass, and what I had just said to Aunt Natalie, and realized this was the whole point. Nuclear or not, they were my family of origin. They were what I needed to leave, both literally and symbolically.

"They're both walking me down," I said. In the mirror, I could see Aunt Annie smile.

"Will your mother agree to it?" asked Aunt Natalie.

"We won't tell her until the last minute. That way, she'll have no choice."

"What about your father?" asked Aunt Annie. "He's got a problem with his wife there, you know."

"He can walk Phyllis down first, before my attendants, then come back and walk with me and my mother."

"Seems fair," Annie nodded.

"You know, neither one of them's gonna like this," Aunt Natalie said.

There was something poetic about that too.

"Good," I said, and both aunts laughed.

"Okay," Macy said, standing back, "we're ready for the veil!"

This was my cue to change into the outfit I'd drive over to Woodend in—a pair of clamdiggers and the button-down shirt Dan had worn the night before (the only easy-on, easy-off top available that wouldn't interfere with either my hair or my veil). Once there, I'd put on the dress. Dressed, I sat back down at the mirror.

Macy approached with the veil. Annie smiled and Aunt Natalie made a little inaudible oh-goody clap. "Close your eyes," she said. "Don't look 'til it's on."

"Okay." I nodded, breathing in and out as the bobby pinning jostled me.

"So beautiful!" Aunt Natalie sighed. I could hear her hand cover her mouth.

"You can look now!" Macy said.

I exhaled and opened my eyes. I was me, exponential.

Thirty-one

As for the wedding itself—I'm afraid I'm an incredibly unreliable narrator. Nearly all of the memories I have of that day fall into one of three categories: Total Blur, Helped Along by Pictures, and I'm So Positive It Was *Exactly Like That* Even Though the Picture in My Mind's Eye Includes My Own Likeness—a category achieved by looking at the same photographs way too many times.

At the risk of being accused of holding a naïve belief in fairy tale endings, I could tell you that it was amazing, that it was everything I'd hoped for and more, that it made all of the pain and pains in the ass that went into it seem, not just okay, but even, somehow, right.

But they say "show, don't tell." So instead, I figure I'll do what I'd do if Dan and I had you over to our apartment and you asked, "What was your wedding like?": namely, show you the video.

Dan would sigh, thinking that's his job, and I'd put the tape in the VCR. Then we'd all take a seat on the comfortable Crate and Barrel couch we got from returning nearly everything on our registry and I'd grab the remote and press Play.

The video opens with two big, interlaced gold hearts in front of a pinkish background. Then, accompanied by a piano playing *ain kelohainu*, the words "Two Shall Become One" float across the screen. (At this point either Dan or I would say, "This is one of the few cheesy parts," and I would announce that my mother was completely responsible for the video.) Then the title, "The Wedding of Rachel Beth Silverstein and Daniel Joseph Gershon, June 14, 1998," emerges in somewhat flowery ("it could have been much, much worse") script. *Ain kelohainu* continues as we cut to a pan of green grass and a slightly overcast sky, stopping when a large red-brick house comes into view and the words "Woodend Manor, Chevy Chase, Maryland" appear at the bottom separated by a C-SPAN-esque red line.

There is more grass panning, then a close-up of my white rose bridal bouquet, which zooms out to the wedding party posed—half-sitting, half-standing—around a picnic table. Naomi, standing next to me, scrunches her hair, Julie mouths "take off your glasses" to Connor. Their bouquets have stems on them. Then the camera pulls back and we see the photographer at her tripod, my father standing with Phyllis, Carol joining them, saying, "Doesn't she just look beautiful?", Phyllis giving her quick double nod and saying, "It's a start."

(The videographer didn't catch the first moment Dan saw me in my dress, but the photographer did. I am walking out the French doors and onto the patio, and Thomas is holding up the back of the dress. Dan is standing on the patio, his likeness caught in profile. We both have smiles so wide, it's amazing our faces can fit them. At some point—after the picture was snapped, I think—I said, "Bridey enough for you?" and he smiled and said, "Perfect.")

There are more picture pans, the bride by herself turning awkwardly, saying, "This is how I should stand?", Joyce, hands folded over, shoulders hunched, asking the rabbi some unintelligible, but no doubt nervous, question. Gregory and Thomas milling with Annie and Naomi as Dan and I pose with his parents and brothers. Then, as Dan stands awkwardly for a solo portrait, Aunt Natalie shuffles a cousin over to me and I say, "You're Helen! Of course I remember you!"

The scene then cuts to the rabbi. We are indoors and there's a bit of an echo. Instead of the Yankees *kippah*, he has opted for black suede. He says, "This is the part of the ceremony where we take a breath, relax, and focus on why we're here today, instead of worrying about all the extraneous details that have occupied us up to this moment." The camera pans out and you can hear both Dan and me laugh, a nervous hehhehheh to which we now react by saying "Me love cookies." (It's possible that other people were laughing, too, but since Dan had a microphone planted subtly in his tie, we're the only ones you really hear.) You see us sitting at a table with Richard and Jan Levy, our *ketubah* signers, our brothers and Dan's parents standing behind us. (You can't see Stuart and Annie; they're on the side of the table with the video guy, taking pictures.) The rabbi continues, "It's also a moment for us to look back on your lives, to honor the people who have helped bring you here and include them in the celebration. So, in this vein, I will say a prayer to invoke the spirit of people who aren't here physically but who, spiritually, are very much a part of this day—grandparents, in particular, who are, in a very real sense, responsible for bringing you both here." He opens the *Siddur* in his hands and starts chanting in Hebrew. I sniffle and the camera widens. Everyone looks serious. Dan and I hold hands, and I dab a bent finger in the corner of my eye, so as not to smear my makeup, just the way Macy had advised. Soon the rabbi is finished and we all say Amen.

The rabbi closes his prayer book and says, "We pray that they take joy and pleasure in this moment and that we feel their presence with us today." The camera tilts to the left, and we see Joyce up close, bent over and wiping her eyes. She notices the camera, then heaves her shoulders and wipes again. Aunt Thelma stands behind her stone-faced, arms folded across her stomach. Jerry is standing in the distance behind them, staring at the floor. Phyllis is standing next to him, whispering something to Aunt Natalie. (Whenever the camera catches her at this part of the service, she is doing this. It reminds me of myself in services at summer camp when I was fourteen.)

The rabbi puts his prayer book down and continues. "The second thing we're going to do is sign the *ketubah*—the traditional Jewish wedding contract." He holds up our *ketubah*, which is wrapped in plastic, and there's some editing here and some "Me love cookies" laughter as Rabbi David struggles with the wrapping, apologizes for being nervous, then hands it off to Marty to deal with. He explains that the *ketubah* was originally a prenuptial agreement meant to protect the bride, but that Dan and I have chosen a more contemporary, egalitarian one to better reflect the nature of our relationship. The camera zooms in and out of close-ups on the *ketubah*, me, and Dan (in that order). The rabbi begins reading the document. "On the fourteenth day of the month of June, in the year nineteen-ninety-eight here in Woodend, the Garden of Eden"—here everyone laughs—"in Chevy Chase, Maryland, on the twentieth day of the month of Sivan in the year five thousand seven hundred and fifty-eight, the bride, Rachel Beth Silverstein, daughter of Jerold and Joyce, and the groom, Daniel Joseph Gershon, son of Martin and Carol, stand under the *huppah* before family and friends to make a marriage covenant in accordance with the laws of Moses and Israel," then the rabbi stops and says, "No, wait a minute, why don't you two read it?"

I point and say, "From there?" and Dan and I begin in unison:

"We promise to uphold a warm and loving partnership throughout our lives"—you can hear the tears in my voice and I dab at my eyes again—"and to support and nurture each other through unity and difference, joy and sadness. We commit"—and here we're both teary so we laugh, then start again—"we commit to a marriage which fosters trust, laughter, love, and companionship. Together we promise to establish a home in which Jewish tradition sanctifies our days and loving-kindness our actions. All here written is valid and binding."

At this point, either Dan or I might point out the real-life *ketubah* hanging on our living room wall. On video, Richard Levy says something about having his "official business" pen and everyone laughs—hehhehheh—and the *ketubah* gets passed as Dan and I, and Jan and Richard, and then the rabbi all sign it. (We usually fast-forward over the details of this.)

The rabbi continues, and, at this part of the video, it never fails to annoy me that Phyllis is in the shot and *won't stop talking* throughout both his speech and the reading that follows it. But you might not be as sensitive to this as I am, so you might actually be able to concentrate on what the rabbi is saying, which is: "We've now come to the last part of what I like to call the pregame ceremony"—hehhehheh—"which is the *bedeken*, where Dan, you will place the veil over Rachel's face. This part of the tradition goes back to the marriage of Jacob and Rachel. As the story goes, Jacob worked years to marry the love of his life Rachel, only to be tricked at the wedding by his father-in-law, Laban, into marrying her older sister Leah. It's not an explanation I particularly like for the *bedeken*, except for the part that has to do with knowing that you've got it right, that this is the person you're here for. So, Dan, before you place the veil over *your* Rachel's face"—this draws a laugh, who knew the name Rachel had such comedic potential?—"you should both take a look at each other and remember why it is you've chosen this person. You can turn to each other and, when you're ready, Dan, you can lower the veil."

And we turn to each other, and the shot is a little higher and you can see that we've been holding hands the whole time, because we smile at each other and let go and Dan stands up to lift the veil. He lifts it and I say, "Not the whole thing," and Aunt Natalie rushes in from the side to make sure he only takes half and it falls right.

Then there's a weird, flipping-in-from-the-corner effect and we're back outside. It is sunny now—that part I remember for real, because when we left the *ketubah* signing room, I noticed the sudden sunshine and caught Annie's eye and mouthed, "Grandpa Sol?" and she shrugged and said, "Who knows?"

But that's not on the video. What is on the video is the procession, through a clearing between the two sections of guests, accompanied by a keyboard and an alto saxophone playing a selection from Handel's Water Music (their suggestion). The camera is at the end of the aisle, facing the procession head-on. First, the rabbi makes his way down the stone steps between the trees to the flat clearing where the guests are seated. Among the guests, Thomas's mother is very distinct, sitting on the aisle in a turquoise Chanel suit. Across from her, Macy wears a floral dress and holds hands with a mustached guy roughly three times her size.

The *huppah* (Grandpa Sol's *tallis*) and its bearers (our brothers—Adam and Joel, Matthew and Gregory—each holding a white, vine-wrapped pole) arrive and walk down the aisle. Then comes Connor (nice and slow, the right man for the job), then Andrew (looking stoned), then Rob (looking nervous), then Will (looking strangely like a Secret Service agent). Then Dan walks with his parents on either side, at which point there is laughter (both on the tape and when watching it) because Carol is using both of her hands—one at his elbow and one holding his—as if clinging, and because Dan looks very serious and straight into the camera.

My father walks Phyllis down next. Annie later told me that when she informed my mother and father individually of the procession arrangement during the prewedding photo shoot, they had each opened their mouths to protest. But, before either could get a word out, she raised her finger and said, "This is your daughter's wedding, and this is not up for debate." Never had her nursery-school teaching skills come in so handy.

If you know what you're looking for, you can still see signs of displeasure on the video. Jerry walks down with Phyllis, holding her hand. Aunt Annie (seated in the front taking pictures) motions toward the seat in the front row she saved for Phyllis, but my father doesn't see this and Phyllis, somewhat huffily, finds a seat on her own farther down the aisle. My father, heading back at the far side of one section of guests, disappears from the shot. At the time (this is *not* on the video), my mother, standing next to me, said loudly, "Oh, look, he's finally leaving Phyllis and coming back to me!" Which caused both Thomas and Naomi, who heard it, to suppress giggles, and me to roll my eyes. (Later, Thomas would say, "You have to admit it was a funny line.")

But, on the video, all you hear is Handel and the birds in the

trees and the procession continues. Naomi walks down, fully
vamping on the catwalk, waving to someone in the crowd and
smiling flirtatiously at no one specific. The other bridesmaids
follow her, looking nervous and trying to smile. Thomas, who
has exceptionally good posture, finishes off the music.

There is quiet for a moment, and you can hear a camera click,
then the musicians strike up "Ode to Joy" (my pick) and the
bride—me!—appears in the lane with her parents and starts
walking. To my left, Jerry is sort of smiling. To my right, Joyce
occasionally finds someone at whom she can make a face, then,
as we approach the end, gets teary. I am veiled, so you can't see
my tears, but I remember them being there and thinking,
"Damn, they've got my arms and I have these stupid flowers, so I
can't do Macy's trick." But once we're at the end, I am smiling—
which you can see through the veil—as Dan comes to get me and
I let go of my parents and take his hand. I walk up the stone steps
to the little table under the *huppah* with him, never once looking
back.

The camera switches to a long shot from behind the audience
(apparently the videographer had one set up in the back and one
hidden in the bushes in front of the *huppah* for close-ups. Neither of us was aware of it at the time—we might say something to
that effect at this point in the tape). In the wide shots, you notice
the photographer, running around taking candids, and a particularly bushy-haired friend of Dan's parents seated in the back row.
All of the men are wearing the light blue suede *kippot* saying
"Rachel and Dan's wedding" and the date on the inside, which
Annie had (luckily) reminded me to order.

The rabbi says: "We begin by welcoming not just the two of
you, but everyone who is here with us today to honor this sacred
moment. Those who are here physically and those who are not,

but whose presence we have invoked to share in the joy of this day." He sings a blessing of welcome in Hebrew, and again you can hear the birds chirp. The camera switches to a close-up shot of Dan and me, though it's really more of Dan and me in three-quarter profile. "May you who are here be blessed in the name of the Lord. Sanctify this moment by invoking our awareness of everything that we hold sacred in life, all the holiness that we perceive in this world." The rabbi chants some more and Dan and I sneak glances at each other. "May God who is supreme in power, blessing, and glory bless today this groom and this bride." He continues, "And we pray for this moment. We pray, God, that all of us can see the sacred dimension of life. We pray that You will guide this groom and bride to the realization of sanctity, and devotion to each other—every day just like today. Help them to renew their love continually as You renew creation day after day. May their concern for each other reflect Your concern for all people. May their faithfulness reflect Your love. Throughout the years, may they hallow their life together, may the home that they establish together be a blessing for all Israel and for all people. May their life together embrace and nurture the promise of this moment, so that all who know them will call them truly blessed. And let us all say: Amen."

There are smatterings of Amens, the loudest from Dan, who is still wearing the mic.

The camera switches to a long view and we're seen from behind. (I might note that I like this shot because you get a good view of my dress from the back.) The birds still chirp.

"We now say a blessing of betrothal, by which we give thanks to God for the creation of relationships." And the rabbi says the blessing. The camera is now tight on us, but the angle has changed, so you can see the rabbi's shoulder and Joel smiling and holding his end of the *huppah* and Will looking ever more like a Secret Service agent in the background.

"Whenever we celebrate, we do so with a full cup, a symbol of joy," the rabbi says, and hands Dan the Gershon family *Kiddush* cup, brought down for this purpose. Dan takes the cup and the rabbi says, "Blessed be God who lifts us up through holy celebrations like this, who wakes us to seek love and to sanctify our love through *huppah* and marriage. Blessed be God who makes the Jewish people and all who dwell in the world holy, and let us say: Amen."

Then Dan sips the wine and starts to hand me the glass, and the rabbi says, "I'll hold it," because my veil is still on, but he's too late, because I'm already in the middle of lifting the thing myself anyway. Will and Connor are both laughing at this. Dan laughs too—hehhehheh—and I take a sip of wine and put the cup back on the table.

The rabbi says, "Rings?" and looks around, and Will, all business, rushes in, reaching into his inside pocket. He stands between us and hands the rings to the rabbi, who then hands one to me and one to Dan. Will then does this ducking, almost-bow thing and makes to leave, and I smile and say, "Thanks, Will," and laugh, and he turns around and smiles. Back in his place, you can almost hear his sigh of relief as his shoulders lower. The Secret Service look is over. He is almost relaxed. There are trees all around him and it's very green.

The rabbi continues: "The giving and accepting of something of value—in this case, of rings—tells us something about the heart of a relationship—the ability to give, and the ability to accept and receive, to understand our interdependence, our complementarity."

We switch to the long, from-the-back view, and the rabbi says, "Dan, if you could, repeat after me: *Charay at—*"

"*Charay at—*"

"*Mikudeshet—*"

"*Mikudeshet—*"

And here the camera switches to the close-up shot, and we can see that as Dan has been saying all of this he has been looking, not at his bride, but at the rabbi. The rabbi says, "*Li—*" then points Dan in the right direction with his bearded chin.

Dan says "*Li—*" and I roll my eyes and Will, Andrew, Rob, and Connor are all laughing and Dan is smiling and trying not to.

"*Bitoba'at zo—*"

"*Bitoba'at zo—*"

"*Kidda'at Moshe—*"

"*Kidda'at Moshe—*"

"*Viyisroel.*"

"*Viyisroel.*"

"Behold with this ring—"

"Behold with this ring—"

"Be consecrated to me—"

"Be consecrated to me—"

"As my wife—"

"As my wife—" You can see Naomi tearing up in the background.

"According to the traditions—"

"According to the traditions—"

"Of Moses and Israel."

"Of Moses and Israel."

He puts the ring on the middle finger of my right hand and the rabbi says, "Okay, Rachel, look at Dan," and I nod, yes, good idea, "and repeat after me: *Charay atah—*"

"*Charay atah—*"

"*Mikudash—*"

"*Mikudash—*"

"*Li—*"

"*Li—*"

"*Bitoba'at zo—*"

"*Bitoba'at zo—*"

"*Kidda'at Moshe—*"

"*Kidda'at Moshe—*"

"*Viyisroel.*"

"*Viyisroel.*"

"Behold with this ring—"

"Behold with this ring—"

"Be consecrated to me—"

"Be consecrated to me—"

"As my husband—"

"As my husband—" My voice catches and I steady my shoulders.

"According to the traditions—"

"According to the traditions—"

"Of Moses and Israel."

"Of Moses and Israel."

And I put the ring on the middle finger of his right hand, and, because of the way he's turned, you can now see Marty, standing behind Dan, beaming. The rabbi says, "Mazel tov," and Dan and I both smile.

The rabbi goes on to explain that just before the ceremony, witnesses watched the signing of this *ketubah*, holds it up for all to see, then reads the English translation that Dan and I had read in the room. Then he makes the joke that "this is yours to keep."

He adjusts his glasses, then, as someone coughs in the background, goes on: "This is the time in the ceremony when someone is supposed to offer wise words about the secret of warm, loving, loyal, and lasting relationships. The truth is, no one has found that secret yet. But we do have some pretty good clues. Our tradition teaches us to understand ourselves as being incomplete without other people. Finding somebody who helps us realize aspects of ourselves that, until we met that person, we didn't know were there—that is what a marriage is supposed to be about. And even from just the little bit of time I've spent with the two of you, eating fantastic nova at Barney Greengrass"—this gets both a hehhehheh and a laugh from the crowd—"I have to say, honestly, that there is a wonderful chemistry, an intangible connection, between the two of you"—here, I dab at my eyes full-on, with a hankie—"that you, I can tell, appreciate and love about each other and is written all over you when you are together. I can see that spirit reflected in the faces of the people around you here, who know you even better than I do. That makes this occasion a great joy to celebrate.

"You have welcomed us—really, a Jewish wedding is a *channukat ha'bayit,* a dedication of a home—and you have welcomed us into the home you've created today. It's a home that has at its root your grandfather's *tallis,* which was wrapped around you last week at your *auf-ruf,* which reminds us of all the generations upon generations that have come before you to lead you to this day. *Yivarechecha adoshem viyishmarecha*—may God bless you and guard you—*ya'air adoshem pa'anav eilecha viyichunecha*—may God shine on you and teach you compassion, for yourselves and for others—*viya'asem lecha shalom*—and may He grant you peace, peace in your home, peace in your hearts, and peace in yourselves, together." And we smile as everyone says Amen.

"Kiddingly, I said before that we were here in the Garden of Eden. But every Jewish wedding takes us back to that first couple, in that first place, a place of perfection. The seven wedding blessings that I'm going to chant, and that your aunts will read in translation, recall for us the Garden of Eden. They keep us hoping for a time when the world will reflect the wholeness, the holiness, and the joy that we feel today."

He comes around to our side of the table and wraps us in a *tallis*. Dan leans in and whispers, "What's up, bride?" (which no one could hear at the time, but everyone can on the video) and I laugh. We hold hands. The rabbi then begins chanting the blessings in Hebrew, and the camera switches from front to back, then, back to front, panning out from the rabbi's face to us, our brothers, the wedding parties. When he gets to *kol sasson, v'kol simcha, kol chatan, v'kol kallah*—the voice of joy and the voice of gladness, the voice of groom and bride—I sing along.

When the rabbi is done, everyone says Amen and the camera goes to the wide shot as Dan and I turn around to face our guests. (I might remark that I like this shot because it shows the front of my dress.) There is a close-up on Aunt Natalie, who stands from her place among the guests and says, all business, "Be blessed, O infinite God, power and majesty of all, for creating the fruit of the vine. We bless You now, O sovereign spirit of the world, for creating the universe to augment Your glory. Be blessed, O infinite God, the power and majesty of all, for creating the individual."

Then the camera goes close on Dan's aunt Eleanor, who stands up on the other side of the aisle and says in her best retired-high-school-English-teacher delivery, "We bless you now, O sovereign spirit of the world, for fashioning human beings who reflect the divine, one at their core, complementing each other in their differences. Be blessed, O infinite God, for fashioning woman and man. May our land be happy and rejoice, as a mother whose children return to her in joy. We bless You now, *adoshem*, for letting Zion rejoice with her children. Let these loving friends rejoice. May their joy be a paradise on earth. Be blessed, O infinite God, for causing this groom and this bride to rejoice."

Then the shot goes close on Aunt Annie, who stands, lets out a deep breath, and says, "We bless You now, *adoshem*, O sovereign spirit of the world, for creating joy and happiness, bride and groom, mirth, song, gladness and rejoicing, love and harmony, peace and companionship. O Eternal One, our Boundless Power, may there soon be heard in the streets of Jerusalem, voices of joy and gladness, voices of bride and groom"—here she really gives it some gusto—"the voices of lovers crying in joy beneath their *huppahs*, of soulmates shouting at their wedding feasts. Be blessed, O Infinite God, for letting *this* bride"—and here she looks up at me and I dab at my eyes and her voice catches—"and *this* groom rejoice together."

Then Dan and I turn around and, amidst many hehhehhehs, sip our second cup of wine. The rabbi comes over and lays a handkerchief near Dan's feet.

"Everyone knows," he says, "that the last part of a Jewish wedding is the breaking of the glass, which recalls for us the destruction of the temple. We live in a broken world. We break the glass to remind us of this brokenness and to take with us the vision of perfection that, through your help, we've sharpened here today. It is a gift you can carry with you at those times when you feel you're at the shoals of the relationship, the remembrance of this beautiful, joyful, sacred day." He then tells the crowd that we've opted to spend the first few moments of our married life together in the solitude of *yichud*, and so will join our guests afterward.

"So now, without further ado, by the power vested in me in, I guess, the state of Maryland"—heheheh—"but more important, in accordance with the laws and traditions of Moses and our people, I pronounce you husband and wife."

And Dan smashes the glass, and we laugh and kiss and everyone claps and the musicians start playing "Linus and Lucy" (better known as The Peanuts Theme—my choice) and we turn and, smilingly, walk back down the aisle, me making sure not to trip on my dress.

Then our parents file out. First, mine, at the same time, but separated by a yawning gulf of inches. Toward the end of the aisle, my mother inhales, rolls her eyes toward my father, and— "Give me strength, I need it!"—reaches for the hand of some friend in the audience. My father looks as if he doesn't know quite where to go. Then Dan's parents come down, holding hands and beaming. Our attendants file out one by one (my side first, then Dan's) with smiles on their faces. The *huppah* comes down last, our brothers looking satisfied with a *huppah*-bearing job well done. There are smiles and laughter and a happy buzz from the rising crowd as they get up, smooth their skirts and adjust their blazers, and look backward to the place where the recessional has recessed. Someone says, "be-a-u-ti-ful" as the camera pans upward, to the treetops.

We cut to a white background on which the words "Mazel Tov" appear.

At this point, I would hop up off the couch, and put in the second video, the one of the reception.

We get the same hearts and "Two Shall Become One" as on the first tape, as well as the lawn pan and the C-SPAN graphic, but now the music is "Donah, Donah, Donah," an Israeli folk song involving a calf and winds laughing with all their might—fortunately, it's just that piano again. The Woodend shot switches to a

close-up of the instruction on our seating assignment table—
"Match the photo in your card to the photo on the table"—
which zooms out to the color Xeroxed collage-on-posterboard
we'd glued it to. You see Dan as a baby, me as a four-year-old,
Dan playing soccer, me lifted on a chair at my bat mitzvah. Then
we switch to a shot of one of the photos (four-year-old Dan pet-
ting a goat), laminated and in a silver holder, and we widen to see
an empty table, a colorful, somewhat wildflowerish arrangement
in the middle (no Mason jars, yes Gerber daisies). This goes on
for a few more pictures, and ends in a pan of the patio. We then
switch to a shot of the cake, a simple white one decorated with
flowers similar to those on the tables, no bride-and-groom statue
(this despite protests from Joyce, who, after we'd taken over the
wedding, had miraculously been able to find a bakery to make it
without her usual drama).

Now we switch scenes to the actual party, and music to the
actual music—"Isn't It Romantic?" As Dan and I, standing on a
balcony, pose for more pictures, the camera moves past us and
looks down, to the area below where our guests mill about the
not stuffily manicured lawn, cocktails in hand. (There's no
hehheheh laughter on this tape; the microphone has been
removed from Dan's tie.) The camera cuts to ground level, and
we see Stuart with some of my mother's cousins, Joel with some
of Dan's parents' friends, Connor and Julie talking to Naomi and
Erin. The rabbi adjusts his glasses as Dan's aunt Eleanor says
something to him including the words "so spiritual." My father
stands with some of his Scranton posse and tells a story: "When
we realized it was a pretty weird place for Jews to go, we asked
Wally's father, 'How'd you come to Scranton?' You know what he
said? 'On a bus!'" There is laughter all around.

The music changes to "New York, New York" and people

begin filing into the house, and back to their tables, finding their seats.

Then we have another weird graphic effect where the two sides of the frame come into each other like puzzle pieces, and the next shot is of Dan and me dancing our First Dance to "I Could Write a Book," smiling at each other and whispering. The room is empty at first, but the guests, seated on the patio, soon realize what is going on and start coming in through the french doors. Dan dips me. There are cheers. The song ends, and immediately transitions (by way of the drums) to "Chava Nagilah." People begin reacting to this, clapping and readying themselves for the *hora*. But not my father. In the corner, Phyllis whispers something in his ear, and he makes his way over to Dan and me, his hands in a ready-to-cut-in position. Over the music, you can hear me say, "Of course you can dance with me—it's the *hora!*" And he smiles and says, "Oh, it's the *hora*," and then, not joining either one of the circles that have begun to form around us, walks back to where he came from.

At this part of the video-watching, I usually shake my head and roll my eyes, saying something about my father designing satellites and therefore being, somewhat legitimately, spaced out. But it really makes me sad. He finally wanted to be the Father of the Bride, but it was too late. He never got the chance.

But back to the video: "Chava Nagilah" is played, people (mostly our friends, the non-Jews in particular) get into it, Dan and I dance with just the bridesmaids, get lifted on chairs and hold a handkerchief between us. At some point, I'm leaning dangerously forward, but I grip the chair and don't fall. Esther and Frieda stand at the sides, clapping with extra vigor. The *hora* ends, everyone claps, I hug Uncle Stuart, and the shot dissolves.

We cut to couples dancing to "They Can't Take That Away

From Me"—the Levy-Wus, my friend Jonathan and his wife Leora, Phyllis and Gregory, Dan and his mother. (At this point in the viewing, I might drily say, "Nice song, huh?" to point out the irony you no doubt already noted.) I am not dancing; I'm in a corner talking to Joel and my cousin Kenny. I'd looked for my father in the post-*hora* music switch but, since he hadn't danced the *hora*, couldn't find him.

The next shot is of Grandpa Sol's sisters, saying the *motzi* and cutting the *challah*. Dan and I kiss them, then we cut to the buffet, at which point in the viewing Dan usually says, "Good-looking food, too bad we ate none of it." On tape, as we file into the room with Will, Naomi, Connor, and Julie, Will says, "Yeah, baby. Bride and groom's table gets first crack."

We mill about as our guests enjoy their meals. Gesticulating, I tell my mother's cousin Roger and his wife Renee that "we wanted it inside and outside, that way, in case it rained" while Matthew, standing next to me, nods, pretending (unconvincingly) to be interested in what I'm saying. Dan talks to Wally Frankel, the stockbroker from my father's Scranton posse. You can hear him saying, "So, yeah, I'm not sure of my specialty yet, but once I start rotations, we'll see . . ." I lean in to Aunt Lilly, who is shrouded in a pink silk caftan. She grabs my wrist and says something and I nod. (What she said was: "You are an *exquisite* bride, gorgeous and radiant. You are *glowing*. You've always been my favorite of your generation.") I smile and kiss her cheek. In the back corner of the frame, my father's cousin Irwin inspects another cousin's shoulder, then shakes his head and says, "Nothing to worry about."

We then cut to the toasts. The first one is from my father. The shot is tight, then widens to show Phyllis, standing next to him in the corner of the tent, trees in the distance behind them. He says: "As many of you would expect, standing here now, I feel a sense of relief." There is a smattering of laughter. "But it's not the kind of relief you might expect. There used to be a tradition—in the movies at least—where in the ceremony, it was always asked, 'Does anybody have any reason why these two should not be married?' And I've been thinking that I did have a secret that I hadn't shared with Dan. And now that everything's legal and binding, I feel I can disclose it. When Rachel was one year old, her pediatrician told us that she was going to be six foot two." Now everyone laughs. "Now, I have no idea when she's planning to grow another foot or so, but Rachel is a person who does things in her own way, and when she puts her mind to something, she gets what she wants. So I don't know when you're planning on doing this, Rachel, but, Dan, I thought you should be prepared just in case." There are laughs, then he continues. "Uh, we've been very happy to have Dan join our uh—to have him join us. And I'm glad everyone could be with us and we're very happy, and we wish the best to Rachel and Dan." He raises his glass, and as you hear others clinking, he takes a sip.

Then Richard Levy makes a toast, a very good one in fact—he is a man whose time in academia serves him well at such occasions—but since it's mostly about his days at Harvard with Marty, then on family trips with the Gershon brood, we'd probably elect to fast-forward.

Then it's Uncle Stuart's turn. He "officially" welcomes Dan to our family, then says, "In the past few years, I've gotten to know you and your family, and I can see that your roots are embedded with love, fun, sensitivity, and warmth. What impresses me about you is your intelligence, your humor, your love of family. However, what I truly admire is your unique ability to fall asleep anywhere." This draws perhaps the biggest laugh of the night, and is followed by extended applause. "O.J. Simpson is leading the LAPD in a car chase, Dan's catching his Z's. Michael Jordan scores forty-six in a playoff game, Dan's getting his beauty rest." The camera shoots to our table, where both Dan and I are doubling over. "I know that you are well-prepared, and certainly *well-rested* to assume your duties as a husband." He continues, on a more serious note, wishing us well throughout "whatever joys and, unfortunately, sorrows life holds for you." And everyone says, "Hear, hear," and glasses clink.

Then Dan's brother Adam—who was in charge of the toasts—announces, "We're gonna hear from the groom's party now," and Connor, Andrew, Rob, and Will make their way to the microphone.

Connor speaks first. "We are all friends of Dan and Rachel's from Columbia—Barnard in Rachel's case"—the mention of Barnard draws yelps from the Jewish Spice Girls—"and we've decided that, rather than just appointing someone to give one toast, we'd try and do something a little more flowing"—he is laughing a little—"um, my part is to talk about the beginning, which is to talk about family. And while we've known Dan and Rachel a long time, we all met Dan our very first year at Columbia. One of the things that I think we all felt leaving home and going off to college was a loss of the support system and the warmth and the love we all got from our families. And those were all things that we immediately felt in Dan Gershon." There are awwws from the crowd. "So we wanted to acknowledge that, and now I'll pass it on to Robert Murphy."

Rob takes the mic and, in true good-manners form, proceeds to "thank the parents" for "putting this all together" and says how "lovely" it's all been. He then passes the mic to Andrew, who says, "I could tell you two hours' worth of Dan-falling-asleep stories"—more laughter, from both the crowd and his fellow toast-ers—"but I won't indulge myself in that. It's just really great to be here. Not so long ago, it seemed like we were all going our sepa-rate ways—Dan was starting med school, Connor was applying to grad school—it looked like, maybe, it was the end of an era. But we've all really stuck together and it's kind of confirmed how strong a core relationship was there. And I'm just looking for-ward to seeing this thing grow, and having our kids play together"—there are awwws from the crowd at this. "So, con-gratulations, you guys."

Will is up next. He says, "I'm normally the verbose member of this crowd"—there is laughter at this—"but, in the spirit of the day, I'm gonna keep it short and sweet. Congratulations, Dan, for finding a woman whose intelligence is matched only by her beauty, whose warmth is matched only by her strength, and for being the first one of your friends with the guts to step it up and be a real man." There are shouts of "hear, hear." "But, seri-ously," he says, "we love you both, and we wish you all the hap-piness in the world. Cheers." And there is applause.

Adam says, "And now the bride's party," and Naomi grabs the mic, and holds it like a veteran. She says, "I'm Naomi Rifkin," and explains that she's been elected—by unanimous vote—to represent the bride's wedding party. At this point, either Dan or I will announce that we've entered the Borscht Belt phase of our wedding. "Rachel Silverstein is one of my favorite people in the whole entire universe, and I think my most visceral and intense *thought*, you know, that comes to mind when I think of Rachel is this story I have about going to dinner at one of our favorite places on the Upper West Side—a Chinese restaurant on Amster-dam called Silk Road." There is some applause and she says, "Good, so you've heard of it. Well, on this particular night,

Andrea, another member of Rachel's wedding party, was there too. Now this place has amazing, amazing Chinese food—they make these specialty soups, I recommend the chicken cucumber," people laugh, "but they also give out free wine or soda, so naturally, there's always a big line out front, especially when the weather's nice. I mean, they give you the free wine or soda while you wait, so what the hell?" A steady flow of laughter has built up around her buildup. "Anyway, it was the summer, and there was, like, an hour wait, and there were a lot of people out there waiting and we thought, 'Hey, we're on the Upper West Side, we just graduated from Barnard, there are some older professionals here, this is, you know, a good opportunity for us to, you know, pitch ourselves and maybe get jobs.'" Everyone laughs and she nods and says, "You know, sure. What else are ya gonna do? So we start going up to people and saying, 'What do you do? We just graduated from Barnard, and you know, we're so intelligent,'" more laughter, so she stops, shakes her hair, and says, "Of course. So we go up to this one guy and say, 'Hey, what do you do, we just graduated from Barnard and we're looking for jobs.' And the guy says," and she lowers her voice here and raises the microphone, "'I'm a gangster.'" Naomi, pro that she is, steps back and lets the crowd digest this before continuing. "And Rachel," she says, "looks him straight in the face and says, 'Does entry-level gangster have full medical and dental?'" The crowd goes wild. "And that's Rachel in a nutshell. There it is." As the crowd catches its breath, she brings it down a notch, "And Dan—Dan is an amazing person. On my way to this wedding people kept asking, 'Oh, do you like the groom, do you like the groom?' and I was so happy I could say, in full honesty, 'I *love* the groom.' I think they are just an amazing couple, and this is just an amazing day, and it's a very emotional day for me, I mean, I cried at the ceremony—face it, I'm *kvelling*." The crowd is so with her, dying. "And I just want to say, Mazel Tov, *L'chaim*, and anything else in Yiddish—pu, pu, pu." The crowd applauds. Classic Naomi shtick—I liked her in spite of, and sometimes because of, it.

There are more toasts, from Matthew and my oldest friend, Ben, from Dan's brothers, and, finally, Marty, but we've found that, watching the video, people's eyes start to glaze over at a certain point in the toasting, so I'll fast-forward to the part where Adam directs everyone inside for the cake cutting.

Inside, Dan and I stand next to each other, the cake to his right, in front of the band and the two microphones they've set up for us on stands.

"Before we cut the cake," Dan says, "we want to thank all of you for making this a truly incredible day for both of us. A lot of work went into this," and he looks at me, "and I think we can honestly say that it was worth every minute."

"It was," I say. "And we do want to thank you all for coming. We hope you could each feel at least a fraction of the joy that the two of us are feeling now—the joy they refer to many times in the seven wedding blessings, including the quote we chose for the top of our invitations—the voice of joy and the voice of gladness, the voice of groom and bride. So, in that spirit, without further ado, we give you our first duet as husband and wife!"

And there are more cheers as the band strikes up—dudu*du*, dudu*du*, dudu*dow*, du*dow*dudu*dow*du*dowdow* . . .

And Dan leans into his mic and starts singing, "Don't go breakin' my heart."

And I respond, leaning into mine, "I couldn't if I tried," though you almost can't hear me over the laughter and cheers.

"Oh, honey, if I get restless—"

"Baby, you're not that kind."

The camera pans the audience, who are laughing and clapping and dancing and looking utterly surprised. Usually, if the person watching the video wasn't at the wedding he or she says, "I can't believe you did this!" and one of us says something about needing to end with a musical number.

In front of the band, we sing together, "Oooh, hoo, nobody knows this—"

I sing, "But when I was down—"

And Dan sings, "I was your clown."

"And right from the start—"

"I gave you my heart—"

And together, we sing, "Whoa, hoa, I gave you my heart!"

We do the other verses, which I won't go into here, but suffice it to say, there are enough "don't go breakin' my"s and "I won't go breakin' your"s to satisfy even the strictest Sir Elton John purists.

We finish and there is a hearty round of applause. We cut the cake with full "we're cutting the cake!" pomp. We feed each other and I pronounce it "yummy." There is more dancing (to "Under the Boardwalk"—Laura is dancing with Rob, so I point out that they met at our wedding and have been dating ever since). Slowly, the scene reverts back outside, where the sun is setting, then cuts to the bouquet toss. Everyone scrambles away from the bouquet, except Naomi, who picks it up off the ground and says, "Can I have a baby instead?" Thomas is heard immediately, offering to donate sperm.

As the party winds down, the video music switches to "Tzivvivon, Tzov, Tzov, Tzov," a Hanukkah song that, literally translated, means, "dreidel, spin, spin, spin," and Dan and I say good-bye to some of our guests. We then cut to the scene out front, where Dan's wedding party had decorated our rented Toyota with shaving cream hearts and toilet paper streamers. I say, "Very cute, guys." As we get into the car and drive away, our friends sing "We Go Together" from *Grease*.

At this point in the video-watching Dan, either laughing or groaning, will say, "Get ready for the cheesiest part. They saved the best for last." And I'll say, "The sad thing is, I sort of love it."

You will soon see what we mean. Because, as the camera watches us make our way down the drive and the dreidel-spinning song spins on, two three-D–esque words appear on the screen: "The End," then flip over and change to "The Beginning."

It's cheesy, I know. But it's a *wedding video*. And, for capturing the wedding, it does the trick.

But what it doesn't capture, what it can't convey, is how wonderful it really did feel. And even now, I'm still not sure whether it was wonderful in spite of all the headaches or because of them. But I am sure of this: It felt like us. And that felt magical.

Up Close and Personal With the Author

WHAT INSPIRED YOU TO WRITE THIS NOVEL?

The short answer is planning my own wedding. But it wasn't just that. Around the time I was planning my wedding, I was asked to write an article about "the new brides"—magazine-speak for how the attitudes of women in my generation toward planning their weddings differ from those of women in previous generations. I guess at the time—and this was five or six years ago—the huge, elaborate wedding had just started to have a kind of revival. It seemed that these types of wedding were—and still are—everywhere, and that left some people scratching their heads over a "return to traditionalism." The idea of the *Free to Be You and Me* generation wanting to wear the big, white gowns and have the big, fancy parties struck some people as strange or contradictory. I really never saw it that way. I saw women my age returning to more traditional weddings, but doing it on their own terms, which interested me. Plus, a lot of the stuff about weddings—articles, TV shows, movies—seemed to be missing the boat, or at least seemed untrue to the experience I and everyone else I knew had planning their weddings. Eventually, I thought, why not set the record straight, and tell the story of what this is really like? And that's when I started writing.

WHAT ABOUT WEDDING-THEMED MATERIAL STRUCK YOU AS UNTRUE TO THE EXPERIENCE OF PLANNING A WEDDING?

Well, I think it's pretty commonly accepted that planning a wedding is a stressful thing. But what you most often hear about are battles over the surface things—like the band or the caterer or the flowers. I have yet to meet anyone whose main wedding-planning issue was "we have to have this band" or "I want these centerpieces." Even if those kinds of details became contentious, it wasn't really about music or flowers, it was about the stuff underneath—old family baggage popping up or the ever-present question: "Whose wedding is this"—which is really about control. Even "bridezillas" who want all the details to be just right are really channeling some other anxiety into all of that planning.

WHAT DO YOU THINK MAKES PLANNING A WEDDING SO STRESSFUL?

Hmmm. Well, every wedding is stressful in its own unique way. But I think Rachel's experience highlights the main thing, for people of her age at least. Rachel's in her mid to late twenties, which, these days, is a pretty common time to get married. She's been living independent of her parents for a while and really considers herself to be a full-fledged adult. But she's still not financially independent enough to throw her own wedding—at least to throw the biggish, traditional affair she wants. Because of this, it's as if she's sucked back into a sort of late adolescence; she has her own point of view and can assert it, but, ultimately, she's dependent on her parents. Not everyone's parents are as difficult as Rachel's—they are particularly frustrating to deal with. But I think even in the best-case scenario, a wedding is the last gasp of your childhood family, and any of those dynamics are bound to rear their heads.

IN THE INTRODUCTION, YOU TALK ABOUT THE DIFFERENCE BETWEEN GETTING ENGAGED AND PLANNING A WEDDING. WHAT DO YOU THINK THAT DIFFERENCE IS?

I think when people first get engaged, all they see is the romance. Every bride I know ran out and bought the stack of wedding magazines and dove right in. But once you're in the thick of the planning, you can't even look at those magazines. They're just too overwhelming. It's like there's some kind of curve—I bet you could chart the fall-off point, because everyone has one. I know someone who rushed out and bought a ton of wedding magazines only to give every last one away two months later—and she still had almost a year until her wedding. Just having the magazines in her house stressed her out too much. I think it's about the difference between the idealization of the event and the work it takes to get it all to come together.

BUT DON'T YOU THINK WEDDINGS ARE ROMANTIC?

Absolutely! I love weddings. In fact, I think I've cried at every wedding I've ever been to. That's the funny thing—the wedding itself always ends up being beautiful. It's just the steps along the way. . . . I think everyone loses sight of the forest for the trees, but then, at the actual wedding, all you see is the forest. Or at least you should. If you're at a wedding ceremony, and all you're thinking about are the flowers, you're really missing the moment. Especially if it's your own wedding.

WHY DO YOU THINK WEDDINGS ARE SUCH A BIG DEAL IN OUR CULTURE?

I think weddings are important because they are such hopeful, life-affirming events. I mean, what could be more optimistic than pledging yourself to another person for the rest of your life? Every culture has some sort of wedding ritual. I think weddings are such a big deal in America in particular because they unify us while celebrating our differences—we come from different religions and cultures, each of which puts a different spin on this one same event. I think people love to go to weddings in traditions other than their own; it's a way we can all relate to each other.

IN THAT VEIN, COULD YOU TALK ABOUT RACHEL'S RELIGION AND WHY IT'S SO IMPORTANT TO HER?

Sure. First of all, a wedding is, above all, a ceremony, so I think gravitating toward religion is the natural thing to do. I know a lot of people who lived their lives fairly a-religiously, but when they got engaged, wouldn't have dreamt of having anything other than a religious ceremony. I don't think that's quite the case with Rachel and Dan though.

Right from the beginning, Rachel and Dan know they want a wedding that "feels like them"—something everyone I know has said was a priority for their wedding. Being Jewish is a big part of who they are—for Rachel especially, it's just a given. I think Rachel would describe herself as religious, but she's religious in a very contemporary way—one that allows her to sow her wild oats a bit before she gets married. I do think that attitude might be more unique to women of my generation, which is another reason I wanted to emphasize it.

RACHEL IS SUCH A DIE-HARD NEW YORKER. COULD YOU TALK ABOUT WHAT THE CITY MEANS TO HER AND WHY YOU CHOSE TO MAKE IT SUCH A BIG PART OF THE BOOK?

I think New York is Rachel's first great love. It's also a key part of her identity, as I think it is for many people who live here. She's created a life for herself in this city, a life away from and independent of her parents, and I think that's why she's so stubborn about it. That was one of the main reasons I had her go back to Washington for her wedding—she literally had to go back there, to a place she thought she'd left behind, in order to move forward in her life with Dan.

WHY DOES RACHEL "FREAK OUT" IN CRATE AND BARREL?

The obvious reason, and the one she's first aware of, is that to her, a wedding is really not about the stuff. At least she doesn't want it to be. I think Rachel is very much a person who looks at things and questions why she's doing them, and the whole registry thing is something she can't just blindly go along with. But the one thing she really hasn't examined, at least until that point, is her dead-on certainty about marrying Dan. That's the moment when she really says to herself: What am I doing and why am I doing it?

DO YOU THINK RACHEL AND DAN WILL LIVE "HAPPILY EVER AFTER"?

I do. But I think they were already living "happily ever after" and the wedding just cemented it—which, in my opinion, is what a wedding should do. It is, after all, about a lifetime, not just one day.

Like what you just read?

Then don't miss these other great books!

Bite
C.J. Tosh
0-7434-7764-2

Liner Notes
Emily Franklin
0-7434-6983-6

My Lurid Past
Lauren Henderson
0-7434-6468-0

**Dress You Up
in My Love**
Diane Stingley
0-7434-6491-5

He's Got to Go
Sheila O'Flanagan
0-7434-7042-7

Irish Girls About Town
Maeve Binchy, Marian Keyes,
Cathy Kelly, et al.
0-7434-5746-3

**The Man I Should
Have Married**
Pamela Redmond Satran
0-7434-6354-4

**Getting Over
Jack Wagner**
Elise Juska
0-7434-6467-2

The Song Reader
Lisa Tucker
0-7434-6445-1

The Heat Seekers
Zane
0-7434-4290-3

I Do (But I Don't)
Cara Lockwood
0-7434-5753-6

Why Girls Are Weird
Pamela Ribon
0-7434-6980-1

Larger Than Life
Adele Parks
0-7434-5760-9

Eliot's Banana
Heather Swain
0-7434-6487-7

How to Pee Standing Up
Anna Skinner
0-7434-7024-9

Look for them wherever books are sold or visit us online at www.downtownpress.com.

Great storytelling just got a new address.

PUBLISHED BY POCKET BOOKS

09503